Things Left Unspoken

a novel

EVA MARIE EVERSON

Revell

a division of Baker Publishing Group
Grand Rapids, Michigan

© 2009 by Eva Marie Everson

Published by Revell
a division of Baker Publishing Group
P.O. Box 6287, Grand Rapids, MI 49516-6287
www.revellbooks.com

Printed in the United States of America

Library of Congress Cataloging-in-Publication Data
Everson, Eva Marie.
    Things left unspoken : a novel / Eva Marie Everson.
       p. cm.
    ISBN 978-0-8007-3273-8 (pbk.)
     1. Family—Fiction. 2. Georgia—Fiction. 3. Domestic fiction. I. Title.
PS3605.V47T47 2009
813'.6—dc22   2008047708

the breeze skipped on my shoulder and tickled my ear. *"I'm not there..."*

"Hmm?" My voice was barely audible, but my mother turned and gave me a harsh look.

"Jo-Lynn." She whispered my name in admonishment, as though I were a child, then nodded toward the youthful pastor who stood shivering on the other side of the casket, reading from a book of prayers. He'd never once laid eyes on Uncle Jim; other than speaking recitations, there wasn't much else he could say.

Uncle Jim had never been one for going to church. For the life of me I couldn't remember a single time I'd seen him sitting in one of the hard pews at Upper Creek Primitive Baptist Church or standing rigid with a hymnal spread against his open palms. But I'd heard him talking to God in the fields behind the big house; listened in the cool of the evenings as he sang, "In the sweet by and by . . ." while rocking in one of the front porch rockers that lined the wraparound of the old Victorian he and Aunt Stella called home.

He wasn't a "religious" man, but his prayers before dinner were more like conversations with the Almighty than "grace."

"Most beloved heavenly Father," he would begin, then he would thank God for every single item on the table, for the hands that prepared them (typically Aunt Stella's), and for those who would be blessed by them. "Keep our bodies healthy for thy service on earth and purified for thy kingdom in heaven."

I remember raising my head ever so slightly, peeking through one eye at him. His ruddy face and drooping jowls

1

It snowed the day we buried Uncle Jim. Not the kind of snow that flurries about your face or drives itself sideways, turning the world into a blinding sheet of white. This was angels dancing on air.

When the first flake touched my cheek I felt the icy wet kiss and looked up, past the rows of granite markers—some shiny as silver and others cracked and gray—and into a fortress of old oaks, Spanish moss dripping from barren limbs. Another flake landed on my eyelashes. I batted them, then raised my gloved hand to brush it away.

I looked at my mother, who caught my movement. We sat shoulder to shoulder in the front row of chairs reserved for the family, as though we were aristocrats who'd managed to snag the best seats at the opera. Our eyes locked as she reached for my hand, then squeezed.

I took a deep breath and looked away. The pain of loss in her eyes was too much; especially at this moment, with Great-uncle Jim not six feet away, entombed by polished cherry and cold white satin.

A gust of wind blew against my back, and I glanced toward the open sky nearly white with the cold. I lifted my chin, and

Ren·o·vate (rĕn'ə-vāt')

1. To restore to a former better state (as by cleaning, repairing, rebuilding . . .)
2. To restore to life, vigor, or activity

Pre·serve (pri-zŭrv')

1. To keep safe from injury, harm, or destruction: Protect
2. To keep alive, intact, or free from decay: Maintain
3. Fruit canned or made into jams or jellies

Dedicated to
John Edward Collins and Lenore Nevilles Collins
Della Collins Atwood and Jimmy Atwood
My great-grandparents, great-aunt, and great-uncle.
These are not your stories, but you inspired them.

quivered. His eyes were squeezed shut; tiny slits behind black-rimmed glasses. His hair, dark blond and thinning, shimmered in the glow from the overhead kitchen light.

At the big house, breakfast, lunch, and dinner were eaten in the kitchen. We never ate in the formal dining room, though it was certainly laid out, ready for guests. Uncle Jim said it was just a waste of space, and if *he'd* built the house, he would have left off that room. Growing up, I imagined that if *I'd* built the house, I'd use it for every meal.

My great-grandparents—Aunt Stella's mother and father—had built the house before they married in the late 1800s. It was 1896, to be exact, when my grandmother came to live here as a bride at sixteen to her dashing "older" groom, ten years her senior. As the story goes, he met her, fell in love with her, married her against the wishes of her family, and then carried her over the threshold of this sprawling two-story with tucked-away rooms, long hallways, and an honest-to-goodness brick well on the back porch. Still to this day one can drop an old wooden bucket down into its depths and then, using a beat-up, long-handled tin dipper, sip of something so sweet and clean it almost doesn't seem real. Liquid heaven, Uncle Jim used to call it.

In the early days, beyond the rose-covered trellises on the back porch, perfect rows of vegetables for canning and freezing were planted, both for our family and for neighbors in need when there was abundance. Standing behind the small garden was the farm. It extended alongside the highway that ran beside the left side of the house. The crops stretched toward the horizon and out of sight, interrupted only by the leaning of an old barn, the rise of a tin silo, or the deliberate movement of a John Deere tractor.

But those days were long gone. That was a time when everything seemed to be about life and living. These past few decades, the earth hasn't been tilled or loved. No planting, no praying for rain, no harvesting. Nothing to show for what had been except the gray of the packed soil and an occasional twig rising up from out of the ground, a remnant of the last crop. Of what my great-grandparents had built, only the big house remained, and it was a part of the remnant of what had at one time been a thriving farm in Cottonwood, Georgia.

I blinked several times and brushed away those memories of life. There was too much heartache in the moment to allow myself to remain within them. Now was a time to reflect on death and dying. I could sit here and commiserate, and no one would be the wiser as to the depths into which I was falling. But I knew . . . I knew that when the funeral was over—when the casket had been lowered into the ground and the last clump of dirt had been patted down and the clusters of floral arrangements had been placed strategically about the mound—I'd see that old, proud house filled with family and friends eating fine Southern cooking off Chinet plates, reminiscing about the time Uncle Jim did thus and such and then throwing back their heads and bellowing at their memories.

But I . . . I would move about the house I had loved my whole life, touching old photographs—their frames caked with dust—seeking a flicker of solitude where I could grieve in my own way for the man I'd loved more like a great-grandfather than a great-uncle. A man who, it seemed, was always right where I needed him to be.

Except now. When I needed him most.

2

Just as I expected, the house was filled with folks sipping hot coffee, dipping their forks into Mrs. Patterson's banana cream pie, and alternating between thunderous exchanges about Uncle Jim's antics and the quiet moments that came with the memory of his death.

I had left Mother and Aunt Stella in the kitchen, fretting over where to put all the food that had come in. "You won't have to cook for a month of Sundays," Mother was saying.

As I pushed my way through the heavy swinging door, I glanced over my shoulder at the two of them. They were a picture of opposites. Mother, tall. Her aunt, short. Mother's hair, dark and wavy and straight from a bottle. Aunt Stella's hair, thinning and cottony white and straight from nature. Mother's posture always upright. I can't remember when Aunt Stella didn't hump over. When Mother speaks, her voice is quiet but firm. Aunt Stella, a smoker from the age of nine, has a raspy voice. Though she is a gentle, sweet soul, most of the time her words sound harsh and a compliment sounds more like a reprimand.

I smiled, released the door, and walked down the long, cold hallway toward the living room, where most of the people had gathered. In my desire to suspend time, I took deliberate steps then stopped. I drank in the sights and sounds of the old house. I called upon imagination and heard the laughter of all those who'd called this their home. The children who had run through this hall, then up the stairs. The adults who'd called after them. "Stop your running in the house, now!" they'd say. And the children would call back, "Yes'm" or "Okay, sir." I turned a slow circle, dipping my neck back, and peered upward. Ceilings of dull white paint—bearing water stains amber with age—towered at twelve feet. The walls were cracked and peeling. The floors—made from wide heart of pine boards—could have used stripping and refinishing years ago. Four oblong wool rugs, their design faded beyond remembrance, ran the length of the room. As I started toward the living room, they muffled my steps with a familiarity I found strangely comforting. They brought a rhythm I'd long ago lost. This was the sound of my childhood, when I'd known exactly where I was going and what I was doing, if only for the day. This was the tapping of heels on wood and the padding of soles on carpet.

I reached the closed French doors leading to the living room. I opened one of them slowly, not wanting to be jarred out of my reverie. I closed the door behind me, and life returned in an onslaught of conversation and heat from the fireplace. I spotted my father right away, sitting in the middle of the overstuffed and outdated sofa. Uncle Bob, Mother's older brother, sat next to him. They were engaged in conversation, as always when the family got together. I couldn't hear them over the other banter, but I caught words like "bow hunting" and "next deer season." These were the words all Southern men knew, possibly from birth.

I made my way past the clusters of people toward a small table in front of one of the half dozen floor-to-ceiling windows in the room. Atop it sat an antique lamp, the tattered family Bible, and a small box stuffed with black-and-white photographs with curling edges. I knew the box well; digging into its contents was one of my favorite things to do when I came to the big house.

"Jo-Lynn."

I turned. "Doris, hi." I stepped forward to give Uncle Jim and Aunt Stella's daughter a quick hug. "I'm so sorry for your loss." I drew back and looked at her. If the frayed edges were any indication, her long blonde hair had been bleached one too many times, and it appeared her makeup had been applied with a shaky hand.

"Daddy was a cap pistol, wasn't he?" The question was rhetorical. "He's going to be missed." She took my hand and squeezed it. "I know you'll also be lost for a while. The two of you were always so close." She wrinkled her nose at me and shook her head ever so slightly as if by making a face everything would suddenly be okay again.

"He was the closest thing to a grandfather I had on Mother's side." Mother's parents had died within six months of each other—one of a heart attack, one in a car accident—when I was five.

"I was only six when my grandfather died, but I remember it so well. It was February, and it was raining. Mama always told me it was sleeting, but I don't remember that part. I just remember coming back to this house and searching every room in the house for Pops and not being able to find him."

"And now you've lost your father."

"And you've lost an uncle."

Even though technically Jim was my *great*-uncle, in the South an aunt is an aunt and an uncle is an uncle, "removed" or not.

She squeezed my hand again. "Your parents get to a certain age, you begin to expect the day when . . . well, you know . . ."

Doris turned her head as her eyes scanned the room. "I haven't seen Evan."

"Evan couldn't make it . . . his work. And the holidays being just two months ago . . . he felt he should stay . . . he . . . he sends his condolences, of course."

Doris's smile was wry, and I wondered if she could see through my lie. The truth was, Evan hadn't come because I'd asked him not to. We hadn't said a civil word to each other in weeks, had only tolerated each other for the past few months. In spite of his attempt to reach out to me when I'd received Mother's call telling me of Uncle Jim's death, I'd brushed him away. "Please," I'd said. "Just leave me alone. I'm a big girl; I can drive myself halfway across the state." I'd shaken my head. "Besides, I just don't want to be with you."

"So, his business is good, then?" Doris now asked.

"Business is very good. It's amazing how many people are moving into the area . . . It's an architect's dream world over there." I forced out a laugh. "Evan and his partner are among the most successful neighborhood developers in the entire Atlanta area."

Doris looked down at her hands, studied the elaborate diamonds and long red nails gracing her fingers. "And you? How's your business?"

I crossed my arms and squeezed, attempting to stop the quivering rising from within. "Um . . . it's going."

Doris's brow lifted. "As in going, going, gone?"

I nodded, unable to say anything at all. Truth was, my work as an interior decorator for the design firm of Stanley, Stanley, and Miller had come to an end. By mutual decision, I'd left more than a month before. With my life and marriage at a crossroads, my creative juices had dried up. I wasn't able to give to the clients and, therefore, was of no use to the company.

I raised my hand and shooed away the memory. "As in going, going, gone. I've taken a leave of absence. For about a month now." I gave a nod to Doris. "But, I'll go back to work. In time." *As soon as I can figure out who I am and why I'm here in this world* . . .

Doris looked relieved. "Well, thank you, Jesus."

"Excuse me?"

She reached over and touched my arm with her fingertips. "Jo-Lynn, Mama and I need to talk to you later." She looked around the room. "After everyone is gone. You stick around, ya hear?"

"What's going on, Doris?"

Doris didn't answer. Instead, her attention shifted as a hush swept over the room. I turned to watch as Aunt Stella made her way through the French doors, past a few mourners, and to the closed door leading to the bedroom she'd shared with her husband for more than sixty years. She moved like a woman on a mission, opening the door with a jerk and closing it firmly behind her, the old glass and brass doorknob rattling in the wake.

Moments later, we heard the wail . . . the gut-wrenching cries of a woman who knew she would sleep alone every night for the rest of her life. The sobs of a wife no longer with a companion to share the days . . . to cook for . . . to clean up after . . . to make love to.

Uncle Bob stood. "Y'all leave her alone, now." He adjusted the waistband of the dark pants around his hips. "She'll be all right."

I turned back to the window, peering through the lace curtains yellowed by years of cigarette smoke and neglect, to the barren land on the other side. In many ways, Aunt Stella and I were very much alike. The only difference being I couldn't find it within me to cry.

3

"What do they want to talk to you about?" Mother asked as we tied off the yellow plastic strings of the last few trash bags.

I looked up at her from my bent position in the middle of the kitchen. "I have no idea."

"Aunt Stella can be a sly one. Whatever it is"—Mother handed over a trash bag so I could haul them all out together—"it's probably a doozy." She pointed at me with a perfectly manicured finger and arched her Audrey Hepburn brow.

"I'll meet you back at the house." I headed toward the back door.

"You'll call me as soon as you get in your car, Jo-Lynn Hunter," she said . . . and suddenly I felt like a teenager with a curfew.

Mother has a way about her, which I suppose is the birth-right of all Southern women. With a look, a word, or the tone of her voice, she gets just what she wants. And by the very nature of her position within the community, her social sensibilities, and her ability to gently but effectively rule the roost of her home, she is accustomed to nothing less than compliance. So I said, "Yes, Mother." But as I looked over my shoulder, I winked at her.

A half hour later I was waving good-bye to the last of the

guests, Aunt Stella and Doris beside me on the front porch. Without a word we watched their taillights heading down the endless black ribbon stretching toward their nearby homes or to Raymore, the nearest town to Cottonwood and my hometown, then turned to one another and sighed.

"Glad that's over," Aunt Stella remarked as though she'd just come from a bad school play.

The screen door moaned as I opened it, then allowed both her and Doris to walk past me before I joined them inside and closed the old wooden door. It rattled into place, and I turned the dark key in the keyhole and then shook my head at the lack of security about the old place. "You should think about dead bolts."

Doris stood in front of the fireplace, stabbing at the logs with the poker. The flames of a near-dying fire hissed and popped as they became more intense. Aunt Stella collapsed into her favorite chair, pulled a cigarette from the burgundy leather case I'd given her for Christmas several years before, flicked a plastic lighter, and drew on the cigarette I knew she'd been craving for hours.

"And you should think about quitting that," I added.

"Good luck, Jo-Lynn," Doris muttered with a chuckle.

I took a seat in the old box-like chair next to Aunt Stella's, then looked from her to Doris and back to her again.

Aunt Stella took a long drag from her cigarette, then exhaled the smoke toward the ceiling. "Doris, sit down, hon. We need to talk to Jo-Lynn."

"I know, Mama," Doris said, then took a seat on the sofa, the same sofa that Daddy and Uncle Bob had been sitting on a few hours earlier.

"So . . . what's going on?" I asked, forcing a smile.

Aunt Stella turned to me. "How's Evan, shug?" she asked.

"Evan? Evan's . . . fine." My fingers flittered about the hollow of my throat. "He's good. Evan's good. And fine. Good and fine."

Aunt Stella took another drag, keeping her eyes on me the whole time. "You want to try that again?"

I sighed. "What are you asking me exactly?"

"A man doesn't stay home when his wife is going to the funeral of a favorite family member."

I felt the heat rising to my cheeks, then looked over at Doris, who had cocked a brow toward me. "Oh," I said.

"Tell me what's going on, shug."

I laid my head against the back of the chair. "We've hit a bump in the road, Aunt Stella," I said.

"What kind of a bump?" Doris asked. Doris never was one to stay within the boundaries of "Mind Your Own Business."

I raised my head and looked at her. "A midlife one, I suppose. Evan's been blessed—or cursed—to make enough money to buy his way out of it, and that's exactly what he's done. He thinks life is about country clubs and big-boy toys. Boats, hot cars, and to-die-for getaways. It's Disneyland every day and it's . . . it's just not what I want, quite frankly. I want a husband, not a sugar daddy. I want a marriage, not a vacation." I looked at the small stack of magazines sitting askew on the coffee table in front of Doris, forced myself to not get up and straighten them, then turned back to Aunt Stella as I tucked my feet up under my legs. "This should be a time when we're taking some time for ourselves. With ourselves. We've both worked hard for a good number of years, but Evan seems to be . . . I don't know . . . it's like he's in another world."

"Do you think he's having an affair?" Doris asked.

"Evan's not having an affair," Aunt Stella declared. "He's no fool." She crushed her cigarette in the glass ashtray sitting alone on the table between us. "But he's a man, and men . . . go through these things."

"Did Daddy?" Doris asked, stealing the question I was wondering.

Aunt Stella rolled her eyes. "Did he ever. God knows how much I loved that man, but there were times I could have kicked him as good as looked at him."

"Mama!"

"And it was about this time in his life as it is in Evan's. Doris, you were grown and gone." She turned to me. "Jo-Lynn, for whatever reason you chose not to have children . . . but the timing is the same."

"It's not like I *chose*, exactly. It's just that Evan didn't want children, and I went along with him."

"I've always wondered what man doesn't want a son to play ball with," Doris said. "Or why you didn't want a little girl to froufrou up badly enough to just get yourself pregnant and worry about Evan's reaction later."

Bless her heart, that Doris. What does a woman with four sons and a daughter know about the cravings of someone who chooses not to have children? I hadn't chosen this because I felt the world wasn't good enough for a child today or because I wanted to get my career going and then I would start a family. I chose not to have children because it was the wish of my husband, a man who said he couldn't bear to share me with another living soul, not even a child. A man who attempted to give me the world, but in the end, robbed me of my place in it. A man who said I was enough for him and he wanted to be enough for me. But we hadn't been; certainly he had not been for me. "Well, it's too late now," I said, hoping to dismiss the subject.

We drew quiet until Aunt Stella said, "Doris, shug, there's not any more wood in the house. Go get another log for the fire."

Doris pushed herself off the sofa. "I know when I'm being asked to leave the room," she said, then slipped out the French doors leading to the hallway, not quite closing them behind her. I felt the whoosh of cold air from the unheated back of the house.

Aunt Stella turned to me. "Now you listen to me, Josephine Milynn Hunter. Listen to me good. One thing I know is men. How I know them, we won't even get in to. But, I know them. And if your Uncle Jim was here right now, he'd tell you the exact thing I'm going to say. You two need a time away from each other." She looked away for a moment as though she had to think what to say next, then turned back. "To reevaluate. To see your marriage for what it really is. What it's worth." She pulled another cigarette from the case and lit it. "Marriage is a good thing and a husband is a good thing." She winked at me. "A real good thing. Sometimes, though, a marriage has to be . . . shaken up. It isn't always about passion up under the covers. You know what I'm saying, don't 'chu, shug?"

I felt my brow knit together. "I guess so."

"Look around yourself, here. What do you see?"

I looked around. "An old room in an old house."

Aunt Stella chuckled. "Mercy, I hate to clean. I haven't so much as touched this house in years, 'cept as I had to. Doris . . . now Doris would come every so often and do her best, but she has her own place to deal with." From down the hallway beside me I could hear Doris's footsteps making the same sounds mine had made earlier. Tap-tap-tap-thump-thump-thump-tap-tap-tap.

I nodded for no apparent reason as Doris walked back in the room. Her arms hung long before her, weighted down by the tote filled with logs. Her stout frame seemed to heave under the burden. "Did I stay gone long enough?" she asked, her voice strained.

18

"It was enough," Aunt Stella answered.

"Have you told her yet?" Doris laid the tote on the hearth, brushed the debris from her hands, then returned to the sofa.

"Told me what?" I asked, looking from one to the other.

"Here's the thing, Jo-Lynn," Doris said. "There's a woman—Karol-with-a-K is her name. Karol Paisley. And she's wanting to bring Cottonwood back to its former glory."

"To its former glory?"

"The way it used to be," Aunt Stella supplied. "Back when."

"What is it she's wanting to do, exactly?" I asked.

Doris shifted, crossing her legs and kicking off her black heels at the same time. "Oh, goodness me, that feels good." She wrinkled her nose. "What she's doing is this: Ms. Paisley works for some firm that is buying up Cottonwood—the town—and one by one some of the houses. The more prominent ones, I suppose. I don't know about the others."

"They are actually buying the town? Buying Cottonwood?"

"As you may know, a hundred years ago Cottonwood was the county seat. It was a hotbed of activity. Of enterprise and opportunity. Little by little, though, all the young people moved away, and when that happened, the town eventually dried up to the way it is now."

It was true. One by one, the small businesses in downtown Cottonwood had closed their doors. Currently there was nothing more than a feed and seed and a small general store owned by Uncle Bob, complete with a single gas pump and an old sign that still read "Gas 39.9/gallon." All the other buildings were boarded up or caving in.

"So what does this have to do with me?"

"Miss Paisley wants to buy this house and turn it into a museum," Aunt Stella answered.

"Buy this house?" I sat upright. "Our house?"

19

Aunt Stella ignored me. "But I told her no doing unless she hired you to redo . . . refurbish . . ."

"Renovate?"

"Whatever you call it . . . from top to bottom." She ground out her second cigarette as she heaved herself from the chair, then crossed the room. When she reached the table with the box of photographs, she turned back to me. "This box right here is filled with pictures of the way this place used to be."

I stood and joined her. "I know," I said in a whisper.

Doris spoke from behind us. "Mama wants you to use the pictures as a guide."

I looked at her. "Doris, how do you feel about this? This is, after all, the house you grew up in."

Doris crossed her arms over her ample middle. "Karol told me the company will buy everything in Cottonwood. The key, she says, is to get Young America back to the town. To bring in small businesses. She says that by remodeling some of these old relics, she can then advertise Cottonwood as a place for those who work in bigger towns like Raymore to live . . . to raise their children."

She hadn't really answered my question.

Aunt Stella picked up the box of photographs. "She's willing to pay a right pretty penny for this old hunk o' junk." She placed the box in my hands. "Here you go, Miss Priss. What do you say?"

"I, uh . . . I'd have to speak to Evan."

Aunt Stella patted the side of my face with her gnarled fingers. "Like I said, it may be just what your marriage needs right now." She reached for Doris. "Help me, shug. Help me to bed now. I'm tired."

Doris took her mother's hand and led her toward the bedroom. "Come on, Mama. That sure sounds good. I'm tired too."

I watched them shuffle across the room. Doris opened the door for Aunt Stella, then looked at me from over her shoulder. "Lock up, will you, Jo-Lynn? I'm going to sleep in here with Mama." She started to look back, then shifted her attention once again to me. "You can stay the night, if you'd like. Your old room is always ready for you, ya know."

I took a few steps forward. "Doris, we need to talk about this . . ."

"We'll talk in the morning, okay? Mama's tired and so am I."

4

I walked around the house, making sure all the doors were locked and windows bolted. It would be just like Aunt Stella to open either of them in the dead of winter and then forget about it. I studied each room as I went along, wondering how I might bring them back to their former glory, as Aunt Stella put it.

The walls, floors, and ceilings would need to be stripped and either repainted, repapered, or refinished. The thought of it made me more tired than I already was. I looked up at the chandeliers in each room. They hung forlorn and lonely. Half the bulbs had burned out on most of the fixtures. Others—those that could have boasted brilliant light from a dozen or more bulbs—were dimly lit by a single low-wattage bulb. All were dust-caked and woven with cobwebs.

The kitchen and baths were another story. I wondered about the plumbing and the fixtures. The tubs were claw-foots, and there wasn't a shower anywhere in the house. "If God had wanted us to take showers," Uncle Jim had said to me once, "he'd-a told us to stand out in the rain."

I smiled at a memory of the day when a fierce rainstorm had rushed in from the fields. It was the middle of a hot summer's afternoon in my seventh year and we'd been out on the tractor all day, Uncle Jim operating it with me riding shotgun, thanking God I wasn't inside the stifling kitchen where Mother and Aunt Stella were canning vegetables. Uncle Jim and I had already made it back to the house and had drawn water from the well to sip on while we sat at the top of the back porch steps. The air was heavy and the insects hummed.

"Yonder she comes." Uncle Jim nodded toward the fields.

I sat with my knees spread wide, my elbows perched on them, arms swinging between my legs. I looked up, wondering at his words, to see a sheet of rain moving toward us.

"I thought we'd get some rain today. Praise God, praise God . . ." And then he sang, "From whom all blessings flow . . ."

"Look at that," I'd said, wiping beads of sweat from my forehead with the palm of my hand. I felt my bangs stick straight up, but I didn't care. "I've never seen such a sight."

The glint I loved so much appeared in his eyes. "Tell you what let's do. Grab that bar of Octagon on the ledge there."

I jumped up to do as I'd been told. When I handed the large, gold block of laundry soap to Uncle Jim, he rushed down the steps just as the rain reached us. He peeled off his shirt and began scrubbing the day's work from his arms. I giggled the way little girls do, unbuttoning the cotton print shirt Mother had made for me on her new Singer, and joined him in the downpour that thrashed against our bodies.

Seconds later, no doubt drawn by our laughter, Mother and Aunt Stella stood stern-faced on the back porch, scolding us as though we were both infants. "Jim Edwards, what in the world are you thinking? You could be struck by lightnin'— and that precious child too!" Aunt Stella's words were barely audible over the storm.

Uncle Jim and I stood like two frightened deer staring down the barrels of shotguns in the middle of hunting season. Then Uncle Jim looked down at me, back at his wife. "Go on with yourself, Stella. It's just rain. There's not a rumble in the sky."

"Never mind that, then," she called back. "You've got that child near naked."

Uncle Jim looked at me and, this time, winked. I giggled in spite of the fact that my mother's look said she was ready to send me to the groves for a whipping switch, which she'd never actually done but had often threatened. "She's got more clothes on now than she does when she runs from the tub to the bedroom, I'm thinking." He laughed again, then sobered as Aunt Stella raised her chin. "She's just a child, Stella," he said. "She ain't no growed girl."

Now, standing in the downstairs bathroom, I remembered feeling shame for the first time in my life.

I buried my face in my hands and groaned. Life was so innocent then. No one *really* worried about little girls and boys playing near-naked in a sprinkler's cool delights or on open lawns during a summer downpour.

I stood and walked out of the bath and into the kitchen, where I retrieved the purse I'd left sitting by the pantry, then back into the hallway, where I made my way up the staircase to the second floor. A broad, empty hall greeted me. It was pitch dark, and I widened my eyes in an attempt to see the doorway leading to my old bedroom. It was one of the four upstairs—not counting the nursery—along with a reading and sewing room for the women of the house and a single bath at the end of the hall. When I had my bearings I moved to the opened door, leaned against the frame, and slipped my right hand up the wall until it connected with the light switch.

The room struggled to life in a haze of old quilts and musty, thirsty furniture. I shivered, wishing I'd brought one of the logs from Doris's tote with me. It would have been nice to have a fire in the white-brick fireplace sitting catty-corner in the room. I could then turn off the overhead light and ignore the dust that covered the dresser, chifforobe, and the narrow bedposts and feather carved urn finials of the regency tall post bed.

Tomorrow, I decided, I'd dust the house from top to bottom if I did nothing else. It could easily take all day.

I threw my purse in the center of the bed, then climbed on beside it, hiking my knee-length black skirt up over my thighs until it bunched around my waist. Still kneeling, I pulled my dark brown hair from the clamp that had held it into place all day, felt it swirl around my shoulders. The mild headache I'd been unaware of until now seemed to dissipate as the roots of my hair sprang back to life.

I lay back on the bed and stared at the ceiling, noting every crack that ran along it like rivers on a map. They had been there as far back as I could remember. As a child I'd lain here many a summer morning and imagined where the cracks might lead to, if they led anywhere at all. When I'd asked Uncle Jim about them, he stated simply, "It's where the house settled, that's all."

A house settling, I now thought. As though it were content—finally—with where it'd been built.

I lifted my hips and reached for the band of my control-top pantyhose in one fluid movement. I tucked my thumbs in, then tugged that which had held me captive all day, sliding it toward my feet, groaning as though in ecstasy. Reaching my ankles, I kicked off my shoes and removed the pantyhose, dropping them all to the floor. "Ahhh, that feels good." I unbuttoned my suit jacket, peeling it away, followed by my blouse and skirt, tossing them over the edge of the high bed where they joined the rest of my clothes.

I shivered, then scampered under the mounds of covers and between ice-cold sheets. I felt my jaws lock, and my teeth began to chatter. I glanced toward the large dark chifforobe. Stripped of dust and time, it would be a glorious rich mahogany. I also knew that on the other side of the mirrored door was the thick robe I kept for the occasional bath I took here, but I was too cold to get out of bed and get it.

I pulled my purse toward me, then dug into its insides, searching blindly for my cell phone. A minute later, I placed a call to my mother. "What's she up to?" she asked by way of greeting.

I closed my eyes, picturing Mother sitting in her favorite chair in the family room, wrapped up like a little girl's birthday gift in a satiny pink housecoat. "I'm exhausted and it's too complicated to explain," I answered. "I'm spending the night here."

"You'll do no such thing. You get yourself in the car and get home. I won't be able to sleep until you tell me what's going on."

I kept my eyes closed and shook my head. "Mother-dear, I'm too old for you to boss me around and I'm too tired to argue with you. Let's just say that Aunt Stella wants me to move in here and restore this old house."

Mother was as quiet as the countryside around me.

"Mother?" I opened my eyes in my quilted cave. I was beginning to warm up, as long as I didn't move.

"I'm here."

"And?"

"What in the world does she want you to do that for? Not that I wouldn't give my soul for the opportunity to decorate that old relic, but . . . why now? At her age?"

I sighed. Obviously I wasn't going to get out of explaining this to her. "Some woman is buying up Cottonwood. Or at least buying it for some company."

"Buying up Cottonwood?"

26

"Look, Mother. I'm really, really tired. I'm in bed and I'm heading off to dreamland. I promise I'll explain everything in the morning."

Another moment of silence passed before she said, "Evan wants you to call him."

I sat upright, exposing my flesh to the room's chill. "Why did he call you? Why didn't he just call my cell?"

"You'll have to ask him, dear. But do call him back tonight. I don't want him calling here again. It makes me uncomfortable, feeling like a go-between."

"Mmm."

"Jo-Lynn."

"Mother." I burrowed back under the covers.

"Too sassy for your own good." She paused. "Good night, my love."

"Night, Mother."

I ended the call, then stared at the slide show on the face of my cell phone, contemplating whether or not I wanted to have a conversation with Evan. I opted for calling, figuring I'd wonder all night what the man wanted anyway; I might as well do it and get it over with.

Evan answered on the second ring. "Jo-Lynn?"

"Mother said you called."

"Yeah."

I swallowed before continuing. "What do you want?"

"I just wanted to know how you're doing. How the family is doing."

I pulled the cover over my head and rolled over to my side. "It was a funeral, Evan. The whole day was sad." I almost told him about Aunt Stella's crying but decided against it.

"Bet Mrs. Patterson brought some of her banana cream pie, huh?"

"Yeah."

"I knew I should have gone with you."

His attempt at humor didn't work with me. "It wasn't your choice, Evan." I pressed my lips together. "It was mine."

I heard him sigh. "So, when are you coming home?"

I wondered if he missed me or simply my presence on his arm at the country club. I wanted it to be the former but feared it was the latter. "I'm not sure."

"But in a few days?"

I placed my free hand on the pillow beside me, rubbing it lightly with my fingertips. "That depends."

"On?"

I smiled then. "I may have a job here. I'll call you tomorrow and fill you in. Good night, Evan." I slapped the phone shut, ending the call.

5

I woke the next morning to the scent of fresh-brewed coffee making its way from the kitchen, down the hallway, up the stairs, and all the way into my room. I rolled over, stretching as I went, shivering in the early morning cold. Pulling my arm out from under the mound of covers, I stole a quick glance at my watch. It wasn't even six o'clock, but I'd slept all night with the overhead light on, so the room was as bright as noontime in the middle of summer.

I leapt from the bed and ran over to the chifforobe. I opened it and yanked the robe from the hook on the opposite side of the door. I slipped into it, tied its sash around my waist with a tad too much force, then scurried to the dresser, where I hoped I could find a pair of socks. Drawer after drawer revealed only a hodgepodge of old books, papers, yellowed color photographs and some fading black and whites. Finally, in the bottom right-hand drawer, I found an unopened six-pack of white sports socks.

I made a quick trip into the upstairs bath, where I rummaged through the drawers next to the sink, through old tubes of ointments, various sizes of Band-Aids, broken pocket combs, some emery boards, and a nail clipper until I found a travel-size tube of toothpaste and toothbrush I'd brought with me on my last visit. I brushed my teeth, splashed ice-cold water over my face, and reached for the only towel in the room, hanging over the inside doorknob.

It smelled musty.

When I reached the bottom of the stairs, I turned my left foot upward and frowned; the sock was already soiled from walking down the staircase. I made a mental note to wash the floors with a vinegar and water solution as soon as I was done with the dusting. I padded into the kitchen, following the aroma of Maxwell House.

"Morning," I greeted Aunt Stella and Doris, both of whom were sitting at the kitchen table, reading sections of the *Savannah Morning News*.

"Did we wake you, Jo-Lynn?" Doris asked. "Mama, I told you we were being too loud." She folded the local section, then laid it on the table beside her. "Mama, hand me your part, please. You're hardly reading it."

"It's the comics. What'd you expect?"

I smiled as I poured a mug of coffee and joined them at the table. "You didn't wake me," I said, sitting. I reached over and patted Aunt Stella's old and wrinkled arm. Her skin seemed so thin, so fragile. "How you doing this morning?"

She nodded at me. "At least I wasn't sleeping alone." She nodded toward Doris as she passed the comics to her. "Sleeping in that bed by myself is something I never intend to do."

I took a sip of my coffee. "Evan called last night."

"Did you tell him about staying here, Jo-Lynn? Did you talk to him about the offer Mama made you?"

I shook my head. "Not really. I dropped a hint." I winked at Aunt Stella. "You know, just enough to drive him crazy."

Aunt Stella peered into her coffee mug. "Doris, shug. I could use a little more coffee."

Doris dropped the comics, looped fingers into the mug's handle, and swept over to the counter where the half-empty coffeepot waited. Aunt Stella turned to me. "Now, shug. You want to be careful here. You don't want to end your marriage over this."

I shook my head. "It's not over this, Aunt Stella. Believe me."

Doris rejoined us at the table, placing Aunt Stella's coffee before her. "I'm planning on calling Karol Paisley this morning. I thought maybe you'd like to meet her."

"We need to go by the cemetery," Aunt Stella commented, as though that altered anything Doris wanted to do.

"We will, Mama."

"We need to check your daddy's grave."

I knew better than to comment. It was the Southern way. In fact, I was somewhat surprised Mother hadn't insisted we head back to the cemetery before yesterday's sun had set.

"I know, Mama." Doris looked at me. "Jo-Lynn, you want some breakfast, hon?"

I shook my head. "No. I'm going to head upstairs, get dressed, run over to Mother's. I need to shower and change and then I'll be back." I finished off the cup of coffee I'd steadily sipped from.

"Bring your mama back with you," Aunt Stella said. "She'll want to go with us to the cemetery."

"I'm sure she will." I stood. "Alrighty then. What's say I come back around ten or so?"

"Ten sounds good," Aunt Stella said.

We rode to the cemetery in Mother's new Caddy. Mother drove slowly while Aunt Stella, who sat up front, reminded her that the roads might be icy. Doris and I shared the soft leather of the backseat.

"It's not cold enough for the roads to be icy, Mama," Doris said.

"It snowed yesterday," Aunt Stella reminded her while staring straight ahead.

"Flakes, Mama. Weatherman says it's forty-seven degrees outside."

Aunt Stella didn't respond.

I turned my head to look out the window. The entire countryside was barren; gray, brittle grass lay flat against the soil and naked trees reached like an old woman's fingers toward an ashen sky. Old farmhouses continued to stand proud against the landscape, appearing sturdier than some of the newer ones, many of which were overgrown and overshadowed by untended foliage. I spied an older teenage boy, clad in jeans, shirt, and a denim jacket, driving alongside the road on a four-wheeler. He wore a dirty baseball cap, and his long blond hair, tucked behind his ears, hung on his shoulders from beneath it. As we passed I craned my neck to look back at him, and for a moment it seemed his eyes locked with mine. He nodded, then rolled his shoulders and turned off to the right, down a ditch, and through an open field.

I turned my attention back to what was happening on the inside of the car. Doris was staring at me, a quizzical look on her face. "You know who that is, don't you?" she asked. "That's Bettina Godwin's grandson." She leaned forward. "Mama, what's that boy's name?"

"What boy?" Aunt Stella asked, her gaze never leaving the front windshield. "Turn up here, Margaret," she instructed Mother.

"I know, Aunt Stella. I've been driving to this cemetery

nearly my whole life." Her words weren't unkind, but the irony of it wasn't lost on me.

"Just didn't want you to miss it, shug," she said, then turned her chin over her shoulder and said, "Terry. Terry Godwin. He's a rascal, that one is. And he's hardly a boy. I think he's near-bout twenty years old."

Doris turned to me. "You remember Buster Godwin, don't you, Jo-Lynn? His mama and daddy lived out on Bird Lane."

Mother slowed her car as she took a sharp left turn, then sped up again as she drove up a slight incline toward the church property. The old cemetery ran adjacent, rolling toward a field of harrowed dirt that died out on the horizon. I immediately spotted the fresh mound near the back, the Shepherd Funeral Home canopy still standing guard over the floral blanket and the cluster of arrangements sent by family and friends.

"Margaret, we need to see about getting these flowers home before they die in the cold," Aunt Stella said. "You send that husband of yours on over with his truck, you hear, and he can bring them to the house."

"Yes, ma'am."

"Mama," Doris interjected, "I was telling Jo-Lynn about Mr. Buster Godwin Senior."

"What about him?"

"I was telling her that his mama and daddy lived out on Bird Lane."

"Well, who gives a rat's rear about that?"

Doris sat back with a huff. "I just thought she might remember them, is all." Doris looked at me. "They're both dead now anyway, Jo-Lynn."

"Bunch of white trash. Never cared for them much. None of 'em. The day Senior died nobody cried." Aunt Stella sniffed.

"Mama!"

Blessedly, Mother pulled the car up the asphalt drive, rolling it toward one of the gravel roads that ran between thick rows of the dead. I looked over at Doris, who sighed as I rolled my eyes.

"That's not altogether true, Aunt Stella, and you know it," Mother said. "I'm quite certain his family mourned him then as we are Uncle Jim now." She momentarily looked back toward Doris and me. "When we were younger, Bettina Godwin—then Bettina Bach—and I were good friends." She looked at Aunt Stella again. "Anytime she came over to the big house, you were nothing but sweet and kind to her."

"Mama? Sweet and kind? Do tell, Cousin Margaret."

"Bettina comes from good people," Aunt Stella said, never looking back. "Hurry up, Margaret, and stop the car. I need a cigarette and your Uncle Jim's grave needs tending to."

The tires of Mother's car crunched along the road then rolled to a stop. Doris reached over and took my hand. "Mrs. Godwin's people were the Bachs. You know, Valentine and Lilly Beth Bach. Miss Lilly Beth died way before our time."

I nodded. "I remember him, yes." Valentine Bach—a man I thought born old—had been a local builder as long as I could remember. He drove a beat-up truck and was always, *always*, clad in worn overalls, faded from years of wash-n-wear.

I opened the door and slipped out of the car's warmth and into the chill of the day. "Mercy," I muttered, then reached around and opened Aunt Stella's door for her. "Tuck your scarf around your neck, Aunt Stella," I told her as Doris and Mother came from around the other side of the car.

And she did.

Aunt Stella looped her arm in mine and headed toward Uncle Jim's grave. "Valentine and your Uncle Jim were good friends," she said, squeezing my arm.

"I don't remember seeing him at the house yesterday," I whispered, as though not wishing to disturb the dead.

Doris and Mother walked behind us, the sound of our footsteps growing more solemn as we drew closer to the mound. A gust of wind whipped through the nearby oaks, howling a bit, and I shivered.

"Mr. Bach was never much of one for a funeral," Doris said. "But his daughter Bettina was there. She married Buster Godwin Senior."

"That boy was pure white trash," Aunt Stella repeated her sentiments.

"Mama!" Doris all but stamped her foot. "Anyway, Jo-Lynn, she was there with her son Buster Junior, though with so many folks there you may not have noticed them. They kinda stay to themselves sometimes. Well, mostly Miss Bettina. Margaret, did you get to say hello to Miss Bettina?"

"We spoke for a moment or two."

"That was nice," I said for lack of anything else to say. "I'm sorry I didn't get to say anything to them." I winked at Aunt Stella beside me. "Or to Mr. Bach, who didn't bother to show up."

"Wait till he has his own funeral," Aunt Stella said. "He'll show up then."

I looked back at Mother, who shook her head and sighed.

6

I called Evan at about eight that evening, this time dialing his cell phone. I knew he would have, by now, gone to the club to unwind followed by dinner with Everett, a man who is both a business partner and as close as a brother to Evan. Their very names said together sound as though the same parents reared them. Evan and Everett. No doubt the names had been said together more times than Evan and Jo-Lynn.

"Evan and Everett are in the boardroom."

"Evan and Everett have gone to the golf course."

"Evan and Everett are hunting in Alabama this week."

"Evan and Everett took a two-week vacation to go deep-sea fishing in the Gulf."

Wives on such a trip were optional, which was just fine with me, seeing as I absolutely loathe everything about Everett's wife, Kit. Try hard as I may—and as much as Evan pushed me to feel otherwise—I couldn't find a single redeeming quality about that woman. Something told me she'd ignore her own mother if it meant gaining another shred of social status.

Evan answered his cell phone on the third ring. He sounded winded.

"What are you doing?" I asked, mentally kicking myself for being curious.

"Treadmill," he puffed into the phone's mouthpiece.

I frowned. I was sitting on the back steps of the big house, wearing jeans and a thick pullover sweater and wrapped in an old quilt. It was freezing cold outside, but this was a call I wanted to make in private and Doris had been hovering since supper. I also wanted any excuse to end the call, if necessary, and figured that "Evan, I'm freezing to death" was as good as any.

I decided to get right to the point. "Evan, I've decided to stay here for a while. To take Aunt Stella up on her offer to renovate the house."

Evan didn't answer right away, but I heard the whir of the treadmill coming to a slow stop.

"Evan?"

"What?"

"I said I'm—"

"I heard what you said, but it doesn't make any sense, Jo-Lynn. What do you mean? What are you talking about?" His breathing, though still labored, became steadier and less audible.

"I thought I told you last night . . ."

"You told me you would talk to me today. And I've been waiting all day. Everett and Kit invited me to dinner at the club, and I passed on the offer of a decent meal with good people just so I could take your call. And this is what I get? My wife isn't coming home?"

He didn't say it, but I got the distinct impression he wanted to add "where you belong" to his tirade. "So why didn't *you* call *me*, then?"

"You said you'd call, Jo-Lynn. I'm just trying to keep everything civil here."

I closed my eyes for a moment, electing to remain silent. The evening wind was beginning to pick up; it whistled around the corner of the house, making its way to the old barn and stables. I imagined it turned right to blow across the field where what remained of the farm lay broken and neglected. On its wings was the sweet aroma of chimney smoke.

"There's a woman here," I said, "named Karol. Karol-with-a-K Paisley. She's buying up Cottonwood for the purpose of restoration. Aunt Stella says she won't even consider selling the big house unless I'm the one who renovates it. Karol is coming over in the morning to talk more about it, and long story short, I've decided to take the project."

"And how long do you think that will take? This . . . project?" What had earlier felt like something I could sink my teeth into suddenly sounded as though I was playing with Lincoln Logs.

"Three months. Maybe longer," I answered with a shrug, knowing that Evan, of all people, would realize that an undertaking like this could take close to a year. Or longer. Aunt Stella would be unaware of it, of course, and Doris would be oblivious to it. But Evan would know.

"I don't want you gone that long, Jo-Lynn. You and I both know you are looking at more than three months from home. I'm not a client who doesn't know the difference. Don't try to pull anything over on me."

I pulled the quilt in tighter and drew my knees closer to my chest. "Evan, you're the one that—"

"Jo-Lynn." He spoke firmly, and I hushed. "I know I'm the one who started this little midlife crisis we seem to be in."

We? I thought. *Yes, yes. You started it, and I jumped right into it. You wanting more, me wanting . . . something. Anything at all.*

"I don't need to be reminded. But that doesn't mean I want my wife living off in Cottonwood, Georgia, population fifty. If that many." He took a deep breath and exhaled. "Look, come on back, you hear? Everett and Kit want to have us up to their mountain cabin next weekend. Everett even suggested we make it a four-day weekend. You come on back, we'll have a nice little vacation with our friends, and we'll start to put this time in our lives behind us. You don't need a house to decorate to find yourself, Jo-Lynn."

"To decorate? Is that what you think this is? Throwing a few draperies up and coordinating throw pillows? I'm doing more than that, Evan. I'll be restoring something that is a part of my history and heritage."

"That's ridiculous. You're my *wife*."

I closed my eyes and tilted my head forward until my forehead touched my knees, then pressed so hard I saw little flashes of color behind my lids. Without opening them, I said, "That's just it, Evan. I don't want to just be your wife. Do you realize how little I have to show for myself? I'm a middle-aged woman with no children to be proud of. I don't have a job—and please don't say that being your wife is my job. That's hardly an accomplishment. What you need, Evan, is a woman to show off at country club social functions. What do they call them? Trophy wives? Someone to tag along on these weekend excursions Everett feels obligated to bring Kit to. And let's face it, that's only because she'd skin him alive if he didn't. Which brings me to another point, Evan: Everett and Kit are *your* friends. Not *our* friends. *Yours*. I personally cannot stand Kit Jansen and you know it."

He was silent. I pictured him leaning on the arms of the treadmill, one knee bent, hip cocked out. I pictured his face, boyishly handsome in spite of the receding hairline and Van Dyck beard cropped close. I watched with my mind's eye as the sweat poured past his sideburns, along his jawline, and onto the thick hand towel he always kept draped over his shoulders during a workout. I saw his face turn red, blanch, then turn red again.

"Hello?" I opened my eyes and gazed past the inky outline of naked trees and into the blue-black of the evening sky. I focused on what appeared to be a tiny roof on a tiny house, peeking out from between the branches of high-growing shrubs and thick-leaved trees. I squinted to bring my vision back into focus, trying to determine just what it might be and wondering why I'd never noticed it before.

"She can be a bit much, I agree," he said finally.

"A bit much?" I redirected my thoughts as I shook my head. "No. We're not going to use Kit Jansen as our common ground, Evan. Not now. Not in this conversation. I'm coming home to-morrow to pack some things for my stay here, but I am staying here for the next three months, six months, or twelve months, if that's what it takes. I'm staying, and if you want to come down on weekends or if I feel like coming up sometime, I will. But I am doing this. I'm bringing back the former glory of the big house because it's what I want to do and it's what any interior designer would want to do. It's a stab at something great, Evan, and I haven't had a stab at something great in a very long time."

I stopped in my tirade so fast I nearly choked on my tongue, then pressed my hand against my breast and waited for Evan to explode. But he didn't. He merely said, "Well, I tell you what, my dear. Either come home to stay or don't bother to come home at all."

I felt my jaw go slack. The wind hollered as it cornered the house. I stood; it was telling me to go inside. "Fine then, Evan. I won't come home. All I need is some good work clothes anyway, and they've got a mall in Raymore. It may not be Lenox Square, but it's got a Belk and a Wal-Mart. You might not be able to survive on such, but if I don't do this thing I may not survive at all." I paused for the briefest of seconds. "Call me should you change your mind."

"About what?"

"About anything," I said, then disconnected the phone.

7

"You're not going back for your clothes?" Doris asked. I sat at the old Formica kitchen table, sipping on a cup of hot decaf she insisted I drink after my return inside. She stood at the kitchen sink, washing out the last of the supper dishes and looking over her shoulder at me. "Or your cosmetics or anything?"

I shook my head and stared at the cream-colored drink in the old coffee-stained Currier & Ives cup. "No," I said, barely above a whisper. I picked up the silver spoon next to the cup and stirred my coffee as though it actually needed it. I heard the water in the sink draining and Doris wringing out the dishcloth. I looked over at her, watched her folding it over the faucet, as she'd no doubt done countless times. Soon, this kitchen would no longer be the one she'd grown up in, the one she'd learned to cook in, eaten meals with her father and mother in. Soon, everything—from the faucet to the chipping white metal cabinets that Uncle Jim had put in sometime during the fifties—would be ripped out and tossed. My eyes scanned the room, already planning what I would do with it, the type of cabinets I'd have installed, the hardware, the countertops . . . everything.

"Mama would be very upset to hear this." Doris brought

my attention back to her. She crossed her arms, walked to the table, and sat across from me, then quickly stood again, saying, "I think I'll have a cup of coffee too."

"Promise me you won't say anything," I said as she poured from the old Mr. Coffee into a cup that matched the one on the table before me. "And don't judge Evan too harshly. He's a man and he's got a misplaced sense of pride."

"Oh, Jo-Lynn. I'd string my man up by his toes if he did anything like this."

I laughed, picturing Doris stringing Mickey up. For Doris, most of life had been black and white. No shades of gray. "Doris, please don't think this was an easy decision. It wasn't. I'm more scared now than I was the day I left for college. And goodness knows I was terrified then."

Doris returned with her coffee and sat with a plop. "Why are you scared?" She spoke as though being let in on a big secret.

"I don't know. I haven't lived without Evan for anything longer than one of his business trips or fishing expeditions. But those were . . . those were *his* trips and I knew he was coming home." I took a sip of my coffee; it went down hot and slow, past the knot that had formed between my throat and my heart. "I shouldn't be talking about this. Not with you, not right now. You've just lost your father and . . ."

"No, no. I want you to talk to me." I heard the change in her voice, wondered where it came from. There was, I thought, probably a great deal about Doris that would surprise me had I gotten to know her better as an adult. "I want you to feel free to talk to me."

I looked at the old light fixture overhead. Soon enough it would be one thing of many in a pile of scrap and junk. When I looked back at Doris, who sat waiting to hear the rest of what I was holding inside, what I'd held inside for too many years, I shook my head. "I love my husband but . . ." The words came out in the saddest of whispers.

"But?"

"It's not enough." A tear slipped down my cheek, and I swiped at it as though angry at the betrayal of my emotions. I shook my head again. "Just don't say anything, Doris. Not to Mother. Especially not to Aunt Stella."

"Oh, Jo-Lynn. You know I won't say anything. But if Mama found out this decision had made you cry, she'd be plenty upset and you know it."

"I know. That's the last thing she needs right now, so let's just keep this between us."

"I will. I promise." Doris sipped her coffee and I did the same. When she set her cup back on the table, she said, "What will you do, then? For clothes?" Before I could answer she said, "Do you want a piece of cake? We have plenty. Mrs. Patterson's sister Melba brought over a caramel cake today, God love her, like we need any more desserts around here." She patted her abdomen. "Or here."

I opened my mouth to say no, but Doris was up again, bustling out of the kitchen, through the swinging door that led into the dining room, and back again with a glass-covered cake plate. "I have to tell you, nobody but nobody can make caramel cake quite like Miss Melba."

A bite later and I had to agree with her. I could practically feel the butter sliding into my arteries.

"Mother and I will go shopping in Raymore," I said when the slice was half eaten.

"What?"

"Shopping. For clothes. You asked me what I'd do for clothes."

Again Doris frowned. "Oh, Jo-Lynn. Such unnecessary expense."

I grinned at her. "I have Evan's credit card with me," I said with the first lilt in my voice I'd heard all day.

Doris smiled back. "Now that Mama would be proud to hear." She took another sip of her coffee. "By the way, while you were out back talking to Evan I finally got Karol Paisley on the phone. She's the hardest thing in the world to get to answer, let me just tell you now. Anyway, she'll be here tomorrow afternoon, she said. Around two. Does that work for you?"

I nodded, then drained the last of my coffee and said, "It works just fine." I stood.

Doris and I were silent then, the only sound in the room being the occasional clinking of Doris's fork tines against teeth as she fed herself more cake. Finally, she said, "I'm moving Mama in permanently with Mickey and me. I talked with Mickey tonight, and he thinks it's the right thing to do." Mickey and Doris lived about a half hour from Cottonwood in the opposite direction of Raymore. While Raymore, a small university town, was bursting in growth, Luverne, Georgia, was a community still nestled into the simpler way of life.

Doris sipped at her coffee and coughed a note of a laugh. "One thing's for sure, even living here her whole life, Mama never felt any connection with this house. She'd move to the moon just as quick as she'd move to my house." She shook her head. "Still, this sure is going to take some getting used to." She took a deep breath and exhaled. "Not for her, mind you. For me. But I think it's the right thing to do. You don't need Mama rambling around in this old house if you're going to be able to do what you need to do, and Mama sure doesn't need to be around all the dust I'm sure is going to be flying from one end to the other."

I nodded. "No doubt."

"I'll get her out of your hair within the next few days. We'll pack some of her personal things . . . her clothes . . . things of Daddy's . . ." The last three words were spoken in a whisper. I would have missed hearing them at all had I not been at the table with her.

I nodded again and tried to think of the right words to say. Right then, all I could think about was that Evan had practically kicked me out of my home and Mickey—a blue-collar family man Evan had always looked down on—was welcoming his mother-in-law into his. The difference left me feeling sad and empty. It was not a thought I wanted to share with Doris. Instead, I stood and gave her a quick hug. "I think I'm going to bed. I'm so tired I can hardly think."

"Well, darlin', you should be what with all that dusting you did today. Now don't you worry one iota about the dishes here. I've got you covered."

I smiled at her, said good night, and then made my way up the hallway and to the second floor.

All that dusting, I thought. I'd barely made a dent in it, having dusted only two of the bedrooms upstairs before I was overcome by an odd sense of asthma and lemon oil. I took the hottest, soapiest bath possible before dinner, and now I was ready to climb into the freshly polished bed. But this time, in pajamas and with a log on the fire.

I awoke with a start. Fat shadows played on the ceiling overhead and the room was ice cold. I raised my head and looked over at the fireplace, then let out a sigh. The fire had gone out. I burrowed myself deeper into the mattress and pulled the old quilt up under my chin, fisting my hands in the process. I closed my eyes against the gray of the room and wished for sleep to return quickly.

Somewhere in the silence I heard the low whistle of wind through the thin draperies. I opened my eyes again and saw the billowing of lace curtains. I sighed, remembering that I had raised the window when cleaning it. I left it up to allow fresh air into the room and certainly had closed it before leaving the room. Apparently, though, not well enough.

I forced myself out of the bed and over to the window, pulling back the drapes and reaching for the sash. A quick look at the latch and I realized I had not slipped the metal through tightly enough. As the wind outside had picked up, I reasoned, it must have forced the window back up enough to fill the room with cold air and put out the fire.

It was then that I saw two men, both dressed in dark clothing, hands stuffed into the pockets of thick jackets. They moved deftly from the side of the house toward the old barn, chins tucked to their chests, occasionally glancing over their shoulder. One carried what appeared to be a cylinder of some sort tucked under his arm; the moonlight reflected off a bit of metal.

I started to open my mouth, to call out to them, but then stopped as the two men slipped into the shadows of the fields. At this hour, the only good my shouting would do would be to wake the dead.

8

Cottonwood, Georgia
1938

She had thought it a perfect day for fishing, and she said so to her papa.

"Papa," she'd said, "do you want to go fishing with me this afternoon? I was thinkin' maybe just before sunset. Fish oughta be biting good by then."

Papa had smiled down at her; him not even five-foot-seven and, at seventeen, her barely over five feet tall. "You look like your mama standing there." He pulled the old porkpie straw hat from the top of his head, then wiped the sweat from his brow and crown with the long sleeve of his shirt. "Did I ever tell you your mama and I went fishing on our first date?"

She smiled at him. "You tell me all the time, Papa."

"Your mama's a good one for fishing."

"So will you or won't you?"

"Can't, baby doll. Papa's gotta finish off these fields. How about a game of Monopoly later on tonight, though?"

It would have to do. Because of the Great Depression, as everyone called it, Papa had been working that much harder to keep up, and food—once in great supply— was brought in by your own hand or not at all. The year before, during the Recession of '37, she'd overheard Papa and Mama talking about how much longer this could go on and whether they'd survive it at all. Papa said they were blessed to have kept the farm.

She was old enough to understand, but as Papa's baby, too spoiled to care. As it was, she might not be much help with the household chores, but if she could bring home some fish to fry, Mama'd be pacified and Papa'd be proud.

That warm evening, as the sun had dipped behind the pecan grove and the crickets had already come out to serenade, she strolled through the wiregrass with a cane pole and bucket of earthworms she'd dug up near Mama's garden and headed for the pond near the back of their property.

Poor Man's Pond, they called it, though she didn't know why. It'd been called that as far back as anyone in Cottonwood could remember, but until the Great Depression, no one here'd really been poor. Every man and woman was self-sufficient, no one depending on governmental handouts and ABC programs brought about by the president.

Gnats began to dance around her. She blew them from her face by cupping her bottom lip and exhaling hard and fast. Some of them flew away, others stuck to the sweat on her face. She didn't care. It wasn't like anyone was going to take stock of what she looked like, measuring her up against one of her beautiful older sisters, as was often the case.

Not that she wasn't pretty in her own right. Pretty as a picture, Papa always said. But she could tell sometimes when that faraway look came to Mama's eyes that she worried her baby girl would never find a man, get married, and settle down.

"Maybe I'm not the marrying kind," she'd say to Mama whenever the subject of "stopping all her running around" came up.

Mama would immediately draw back and say, "Hush your mouth, girl."

Papa would wink and she would giggle.

She arrived at the pond, set her bucket on the bank, and then dropped down beside it. She wore her papa's overalls and a long-sleeved cotton shirt because Mama said that if she were going to dress like a boy the least she could do was to keep her arms from blistering or becoming a feeding ground for mosquitoes big as crows.

She hooked a worm, then cast the line into the water, propped her elbows onto her raised knees and waited. She stared up at the trees, thick with foliage, and watched them bend just so in the afternoon breeze. She blew at a few more gnats, then rubbed her ear with her shoulder to shoo those that hummed along the lobe. Thinking she heard a rustling in the grass behind her, she turned and stared, but saw nothing. A person could get kidnapped—like that Lindbergh baby— back here, she thought, be dead and buried and no one would ever find the remains.

A tug on her line brought her back to the here and now. She brought her attention to the murky water and watched the line jerk with a tiny nibble, followed by another, and then the cork went under and the line pulled taut. She stood and pulled back, bringing the pole up and the line and her catch up over the water's edge.

"That's a good 'un," she heard a male voice say.

Dropping the pole, she spun around, then stood captivated by the most amazing pair of blue eyes she'd ever seen.

9

I hardly slept the remainder of the night. Not only was the room intolerably cold, but I couldn't seem to get the two men off my mind. Exhausted but restless, I slipped an arm out from under the bedcovers and over to the old clock tick-tick-ticking on the bedside table. I pulled it to me then cocked it toward the moonlight shimmering through the curtains. It read 4:02.

I groaned in surrender and climbed out of the bed, knowing my days of sleeping in were nearly at an end. For a while, anyway. I might as well start this day off right, I reasoned, and get on with it.

I padded down the stairs and into the living room. In spite of my efforts to be quiet, the floors groaned under my feet and the French doors creaked as I pushed them open. I slowly pulled a couple of logs out of the hammered copper tub near the fireplace where Doris had stored more wood before we'd gone to bed, then rose on my tiptoes and inched my way back into the hallway, toward the staircase, looking back to the closed bedroom door with every step. Once at the stairs, I took them two at a time.

I could feel the rough bark of the pine logs, even through the thickness of my robe and the flannel of my pajamas, as

I tried to balance them in my arms. I breathed in deeply, intoxicated by the scent of pine, mixed with the muskiness of the house and the cold of the air. For a moment, I didn't regret at all my decision to rise in the darkness.

Once I got a small fire going in the fireplace, I crossed the room to the window I'd closed no more than two hours earlier. I sliced the center of the lace curtains with my fingers and drew one side back, then peered out. The world was still and appeared to be without color. I looked for a twitching of the old tree branches, something to let me know the world might be in darkness but was nonetheless alive, but they were not in a giving mood. I shrugged, though I don't know why. It just seemed the right thing to do. I released the drawn curtain, then moved over to the wardrobe, pulled out an old pair of jeans and a dark blue sweatshirt with MAUI stitched in gold lettering I'd once brought from my stash of clothes at my parents' home, and got dressed for the day.

I inched my way out of the big house a half hour later, creaked along the wooden blue-gray slats of the wraparound porch, and skipped down the cement steps leading up to it. My car was covered in a thin layer of frost. I swiped at the bit of it along the door handle, then opened the door with a click and slipped inside. I started the car's engine, thankful for the muted purr of a Lexus SC. I ran the defrost on high, then twisted the windshield wiper control for a few quick swipes to clear the moisture forming on the other side. With the glass now frost free, I was able to peer out the windshield to Aunt Stella's bedroom window. I pictured her sleeping on the other side in the simple maple tulip-top bed she and Uncle Jim had slept in since the first night of their marriage. I thought about what Aunt Stella had said in the kitchen a few days earlier; that she never intended to sleep in that bed alone. I shifted my eyes to the left, then up to the window of my bedroom—Aunt Stella's childhood bedroom—and pictured the bed there. For the most part, until this project I'd found myself at the center of was complete, I would sleep there. And I would sleep there alone.

I shivered. *Evan.* Where had we gone wrong?

The ride toward Raymore gave me plenty of time to think of an answer, though not necessarily one that satisfied the question.

10

I grew up in Holly Hill, an old section of Raymore—not Cottonwood-old, but old in comparison to the remainder of the town—where stately houses boasted one-acre lots with front lawns that curved down ever so slightly to the wide streets weaving through the neighborhood. Too posh for sidewalks was Holly Hill. Our house, a Georgian colonial, stood on the most elevated piece of property, earning it the name "the house on the hill." My whole life, whenever I met someone new, inevitably I'd hear, "She lives in Holly Hill . . . in the house on the hill," as though it were the governor's mansion. As far as Margaret Tatum-Teem—my mother—was concerned, it might as well have been.

Mother has a natural flare for decorating, and Daddy has a natural and inherited knack for making money. Between the two of them, our home was a showcase framed on the outside by large magnolia and dogwood trees and thick azalea bushes and on the inside by traditional furnishings.

I arrived at the house a little before eight o'clock, just in time to see my father—dressed in navy blue pajamas and a matching robe—bending over near the middle of the front lawn to retrieve the morning paper. Straightening, he turned toward my car. I waved. He raised the paper in return, then began walking toward the driveway at the right of the lawn. I stopped the car, shut off the engine, and got out.

"What's got you out so early?" he asked.

I smiled toward him, a man still   handsome for his age. "I've got a load of shopping bags from Wal-Mart in the back seat here," I said as he neared me. "Did you know Wal-Mart is open twenty-four hours a day?"

The tanned skin around Daddy's face wrinkled in waves as he smiled. "What in the world were you doing in Wal-*Market*? Your mother will have a conniption when she finds out." He leaned toward me and gave me a kiss on the forehead. "Good morning, sunshine."

I patted his already-shaven cheek and said, "And good morning to you too." I opened the back door of the car and began pulling Wal-Mart bags from the interior. "Got an extra arm or two?"

Daddy extended his arms. One at a time, I slipped the bags over them until he swore his arms would break, then grabbed the rest for myself. As we made our way inside I explained. "I bought some necessities. Toiletries . . . work clothes . . . socks. There's a portable TV for picking up the two or three Savannah channels—hopefully—from my bedroom at the big house. I've got it in the trunk along with a new kitchen fire extinguisher, just in case that old stove blows or the wiring gets crossed during the renovating."

"Not an altogether bad idea," Daddy said with a nod. "You're a smart girl. You remind me a lot of your daddy." We reached the door, and I stepped forward to open the door with my free hand. "Shhh," Daddy whispered. "Your mother is still getting her beauty rest." He winked at me.

We entered through the front door as though coming into a sanctuary, the only way Mother would have it, getting her beauty rest or not. I dropped my packages onto the marble floor of the entryway, then began unloading those hanging from Daddy's arms. "I'll take these upstairs in a minute. I need to reorganize a few things, see what else I might need now versus later. I was hoping Mother might be up to hitting the mall with me before I have to head back to the big house."

"I've never known your mother to pass up shopping. Coffee?"

"Please."

I followed my father to the farmhouse-style kitchen that showcased an English pine washstand Mother had inherited from her mother, Adeline, who'd been given it as a wedding gift from Adeline and Stella's parents, Loretta and Nevan. My growing-up years were surrounded by the giftings of my great-grandparents. Washstands, old front porch rockers, delicate china, quilts, and bedcoverings crocheted from tobacco twine. Beyond those things I could touch was the sense of family that came with each one; knowing I was a part of something I could neither see nor fully comprehend.

I sat in one of the white wicker breakfast chairs and waited as my father poured cups of coffee. I listened to the familiar sound of him adding cream and sugar as my eyes rested on a rooster-shaped ceramic cookie jar at the end of the washstand. "Mother got a new cookie jar, I see." Mother recently agonized over the fact that my brother Stephen's youngest child had accidentally toppled her beloved grandmother's cookie jar to the floor. It had shattered beyond repair. Heartsick but determined, Mother began an earnest search to replace the heirloom.

"She did. Found it at the antique market." He shuffled over to the table. "Here you go," he said, placing my coffee in front of me. "Prepared as the lady prefers."

"Thank you, Daddy."

He sat across from me and wrapped his large hands around

his coffee mug. His shoulders sagged as he leaned forward and looked me in the eye. "So what's going on, sugar bean?"

I took a tentative sip of the hot coffee and said, "What do you mean?"

"You know what I mean. Evan called me at the office yesterday." My father is a vice president at Tatum-Teem, a family-owned pharmaceutical company started by his grandfather and brought to glory by his father. Daddy operates the Raymore division, his three brothers and one sister operate four others, and their uncle is president of the corporate office in Charlotte, North Carolina. With my father's age and the always burgeoning business responsibilities, I knew the last thing he had time for was Evan's antics.

My shoulders mimicked his. "Oh, Daddy. I'm sorry. He shouldn't be involving you in this. You've got enough on your plate."

"Stephen carries the majority of my weight at work these days," Daddy said with a shake of his head. "And your mother doesn't let me lift a finger around here. The least I can do is to tend to my only daughter's problems."

"I'm nearly fifty years old, Daddy. I'm no longer a baby, and I surely don't need my husband calling my father as though I were."

Daddy smiled. "You'll always be my baby."

I returned the smile. "And you'll always be my daddy."

"And Evan? Will he always be your husband?"

I took another sip of coffee. "Where'd we go wrong, Daddy? I asked myself that very question this morning . . . on my way to Wal-*Market*. Have you ever known two people more passionate for each other than the two of us? Before, I mean?"

"Your mother and me."

I pretended to blush. My parents' love story was nothing they'd ever bothered to hide from Stephen and me. Mother was the epitome of decency and decorum in public, but she doted on my father in a way I had once hoped to imitate but had never quite mastered.

"I remember the first time you brought him home to meet the family," Daddy said. "Remember that?"

I nodded.

"I told Margaret before you got here that I was concerned about him being five years older than you and with you fresh out of college and just starting your career, that he might be ready to get married and start a family right away . . . might not give you time to find your own place in the world. Then we met him. I saw the way you looked at him . . . the way he looked at you. I told your mother that if he continued to love you with even half the affection he seemed to have for you then, it would be more than most women experienced in a lifetime."

I closed my eyes at the memory. Evan had treated me like a storybook princess. He had taken me to the best restaurants Atlanta had to offer, to hit shows, to exotic getaways. Though our ardor had been more than heated at times, the entire two years we dated he never once crossed a line my father would not approve of. Trips to Europe and the Caribbean always included separate sleeping arrangements, sometimes even to my chagrin. But Evan was determined to see me walk down the aisle in sanctified white and, two years after we met, I did. By the time we said "I do" I would have done anything for this man, even agreeing never to have children.

11

Evan, the oldest of seven children, had surprised me with a Christmas trip to Ireland. One of our afternoon outings had been to Thoor Ballylee, the onetime Yeats family home. There, on the lush green lawn, he'd told me of his intentions—to build a career unlike anything either one of us could imagine, to marry me, and to have a home filled with love and friends and a lifetime of memories.

My mind reeled from the magic of the moment, and I felt light-headed, as though I'd been transported magically into a dream or a fairy tale. "And children," I whispered, my eyes looking deeply into his. "Lots and lots of children."

"Jo-Lynn." His voice was soft but firm. "We need to talk about that. I want you to understand something . . . I don't want children. Call me selfish and . . ." He looked down, his long lashes sweeping against his high cheekbones, then back to me. "I suppose I should have told you before, long before now . . . but . . ." He kissed the tip of my nose, my cheeks, between my brows. "I love you so much. I can't bring myself to think of living without you. It's a sacrifice for you, I know . . . but I just don't want children. What we have . . . this love . . . this incredible love . . ." His breath, a mixture of the hot tea we'd enjoyed earlier at a small café and spearmint gum, blew warm and sweet against my face. I stepped closer to him, so close he took both my hands in his, lacing our fingers and pulling our arms taut by our sides. "You are everything and more for me." He whispered as though a man in emotional torment.

I felt a tear slip from the corner of my eye and down my cheek. I'd never known a moment like this; a moment of such intensity and fervor. "Evan—"

"No, let me finish. Hear what I'm saying and then you have to make a decision." I nodded and he continued. "I want you to make it with a clear understanding . . . no misinterpretations or allusions to what I'm saying to you . . . you are everything and more to me and for me. You are more than I could ever hope to have and yet, by some gracious gift of God, you are mine. It's enough for me, Jo-Lynn. More than enough. And *I* want to be everything and more for you—"

"You are . . . you are . . ." I kissed him, giving his lips tender pecks over and over as though hungry for the anguish to end. I'd never seen him like this before, didn't think I could bear to see him this way ever again.

"Then you agree? It's a deal? You'll marry me with no expectation of children?"

I wrestled my hands free of his, threw my arms around his neck. His arms encircled my waist, squeezed so hard I could barely breathe. "Yes, Evan. I will," I managed. "I will marry you, and no, we won't have children. We'll have each other and that will be enough." I pressed my lips to his with such force I nearly bruised us both. "It's a deal."

We married soon thereafter, giving Mother and me just enough time to plan the fairy-tale wedding of my dreams, the social event of hers, and allowing Evan time to plan a honeymoon that would signify the extraordinary future we both believed we'd have.

And for a while, we did. We had it all. Or, nearly all . . .

"I didn't realize," I said now to my father, "exactly what I was giving up when I married Evan."

"The no-children clause?"

I swallowed past the knot forming in my throat. "I thought Evan's love would be enough, but . . ."

"Children are a blessing, no doubt about that. I can't imagine life without you and Stephen. But not having children isn't the end of the world, nor the end of a marriage, Jo-Lynn."

My chin jerked. "Do you think it's me? Do you think I'm the cause of all this?"

Daddy raised his hands in mock surrender. "I'm not saying any such thing."

"Just what did Evan say to you yesterday?"

"Only that he doesn't understand what's happening to you right now."

"To *me*?"

"Don't get angry with me, pumpkin. I'm just telling you what the man said."

"What who said?"

Daddy and I both jumped at the sound of Mother's voice. Turning, we saw her standing there, resplendent in a pink satin gown, fresh-faced even at sixty-eight years of age and first thing in the morning.

"No one," Daddy answered, then gave me a look of warning. He rose from the table. "My, my. Don't you look prettier every day than the day before?"

"Don't avoid the question with flattery, Horace. We've been married too long for you to try such foolishness." She looked from my father to me then back to my father again. "And furthermore, why are there Wal-Mart bags in my entryway?"

12

Cottonwood, Georgia
1938

It was a risk and she knew it, but a risk she figured worth the chance.

Without saying so much as a word, she gathered her cane pole and paraded out the back door as though she were making her way to the old outhouse that hadn't been used in a decade. But Mama was at the well, drawing water for their ritual Saturday evening lemonade. Mama said the well water was better than anything that came from a faucet. "Whoa, little girl. Where are you heading off to?"

"I'm going fishing."

"Like that?" Mama eyed her up and down. "Kinda dressed up, aren't you, shug?"

She looked down at the blue-gray dress that fell in soft pleats from the belted waistline and ended in a hem two inches below her knee. "This? It's not that nice. And it's from last year, besides. And look, Mama. I'm wearing socks and shoes, so it's not like I'm up to something."

Mama cocked a thick brow. "Who said anything about you being up to something?"

About that time her papa came out the back door, the screen flying open and then slamming against the door frame. "Who's up to something?" He propped his straw hat upon his head. "Sugar lump, where you off to?"

"I'm going fishing, Papa. I have my cane pole and my worms. See here?"

"In a dress? You're going fishing in a dress?"

She sighed like she'd heard Greta Garbo do in a movie once over at the picture show, then fingered the lace of her linen handkerchief she'd tucked into the fabric belt at her waist. "Well . . . aren't we having ice cream later? It's Saturday, isn't it? And Mama, don't you always insist we girls dress up a bit? I was going to fish for a spell, then come back and change into some proper shoes." She stuck out a foot so her father could see the scuffed everyday square-toed lace-ups.

"Well, go on," Papa said, pulling a thin cigar from his pocket and heading over to one of the porch rockers to smoke it. "Go on so you can get back in time for your mama's peach vanilla, now."

"I won't be late," she called as she raced down the steps and across the back lawn, through the path she and her brothers and sisters had long ago etched into the landscape toward Poor Man's Pond. When she arrived, breathless and a little anxious, she looked around the bank for a sign of the man-boy she'd met earlier in the week, met him twice in fact. Once that first day, the next time two days later. Both of those times had been on accident. This time, she hoped he'd be here again.

But he was not. Feeling let out like an old automobile tire, she set her bucket of worms down and then pulled one of the wigglies out with the crook of her finger and hooked it on the line. She sent the worm sailing through the air and into the water with a plop of the cork, then braced her feet apart and waited. The least she could do, she reasoned, was bring home a few fish for Mama to fry up in the pan for their breakfast the next morning.

"See you came back."

She turned with a start, but this time she didn't drop her pole.

"Hello," she said slowly. She looked back at the water, trying to pretend she wasn't all that interested in his arrival. "Wasn't sure if I'd see you out here today or not."

She heard him chuckle, then eyed him slowly as he settled in next to her and got his line ready.

"What's so funny?"

"What's the dress about? I ain't never seen no girl that can fish like you before, but I can honestly say I ain't never seen no girl fishing in a dress, neither."

She bristled and blushed appropriately. "I'll have you know we have a social outing later. All I have to do is change my shoes and put some stockings on. So there."

"Stockings? Should girls like you be talking to boys like me about stockings?"

"Well, I don't know." She looked out at the cork resting on the water, saw it bob a couple of times, and she lowered her voice to a hair below a whisper so as not to scare the fish. "Maybe girls like me shouldn't even be fishing with boys like you."

He gave her a funny look, then glanced back at the water. "You got one."

He reached toward her as though to help her bring it in, but she jerked her shoulder. "I can do it."

They fished in silence for the next half hour; him bringing in about six fish and her bringing in about nine. "A fine mess you got there," he said. "Fine mess."

"I'll have Mama fry 'em up in the morning."

"Good eats."

She licked her lips, tasted the salt on them, then worried she might have beads of sweat all over her face. She pulled the handkerchief from her belt and patted around her lips with it.

"That's pretty," he said.

She looked at him then, allowing her green eyes to meet his blue ones, then discreetly glanced over the sweep of the light brown hair over his forehead, the broad brow and naturally flushed cheekbones. His ears were too small for his head, she reckoned, but his lips were full and . . . She didn't dare to think beyond that. "My grandma made it for me. See?" She extended the frilly piece of linen toward him, and he took it. "It's got my initial on it. Right there." She pointed to the fine lettering in the center of colorful embroidered flowers.

"S," he read. He looked up at her then, caught her eyes with his, and held them. "You're pretty; anyone ever tell you that?"

She didn't answer. Couldn't really. His was the first male voice other than Papa's to say those words, and she'd not prepared herself for it.

"You blushing?"

She turned to gather her fishing equipment. "I gotta go. Mama'll skin me alive if I'm late for ice cream."

"Y'all are having homemade ice cream tonight?"

"Mmm-hmm."

"My mama makes the best butterscotch in the world." He paused. "I guess you'd better be going."

He turned as though nothing had happened, nothing had been said at all, and went back to fishing. She stepped away from him, from the heat of him, and began to trek up the muddy embankment to where the wiregrass grew and a dirt path would lead her home. "Bye," she called over her shoulder.

64

"Bye now."

She'd gone only about ten yards when she heard the sound of footsteps running hard and fast behind her. She stopped and turned and he was there, coming toward her, slowing in his step.

"What are you doing?" she asked.

He stopped just a yard short of her, fought to catch his breath as he extended the off-white embroidered handkerchief as though it were a bouquet of flowers. "You forgot this."

"Oh." She blushed again, deciding that it was his fault; had he not told her she was pretty she would have remembered to retrieve it from him. She reached for it, and he took the necessary steps to close the gap between them. Her fingertips brushed along the back of his hand, tanned but not rough like her papa's. She jerked back as though burned, but he grabbed her hand before she could fully retreat.

"You're pretty," he said again, his eyes squinting in the red light of the sun, then leaned over and gave her the swiftest of kisses on her cheek, then her lips, then her brow.

She felt her flesh go to goose bumps and she shivered, hoping he hadn't noticed either one.

He stared at her for a moment. "I best get back to the pond," he said, then turned and began to walk away.

"Wait," she said, and he stopped. She extended the handkerchief toward him. "Keep it. So you can think of me sometime."

He took the offering, smiled, then turned back for the pond.

She watched him. Just stood there and watched him until he turned back around and said, "I'll see ya later, Stella."

"Yeah, maybe so, Valentine," she called back. She ran the rest of the way home.

13

Mother and I arrived back at Aunt Stella's at 1:30 that afternoon, ready for the meeting with Karol-with-a-K Paisley. I was wearing a new pair of lined wool slacks and a matching sweater in baby pink cashmere I'd purchased with Evan's credit card. My trunk was filled with bags of purchases.

Though I'd never known Mother to pass up a shopping spree of any kind, she had been my unwilling companion that day. "You're a foolish child, Jo-Lynn, even if you are mine," she said. We were standing in line at a bookstore where I'd picked up a few books.

"How's that, Mother?"

"Leaving your husband in the middle of his midlife crisis to decorate a house, I ask you."

"I'm not decorating it, Mother. *You* have always enjoyed decorating. But *I* am a designer. By profession. There is a difference." I took a deep breath and shifted the books from one arm to another. "Besides, if I can pull this off, I will have left a legacy in Cottonwood. Don't you see that?"

We took a step forward as the cashier—a young woman with blonde hair streaked red and green and a body laden with so many piercings she looked like a Christmas tree—

finished with a customer and brought up another one with one word: "Next?"

"What do you mean 'a legacy'?"

I shook my head. This woman with two children, both of whom appeared to be successful by the world's standards, would never understand what was stirring inside my heart. I wasn't so sure I understood it myself. I wasn't so sure it didn't go deeper than that. "Mother, listen for a minute. If you can, without judgment."

"I resent that," she said, but her voice was kind.

"You grew up as Margaret Seymour of Cottonwood, and that meant something. Then you married Daddy and became Margaret Tatem-Teem, and that meant something. I can't remember a time in my life when you weren't involved in some sort of social club or church group. You lived in the house on the hill, a place people nearly frothed at the mouth to be invited to for Fourth of July picnics and Christmas parties."

Mother's head tipped to one side. "Hmm . . ." Like a princess remembering.

"People highly regarded you and your life stood for something. Always."

Mother looked me in the eye. "How does that affect you?"

"I grew up Jo-Lynn Tatem-Teem and that was something, yes. And marrying Evan was something wonderful. I've enjoyed my career, but . . . I'm not like you socially or civically. I can't even say I've had a drive to be. But now . . . I realize I've really contributed nothing to this life. I've lived it, but that's all I've done."

We took another step forward. "Just trust me, okay?" I said, which—by the shrug of her shoulder—wasn't quite good enough for her, but she settled for it.

I found Karol Paisley to be quite likeable in spite of her commanding disposition. When Mother and I entered the big house without knocking, Karol, Aunt Stella, and Doris were sitting in the living room, a large fire crackling in the fireplace and the three women engaged in conversation and laughter. Seeing us, Karol straightened, drawing her nearly six-foot frame off the sofa, then crossed the room with her right arm extended. "You must be Jo-Lynn."

I took her hand, and she pumped mine as though we were two men, then reached for Mother's. Mother has never been much of one for shaking hands; she clasped her hands together low and in front and said, "I am Margaret Tatem-Teem, Mrs. Paisley. Very nice to meet you."

Karol smiled knowingly, keeping her eyes locked on Mother's. "Ms. Paisley. I'm not married." She looked back to me, her entire body turning, and said, "But, please. We're going to be working together. Call me Karol. And that's Karol-with-a-K."

14

"Karol," I repeated with a smile. "As Mother said, it's very nice to meet you."

Doris stood from the chair I'd sat in a few nights earlier, the night I'd first heard the name Karol-with-a-K Paisley, and joined us. "Jo-Lynn has the most extraordinary taste in decorating—she gets that from my cousin Margaret here. Her home in Atlanta is a veritable showcase even by Druid Hills's standards." Doris raised her brow. "It's an Ivey and Crook built in 1925; isn't that right, Jo-Lynn?"

"1927. But Ivey and Crook may not mean a thing to Karol."

"Of course it does. Anyone who knows anything about architecture knows about Ivey and Crook. Your home must be quite special."

"Thank you." I lightly touched the small of my mother's back. "But if you really want to see a showcase, you must come to Mother's sometime."

Mother frowned and I smiled. By what I recognized as sheer will she drew a smile on her face and said, "Absolutely. You must come by. Where are you staying while you are in town, *Ms.* Paisley?"

A groan came from Aunt Stella. "Mercy, are you going to talk niceties all day or are we going to talk business?"

"Mama! For heaven's sake." Doris sighed. "Yes, let's go into the dining room, shall we?"

With that Doris led the way, followed by Karol and then Mother. I remained next to Aunt Stella's chair, watching the threesome turn out of the hallway and into the dining room, then offered Aunt Stella my hand. "Shall we?"

Aunt Stella *humphed* but took my hand. When she'd steadied herself, I patted her hand in mine. "She's quite a force to be reckoned with, isn't she?"

I felt her hand squeeze mine as she said, "That's her daddy's doings. He made her a stubborn cuss."

For a moment I was lost, then understood her confusion. "Not Doris. Karol."

"She's got spunk," she said. "What do you think of that haircut?"

Karol's hair, bleached blonde, cut close to her head and spiked here and there, was a style I'd grown accustomed to in Atlanta, but it was something of an anomaly in Cottonwood. "I like it, actually. I could never get away with it, but she can."

"Because she's got spunk, that's why." Aunt Stella shuffled toward the door—her feet dressed in Naturalizer soft-leather mules—drawing me with her. "Never saw her in anything but a pair of dungarees either," she added. "That goes to show that she's practical. If I don't know anything else about her, I can tell you that much."

By now we'd reached the dining room. I inched in with Aunt Stella still holding my hand, our arms now linked like a chain support for the aging woman. I glanced around the room; the old thick draperies had been pulled to either side of the large windows. Filtered sunshine struggled to brighten the room as it passed through the grime on the inside and the rusty screens on the outside.

"Mama, come sit down here." Doris motioned to the nearest master chair, one of the eight heavily carved, gold silk upholstered chairs. The material covering the seats and backs was flawless from lack of use.

I helped Aunt Stella into the chair, then took the one to her right. Mother stood at the fireplace, her fingertips dancing over an antique cranberry hobnail pitcher that gleamed and sparkled and had belonged to Aunt Stella's mother, my great-grandmother. Granny Nevilles, Mother had always called her. Doris had set the table—Granny Nevilles's circa 1900 solid quarter-sawn oak carved Dolphin pedestal—with the Staffordshire china Aunt Stella had been given by her parents on her wedding day, Christmas Day, 1946. I watched as the recent widow laid a hand across the dessert plate, patted it, then placed her hand back in her lap.

My heart ached for her. Theirs had been a whirlwind romance; they met, fell in love, and married within a two-month period. "That woman knew a good thing when she found it," Uncle Jim used to say.

Karol took a seat across from me, craning her neck to take in the room. "This house has got such character. I can hardly wait to hear what you plan to do here, Jo-Lynn."

"I'll get the cake and coffee," Doris offered.

"I'll help," Mother said.

15

The two women disappeared through the swinging door leading into the kitchen. Karol, Aunt Stella, and I sat in silence until less than a minute later when they burst back into the room, Doris carrying the Mr. Coffee carafe and Mother carrying the remainder of Miss Melba's caramel cake under the glass top of a cake plate.

"Here we go," Doris sang, then began serving the coffee, beginning with Karol and making her way around the table.

When we'd all settled at the table and taken a bite of cake, Karol praised it to the skies and Aunt Stella said, "Melba's cakes won blue ribbons back when the county fair was an annual event."

I only had the vaguest of memories of the county fair.

Karol leaned back in her chair and crossed her legs, then looked up to the ceiling. "Wow. A remarkable fresco."

"Worse for the wear, I'm afraid, but my hope is that with a good cleaning and a little restoration, we'll be able to uncover the original pattern."

"Stunning." She looked back at the eyes watching her. "Well, why don't I start the meeting off by telling you a little bit about myself?"

"We'd like that," I said.

"Let's see . . . I'm originally from Fairbault, Minnesota—frigid north in the winter, as I remember it. But I moved to Vegas with my father after he and Mom divorced. I know, I know, you're probably wondering why I didn't stay with Mom. Well, I'll tell you." Karol sat up, picked up her fork, sliced off another bite of cake, then put it in her mouth and swallowed. "Mom decided two things the year she divorced Dad. One, to divorce Dad . . ." She took a sip of coffee. "And two, to move to Los Angeles and become a really big star." Karol fanned her hands around her pretty face and cut her eyes upward as she said the last three words. Then she laughed.

"Anyone we know?" Doris asked. "Someone from the movies? Television?"

"Ever hear of Chuck Katz?"

We all paused and pondered. Finally I said, "The game show producer?"

Karol took another bite of cake and nodded. "Mmm. That's him. He's stepdaddy dearest. So, while Mom never got her star on the Hollywood Walk of Fame, she did manage to rub shoulders with some of the biggest names Tinsel Town had to offer."

"Like who?" Doris asked, nearly slipping off the end of her chair.

Karol laughed again. "You name 'em, Mom's had them over for dinner. Or cocktails." She picked up her cup of coffee again and curled her little finger properly into the air.

We all laughed then. Except Mother, who added, "You never said where you were staying."

"Oh. The Southern Hawk . . . that little inn near the university in Raymore. I guess the hawk is the university's mascot? Anyway, it's a room. In my job I stay in so many hotels and motels along the way, one begins to look pretty much like the other."

"What is it exactly that you do, Karol?" I asked. "Maybe you can give some clarity as to what you plan to do for Cottonwood too."

Karol's blue eyes danced beneath dark lashes. "I'm so glad you've asked me that. Let's get right to it. I work for a company called M Michaels. Ever hear of it?"

"They're a land management and investment company."

"That's right. You've done your homework."

"No, I just know . . . with my job . . . well, anyway, I've heard of them. I can't really say I know much about them. Please, continue."

Karol looked at the others at the table. "For those of you who don't know, M Michaels is based out of Vegas."

"I'm sorry to interrupt," Doris said. "But what is a land management and investment company?" She reached over and sliced another piece of cake from the cake plate and plopped it onto the dessert dish before her.

"Good question, Doris. M Michaels—by the way, that's short for Matthew and Mark Michaels. They're brothers, co-owners—M Michaels finds properties and cities worthy of a little facelift and brings them back to life. They hire various companies—real estate developers and designers like your Jo-Lynn—who serve in a subcontractor role. I work as a co-ordinator for everyone in the mix." She put her focus on me again. "The plan of the company, Jo-Lynn, is this: M Michaels wants to purchase each one of the abandoned houses here in Cottonwood. We'll offer a good price, a fair price, to the owner and then most likely tear them down. Some of these houses are just begging to die anyway." She gave a little nod. "We'll start with the houses, but we'll quickly move to Main Street."

"And what about the houses where people live?"

"We'll offer to fix them up. Get them up to the standard

of housing we'll be building. The look and feel of the newer houses will have the look and feel of an old Victorian, but obviously . . . the older ones . . . well, we'd need to do some work."

It made sense to me. "And the businesses? The ones—one or two—that are still in existence?"

"Oh, not to worry. No one will lose their business. M Michaels is prepared to renovate and let them keep their property. In the end, it's a good business decision because it will add to the whole. Does that make sense?"

"Yes. With the total renovation, Cottonwood will draw people, young and eager merchants, families with children. Cottonwood will be booming again in no time."

"Exactly. We'll fill the downtown area with antique shops—very big these days—and cafés and things like that."

Doris raised her hand. "Explain this to me again. What will happen to people who live here already? Like Uncle Bob and Aunt Mae-Jo? When you renovate, will they be kicked out of their home? And, if so, what do you plan to do about them?"

16

Doris made a good point, and Karol nodded in understanding. "According to the 2000 census, there are fewer than 30 families residing here, most of them beyond the actual city limits and mostly farmers. In 2000, Cottonwood had a total of 133 people. I'd be willing to bet that in the last seven or eight years, those figures have gone down. The median income per household is just a tad over $20,000."

"How do you know that?" Doris asked.

"It's my job."

"Most people in Cottonwood have been here all their lives," Aunt Stella said. "Most people here can trace generations of their families to the soil beneath their feet."

Karol didn't answer right away. "Well, let's cross that bridge when we get to it." She turned to me again. "I understand you are an out-of-work interior designer."

"I'm on leave," I said. "I needed some time off."

"She's the best," Doris said. "Wait till you see what she does with this old place."

"What *do* you have in mind, Jo-Lynn?"

I shifted in my seat. "Let me ask you a question first: do you want this house brought back to the time period of Aunt Stella as a bride or her mother as a bride?"

"When was the house built?"

"1896," Aunt Stella provided.

Karol thought a moment before answering. "Well, I'll tell you, we chose this house for the museum because of its size, its location on Main, and the history your family has within Cottonwood. So, I'd have to say we'll go with the way the house would have been in your great-grandmother's day." She smiled. "So, what have you been thinking?"

"My mind has been racing with ideas," I said. "I'll have to look for a contractor, of course. There's probably some termite damage to deal with. Some of these walls might be original, meaning we're looking at canvas stretched over hand-cut lumber, followed by wallpaper. And on top of that, paint. Some of these tongue-and-groove floorboards need to be replaced, if we can match them well enough, and I think we can." I looked down briefly. "This house was built with heart of pine. When they're refinished and buffed you'll be amazed at how new they look. But all in all, I'd like to retain the old Victorian charm of the place, especially as it was in my great-grandparents' time. So you will use this as a museum?"

"That's the plan. As you probably know, part of M Michaels's work is community planning. Most projects are new developments, but when Mark Michaels happened to drive through Cottonwood about six months ago, he got a wild idea to do something like the Historic Savannah Foundation did back in the sixties and seventies when they rebuilt an old city that time and so-called progress had nearly destroyed."

At the mention of the Historic Savannah Foundation Mother sat straight, having been a member in fine standing since a decade after its chartering in 1955. "Savannah has the history to warrant such a project, Ms. Paisley. What does Cottonwood have?"

Karol raised her chin. "Again, I am glad you asked. There is actually a good deal of pre–Civil War and Civil War history here. Not to mention being so close to Savannah, the history goes all the way back to the years just after Oglethorpe landed on the coast. Native American history abounds here."

"I know that. I grew up here. But one could hardly compare Cottonwood with Savannah. There is not much left here aside from having a few productive farms and the shells of several of the plantations that once graced our county."

"Yes, and we'd like to turn some of those old plantations into B&Bs, perhaps. We'll have to find out who owns them first. I've been researching, but the records have only led to other records buried in the courthouse basement." Karol paused, then added, "Maybe you can help with that, Margaret."

Mother is too refined to faint at Karol's use of her first name, but I knew she would have swooned if it wouldn't have made her look like an overdramatic Southern belle. Instead she said, "I'm afraid I'm far too busy at this time."

Karol smiled in understanding. "Then I'll keep at it." She waved her hands in display of the room. "Now, this place will thrive under M Michaels's investment and Jo-Lynn's work. And this old beauty will be the place to draw the locals and the tourists to see how things might have looked a hundred-plus years ago. People will come here, see the remnant of a simpler life, and, in turn, they'll decide to move to Cottonwood in hopes of gaining the same for themselves."

"Sounds very *Field of Dreams*-ish," Doris commented.

Aunt Stella pushed back in her chair. "Hold on a minute," she said, then made her way toward the butler's pantry. Unlike most—situated between the dining room and kitchen—this one had been built between the dining room and living room and was wider than standard. As a child it was one of my favorite places to be. There were built-in hutches on either side, the drawers and shelves filled with everything from silver flatware, linen tablecloths and napkins, silver serving dishes, and a hodgepodge of moldy, dusty daily journals. It was, for me, a playroom. I could hide within it for hours on end, pulling book after book off the shelf and, in the dim lighting, reading about eras when the big house had been the center of a thriving farm. There were records of purchased and freed slaves, births and deaths and the marriages in between, prosperous years of good crops and the unfortunate years when the land had failed to yield. It was history and it was at my fingertips. I thought to say something to Karol about the journals, to tell her that they would make great displays, but instead said to Aunt Stella, "Where are you going? Do you need help?"

"I need nothing. Y'all just give me a minute or two, you hear?"

"Mama, what *are* you—" Doris began, but stopped as Aunt Stella opened the door to the pantry, shuffled in, then closed the door behind her.

"What is that?" Karol asked. "Is that a butler's pantry? I thought butler's pantries went between the kitchen and the dining room." She stuck her thumb up and pointed behind her.

"It's always been a mystery," I said. "The design is not like anything I studied in school. Including its width."

We sat in silence until Karol asked, "Are you an only child, Jo-Lynn?"

"No. I have a younger brother, Stephen. He works with our father."

"I'm an only child," Karol said. She ran her fingertips along the porcelain skin of her face, beginning at her nose and then pressed her index fingers into her temples. When she straightened, she said to Doris, "What about you, Doris?"

About that time the butler's pantry door opened and Aunt Stella came back into the room, carrying with her what appeared to be an old cardboard mailing tube. "What about Doris?"

"Karol wanted to know if I'm an only child. Mama, what do you have there?"

Aunt Stella rejoined us at the table. "She's my one and only," she said, dropping onto the thick seat of the chair. "I always wanted to give Jim a son, God love him. He wanted a boy, but it just wasn't the way it was. Doris was always my girl and"—she patted my arm—"Jo-Lynn was always tomboy enough to be like another grandson for Jim. This one hung out with him like he was her best friend."

I blinked back threatening tears. "Goodness knows there were times he was," I said. "So, Aunt Stella. What is that?" I pointed to the tube.

"These are blueprints." She opened the cylinder's top by sliding it around and then popping it off. "I had forgotten about them until you mentioned the thing about Savannah." She pulled thick blue papers that crackled as she slid them toward her.

I stood then, walked behind her, as did Karol. Together we helped her uncurl the rectangular papers until we were looking down at a flat drawing of the city of Cottonwood, dated 1938. "Papa had an idea even back then," Aunt Stella said. "I remember he said to Mama once that Cottonwood was going to go under one day. Papa always seemed to know things like that in advance." She paused. "I miss you, Papa." The words came out in a whisper, like a thought she hadn't meant to share. Then she shook her cottony white head and said, "You see here." She pointed to the paper. "Papa saw what this town could be if we began some sort of preservation program before it came to rack and ruin."

By this time, Mother and Doris had joined us at the head of the table. "1938," Mother said. "The year before I was born."

Aunt Stella pointed to a small box at the end of the highway running in along the side of the big house, then glanced up momentarily at Karol. "My sister Adeline and her husband Edwin—Margaret's mama and daddy—bought this house right here. Pretty thing. Bob, their son, still lives there. His wife has kept it up nice. You won't have to do much to it, though. It's as pretty today as it was back when Margaret was a child."

Mother squared her shoulders. "My mother had good taste. And Mae-Jo has had the good sense to leave the décor alone."

Doris pressed her hand to her breast. "Oh, I used to love to play down there. Remember, Margaret? The little carriage house? You and Bettina Bach used to pretend one of you was the mother and the other the nanny. We'd play in there for hours on end."

Mother nodded. "I remember."

I straightened, releasing my hold on the paper. Aunt Stella laid her wrinkled forearm across the right edge to keep it down. I placed my hands on Aunt Stella's shoulders and squeezed. "I wish I could have seen my mother and Miss Bettina as young girls, playing with little Doris."

Aunt Stella didn't answer, but I noticed the slightest nod of her head. Perhaps, I thought, she was remembering the days when young girls in pretty dresses and hair tied up in bows played and giggled and ran in and out of the big house and the home of my grandparents. Now, days of wondering what their futures would hold had given way to the present; some of it good, some of it not.

"Aunt Stella?"

Aunt Stella raised her arm, then pushed Karol's hand away

from the other end of the blueprint. The papers curled inward, and Aunt Stella began to rework them. "Jo-Lynn, make a copy of these, will you, shug?" She pushed back in her chair, sending the four of us scampering to either side. "Let Ms. Paisley here have the copies in case her bosses need them. Papa would have been proud, knowing the hard-earned money he spent on these blueprints had not been for nothing." She stood then, steadied herself by leaning on the table for a moment before sliding the blueprints back into the tube, then turned and handed the tube to me by bopping me on the shoulder with it. "Here you go. You might want to think about framing these originals. For this museum you're going to design out of my memories." She laughed, then reached for Doris. "Doris, shug. Mama's tired now. Come help me lay down for a nap, will ya?"

17

Mother and I were on our way back to Raymore. The sky had turned a deeper shade of gray, but Mother had insisted we stop by the cemetery to check on Uncle Jim's grave. We rode in silence until I said, "Mother, whatever happened to you and Bettina Bach? As friends, I mean."

Mother began to wring her hands.

"Mother? What is it?" I shot her a quick look, then re-focused on the road and driving. It seemed it grew darker outside by the minute.

"Bettina never thought she was pretty enough . . . smart enough . . . Everyone felt that she'd settled for Buster Godwin. He was employed by her father after they married, but he'd hardly hit a lick at a snake. Not like Mr. Valentine. He and Uncle Jim were a lot alike in that. Maybe that's why they were such good friends. I remember that when Miss Lilly Beth— Bettina's mother—died . . . she died young, you know . . ."

I shook my head. "No, I don't know anything at all about her. Or, if I did, I've certainly forgotten it."

"Died just after her thirtieth birthday. Pneumonia. I re-member Uncle Jim saying that Valentine Bach would never be the same without Miss Lilly Beth. He adored her. Simply adored her."

"Like Uncle Jim adored Aunt Stella?"

Mother chuckled. "Oh, he did do that, didn't he? That cantankerous woman . . . he treated her like she was a queen, but no one could put Stella in her place like he could." Then she laughed out loud, and I joined her. "Uncle Jim said that all the women in Cottonwood—the single women—tried to cut a path to Mr. Valentine's door within a week of Miss Lilly Beth being buried. But he wasn't interested then, and I guess he never was." Mother pressed her thighs with her palms. "Uncle Jim said it was the most compassion he'd ever seen Aunt Stella show another human being; that she'd cried and cried for Miss Lilly Beth and what Mr. Valentine was left to do, raising Bettina all by himself.

"You know, when we were young girls, Mr. Valentine was always clean shaven. Not like he is now with his wild scraggly gray beard and long hair. He wore overalls at his work as a builder, of course, but when he came home, he'd go straight to the bath and wash up. After his wife died, he never did dress properly again. He just lived in overalls. It was like the life in him was buried with her."

"But like you said, he had Bettina."

"I used to have dinner over there, back when Bettina and I were very young children. Elementary school age. And always on fried chicken night. Goodness, could Miss Lilly Beth fry a chicken. Even better than Aunt Stella or Mama.

"I remember how he'd come to the kitchen table smelling like soap and aftershave." Mother paused at the memory. "He'd give Miss Lilly Beth a kiss, then nuzzle Bettina's neck. And she'd giggle like little girls do." I could see Mother's head turn toward me then. I cut her a look. "Jo-Lynn, the love of a child cannot replace the love of a spouse." For a moment I didn't answer, so she added, "You know that, don't you?"

"I know that."

I heard her take in a deep breath, then let it go. "Listen, my love. I still don't understand why you'd leave your husband to do it, but I'm beginning to understand your reasoning for taking on that project back there."

"You do?" I glanced at her somber face. "Really?"

"Keep your eyes on the road, please, ma'am. And yes I do. Honestly, I've struggled with whether just to buy you a book on 'finding purpose' and hope you figure it all out for yourself. But there was something you said in the bookstore that made sense."

"That's one for the records."

"Don't be snippy. The point is, I'm here to help you in any way, if you need me." She reached across the seat and slipped her fingers into my hair at the nape of my neck, then scratched with her nails, an endearing thing she'd done as long as I could remember. "You're *my* child, after all." Another quick look at her and she smiled at me. "And I love you."

18

Cottonwood, Georgia
1939

He had become her best friend, even better than Jane Hawkins, who'd gone off to a business school, unlike most girls from Cottonwood, who settled down after high school and got married.

She loved Jane like one of her sisters, but Valentine was different. She could tell him everything and anything. All of her dreams and her fears. She could be angry with him and he wouldn't get angry back. She could tell him her feelings—her honest feelings—about her papa and mama and he understood. She could cry and she could laugh and he would hold her or laugh with her. Whichever one was appropriate.

He was gentle with her, treated her sweet. Brought her penny candies he'd bought from her brother's store. Laughed and said, "If Mister Conroy knew who I was giving these candies to, he'd probably whoop me all the way down this path." And Stella knew Conroy would do more than that if he knew what else they'd been doing.

Sometimes Valentine brought cigarettes, and they'd smoke

them if for no other reason than to keep the mosquitoes away. On cold days he'd bring a little toddy; he said it'd keep them warm. And it did too.

Now she'd been seeing him for a year. More than a year, really. Sometimes once a week, sometimes more, at a specified time, whatever worked best for him. At seventeen-nearly-eighteen, he worked alongside his father as a builder and handyman and never knew when he could break away. But he always managed to find the best time. The right time.

For her.

Stella's schedule was a little easier. In spite of her papa's worried looks and her mama's anxious comments about whether or not she was going to find "a nice boy and settle down," she managed to elude them with her hard work around the house and the farm. Elude them because Valentine said they'd have to keep their love a secret. At least for the time being.

"I don't understand," she'd whispered once, a long time ago—forever ago, it seemed to her—as they lay under an old gnarled sycamore and upon the pinwheel quilt she'd snuck out of the spare bedroom chifforobe, the one where Mama stored all the old linens and quilts and swatches of fabric she said she'd someday make into this or that. She lay flat on her back upon it, felt the softness of it against what little bit of flesh was exposed. Overhead, the canopy of the darkening sky curved above them, the tall stretch of pines and live oaks, bushy chinaberries and weeping willows shadowed against the orange and yellow of the horizon. The slapping of water against the pond's shoreline combined with the occasional leap of a fish and the croak of tree frogs was comforting to Stella. It was the rhythm that carried the beat of lips coming together and then apart and the rustling of clothes as their arms encircled each other, hungry for more. Always for more. "I don't understand," she said again, her emotions spent and raw, "why we can't just tell everyone about us. That we love each other. That we—"

"Shhh," he said, kissing the tip of her nose. "I told you. We're Lutherans. You're Baptist—"

"Primitive Baptist. There's a difference. And I don't care."

"You'd best care. It's an even bigger difference than you know, Stella. My mama and daddy would never understand. They say we have to stick together, we Lutherans. German Lutherans, at that. You gotta understand, girl. We go to a church clear over in Savannah. They speak German in the services, Stella. It's that way with us." He paused, allowing his shoulders to relax and his tone to soften. "But you listen here, now. It's gonna be all right. I promise. You gotta trust me on that."

"I do, it's just—"

"Just don't say you won't come here, to our place. Don't say you don't love me."

Stella squeezed her eyes shut. "I do love you." She opened them again. "But Papa and Mama are wondering why I'm not looking to get married by now. Why I'm not making some kind of plans for my life. They keep saying that my sisters were nearly all married by this age. Or, at least they had someone coming to the house. My folks are all thinking something is wrong with me."

He had chuckled then, nuzzled her neck as he slipped his arm up under her and drew her closer to himself. "I can tell them there ain't not one thing wrong with you, Miss Stella." And he kissed her again and made her forget all about Papa and Mama and the entire town of Cottonwood wondering when she'd walk down the aisle of Piney Wood Primitive Baptist and become a real woman.

For so long, it had been enough. Clandestine meeting after clandestine meeting, sweet kiss after sweet kiss, but now . . .

Now, Stella thought. Now Valentine would have to do something about their relationship, make it known to his family first, to her family after that. Then Cottonwood . . . and the preacher who was always asking her about her purpose in life . . . and Mrs. Foster, his wife, who looked down her nose at Stella as though Stella weren't quite good enough to sit in the pews . . . as though she was up to no good, even when Stella stood nearby, songbook open, singing to the Lord.

Now maybe Papa would stop comparing her to her sisters: Adeline, married and expecting their third child, and Lottie, married to Charles Kavenaugh, living in Rome, Georgia, and mother of two.

"Hey."

Stella heard the familiar voice behind her and she turned. She had already spread the quilt, sat in the middle of it, her feet tucked beneath her bottom, keeping herself busy by tracing the pattern of triangles with her index finger.

"Hey yourself." She smiled at him and he smiled back, showing off white but imperfect teeth that she'd always thought were bigger than his mouth. Not that she cared.

His face lost the smile then. He dipped his hands deep within the pockets of his overalls and he tucked his chin toward the bib.

"Did you just get off from work?"

He nodded. "Yeah." He looked back up then. "Stella, I . . . listen, I . . . I gotta talk to you 'bout something. And it's right important."

She lowered her lashes. "Yeah, I gotta talk to you about something too."

He stared at her for a moment, chewed on the inside of his mouth.

"You gonna sit down?"

He didn't answer right away, then nodded again like an

old dog and lumbered over. Crossing his ankles, he sat, his knee knocking against hers. He drew back, as though it were improper, as though there'd never been a touch between them.

"What's wrong, Valentine?" She reached for his hand, but he pulled away.

"Stella, I . . ."

She watched his Adam's apple bob up and down a few times, then looked into his eyes. For the life of her, she could swear he was about to cry.

"Did someone die?"

"Me."

"What? What are you talking about? Are you sick? Valentine, you're scaring me." She pulled herself up on her knees, sat on the heels of her feet, grabbed his knees with her hands. "Maybe I should tell you my news first? Maybe that will make things better?"

He nodded. "Yeah," he said, the word choking on something in his throat. "Why don't you do that?"

She straightened her shoulders, waited for him to look her in the eye.

"What is it, Stella?" he asked, when he finally did as she wanted.

"I'm going to have a baby, Valentine. Your baby," she added as though he needed to be told. "We're going to be a mama and papa, and we can finally tell your folks and mine and we can get married like we've talked about . . . and . . . what? What is it, Valentine?" She covered her face with her hands. "Oh no. Oh no." Her breath became ragged. "You're not happy. I thought you'd be happy." She dropped her hands and looked at him, studied him. Dear God, what must the man be thinking?

He started to cry, tears pouring down his cheeks. He drew

his knees up to his chest, laid his forehead against them, and whimpered like a boy. "I don't know what to do . . . ," he repeated over and over again until Stella's heart pounded so frantically within her she thought she'd die from it all.

"What do you mean? You love me, right?"

"You know I do." His head jerked up. Blue eyes were washed out to near gray. "You know I do."

"Then why can't you . . . can't we? . . . I'm pregnant, Valentine. Did you not understand that part?"

"And I'm getting married, Stella . . . tomorrow . . . to another girl . . . that's what I came to tell you. My parents . . . hers . . . she's from the church over in Savannah. Her father's the reverend there and . . . and I'm getting married tomorrow . . . and there ain't nothing I can do about it 'cept go through with it."

He leaped from the quilt, stumbled over his feet, then steadied himself as he looked down on her. "I'm sorry. I'm so sorry . . . but I can't . . . I can't . . . You don't know my daddy . . ."

He took off running then, running for home, she supposed. Running for his future, all planned out by his parents, apparently. Running away from her and their child—her child now—leaving her alone to face the rest of her life without him.

19

Evening came chilled and quick; a dark blanket falling over Cottonwood, exposing an outline of trees and the frames of scattered buildings. Streetlights—though few—flickered on as I stood near the road, watching the taillights of Doris's car pierce the darkness like two red eyes catching a last glimpse at what was left behind, then slip around a bend in the road leading to Luverne and what would now be Aunt Stella's new home. I wrapped my thick knee-length sweater tight around myself and shivered, then turned toward the house, stopping long enough to take it in—the large shingled roof, the pointing gables on the second floor and the pediments of the wrap-around porch beneath them, the rising of the chimneys and the smoke that billowed now from two of them. I counted the columns supporting the porch's roof—ten I could see from where I stood—and the brick steps, three on the front and to the right, that led to the refuge of a swing on one end, a glider on the other, and a line of rockers in between.

I ran, then. Ran toward the house that would be my home for the next several months. Ran toward the place I'd know as my haven and my work. I was completely alone now; Mother well on her way to the house on the hill and Aunt Stella and Doris on their way to Mickey and the kids, who were waiting with a pot roast, potatoes, onions, and carrots, all simmering in a Crock-Pot. "They'll wait till we get there, Mama," Doris had said to Aunt Stella as she settled her into the front passenger's seat. "Mickey said it'll be a feast fit for a queen." She kissed her cheek. "That's you, sugar plum."

Aunt Stella had smiled wide. "I know."

My stomach churned as I slid into the glider, reminding me that I, too, had to eat. But for a while I ignored the gnawing hunger and allowed myself to get lost in the squeak of old hinges in need of oil as I pushed myself—feet flat on the floorboards and knees together—back and forth, back and forth, to and fro. The metal beneath me was colder than I'd expected. I don't know why I was surprised; the temperature had hardly reached forty all day.

I turned up the collar of my sweater in an attempt to ward off the wind from my ears. It began its low whistle, a signal that it was time for me to find my way indoors. I stood and stared at my feet, placing one in front of the other atop a single straight board. As I'd done when a child, I took a deliberate step—heel to toe—then another and another until I'd reached the left angle of the porch and was forced to decide whether or not to simply walk like a grown-up toward the door or to continue in my game.

Just then the outside lights of Uncle Bob's nearby store blinked on, revealing its small frame and the wide roof that jutted from its front, supported by thick, white brick columns splattered with tin signs—rusted and disfigured—from the 1960s. They advertised canned goods, motor oil, and Shell gasoline. There was a small red and white sign that read Clean Restroom Inside in bold letters at the top and Everyone Welcome in smaller letters below them. There were two pumps between the columns; the older one hadn't been used in years, the newer one was pumped by locals or those who thought themselves wise to drive from Raymore for the twenty cents a gallon difference in price.

I skipped down the steps of the big house and scurried over the dead grass of the front lawn, along the sidewalk and down the short distance to cross the street at the stop sign. Though with no traffic in sight, I'm not sure what difference it made. I dug my hands into the deep pockets of the sweater, wrapping it around me again, and felt the wind push me along.

The front windows were covered by rusty screens and the front door, kept shut during the winter and summer but wide open in warm weather, was made of solid wood. The old doorknob, I noted, had been replaced by a shiny brass knob and dead bolt, but the sign overhead, "Seymour's Shell Station" (with "Robert and Mae-Jo Seymour, Owners" written in small black letters below), that graced the entry as long as I could remember was still there. To both the right and the left were two advertising benches; one that faintly read "Grayson's Funeral Home" and the other "Miss Gladys's School of Etiquette & Charm." I knew this more from memory than what I could now see. I thought it strange that both businesses were long gone but their commercials remained.

I opened the old screen door—its wire stretched and rusty—then pushed open the door and stuck my head in. I saw Uncle Bob's wife Mae-Jo standing behind the counter in front of the rows of cigarettes and chewing and pipe tobacco, just beyond the old brass cash register. She looked up and smiled; in her early seventies she was still pretty and petite. "Well, darlin', I wondered when you might come over," she said. "Come on in and get out of the cold."

She came around the counter—its patina glossy with age and polish—then wrapped me in a tight hug and rubbed my back hard and fast. "Goodness, child, you're cold as the dead. Come on over here now and sit by the fire."

The inside of the store was like something out of a Maya Angelou short story. The floorboards were old and weathered. The roof was low, causing the room to feel smaller than it was. To the left was the long counter where glass jars filled with candy still managed to titillate the heart of adult or child. An old coffee grinder—painted a dull red and trimmed in black—stood next to a few cans of Maxwell House and Folgers. Just past the counter and near the back door were two chests, one for ice cream treats and the other for sodas. I'd spent many an afternoon dipping my hand into their frosty depths. From the ice cream chest I was most fond of ice cream sandwiches and from the other six-ounce Coca-Colas, to which I would add salted peanuts.

The "fire" Mae-Jo had beckoned me toward was a potbellied stove sitting between two long church pew benches. In front of them were two old tables with two chairs each. Behind the benches were rows of shelves, stocked with canned and boxed goods, household cleaners, and other small grocery items.

"I just came to pick up a few things." I walked over to the stove and placed my hands in front of it. It felt warm and good, and a sudden sense of my childhood came over me. "For supper mainly."

Mae-Jo joined me, then sat on one of the pews, crossed her legs, and began to swing her ankle in tiny circles the way she'd done as long as I could remember. "Don't tell me your mama left you alone over there at the big house with nary a thing to eat."

I shook my head. "Oh, there's plenty to eat. I'm just tired of what's over there. Even after a week, there's enough funeral food to last a lifetime. What I really want is a good old-fashioned peanut butter and jelly sandwich with some greasy potato chips followed by milk and Oreos."

Mae-Jo slapped her hands on her thighs. "Then you have

come to the right place, Jo-Lynn." She stood. "Not hardly a soul comes in here anymore. But we still manage to keep the food fresh, let me just make you rest assured on that one." By now she'd retrieved a shopping basket from the end of the counter and had begun to make her way to the back. I turned to watch her. "If it weren't for Bob's retirement from the postal service and mine from the board of education, we'd starve to death. Do you need bread?"

"Yes, ma'am."

"All right. We've only Sunbeam white, you know."

"Sounds good. I'm good on milk, though."

"All right." She paused, then added, "What do you think about all this that's going on in Cottonwood? This renovation project that Paisley woman is ranting about?"

I looked over the tops of the shelves and saw the graying top of Mae-Jo's head as she moved down a back aisle. I raised my voice to answer. "Obviously, I'm for it. Otherwise I wouldn't be here. I think it'll be a good thing, don't you?"

"Time'll tell." She must have stretched to her tiptoes because she grew a few inches taller, and she peered over the shelves, her large glasses reflecting the dim overhead light. "We've got Skippy crunchy or smooth. Which you prefer?"

"Smooth." I watched her eyes disappear again.

"I can tell you a few of the old-timers have no intention of leaving their homes, but others heard there would be a pretty penny offered, and they practically knocked themselves out running over to the Home Depot in Raymore for packing boxes."

I smiled. "I imagine so."

"I've got some of Mrs. Patterson's homemade strawberry preserves at the counter, or do you prefer Welch's grape?"

I thought for a moment. Mrs. Patterson's preserves were nearly a staple of my childhood. They were gooey sweet and delicious. I answered, "How about one of each?" With the peanut butter I'd have the grape. For breakfast in the morning, I'd slather the strawberry onto lightly golden toast. My stomach leapt at the delectable simplicity of it.

I heard Mae-Jo chuckle. Moments later she was ringing up my total at the brass register, then she pulled a ledger from under the counter. I ambled over to her and watched as she opened it to a new page, scrawled my name on the top with a pen cleverly attached by a string and a thumb tack in the eraser, and said, "There now. You are an official resident of Cottonwood."

"Looks like I am." My eyes caught hers, and she winked at me.

Mae-Jo began bagging my purchase. "Honey, listen," she said, stopping halfway through her task. "I'm sorry you and Evan are having such a time right now. But don't you worry. It'll work itself out. Things like this always do."

I felt myself go weary. "I'm sure you're right."

20

Mae-Jo slid the bread into its own small brown bag, Miss Sunbeam sunny-side up. "Your Uncle Bob will be here shortly, I hope. He and Mr. Valentine were working on something or another for Melba Dawson this afternoon and it's either taking longer than they expected or she's fed them supper."

I leaned my forearms on the counter and laced my fingers. "Is Mr. Valentine still doing his work? I would have thought he'd have retired by now."

Mae-Jo closed the ledger and slipped it back under the counter. "Valentine Bach will work till his fingers fall off or the good Lord calls him home. I don't know what he's got your Uncle Bob a-doing, but whatever it is, I'm past ready for the man to come here and help me close up shop."

I straightened. "Is there something I can do?"

"Nary a thing." She walked over to a candy jar and opened it. "How about some licorice to spoil your dinner?"

I joined her, pulled a Red Vine twist from the jar, and bit into it. It was cherry. "This takes me back," I said. Mae-Jo resumed her "end of the day" labors as I worked my way down my candy. "Aunt Mae-Jo?"

"Hmm?"

"Tell me, who are some of the people here you think won't want to leave?"

Mae-Jo stopped and leaned a hip against the backside of the counter. "Well, let's see. Melba Dawson, for one. She's still living in the house she and Walter built, even though he's been gone now for—what?—nearly a decade, I reckon. But she'll never leave. They raised their children in that house, and Walter practically built it with his own hands for her before they married. His hands and Valentine's, of course. Not too many of the newer homes around here Valentine Bach or his daddy didn't build or lay their hammer to. And when I say 'newer' you know, of course, I mean built within the last sixty to seventy years."

"So, Mrs. Dawson wouldn't move," I said, gently tugging Aunt Mae-Jo back from her rabbit trail.

"Nor her sister, Irene Patterson. She and Marvin are set like old stones around here. Of course, Bob and I aren't going anywhere, and Valentine Bach will most likely never leave. Especially not with Bettina here and her son and his wife, Fiona. They seem perfectly content here. Of course, you know they have three kids, two are twin girls. Prettiest things you ever did see."

"How old are they? The twins?" I reached into the candy jar and pulled out another twist of licorice. "You can add this to my tab," I said, wiggling it toward her.

"Don't worry 'bout that none." She shook her head. "Fifteen or sixteen, I'd say. No, they'd have to be sixteen. I've seen them driving their mama's car up here a few times to pick up groceries Fiona calls ahead for."

"Who else?"

"Well, let's see. Clyde and Larisa Walker. Now, here's a story." She rolled her eyes. "Clyde Walker at least sixty if not sixty-five years old, give or take a year, and he goes on the

99

Internet and finds himself one of those Russian mail-order brides. Everyone in town thought the man had lost his mind and near 'bout expected him to bring home some twenty-one-year-old who'd sink an axe in the middle of his skull one night while he lay sleeping, then take off with his money. Not that Clyde has any. He's got enough, mind you. And he's as tight as Harry's hatband. Nearly nickel and dimes me to death over here, and that man wouldn't put a red cent into that house he's a-livin' in. It belonged to his mama and daddy and pretty much looks just like it did when Old Lady Walker came to it as a bride."

"What about when the Russian bride came to it?"

"Oh yeah. Bob said to him, 'Clyde, why don't you find some nice girl from around here?' but Clyde was quick to point out there wasn't anyone from around here who was single other than Melba Dawson, and they're first cousins."

I burst out laughing. Mae-Jo smiled at her own humor.

"Did she turn out to be okay? This mail-order bride?"

"Nicest thing. She's nearly fifty if she's a day and treats Clyde like he's some Prince Charming, God help us all. Larisa Walker makes the rest of us look like slovenly women, but I like her anyway. Doesn't know much English still, but she tries."

"The South has its own English," I reminded her. "So she's at a bit of a disadvantage."

Mae-Jo opened the cash register and began pulling out bills. "Go lock the door for me, will you? If your Uncle Bob isn't going to come here to help me with this, then I may as well have you stand guard. Not that you'd be any use against someone who really wanted to break in, but at least there's strength in numbers."

I walked over to the front door and bolted it. "I don't know, Aunt Mae-Jo. I seem to remember you're pretty good with a shotgun."

"Who isn't around these parts?"

I turned to face her, then leaned against the door. "That reminds me. Several nights ago I woke up in the middle of the night and saw two men traipsing through Aunt Stella's property. One of them appeared to have some sort of metal box tucked under his arm."

"Did you recognize them?"

"Not at that ungodly hour, no. I could only see them from the back, and I was up in my bedroom so there was the distance. I can't imagine anyone from around here sneaking around at that time of night, though, can you?"

"Can't imagine why anyone would want to be awake when they could be sleeping." She placed a stack of bills on the counter and began pulling change from one of the coin cubbies in the register. "What time did you say it was?"

"I didn't." I returned to the counter. "But probably around three or four. I don't remember now exactly."

"Did you mention it to Stella?" Mae-Jo dropped the pennies and reached for the nickels.

"Can I help you with that?"

"No. I've got it." She began counting the silver coins, and I waited until she was done. "Two-seventy-five," she said, jotting numbers onto a nearby pad of paper. "Plus the fifty-seven cents in pennies."

"Three-thirty-two. No, I didn't mention it to Aunt Stella. No need in getting her upset." My stomach growled so loudly it echoed in the quiet of the store.

"Well, good thing. The Lord knows when that woman gets riled up she's a mess to deal with." Mae-Jo chuckled again, scooped up the dimes, and dropped them onto the counter. "She wasn't always like that though."

"What do you mean?"

Mae-Jo waved at me. "I'll tell you all about that another

101

time. Go on home and make yourself your peanut butter and jelly now, you hear. Bob will be here shortly and if he's not, he's going to find himself sleeping with the dogs. Go out the back door. It locks behind itself."

"Are you sure?" I reached for my purchases.

"I'm sure. Go on."

I was halfway out of the store when I heard Mae-Jo call to me, "And don't worry about those two men. Probably Terry Godwin and one of his friends from over to Raymore he's always running around with. Young'uns these days don't know when to go to bed and when to stay up, I always say."

"I'll see you later, Aunt Mae-Jo."

"Come on back anytime," she hollered. "It's good to have you so close for a while."

I opened the back door. The outside light came on automatically. The wooden steps leading to the ground were rickety. I took each step carefully, then hurried across the way to the big house. As I reached the front door and pulled open the screen, I spun around, thinking I heard something behind me.

My breath caught in my throat. "Who's there?"

Silence. I looked across the porch, down the steps and the lawn and to the road where, on the other side, twig-like branches from small dogwoods cut dark shadows into the large oaks past them.

I jerked at the sound of shuffling feet. "Uncle Bob?"

No answer.

"Terry Godwin, is that you?"

I stood steady, holding my breath in wait for an answer, but none came.

When all sound by the wind stopped, I turned back to face the door of my new home, allowed the screen to rest against my right shoulder, then turned the jangly doorknob and went inside.

21

The house was empty, or nearly so.

I had driven to Raymore, rented four large self-storage units, then gone to the day labor camp, which wasn't a camp at all but a place where men—and occasionally women— gathered in wait for someone to come along and hire them for the day, cash only. That particular morning they stood under the branches of an old oak and huddled around three rusted-out metal trash cans, small fires crackling in each one. The ground around their feet was littered with twisted pages from the newspaper, tossed wrappers from various types of snacks, discarded bottles, and cigarette butts.

They were dressed in layers, mostly cast-off clothing. Their shoulders were hunched against the cold and the hardship of life; their hands covered by mittens, most which needed mending. I sat for a few moments across the street in a bank's parking lot, watching as they rubbed their palms together, then cupped and blew into them in an effort to warm their faces. This February morning was brutal.

When I opened my car door and walked toward them, they straightened then turned toward me. "Gentlemen." Two women were there, one blonde and petite who appeared to be in her late twenties, the other a black woman who appeared to be in the middle thirties. "Ladies."

"Yes, ma'am." "What can we do for you, ma'am?" "How can we help you today?" the men asked at the same time.

The women said nothing.

"Who of you can drive and has a valid driver's license?"

Four hands shot up, including the blonde woman's.

"I will need every single one of you for today and tomorrow, so if anyone comes asking you to work, tell them you are already spoken for. Right now, I need the four of you who can drive to come with me if you have your license with you. Do you?"

They all nodded.

"Show me."

They walked toward me, reaching for wallets in the back pockets of their baggy pants and dirty jeans. When they'd made it to where I stood, they extended their licenses. I looked at each one, beginning with the woman's. "Jerusha." I looked up from the square of plastic. "How are you today?"

She smiled at me, displaying perfect white teeth, then grabbed her shoulder-length unruly hair and jerked it to one side in a makeshift ponytail. "I'm good, thank you."

"Are you strong enough to help me load up some household items?"

"Yes, ma'am." She smiled again.

I asked the same questions of the men, James—who insisted I call him Jim-bo—Delrue, and Percy. Then I shuffled them toward my car, where they climbed in and went with me to the nearby U-Haul dealership. Within an hour, the four drivers were behind the wheels of a truck each, all loaded with the remaining men and woman, whose name was Coral. They drove in a convoy toward Cottonwood and spent the rest of the day boxing the house, carefully labeling each container, and then packing the trucks with what would later be unloaded into the storage unit.

The only room off limits was my room, and I kept it locked.

Irene Patterson and her sister Melba arrived at noon with platefuls of fried chicken and bowls of potato salad and hot vegetables, a bread basket filled with rolls, one of Miss Melba's famous cakes, and gallons of sweet iced tea. I promised them a check just as soon as I settled up with Karol, to which Miss Irene said to Miss Melba, "Just think, Sister. We're now officially a part of the rebuilding."

Half an hour later the crew went back to work, full and happy.

It was mid-afternoon when Percy entered the house through the back door and said, "Miss Jo-Lynn. Have you seen what's out there in the barn?"

The women and I were boxing the kitchen and pantry. I stood on a step stool and was stretched toward the top shelf where everyday china, caked in grease that had somehow managed to seep upward and through cabinet doors, was stacked. I had been handing it, piece by sticky piece, to Jerusha, who took it to the deep porcelain sink filled with warm sudsy water. Coral's arms were wet up to her elbows as she washed each piece with a scrubbie-sponge, then set them gingerly on the paper-towel-lined counter.

I peered over my shoulder at the massive black man with tender deep-set eyes. He stood clutching his ribbed beanie in front of him like a schoolboy. "I haven't. Is it something I should see?"

"I would want to if I were you. This being your family home and all."

I climbed down from the stool. "Jerusha, you'll take over from here for me?"

"Sure," she said, then bounded up the step stool.

I followed Percy out the back door, grabbing my jacket from the back of one of the kitchen chairs as I passed by. When the door shut soundly behind me, I shoved my arms into the jacket's sleeves, then ambled down the back porch steps and along the winding thicket-covered path toward the unpainted barn and connected stables, nearly unseen by the overgrown shrubs around it.

Percy's heavy footsteps fell behind mine. I momentarily peered over my shoulder. "How tall are you, Percy?"

"Six-seven."

I shot him a quick smile. "Remind me to keep you close if I'm ever stuck in a dark alley."

Behind me came the rumble of amusement.

22

Cottonwood, Georgia
1939

She'd waited as long as she dared.

"Mama." She stood in the doorway of the kitchen. Mama's back was to her; she was at the sink, washing the chicken she'd be serving for supper, Stella figured. "Where's Papa?"

Mama looked over her shoulder briefly. "Shug, go get me some of my canned field peas from the pantry."

Stella did as she was told, set the glass Mason jar on the counter next to her mother, then repeated her question. "Where's Papa?"

"In the barn, I s'pose."

Stella looked down a flicker of a moment, then breathed out a sigh she'd not realized was pent up. She turned, made it to the door, with one foot in the hallway. Her mother said her name, and she stopped, turned around. "Yes, ma'am?"

"Get your papa's sweater over that chair there and take it to him." Stella watched her mother dip her head and gaze through the window at the October sky. "It's turning colder by the minute."

Stella returned to the table, pulled her father's sweater from the chair, and left the room without another word.

She would tell her papa first, she'd decided. Somehow she knew it was the right thing to do. The best way to handle the situation. Mama would become hysterical, might even fall on the floor in a faint, but Papa would know what to do. Papa was a secure shelter in any storm. And this was the worst storm of all.

Stella walked along the curving path toward the barn; her mother's perennials—daisies standing tall and proud above the vivid pink Autumn Joy, whose blossoms and fleshy leaves were bunched together like rusty-red nosegays of broccoli, and pink dahlias—shifted slightly as she passed by, as though they anticipated the news she was about to share and how it would change the home they were planted in. How it would change the woman whose hands so lovingly tended them. Stella felt her shoulders tip forward and her stomach lurch in dreaded anticipation.

She stopped, contemplated going back into the house. Maybe even waiting one more day. One more week. One more month. She looked down at her stomach, ran her hands down her sides, felt the thickness of her waist that had already set in.

She had to get this over with. She had to do it now.

She found her father sitting at his desk in the barn. She'd opened one of the double doors just enough to slip her small frame through it, then closed it behind her. The intrusion of the light she'd let in wasn't noticed by her father, who sat in the back where he kept a desk. Atop it was the Zenith tombstone radio he'd bought years ago, before the Depression hit and spending on such extravagances as out of the question. A gentle tune poured from the speaker.

Stella leaned against the door, breathed in the scent of the place—the hay, the sawdust and the molasses sweet feed, the lingering fragrance of animal flesh that never went away, even when the animals weren't there. She listened long enough to recognize the music from the radio; "I've Got the World on a String" was playing.

"Lucky me," Stella whispered the lyrics. "I'm in love."

Her father was dressed in gray pants and a white long-sleeved shirt, the sleeves of which he'd loosely rolled up to his elbows. Against the unpainted boards and hanging barn implements he seemed out of place somehow. Her father, even working amid animal stalls, was a gentleman. The hat cocked on the right post of his ladder-back chair was testament to that.

She made her way toward him, heard him humming along with the music. As she neared, she saw that he was studying numbers on the page of a ledger. At his right hand was a piece of paper where he was doing his figuring. Math had never been her gift, but it was surely her papa's. If it had been hers— if she'd been better at calculating—maybe she wouldn't be standing behind him now with news sure to bring his world to a halt. Even if only temporarily. Or maybe forever.

Stella was so close to her father now, she could reach out and touch him. Realizing he was still unaware of her presence, she looked down at her feet and shuffled one against the floor scattered with sawdust. Her father turned then. He smiled. He called her "sugar foot" and reached around and turned the radio down then casually picked up a stack of papers and slid them into an envelope with the words *Thursday Nights* marking its center. He opened the bottom drawer of the desk and dropped the envelope inside. He shifted back to her, saw the sweater in her hands, and said, "Did your mama send that out to me?"

Stella nodded, or at least she thought she did. Perhaps she hadn't. She extended the garment to her father. "In case you're getting cold, Papa." She kept her eyes on the bottom drawer.

Papa thought she didn't know . . . But she did . . .

He stood then and took the sweater, wrapped it around his shoulders without putting his arms into the sleeves. He wasn't a tall man, but he was still taller than his youngest daughter, and at that moment the bottom drawer was forgotten and she felt as though she were five years old again. She tipped her head, felt a tear slip down her cheek.

"Stella-child. What is it? What's wrong?" He reached for her, gathered her in his arms, as tender as if she were a newborn.

Stella laid her head against his shoulder, felt the hardness of it against her temple, took in the scent of the man she loved more than any other, and that included Valentine Bach. "Papa," she said at last. "Oh, Papa." Her body racked with sobs then, and Papa tipped her chin to force her to look into his eyes.

"Tell Papa," he said. "Papa'll fix it."

"Will you? Will you, Papa?"

"Haven't I always?" he answered with a wink. "Now you tell Papa what's wrong and watch Papa fix it." He motioned her over to his chair. "Sit down right here and we'll talk it out. That's the first step to any problem, talking it out."

Stella felt herself being lowered to the woven rush of the chair's seat. She took a deep breath, raised her shoulders nearly to her ears, then blew out and let them relax. Her father sat on the corner edge of the desk, one leg thrown over it, the other supporting him from the floor. She watched his leg swing ever so slightly, mesmerized momentarily.

"Stella," he said, coaxing her to speak.

Her eyes traveled up the buttons of his shirt, stopping on the bowtie between his collars. It seemed to her that it winked. "Papa . . . ," she said at last. "You know the Bachs? They're kind of new around here."

"Yes." He spoke the word as though it were multisyllabic. Gave a nod of his head.

"And you know Mr. Bach's son, Valentine?"

"I do. I believe he got married a few months back, did he not?"

Stella felt it then, the first flight of butterflies being released in the pit of her belly. Her baby—hers and Valentine's—stirring to life at the mention of Valentine's wife. "Yes, sir," she said. "Lilly Beth is her name . . ."

23

"It's like a treasure chest," I said to Percy, who stood next to me. We stood side by side just inside the double doors of the barn, both of us in a similar stance, feet spread slightly, fists planted on our hips. I looked up. Muted sunlight snuck through the broken tin and boards of the roof, past the shifted rafters and the grimy layers of time on the windows. "This place is begging to be destroyed. I can't believe it is still standing."

Percy chuckled. "I can't believe we're standing *in* it. But I wouldn't do a thing to the structure of it until you get this stuff out of here."

"Oh no. Of course not." I mentally calculated as I took in the stacks of old furniture—unpainted pie safes, dusty book-cases, other mammoth and varying pieces of furniture, small needlepoint-covered stools in need of recovering, and boxes stacked upon boxes of unknown items. At the very back of the barn, just past the last of the stalls, was a small desk topped with an old tabletop radio and flanked by a ladder-back chair, set aside and washed in sunlight swirling with dust particles. The bottom drawer was out, its bottom edge resting on the ground. It appeared a few of its contents had spilled onto the dirt floor. I wondered how long ago it'd been opened and gone through and then left a mess. "We'll need another U-Haul. Not to mention another storage unit."

Percy chuckled again. "That we surely will, Miz Hunter. That we surely will."

I turned back to the doors. "Help me open these doors so we can have more light," I said, pushing in vain on the right-hand door.

"The whole building has dipped to one side," he said, working on the left door. "And the ground has grown up around the building, blocking the doors near-bout."

I groaned as I pushed, exerting too much effort to say anything.

Percy continued to speak, not having the same physical weakness as I. "The land has a way of taking over when a building is left untended, you see." One more shove and his door was completely opened. He nudged me aside and managed to get the second door past the hard packing of the earth.

We turned again to face the interior of the barn. My chest heaved from my efforts. "Wow." I took several steps, craning my neck as I went along. "Look at that, will you? And that. My goodness . . ."

Percy followed behind me, saying "mmm-hmm" as though he were reading my mind.

I stopped in front of one of the stalls, wrinkled my nose. "It smells like . . . *what* . . . in here?"

Percy shuffled beyond me. "Animal flesh. Feed and seed. All that and a little manure."

I pointed to the desk. "Do you honestly think someone sat down and worked in here? How could they have possibly focused?"

Percy shook his head. "Well, now, Miz Hunter, if you love the farm, you love the smell of it too. You can't have the glory of the crop without some sweat and stench along the way."

He picked up a shovel and drove it into the packed ground. "My daddy used to always say, 'Percy, it takes a lot of manure to make one rose.'" He repeated the shovel-in-the-ground action once more, driving the shovel deeper still. "Believe you me; my daddy knew what he was talkin' 'bout." His lids fell to half mast. "Forced to watch his own daddy when the Klan strung him up for the crime of being a black man."

I stood frozen for a moment, then looked up at the gentle giant. "I'm sorry."

"That was another time," was all he said.

"But the pain remains . . ." Silence fell between us. There was nothing left to say.

I walked then to the desk, sidestepping the bottom drawer's contents, and slid the top drawer open. A shifting behind the desk, a squeak, and I screamed, throwing myself against Percy's body as a large rat ran past my feet, turned back, and, seeming to flatten itself, slipped under the barn's back wall.

Percy laughed as I straightened myself. "Do you think there are more?" I felt creepy-crawlies dance up my spine and I shuddered.

"Oh, I'm sure there are. Why don't you let me and the boys get this stuff out of here before you try to dig around in it."

I looked at my watch. "We'll need another day if we're going to do that," I said. "What about the stables? Anything in there?"

"Pretty much empty in there, now."

"Do you think everyone would be willing to come back tomorrow?"

"You feed us tomorrow like you fed us today, and I can guarantee it."

I smiled at him. "I'll call Mrs. Patterson as soon as we get back into the house. In the meantime, see what you can do about closing the doors for me, will you?"

24

I had taken a hot bath and was slipping into a pair of sweats when I heard rattled knocking on an outside door. "Just a minute," I called down the stairs, then scurried to the end of the hallway in slippered feet to peer out the floor-to-ceiling window at the lawn below. I recognized Karol's car parked in the makeshift driveway. I slid my arms into a long-sleeved tee, then went downstairs and opened the front door.

"Looks like you've been busy today," she said as a greeting from beyond the screened door. "My gosh, even the front porch rockers are gone."

I pushed the door open for her and said, "Come in. Please."

I pulled a scrunchie around my wet shoulder-length hair, tying it off neatly at the nape of my neck. "I hired some men and women."

When Karol looked at me quizzically, I added, "From a day labor place."

Karol stepped past me as she nodded. I closed the door, the sound echoing in the emptiness of the living room. "This room is huge," she whispered, walking to its center.

I followed her. "You don't realize how big a room is until it's empty."

"Did you get the whole house done? In one day?"

I shook my head. "No. There's still one more room in the back. It was a bedroom, but my aunt used it for storage. You name it and it's in there, right down to calendars dating back to the fifties, which would probably draw a pretty penny on eBay. I want to go through a few things before I have the men load it all into a U-Haul, so I told them we'd wait." I pointed up. "And my room is still completely furnished. I'll work around it as long as I can, then I suppose I'll have to go to Mother's to live for a while."

Karol nodded. "So, what's next?"

I jutted my thumb toward the back of the house. "Do you want some coffee? I was just about to make some."

"Sure."

We made our way down the wide hallway. Our footsteps in the cavernous room made the oddest of acoustic combinations; her boots clomped against the floorboards while my Wal-Mart satin slippers gave a whispered swish.

I answered her question as we walked along. "Tomorrow we'll pack up the barn. Or, I should say, the men will. I saw a rat in there today, so I won't be back anytime soon."

"The barn? What's in there? Old tractors and stuff?"

I shook my head as we turned into the kitchen. I flipped on the light; it exposed a room void of everything except a coffeepot, a few recently washed dishes turned upside down in the drain, and the new fire extinguisher I kept near the stove. "Mostly furniture. A few bushel baskets of old fruit jars and other glass items." I pulled the carafe from the coffee-maker and filled it with water. "Some moonshine jars. Gorgeous stained glass windows Mother said were a part of the original house. Oh, and a desk I suspect is filled with old farm records. If I'm right, they'd make a nice touch for the museum displays as well."

"Sounds good. Is that decaf or regular?"

"Decaf. Is that okay?"

Karol nodded. "Since middle age has snuck up on me, I can't stand caffeine after a certain hour."

"You and me both."

The coffee began to brew, and I leaned against the counter. "I'd offer you a chair, but there isn't one, obviously. When the coffee is ready, we can go upstairs to my room. I took up a couple of the front porch rockers and an occasional table and made a little sitting area."

"Sure." She smiled. "Please tell me you have a fire going up there too."

"I do." I collected two coffee cups from the drain and placed them on the counter in front of the coffeemaker, then went to the refrigerator for milk. "Back to subject: while the men are getting the barn loaded up and out of here, I'll start the process of renovating. I'll take some photographs of the rooms, make some drawings. When I'm in Raymore tomorrow, I'll stop by a contractor's office—Mother told me about his company, says he's good and fairly reasonable—and set up an appointment for him to come out and determine what damage we might be looking at."

"Speaking of which, I have something for you." Karol reached under the hem of her leather jacket and into the back pocket of her jeans and pulled out a covered checkbook. "It's a local account I set up for you. I put fifty thousand in it for starters. When you get to about twenty-five hundred, let me know and I'll fill it up again. This will give you the spending money you need for repairs, whatnot. Just be sure to keep accurate records and the receipts. I'll come by every few days and see what you've got."

"Good," I said with a wink. "Because I paid the day laborers out of my own pocket." I took the checkbook and set it on the windowsill above the sink as the coffeemaker coughed and sputtered. "Coffee's ready," I said.

Twenty-four hours later the house was completely empty, the barn's insides had been purged and stored, the desk's contents had been placed in a box and taken up to my room for plundering later, and I'd met with a man face-to-face who—even watered down by age—had the bluest eyes I'd ever seen.

25

**Cottonwood, Georgia
1939**

It didn't matter, really, what the rest of the world thought; Valentine knew the truth. Stella's sudden departure from Cottonwood—her sister Lottie's need for help with the young'uns over in Rome while she recuperated from the flu or some such nonsense—was nothing more than an excuse to hide Stella's condition.

Soon, if his figuring was right, she'd deliver her baby. *His* baby. And there wasn't a day that went by but what he didn't wonder what she'd do about it after that. Maybe give it to one of those orphanages where women who couldn't have babies of their own went and bought themselves one from girls like Stella.

His father had him working hard in what was now the "family business," as he called it. Valentine was learning a lot from the elder Bach; that kept his mind off things most of the day. But early in the mornings and late in the evenings when he walked from and to the house he now shared with Lilly Beth and over to the home of his parents, he thought about Stella.

She wasn't a girl a man could quick forget. Large dark eyes, wide set on either side of a slender upturned nose. They'd always seemed to see to the core of his soul. Her lips, full and pink with a deep Cupid's bow, turned slightly at the corners, giving her the appearance of a young woman holding a shimmer of a secret. Her skin, white and creamy as fresh milk, was marked by a splattering of freckles across her back. Her scent; even in the heat she smelled of soap and vanilla.

He closed his eyes and winced against the memory of first love. He had to—with God's help, he decided—put all thoughts of her behind him. He was married to Lilly Beth now, and he was slowly falling in love with her too. One day, he supposed, he'd love her more than he loved—*had* loved—Stella.

How could he help himself? Lilly Beth was everything and more a man could want in a wife. She kept his house clean, his stomach filled, and his bed warm. A tiny bit of a girl, she was pretty to look at. Maybe not as pretty as Stella, but then again, who was? All in all, Lilly Beth Bach was growing on him. The only thing she hadn't yet done for him was give him the beginnings of a child, in spite of the regularity of their lovemaking.

He could sense that she was worried about it. As the middle of each month approached, he'd see the anticipation growing in her eyes. Then the little bag where she kept her monthly rags would come out of her underwear drawer and a glimmer of the expectation would fade. Sometimes, as he walked up the short drive from the side road to their back door, he'd spot them, washed and hanging on the line, and he'd know that when he went inside, he'd find her lying on their bed, crying. It nearly broke his heart for her, but it gnawed at his insides knowing that somewhere out there was a girl with a swollen belly, ready to burst a new life into the world, and that new life was half his.

He avoided Mr. Conroy's store like the plague, not knowing how much Stella's older brother knew about her condition and the man who'd gotten her that way. A few times Lilly Beth said she needed something right bad from there and he'd go in, but he kept his eyes on his feet and his mind on his purpose. Mr. Conroy was always nice to him; Valentine wondered if that was just his nature.

It had been an odd Thanksgiving season. President Roosevelt had tried to change the date of the celebrated Thursday. No one in Cottonwood was going along with it, and Valentine had heard the rest of the country felt the same way. This time, Mr. Roosevelt was alone in his thinking.

In early December, after the last of the Thanksgiving decorations had been taken from the storefront windows and the Christmas garland and red and green lights had been strung from pole to pole along Main Street, Valentine finished a day's work with his father and, gathering up his lunch pail, said, "Daddy, I'm going to walk home now so as to stop over at Wright's Department Store. I saw something pretty in there I'd like to get Lilly Beth for Christmas."

His father—a stern man, but a good man—had given him a half smile. "Your mama said Lilly Beth had put up a right nice tree for your first Christmas as man and wife."

Valentine blushed. He still wasn't comfortable talking to his father about life as a married man. "Yes, sir," was all he said.

"What do you have in mind for buying her?"

Valentine watched as his father pulled his work gloves from his hands, shoved them into a pocket of his overalls, then reached into the front pocket for his pack of Camels and a box of matches. He lit an unfiltered cigarette, then handed the pack to his son, who repeated his father's action. Valentine exhaled the first draw from his lungs and spit a tiny tobacco stem from his tongue. "I thought a scarf. We don't have much money, and she's not a girl who asks for much."

His father nodded. "Scarf'll be nice."

Valentine took another draw from the cigarette. "What about you? What are you getting Mama?"

"Hadn't thought about it much."

Valentine chuckled. "I gotta go, Daddy. If I don't leave now, I won't make it before the store closes."

He made it to Wright's with only ten minutes to spare. He purchased the powder pink delicate material embellished with white satin rosebuds, had Mrs. Wright wrap it special for him to lay under Lilly Beth's tree on Christmas Eve, then slipped it between his chest and coat for safekeeping.

He stepped out of the store then and into the bitter cold of the evening, burrowed his chin into the wool wrap at his throat, and set his course for home.

26

"Missus, my name is Valentine Bach."

The man I'd known—though certainly not well—my whole life stood at the front porch stoop. I'd opened the door, ready to drive to Raymore to pick up the day laborers, locked it, then turned and found him standing there, clad, as always, in bib overalls.

"Yes, Mr. Bach. I remember you. You're a friend of Uncle Jim's and Aunt Stella's."

Mr. Bach shoved his hands into the angled side pockets of his overalls, well-worn but clean. His gray beard was long and wild, but his hair—what I could see from beneath his wide-brimmed straw hat—lay soft on the shoulders of his flannel button-down shirt. His eyes—even from where I stood before the front door—were a mesmerizing shade of blue. "More a friend of your uncle's than your aunt's," he said, "though Stella and I've known each other for a lot of years."

I paused for a moment, trying to figure out what the old man wanted. Surely not to pay his respects for Uncle Jim's passing. Not with him not having bothered to attend the funeral or the gathering afterward. "Is there something I can help you with?"

He smiled. His teeth bore the effects of years of smoking

cigarettes, but the smile was pleasant all the same. "Actually, I was hoping I could help you out some."

I pulled the long strap of my purse over my arm and gripped it with my gloved hand. "In what way?"

"I understand the big house here is going to be used as some sort of museum."

To my remembrance, Mr. Bach was now the first non-family member I'd ever heard who referred to the old place as the "big house." "Yes, sir. That's true."

"I'm a right worthy contractor. My daddy and I didn't build this house, of course. That was before we moved to town. But I've done some repairs on it through the years for Jim. Daddy and I replaced the chimneys in there before the original ones collapsed, so I know the lay of the house pretty well. And I can't think of anyone who'd do you a better job." He looked at his feet for a moment, then back at me. "To be honest with you, missus, I could use the work. Not a lot to do around these parts anymore. Cottonwood's near 'bout dried up, and Social Security don't hardly fill my prescriptions."

I came down the steps, put my arm on his shoulder, and gently guided him toward the sidewalk. When we'd reached it, I looked down the street to where the remnants of Cottonwood's business district strained to stand. Western-style sidewalks ran jagged and busted under tin rain sheds, rusted by time and weather. They toppled in some places and just stopped existing in others, giving scant shade from the winter's sun, hanging low in the early morning sky, reflecting like a forgotten memory on the dark and broken storefront windows. "She's just a skeleton, isn't she?"

"I remember when she was a beauty. Almost like she was alive herself." He turned back toward the house. "Same goes for this old relic. I remember when it was filled with energy and life. Stella . . . now, she wasn't much of one for keeping house, and your Uncle Jim didn't care one hoot either way . . . but your great-grandmother—Miss Loretta—she knew how to keep a house. 'Least that's the way I've always heard tell. I never actually came inside until after Mr. Nevan and Miss Loretta had passed on."

"Mmm. I wish I'd had a chance to get to know them. To see the house back then."

"Died one week of each other. He got sick with his blood pressure and had a stroke, they said. Family buried him in the ground and not seven days later they were doing the same with his wife." The old man shook his head. "I suppose that's the sign of true love right there. Maybe the purest kind, I reckon."

I felt a knot growing in my chest and moving slowly to my throat. If Evan—whom I hadn't heard from since he'd given me the ultimatum—died, would I follow him to the grave? It was a question I couldn't bear to ponder for long. "I've heard that story all my life. They died before I was born, but I've seen their images in plenty of photographs, and I've seen old black and whites of the way the house used to be." I pointed toward the second story of the house. "I have a box of them upstairs in my room, and I'm planning to use them to help put the house back together the way it was . . ." I chuckled. "Before Aunt Stella."

Mr. Bach gave a pleasant snort through his nose. "I tell you what . . . that Stella. What she lacked in housekeeping she made up for in fishing. Did you know that? That woman could fish all day and into the night if Jim'd let her."

"Yes, sir. She taught me how to fish, but I'm sorry to say it's been a while since I've had the pleasure." I shivered in the cold. "Mr. Bach, I'm afraid I have to hurry off to Raymore right now, and to be honest with you I have an appointment with a contractor there."

125

Mr. Bach blushed like a schoolboy. "I see. I beg your pardon; I should have known you'd want someone with more youth and modern ideas on his side. Here I am, just an old man with old ways." He shuffled a few steps toward the remnant of town, then stopped and turned to look at me. "But if you change your mind, ma'am, and if you don't mind my a-sayin' so, you won't find anyone who knows these old houses like Valentine Bach."

I felt my heart grow heavy. There was something pitiful about the old man, as though life had started to touch him with the most loving of hands, then pulled back without reason. As though he had once lived within a moment's notice of fulfillment, but it had gone unperceived and as quickly as the moment had appeared, it was gone. It was a feeling I knew well. All too well.

"Mr. Bach, I promise if I don't feel 100 percent confident in the contractor's work, you will be the first man I call." I smiled at him and he returned the gesture, though I think we both assumed that the other knew I'd not have a problem with the younger contractor.

"Thank you, missus."

I watched as Mr. Bach hunched his shoulders and ambled up the sidewalk. A moment later he turned back to face me as though looking for one last drop of hope. "Thank you, Mr. Bach," I called. "For stopping by."

He touched the brim of his hat with his right index finger—I could see the black grease under his nails even from where I stood—then silently turned and continued on.

27

I met the crew before eight o'clock at the day labor camp; they had multiplied. Apparently news of Melba Dawson's and Irene Patterson's home-cooked meal along with my fairly decent pay scale for physical labor had stirred seven additional men toward the camp. I wasn't sure what I'd do with seven additional men, but I didn't have the heart to turn them away. Besides, I reasoned, there was probably more to unloading that barn than I realized.

Once I had the men and women on their way in the U-Hauls, I drove to Mother's favorite bit of heaven on earth, Trish's Tea Room, owned by Mother's best friend Trish Stratford. Trish rarely set foot in the place, but her daughter Emme operated it along with two older women in need of something to do and four or five of Raymore's finest high school debutantes hoping to soak in additional Southern culture and charm.

Mother was sitting in one of the pretty chairs at one of the elaborately decorated tables in the small windowed room off from the right of the main room. She looked agitated, even sitting properly and near a china teacup filled with her favorite herbal tea, and of course I knew why. "I'm sorry I'm late. I had an unexpected visitor this morning."

I pulled off my coat and gloves, putting the former on a

nearby coat rack and shoving the latter into my opened purse. When I had sat down and given my order of white peach tea, Mother inquired, "And who might that have been?"

"Valentine Bach."

"What in the world did he want? I hope he wasn't coming by in hopes of finding work."

I nodded. "He was. And quite frankly I've thought about it all the way here and I think I just may have him do some of the work."

"Ian Nicholby will never go for that. His work is cutting edge and not to be compromised with antiquated ideas." Mother waved her hand as though that was that. "Jo-Lynn, I have great affection for Mr. Valentine. The man was like another father to me or at the very least an uncle. But he's a man who builds things by the old rules and from the old school."

Our server returned with my tea, and I waited to answer. After adding the tiniest bit of honey from the hive-shaped porcelain honey pot in the center of the table, I answered, "But isn't that the point? This is an old house. Perhaps what it needs is an old hand that understands it."

Mother sipped at her tea and I did the same. "Perhaps," Mother said, setting her teacup into its mismatched saucer, "you should meet Ian first and then decide. I promise you, you will be impressed. Now, before I forget, have you heard from Evan?"

"No."

Mother's shoulders sank. "Have you called him?"

"No, Mother. I haven't."

She leaned forward. "Why not?"

I leaned toward her as though mocking her. And perhaps I was. "Because . . . Now, can we just enjoy our tea before I meet with Ian Nicholby?"

Ian Nicholby's office was located at the corner of Stonecrest and Magnolia, the oldest section of Raymore. Five or so years ago it had been purchased by companies such as Mr. Nicholby's and renovated as a chic area of town. The streets had been redesigned with cobblestones, reminiscent of a day when horse and buggy was the only means of travel. Lovely to behold but downright aggravating even in my Lexus. I jostled and jerked until I came to a vacant parallel parking spot, about a block from Nicholby's and across the street.

I entered the embellished glass door and stepped onto hardwood floors so highly polished the furnishings in the room reflected on them. The walls were painted a muted olive green, the baseboards and crown molding were creamy white. Down the center of the oblong room's tile ceiling were four Tiffany-styled red rosebud chandeliers, each one lighting a different seating arrangement, each in a different style.

In spite of the doorbell that rang as I stepped into the room, my entry had gone undetected. I strolled casually to the first set of overstuffed chairs—four in all, two facing the front, two facing the back—with a pine trunk coffee table between them. Atop the coffee table was a large photo album, opened, exposing before and after photos of work I assumed Mr. Nicholby had done. I sat in one of the chairs and began flipping through the pages of the album, captivated by the designs in a variety of cabinetry—birch, oak, cherry, and maple—hardware, lighting, countertops—granite, silestone, soapstone, ceramic, and marble—and appliances. I searched for something I might want to use in Aunt Stella's kitchen but, reaching the end of the album, found nothing. Frowning, I flipped back to the beginning and began again.

"That's kitchens." I heard a baritone voice from the back of the studio.

I looked up, startled. The apparent owner of the business

was standing before a widely opened door; through it I could see a small office with an oversized desk and chair.

"You must be Margaret's daughter."

Ian was not what I expected. He was tall, thickly built, and extraordinarily handsome. He walked with his shoulders squared back. His face was clean shaven, his dark blond hair combed to perfection, his smile wide and plastered on. He seemed built to order and at the same time almost too ideal. Like a living, breathing Ken doll.

"I am." I stood and walked toward him, extending a hand for the professional woman's handshake. "Jo-Lynn Hunter. Thank you for taking time out of your busy schedule to meet with me."

"That's why I'm here." It wasn't a particularly rude line, but it wasn't kind either. It was matter-of-fact and it was my first feeling of distaste for Ian Nicholby. It was as if he were saying, *I'm meeting with you because I want to make money, lady. That's my job. Otherwise, I wouldn't give you the time of day. Do you know what it takes to keep a place like this running?*

I knew. I'd worked with many of Atlanta's top contractors. I'd sat in their offices, taken them out for lunch. I'd pored over blueprints and photographs, contracts and invoices. Most of them oversaw the work; few of them ever hit a lick at a snake.

I shook my head just, an involuntary movement. *Hit a lick at a snake.* It was a saying I'd heard my whole life but had never adopted as one of my own. Why had it come to mind now? I knew I'd heard it recently, but where?

"Can I offer you a cup of coffee? Tea?" Ian was asking. "I also have Pellegrino."

I didn't answer right away. I scanned the room, the expensive artwork on the walls—complete with price tags for anyone who wanted to make a purchase. I assumed they were from one of the art galleries in the district and were displayed to tickle the fancy of some designer or decorator.

I blinked. "No. Thank you, no. I met Mother earlier at Trish's."

"Your mother . . . such a lovely home. I always know when she comes to my studio that she will pick out the most exquisite pieces."

Yes, that would be my mother. Nothing less than exquisite would do. "Mother has fine taste, yes," I said.

He paused. "If you don't mind my asking, are you all right?"

I took in a short breath, blew it out. "Yes. I'm just . . ." I rubbed my forehead with the fingertips of both hands. "Whew. I'm sorry. I'm just . . . do you mind if I sit down?" I was already sitting as I asked.

"Of course. Let me get you a glass of water from the cooler."

I nodded, and Ian walked to the back of the room, where a water cooler I'd not noticed before stood in the far right corner.

He'd hardly hit a lick at a snake. I heard the voice again. The faintest of memories, but it was most definitely Mother's tone. But who had she been talking about?

"So the house you're renovating is in Cottonwood?" Ian spoke from over his shoulder as he held a glass under the tap of the cooler.

"Yes."

"And it was built in the late 1800s?"

"Yes. 1896 to be exact."

"I understand M Michaels is buying up some of the homes, leveling some areas, renovating others."

"Yes. Have you met Karol Paisley?"

Ian crossed the room with a crystal highball glass filled with water. As he handed it to me I said "thank you" and he said, "Yes, I have. She's come in quite a few times, actually. I can't quite figure the woman out, to be honest with you."

Ian sat in a chair opposite mine, crossed his legs casually.

"In what way?" I took a sip of water.

"I can't put my finger on it exactly." He shook his head, placed his elbow on the arm of the chair, and lightly rested his temple against his index and middle fingers. "She seems to me to be a woman on a mission but not quite sure what that mission is."

Ian, I decided, was a chauvinist.

Buster Godwin . . . I heard my mother say. *Everyone felt she'd settled for Buster Godwin.*

"So what are your thoughts, Mrs. Hunter?"

I blushed, I'm sure I did. "Concerning?"

He chuckled at my discomfort. "The house. Are you planning to knock down walls? Put up Sheetrock? Rip up the floors and replace with something a little less worn? I'm sure the wood in that old house is begging to be swapped out for something more modern. I have some impressive books . . . photos . . . ideas to show you when we get to that point."

I took another swallow of water. "I don't want to destroy, Mr. Nicholby. I want to renovate. I want to keep as much of the original as I can."

Ian laughed again. "Mrs. Hunter, that house is nearly one hundred years old."

"More than that."

He uncrossed his legs, then crossed them again, left over right, right over left.

"I admit I'm better at working with new product than old. My forte is taking homes at around fifty years of age—like most of the homes here in Raymore—and modernizing them. The old relics . . ."

I shifted forward in my seat, a half smile on my lips. Now I knew . . . I knew exactly where the memory was coming from. Mother, discussing Buster Godwin's work ethic with me. *After they married, he'd hardly hit a lick at a snake. Not like Mr. Valentine.*

"Mr. Nicholby, I have a question for you." I placed the cup of water on the table between us.

Ian uncrossed his legs, braced his feet apart, and leaned his elbows onto his knees. "Shoot."

"Who would you say understands a young woman best? A young man, say in his twenties, or an older man, in his forties?"

I watched as his brow drew together in confusion. "I suppose an older man."

"Why is that, do you suppose?"

"Because a young man—and I speak from experience, of course—is only set on having his desires met and not on truly loving the woman. When we become older, wiser, we learn to . . . *stroke* our women. To caress them, if you will."

I looked at the floor and blinked, then looked back to meet his eyes with mine. "And an older woman? Who can love her best? A young stud or, again, an older, more experienced man?"

There was a pause, long enough that I thought the shadows in the room shifted in anticipated wait for the answer. Ian's eyes never left mine, as though he were trying to read me. Where was I going with this line of questioning, I imagined he was thinking. Was this the method of an interior designer from Druid Hills or was I a woman on the make? I kept my eyes on his, refusing to blink until he answered. And when he finally did, he gave me the exact answer I was hoping for.

"I'd have to keep my answer the same," he said. "The older, more experienced man."

I stood, extended my hand. "Thank you, Mr. Nicholby." He stood and took my hand in his for the required shake. "I'm sorry for taking your time."

28

When I reached Cottonwood, I stopped by the house and found that Percy had organized everyone and every job. I patted him on his muscular biceps and said, "Thank you, Mr. Percy. I have an errand to run and I'll be back. In the meantime, you seem to know exactly what I want done."

Percy appeared more than pleased with himself.

I returned to the car and began a slow trek up Main Street. I stayed well below the speed limit, looking from one side of the street to the other, imagining the town the way it had been and the way it could be, were M Michaels not about to bring it down and start all over again. They, like Ian Nicholby, would destroy much of the old then build the new in an attempt to make the new look old. I felt sad at the thought.

My cell phone rang as I neared the end of the town. It was Mother, as I knew it would be. "What in the world did you say to Ian to have him so upset?" she asked. "He said you practically shunned his work. And what was all that talk about old men and young women?"

"Mother, where is Valentine Bach's home? I know it's somewhere past the edge of town but—"

"Valentine Bach? Why would you want to go there? And

please don't tell me you plan to hire him as a contractor, Jo-Lynn."

"Just answer me, Mother." I hit the literal end of Main Street and pressed on the brakes. To my immediate left was the old town theater. Just past it, on Railroad Street, which crossed in front of Main, was the old train depot. Though no longer in use, it boasted an abandoned caboose with faded red paint and white lettering: R&C Railroad. "I'm at the end of Main at Railroad. Do I turn left or right?"

Mother sighed so deeply I thought I felt her breath on my ear. "Right."

"Thank you." I turned right.

"You'll drive about a block and you're forced to turn left. That's Church Street. Then drive about two or three minutes and you'll see a narrow dirt road off on the left-hand side of the road. Turn off the paved road and onto the dirt." She sighed again, and I knew her thoughts without having to think about it. "That's Old Church Street, though I doubt there's a sign or anything. Just follow the road. You can't miss the houses."

"Houses?"

"Mr. Valentine lives in one; Bettina and her family live in the other."

"I see the dirt road." I turned left.

"I can't imagine what this is about."

I craned my neck until I spied what I was in search of. "I promise I'll tell you . . . later."

I continued driving until the road narrowed and the dirt became packed and rutted Georgia red clay; I slowed my car and leaned toward the steering wheel. Keeping my hands gripped at ten and two, I looked first to the right, then to the left, in search of the houses Mother insisted were there and seeing nothing beyond tall naked trees and bushy pines bound by vines of kudzu. I bounced in my seat for the second time that day, the first time driving the stylish streets of Raymore and now the outskirts of a ghost town in search of an old codger's home.

The sun, nearing its highest point in the sky, shot light onto the metallic paint of my car, sending beams in the shape of a cross. I glanced up, squinting, then back out, wondering how much farther the Bach/Godwin estate, for lack of a better word, could be. Considering Mr. Bach had earlier walked to the house and back, even at his old age, it couldn't possibly be too far from Main Street.

Finally, at about two miles from the main road, I spotted the houses, one facing the road, the other slightly behind the first and to the left, facing to the right, almost as though it were keeping tabs on the first. Both were white clapboard; neither had seen a new coat of paint in years. The first was considerably larger than the second. In front of the larger was what appeared to be the remnant of flowerbeds that had blossomed in the fall, the brown and dried remains bent and twisted above the gray earth. Two adult bicycles were lying on their side between the two houses; a shiny red Ford F-10 was parked in the driveway of the larger home next to a slightly older blue Geo with a bent bumper. A four-wheeler was parked near the front door. Two girls—who I surmised to be in their teens—sat on the front porch steps, both with their hands curled around mugs, obviously deep in conversation, which stopped abruptly when they noticed the approach of my car. One stood, leaned her slender hip against the wrought iron hand railing, and crossed one leg over the other at the ankles. The other, nearly identical, remained seated and took a deep swallow from her drink. From around the back of the house the young man I'd seen a couple of weeks ago—the young man Doris had identified as Terry Godwin—lumbered to the front and said something to the girl who was standing.

She, in turn, said something back to him. The girl sitting then stood and walked into the house as I drove my car into the driveway and parked behind the Geo.

I stepped out of the car then shut the door behind me. I waited long enough for the standing adolescent to properly size me up before speaking. "Hello. You must be one of the Godwin girls." The girl standing smiled, and I returned it. I wrapped my coat around my middle and tied the sash. "My name is Jo-Lynn Hunter. I'm looking for Valentine Bach."

The girl came down the steps as the young man turned and walked toward the smaller house, mumbling, "I'll get 'im," as he went.

"I'm Arizona," the girl said. "Arizona Godwin. My brother Terry . . ." She looked behind her momentarily. "He'll go get Pappy." She continued toward me and I stopped, watching her. Arizona moved like the filaments of a dandelion dancing on a warm breeze. Her hair, long and honey blonde, fell in soft waves to her waist and blew in careless wisps across her face. She grabbed at it with one hand, wrapping it around her hand and clasping it into place near her shoulder. She was wearing a pair of worn jeans that fit her small frame well, though loose around the hips and thighs, with a white cotton shirt that dipped to expose one freckled shoulder and scooped at the bodice. She looked like a flower child of the sixties, yet at ease in the new millennium.

When she was close enough I saw the blue of her eyes, recognizing them immediately. They were her great-grandfather's. "What do you want with Pappy?" she asked. I could smell the coffee on her breath and from the mug she still held in her hand.

Before I could answer, the front door opened, and two women—one a near perfect older version of the two girls—stepped out, Bettina Bach Godwin behind her. Sidestepping

Arizona, I walked toward her. "Mrs. Godwin," I said with a wide smile. "I'm Margaret's daughter, Jo-Lynn. Jo-Lynn Hunter."

She ambled toward me, and I met her near the base of the steps, able then to see her better. Bettina, though petite and still shapely, seemed years older than Mother. My first thought was that the difference lay in her clothes. Mother dressed to the nines every day even when she had nowhere in particular to go; Mrs. Godwin appeared to be in Goodwill's last year's selection. Or, perhaps it was the lack of cosmetics, the way she pulled her white hair back tight into a bun at the nape of her neck, the sadness in her eyes. These were not her father's brilliant blues. These were dark brown, flecked in gold, with deep-set lids and thick brows. Bettina Godwin and my mother had their childhood in common, but the similarities ended there.

The older woman nodded at me. "How is your mama? She's all right, I reckon." It was as if she asked a question and answered it—sure of the outcome—in one remark.

I pressed my hand against my breast. "Oh, my yes." I laughed, nervous but unsure why. There was something in this woman's face and character that unnerved me, but I couldn't place my finger on exactly what it was.

"That's good then, I s'pose." She paused. "Your aunt? How's she doing?"

"She's living with her daughter over in Luverne now," I said. "I think she's doing okay for a woman who is nearly ninety years old and just lost the love of her life."

Miss Bettina nodded. "You be sure to tell her I said hello next time you talk to her, you hear?"

"I'm here to see your father, Miss Bettina."

The younger of the two older women stepped forward then. "Ga-Ga, why don't you go back inside, hon? Finish that apple pie Pappy's been hungry for all day." She spoke in a gentle tone, one that would ever so kindly coax Miss Bettina back into the house.

Miss Bettina nodded at me and said, "My best to your folks," then turned to go back up the steps just as the other girl stepped out the front door and said, "Here ya go, Ga-Ga," while holding the door open for her grandmother.

I remained at the foot of the steps, Arizona now right behind me. I turned to her. "Ga-Ga. I've never heard that term of endearment for a grandmother."

"Terry," she said. "Couldn't say grandma and it stuck."

I smiled. "We Southerners sure have a way of calling our kin, don't we?"

Arizona shrugged. "I guess." Then she added, "Terry went to get Pappy."

The younger of the older women, dressed in worn jeans and a long gauzy top with a faux fur vest over it, skipped down the steps then, extending her hand. "I'm Fiona Godwin," she said.

I took a step back, having no choice, and bumped into Arizona. "Oh, I'm so sorry." I reached for her, stumbling over my own feet.

Fiona reached for me, in an attempt to keep me on my feet. "Are you okay?"

I righted myself. "I'm fine." I readjusted the belt of my coat and said, "You must be married to Miss Bettina's son?"

"Junior, yes." Fiona's eyes smiled before her mouth did, and I saw that she and the girl whose name I did not know bore a striking resemblance. Both with long light brown hair, highlighted around the face with blonde streaks, both with gentle brown eyes—doe-like eyes—broad noses, and lips that, even when relaxed, appeared to be smiling.

"And these are your girls?"

139

The girl on the porch and Arizona joined their mother, both standing on one side of her, Arizona slightly before the other. She leaned back, and the other, slightly taller girl draped an arm over her sister, almost protectively, though not quite.

"Arizona you've met." Arizona smiled again, and I thought what a pixie she was. "My other girl here is Annaleise."

Annaleise didn't smile as her sister had. She just continued to stare at me as though she didn't know what to make of me. "How old are you, girls?"

Arizona looked back at her sister, then to me. "Sixteen."

"They're twins, though not quite identical as you can see," their mother explained.

"Mmm," I acknowledged. "They're not in school?"

"I homeschool my children."

I nodded. "Oh, I see."

"You didn't say why you wanted to see Pappy. Does this have something to do with the renovation of the old house off of Main Street? Miss Stella's house?"

"Yes. I want to talk to Mr. Bach about helping with the renovations."

"Pappy's the best, you know," she said, smiling at me again. The knot lifted from around my chest and all but disappeared. "He doesn't have the physical ability he used to have, but he's not lost anything upstairs in the knowledge department, I can tell you that."

From a short distance I heard a house door open and close. I looked to my left and saw Mr. Bach making his way down the steps of his home. "So you found me, did you?" he said as he shuffled toward me. Terry lurked behind him, leaning against the door frame, one leg crossed before the other, and his eyes firmly set on me.

I stared back for a moment, uneasiness causing me to look

away quickly and over to the old man. "Mr. Bach, I'd like to talk with you about working at the house."

"Your city boy didn't work out like you thought?"

I laughed lightly. "No, sir."

Fiona put her hand on Mr. Bach's shoulder. "Pappy, you want some coffee for you and Mrs. Hunter?"

"Please, call me Jo-Lynn. And I'd love a cup of coffee." I looked at Mr. Bach. "Mr. Bach? How about we go inside and have a cup of coffee and talk business?"

Mr. Bach chuckled again. "Tell you what. Let me go back to my house and get some papers and I'll meet you in the kitchen directly." He looked at his great-grandson, who'd remained at the door of his home. "Boy, what's say you and I start a whole new file for Mrs. Hunter?"

He returned to his home as I followed Fiona up the front porch steps of her home, fully aware that I was about to hire more than a man; I was hiring a family.

29

Later that night I lay in my bed, completely alone and completely exhausted, and cried until I had no tears left. My legs throbbed from all the activity of the day and my head ached. Mother had called several times during the evening, leaving messages with each call, wanting to know why I wasn't answering, demanding to know why I had not hired Ian Nicholby, and—her final—"I suppose you've gone to bed by now, determined that I should sulk and suffer the livelong night. Fine, Jo-Lynn, but remember that I am your mother and do not deserve this."

At least that call made me laugh. It was so predictably "Mother."

But more than my "determination that Mother should suffer," I felt an emptiness I hadn't expected to feel while so tired. In my heart I knew the truth; I missed Evan, and in a strange sort of way, I missed my home. My cup of coffee in the Godwin home had only exacerbated my truest feelings for them both.

The Godwin household was . . . *different*. The house, I learned as I sat with the family members around the old Formica kitchen table, was originally the home of Valentine Bach's mother and father. "We moved here when I was, oh, 'bout sixteen, I reckon," he'd told me.

Though not nearly the size of the big house, it was plenty big enough, with rambling rooms of low ceilings and outdated but clean furniture. Arizona and Annaleise took me on a short tour, showing me with great pride the bedroom they shared. "They decorated it themselves," their mother bragged from the doorway, beaming at the two girls.

"Terry lives with Pappy," Arizona offered. To that point, Annaleise had yet to say a word to me.

"In case he falls or needs anything," Fiona said.

I raised a question. "You know, I think he *walked* to my house . . ."

"Oh no," Arizona said. "He didn't want you to think he was feeble, so he had me drop him off at the end of town."

"Oh, I see . . ."

We returned to the kitchen, where a fresh pot of coffee brewed and just as Buster Junior was coming in the back door. Though I'd seen him at the funeral, I hadn't recognized him for who he was, just as Doris had suspected. He was dressed in a pair of jeans and a long-sleeved flannel shirt worn open over what I quickly recognized as an Atlanta Braves tee. His feet were shod in work boots. He stomped on the back doormat as though they were covered in mud, which they were not.

There was nothing overly stylish about Buster Junior, but he was a man I felt an instant attraction to. Not romantic by any means; it was as if my brother Stephen had walked into the room.

Buster Godwin Jr. was tall and boyishly handsome. His hair—a dark blond—was longer than most men his age wore it, and it curled on the ends as though in rebellion to his deter-mination to look younger than—I suspected—his forty-five or so years. His eyes were the eyes of his mother—deep set and dark. They were tender, serene, and they locked with mine.

"Hey, honey. Are you about ready for work?" Fiona asked

from the counter where she was pouring our coffee. I was seated at the kitchen table with Miss Bettina, still waiting for Mr. Valentine to return to talk business. I had a sneaking suspicion he was making me wait on purpose . . . a shift of power. We both knew that what I knew about design was a drop of water in the ocean compared to what he knew about the overall structure of the houses in this area.

Buster's eyes shifted from mine to his wife, then back to mine again. "I thought we had comp'ny. I didn't recognize the car in the drive." He walked over to me, stood behind his mother's chair, and extended a hand. "You're Miss Stella's niece, aren't you?"

I remained seated as I shook his hand. "Yes. And you're Miss Bettina's son, Buster. I believe I saw you at Uncle Jim's funeral."

"Yes, ma'am," he said respectfully, though I'm not more than five years his senior. "I'm sorry 'bout your uncle. Jim Edwards was a good man."

"Yes, he was."

He squeezed his mother's shoulders and said, "Hey, gorgeous. You okay?" to which she nodded. He then walked over to Fiona and kissed her as though neither his mother nor I were in the room. "I'll be ready to leave in a few."

"Get the dogs penned up?" she asked.

"I did."

Her smile to him brought an unconscious smile to my lips.

"Securely this time?" she asked.

He pinched her nose lovingly. "Yes'm. You won't have to send the boy running after them this evening, I promise you." He turned back to me. "I failed in my duties as a husband last night, I'm afraid," he informed with a grin. "Didn't close the pen up good, and my huntin' dogs got out. Terry had to chase them near 'bout to town." He turned again to his wife. "Where're the girls?"

"In their room."

"Excuse me, ladies," he said and then shuffled out of the room. A moment later I heard him as he called, "Girls? Got your schoolwork done?" There was a pause. "Then I bet Mama could use some help with the laundry out there on the line."

I wondered which "mama" he was talking about, his or theirs.

Fiona joined us at the table with mugs of steaming coffee just as the twins walked through the kitchen and out the back door. Buster Junior—known simply as Junior—ambled in behind them. "Keep after 'em, Fiona. If you don't, they'll get lazy."

Miss Bettina laughed as she pointed to the seat opposite hers. "Sit, boy, and have a cup of coffee before you leave."

Buster Godwin Jr. worked the night shift at a machine parts plant in Raymore. According to Fiona, he'd worked the same shift since they'd married in their college years, promptly dropping out and returning to Cottonwood. "College just wasn't for us," she said. "But loving each other and raising a family was." She blushed. "It's all I ever really wanted out of life, anyway. A man I could love and who would love me . . ." She reached over and stroked her mother-in-law's arm. "My sweet pea here saw to it that I got a man who'd love me to pieces and treat me like a queen. Mr. Buster Senior"—she looked back to me—"might not have been the best provider in the world for Mama B, but he made sure my man grew up knowing the importance of loving a woman." She winked at her mother-in-law, then cut her eyes over to her husband.

I watched Miss Bettina blush to the color of a plum. "It's not necessary to discuss my love life at the table. It might make our comp'ny feel awkward."

My awkwardness wasn't the issue. It was my emptiness. I was experiencing love in action and it was something I'd long ago lost.

I wanted the same from my husband. Lying in bed that night, I imagined him being as passionate with me after all our years of marriage as he'd once been, so long ago. I thought of what our life together would have been like had I brought children into the world. Would he call our son "the boy" and would he make sure the daughter helped in the house, in spite of having had a maid nearly since the day we married?

It would be that way too. A boy for him and a girl for me, as the saying went. I pictured our son and wondered what I would have named him. I'd always favored Bryton, but a cousin on Daddy's side had snagged that one. Not that it mattered. I wasn't going to get pregnant and give birth to a Bryton, so I allowed myself to pick that name for my dream son. As for our daughter, her name would most definitely be Savannah, so given to her in order to please Mother. Savannah's grandmother would have it no other way.

I squeezed my eyes shut, willing a picture of the children to come to mind. Bryton—a younger, slightly larger replica of his father. The same deep dimples, eyes filled with mischief and adventure. Savannah—a lovely young woman with cheeks the color of peaches in season, long flowing light brown hair, and deep-set auburn eyes with flecks of amber. Cupid doll lips.

I opened my eyes and pushed up on my elbows. The vision of my "daughter" was a familiar one, though I'd just now thought of it. I swung out of bed. Using the light from the fire dying in the corner of the room, I went over to a box of framed photographs that had been found in the downstairs bedroom. I pulled it over to the fireplace then sat on my feet and began to plow through it until I found what I'd been looking for: an old black-and-white photo taken of Aunt Stella at seventeen, sitting on a photographer's table, peering over her shoulder, eyes tender toward the camera, lips curled at the ends in a teasing sort of smile. She wore a long white dress with thin straps, loaded in sequins, their shimmer evident even without the advancement of color photography. She was so stunning—especially in the glow of firelight—my breath caught. Then I smiled. Subconsciously, as I had envisioned my "daughter," I had pictured a modern Aunt Stella. But there was something else, I realized now. Something more telling . . . something in the way the young woman in the photograph cast her eyes over her shoulder . . . something in the smile. Drawing closer to it my ears filled with what sounded like rushing water and my heart pounded.

It was then that the call came.

30

I jumped, dropping the photo the six inches to the floor and whirling toward the bedside table, where my cell phone's incoming call song sliced through the moment and brought me back to reality. Mother again, no doubt. I stood on aching feet and hobbled toward the lit phone. I wanted to talk to her . . . to tell her about the photograph . . . about a sense I had that something was stirring in the air . . . something I couldn't quite place my finger on. Mother loved things like that.

But the call was from Evan. Evan, whom I hadn't heard from in days. My heart leapt and sank at the same time, though I'm not sure how. I pressed my lips together, climbed onto the bed, and scooted to the center. I crisscrossed my legs and then flipped the phone open. "Hello."

"I'm surprised you answered," he said.

I decided to be honest with him. "Me too. In a way."

I heard a light chuckle from his end. "Why's that?" His voice, a voice I would recognize in a room full of speakers, was like warm honey, the way it was when he wanted to coax me into something . . . or to make love to me. Which sometimes was, I supposed, one in the same.

His voice alarmed me. Thrilled me. I fell back against the

pillows and drew the covers over me in one movement. "I dunno."

He chuckled again. "I am going to hate myself for this in the morning—being the stubborn man and all—but . . . I miss you, Jo-Lynn."

I closed my eyes. "I miss you too, Evan. I really do. I—" I stopped short. I wanted to tell him about Buster Godwin Jr. To tell him about the way he was with his wife and in front of Miss Bettina—even after years of marriage. About the sound of his voice when talking to his girls. Authoritative yet loving. "I miss you," I finally repeated. It was enough. For now.

"I've been thinking."

I didn't say anything and, for a moment, neither did he.

"Do you want to know what I'm thinking?"

"Do I have a choice?" I forced a lilt to my voice.

"No, not really. You know me. When I have something to say, I say it."

"I know you." I rolled onto my side and pulled my knees toward my chest.

"Remember our trip to Maui?"

Remember it? I had worn one of the sweatshirts I'd purchased while there just days before. "I still have the blue sweatshirt I bought there. I wore it the other day, as a matter of fact. I guess I'd left it at my parents' house after one of our visits there."

"What I'm remembering," Evan said quickly enough to stop my rambling about purchased souvenir clothing, "was the view we had from our suite."

"Spectacular. But I don't think you can get a bad view in Hawaii."

"You may be right. In fact, I know you're right. Jo-Lynn, do you remember the morning it rained, so we stayed in . . . ordered room service for breakfast . . ."

That wasn't all we'd done. That morning I truly was the center of his world. For hours on end, we were in a universe where only two existed. Time seemed to stand still, the only hint of life beyond the sliding glass doors leading to the balcony and on to the beaches and mountains beyond the water was the pelting of rain on the verdant lawn below us. For a tiny but significant moment in our history, Evan had made me feel as though there had never been nor could ever be anything or anyone more important than me . . . and him with me. "I remember the rainbow after the rain. It seemed to come up out of the water and disappear back into it again."

"That's not all you remember." My husband knew me well; he was even capable of reading my thoughts from more than a hundred miles away.

A familiar feeling slid across my belly. Love, perhaps. I closed my eyes and sighed. "Evan . . ."

"Jo-Lynn. I'm sorry for everything I said in anger when you called a couple of weeks ago. I love you, Jo-Lynn. There's no doubt about that; I do. And I need you. I'm practically nonfunctioning without you."

I opened my eyes, pushed back the covers, and sat up, my chin hanging toward my chest. "Do you hear yourself? I, I, I . . . It's all about you, Evan. Not once have you asked me, 'Jo-Lynn, how's it going down there? What progress have you made?' Nothing. And you know what? I want to tell you. I want to share this with you. Not because it's all about me but because I know you'd understand and you'd be excited for me. You'd be fascinated at what I've found in the barn . . . in an old bedroom downstairs. I want you to know about my visit with Valentine Bach today . . . with his family."

"Who?"

"Oh, Evan! Does it matter who? I feel like I'm digging in

here. Like I'm being planted into the richest of soil. I can't explain it. But, I—"

"You? What's so different, Jo-Lynn? What's so different in what we're saying here? You're talking about what you're doing and I'm talking about what *I'm* doing."

"No, Evan. You're talking about what you *want*."

"Aren't you?"

I pounded my fist against the soft mattress. I pounded it again for good measure. But I didn't answer him. I didn't say a word because I knew him as well as he knew me. In a battle of words, I wouldn't win. Couldn't win. And to my horror, in this case, he was right.

"You can't answer that," he said.

Victory, victory, victory. I squeezed my eyes shut, then opened them again. "I have to go, Evan. I'm tired." I swallowed hard. "But to answer you, yes. Yes, this is about what I want. Now answer something for me, if you can. When was the last time I did anything because it was what I wanted to do? I love you, Evan. I do. But I have to do this for me. For me, Evan. And maybe, in a funny sort of way, for us."

"You have to go away." It was a question without the question mark. "You have to go away without me. For us. Yeah, Jo-Lynn. It makes sense. Perfect sense." His tone dripped with sarcasm. "It makes so much sense I think I'll write a book about it. It'll be a bestseller. I'll go on Oprah. Be her next Dr. Phil."

I raised my chin in the icy warmth of the room, took in a deep breath through my nose, and then exhaled it. "I'll keep my eyes peeled for it. Be sure to tell Miss Winfrey I said hello."

I ended the call.

That night I dreamed of palm fronds and rain falling on thick grass. I dreamed of rainbows coming out of the ocean, arching high into the azure sky, and dropping back into the deep blue water again.

31

Mr. Nevan Nevilles
1 South Main Street
Cottonwood, Georgia

Dear Papa,

It's Christmas Day and I am writing you this letter on the stationery Lottie gave me for my present. She says it's like me: pretty and pink. What she means is that with this baby growing inside me I've got that woman's glow and I'm flushed from the extra weight. (Just so you know, I'm laughing as I say that, even though I know you probably are not.) Also, just so you know, I am writing one letter to you and one to Mama. Sometimes, Papa, I think I can share my true heart with you better than with her. But that doesn't mean I don't love her just as much as you. It's just that with you things are different. Please don't tell her I said so.

I know you are probably upset because you have hardly heard from me since I've been gone. I want you to know it's not because I'm angry with you or anything close to it. I understand why you sent me here. It's been okay, I reckon.

Lottie has fretted over me and says she is glad I'm here, but I can tell Charles would prefer I hurry up and have the baby so I can do whatever it is I'm going to do and leave. I think he likes keeping Lottie to hisself, and he forgets that she was my sister before she was his wife. I've tried to do my part around here, Papa. Helping Lottie with the chores and the babies and all, but with me more than a week past the date Dr. Martins said I would have the baby, I'm pretty miserable. Too miserable to do much but lay around all day and grow bigger.

Maybe you don't want to hear about this. I don't know. But I figure you are used to the ways of a woman who is in the family way what with Mama having six babies and one that died along the way. And you may as well hear about it because I know I've got to make a decision soon. Could be as soon as tomorrow.

And I think I've made one.

Yesterday, which was Sunday, Lottie made me get up and go to church with them. You know I usually don't think a lot about God, but I've been going to church pretty regular since I've been here. I guess I figure I need all the forgiveness I can get or, if nothing else, all the guidance. Whether you like it or not or even if you love me or hate me, I don't really and truly feel guilty about loving Valentine Bach. Because I do love him, Papa. Or at least I did. I don't think I feel too much of anything these days toward him. And especially with me growing more miserable with every day and especially in this house. Lottie won't even say his name. Not even to me. But every night before I go to bed, I say it in a whisper and I ask God to keep him and his new wife safe and happy. I think, Papa, that if I do this, God will help my heart heal because I'm going to tell you something, Papa, my heart hurts. I never knew a heart could hurt like this, but it does.

So I went to church, and the preacherman was talking about

153

Mary and Jesus, what with it being Christmas and all. And I got to thinking about Mary being a virgin when she got in the family way, and I thought about how people must have talked about her. Gossiped about her in her small town of Nazareth like people would have talked about me in Cottonwood had I stuck around. And I thought about how much God must love us to give His Son (Lottie says you're supposed to capitalize that part) away to a world that didn't deserve Him. Didn't love Him (God) enough to even recognize Him (Jesus) when they saw Him. Charles said at the dinner table after church that there is a Scripture that says something about God sending the Light of the world but the world knowing Him not and that this is one of his favorite passages. I'm not sure where it's from in the Bible exactly, but Charles said it was there, so I suppose it is. Charles is a pretty fine Christian man, in spite of the fact that he's ready for me to go home.

Papa, I want you to do something for me, will you? I want you to go talk to Valentine. I want you to tell him I want him to take our baby. Even though he doesn't deserve it, Papa, because he didn't love me proper, I want our baby to be raised by him and Lilly Beth. I know I can't do it. Raise the baby. I know I can't be like Mary. For one thing, I don't have a "Joseph" willing to marry me. For another, Mama wouldn't be able to handle the shame of me bringing the baby home. But, Papa, I also know I can't give my baby to no stranger and expect to return to life in Cottonwood like nothing ever happened.

So, I'm begging you, Papa. If I could get down on my knees, I would, and I would be begging you to do this for me. No one ever has to know where the baby came from. Just us and Valentine and I suppose Lilly Beth and maybe the Bachs. But you can tell them for me I won't interfere. Not ever. This will be their baby. And I can live my life knowing where my child—their child—is. Happy and healthy and in a house of love. Because that's the way I imagine it, Papa. I imagine it full of love. As much as Valentine loved me (and Papa, I do believe he did), he loved Lilly Beth more, so that sure must be a mess of loving.

Please don't think I'm crazy, Papa. And please don't think I don't know what I'm doing. All I've had is time to think about it. I can't give Valentine my love or my life, but I can give him our child. I guess that is my love and my life. And maybe God will forgive me all the way and I can find someone to love me one day like I loved Valentine Bach.

Please, Papa.

All my love,
Stella

P.S. I am now writing this part the day after Christmas. I was reading the paper this morning, and it said that yesterday King George over there in England made a speech about the war and all. It said he quoted some poem, and it really hit my heart. I want to share it with you, Papa. The king said, "I said to the man who stood at the Gate of the Year, 'Give me a light that I may tread safely into the unknown.' And he replied, 'Go out into the darkness, and put your hand into the Hand of God. That shall be better than light, and safer than a known way.'"

I got that out of the paper, Papa, and I don't know who wrote it first, but it sure said something to me. I guess no matter what happens after today, I'll be walking out into the darkness holding on to God's hand.

One more thing, Papa. And you'll know it by the time you read this letter. My birthing pains have started. I'm going to seal my letters to you and Mama and go tell Lottie. I'm not afraid, Papa. I'm not. I'm picturing myself holding on to your hand. And I'm holding on to God's hand too.

Still yours,
Stella

32

January 1940

Valentine Bach felt as though he'd been ambushed. Walking home, as had become a habit of late, he heard a male voice calling him by his surname. He was, at the time, passing Stella's house. Turning, he saw her father—Papa, she called him—leaning on one of the side porch columns. He wore black baggy trousers and a white long-sleeved shirt under a loosely fit wool coat. One leg crossed the other, the toe of his dress shoes pointed on the glossy gray boarding of the floor. Valentine instinctively knew why Mr. Nevilles had called after him, but to look at the man he'd have just as easily thought it was to be no more than a friendly hello.

Valentine waited across the street; waited to see just what Stella's father would do. There was not a shotgun in sight, and he breathed an unmanly sigh of relief.

"I'd like to have a word with you, if I might, Mr. Bach." It sounded like a genteel invitation.

Valentine nodded twice, hunched his shoulders, and crossed the street that divided them, coming to a shuffled stop at the stoop. "Yes, sir?" It took all the courage he had, but he met the man's eyes—small and dark—that bore into his with a determination to show, without saying, who was going to be in control of the conversation they were about to have.

Without so much as a shifting of his eyes, he reached into his front shirt pocket, exposing dark suspenders stretched easily over the white shirt, and pulled out a small pipe. Then reaching into his coat pocket, he retrieved a packet of tobacco. Pushing himself away from the column and standing with his feet braced apart, he began the process of filling the pipe, then lighting it, puffing several times for good measure. "I don't usually smoke this time of the day," he said, taking steps toward him. He came to a stop at the top step. "Makes the missus unhappy." Another puff. "But I figure today is a good day for smoking before supper."

"Yes, sir." It was all he knew to say.

"You smoke, Mr. Bach?"

"Cigarettes, sir."

The man nodded, then took a complete step down. "My daughter Stella smokes cigarettes, though she thinks I don't know it." He looked dead on at the young man then. "But you probably know that, don't you?"

"Yes, sir."

"Care to have one now? A cigarette?"

"I think so, sir." Valentine pulled the pack he'd put in the front pocket of his overalls that morning. His hands shook so badly he could hardly pull one out much less light it, but eventually he steadied himself enough.

Mr. Nevilles sat down then, resting his elbows on his knees. "Care to join me?"

It wasn't really a question. Valentine sat next to Stella's father.

"I suppose you know why I called you over."

"I think so." Valentine took a long drag from his cigarette, held it in his lungs for so long it burned, then exhaled.

157

"You're a father, Mr. Bach. The father of a baby girl."

Valentine closed his eyes, felt them sting with tears, then opened them and, looking straight ahead, nodded. "Is she all right?" His voice squeaked like a boy of fourteen.

"Who? My daughter or yours?"

With his peripheral vision, Valentine could see that Mr. Nevilles was looking at him, though he didn't feel harshness from the man. He turned and fixed his eyes on him, noticing for the first time the lines around the older man's eyes and the slight puffiness beneath. Valentine swallowed, cleared his throat, and answered, "Yours."

"She's fine."

They sat silent.

"Your daughter is fine too. Born two days after Christmas."

Valentine sighed, looked forward again, and brought the cigarette to his lips.

"Six pounds, two ounces. Tiny thing. But Stella says she's a pretty sight."

"Like her mother," Valentine whispered. He took another draw from his cigarette.

Mr. Nevilles puffed on his pipe. "I should hate you, you know. I should go inside right this minute, get my gun, and blow you off my front porch steps. I might even should have done that months ago when Stella first told me about the baby."

"Yes, sir."

"I kept wondering what kind of man got a girl pregnant when he was engaged to be married to another."

Valentine felt his shoulders hunch forward another inch. "Not one I'm overly proud of, sir." If he could have, he would have added, *But I did love your daughter. I truly did. And I was a boy . . . just a boy . . . playing out a man's role . . .*

"But I'm a peace-loving man, Mr. Bach."

"Yes, sir."

"And a forgiving one. I believe that is God's way. I believe that's the way he wants us to behave toward one another. Apparently my daughter feels the same way." He breathed out forcefully. "She's got a proposition for you, boy. I can honestly tell you I'm not real sure how I feel about it, but it's what she wants, and Stella's pretty much used to getting her way." He paused. "Most of the time."

Valentine looked back to Stella's father, waited.

"Stella wants you and your wife to raise the child, Mr. Bach. Against my better thoughts and judgment."

"Lilly Beth and me?" Valentine felt his cigarette—what was left of it—fall from his fingertips. He turned his head and watched as it rolled to a rest on the step below the one where his feet were perched. He kept his gaze on it as Mr. Nevilles continued.

"Stella says to tell you she won't interfere. The baby won't be hers, it will be yours. Yours and your wife's. Determined little cuss, that daughter of mine. She says she knows without a doubt she can do this . . . give you the baby. Walk away from it. She's had me contact a lawyer over in Savannah. You and Mrs. Bach will drive there. Stella will give you the baby, sign the papers. It will remain our secret. Her mama and I know, of course." He paused again. "What about your folks, Mr. Bach? Have you said anything to them about this mess?"

"No, sir." In spite of his intent otherwise, he began to cry, then felt Mr. Nevilles's hand on his shoulder.

"Go on ahead, son. Cry if you need to. I'm not so insensitive as to not know you had to have some feelings about all this. I can't imagine it's been easy for you neither since Stella told you."

Valentine swallowed hard. "Yes, sir."

"Whether you tell your mama and daddy or not, you have to tell your wife, son. That much is for sure."

Valentine nodded, his shoulders so hunched now he had to hold his head up by pressing his forehead into the palm of his hand. "I'm so sorry . . . I woulda never done nothing to hurt your daughter, Mr. Bach. I swear to you, I loved her. But my daddy—"

"I don't need your excuses, boy. I just need a yes or a no. You talk it over with your wife and get back to me within the next day or two. Stella plans to come home soon. She said she'll stay in Savannah one week after you and your wife come to get the baby."

Valentine raised his head. "Has she named her?"

"No, sir. She says that's for you to do. But she does have one request."

"Yes, sir?"

"She gives the middle name. She says it's to be Rose."

Valentine could hardly speak. He'd told Stella once that his middle name was Pemrose after his mother's maiden name. He hated it. Never talked about it. The only people his age who knew were Stella and, of course, Lilly Beth, and she'd found out on their wedding day when she spoke her vows. He'd told Stella that no one knew . . . it was their secret. And she'd shared a secret with him too. One he promised never to give away.

He looked at her father.

Never.

And now they had this. A name. And every time he called his daughter by her full name—if Lilly Beth consented to the adoption—he would be reminded of *this* secret. This little girl was his and Stella's, and Stella's love for him would be a part of their child forever.

But she'd never know it. Not if Stella stayed true to her promise.

33

Valentine told Lilly Beth after supper. He sat her down on the couch, held her hand, and confessed everything he thought he possibly could. He cried. And she cried. And then she slapped him soundly across the face. She burst into another fit of tears, then ran to their room. Although she didn't slam the door behind her, she made it clear with a look shot over her shoulder that it was in Valentine's best interest not to follow. For the first time in their short marriage, he slept on the couch. He wrapped the afghan his mother had knitted them for a wedding gift around his shoulders and tucked an arm under his head to serve as a pillow. He didn't even bother to change out of his evening clothes; to do so would have meant chancing a trip into their bedroom. He'd never seen Lilly Beth like this before, and he wasn't sure he wanted to know what might follow.

Lying there in the still and silence of the living room he heard the occasional sniffle and sob from across the way, rising and falling as her breasts did clothed in the white soft-ness of her nightgown. His heart felt shattered, not only for what he'd done to her, but for what he'd done to them. For the first time, he noted, they'd gone to sleep having not loved one another first. He was sure at some point married people stopped being intimate on a nightly basis, but he'd imagined it would be because the wife was pregnant . . . or ill . . . or the husband was away trying to make money to survive hard times. He'd never expected it would be this that would keep him and Lilly apart.

No, not this.

Lilly Beth cried off and on all night. Valentine woke each time the sobbing began, and each time, he sat up, flexed his stiff arm, and contemplated going in to try to comfort her. But the crying would soon subside, and he'd return to his place, slipping back into a fitful sleep.

The next morning Lilly Beth didn't get out of bed to fix his breakfast as she typically did. After unfolding himself from the couch, Valentine peered into the bedroom and, finding her asleep, left her alone. The morning light had managed to creep in through the venetian blinds and lace curtains near their bed, and he was able to clearly see her face. The eyes, though closed, were swollen. Her face was splotchy. He wanted to touch her, to gather her in his arms and tell her everything would be okay. That he was a dog for what he'd done. A big ole yard dog. But that he hadn't loved her back then like he loved her now. He'd hardly even known her. If she'd just wake up, just talk to him, he would tell her he was sorry. That he'd been a boy then. And he was a man now.

He was her husband.

But he could think of not a single "reason" to enter the room, even with hopes of *accidentally* waking her. After all, he'd slept in the clothes he'd changed into after his bath the evening before. He could say he needed his shoes, but they were still by the door. The only thing he needed in the bedroom was his wife.

He washed and shaved in the ice cold water of the small bathroom's basin, then slipped out the door and along the path that cut from their home to his parents'. His mama was frying up bacon and eggs in a cast-iron skillet on top of the stove while biscuits browned in the oven beneath it. He could smell the butter melting over them even from the back porch stoop. As good a cook as his wife was, she hadn't quite caught up to his mother in the kitchen.

After breakfast with his folks he left the house with his father to go work on Johnny Morgan's house addition. His stomach was full but his heart continued to hurt, and it must have showed all over him.

"What's on your mind, son?" his father asked from the driver's seat of the 1932 black Ford pickup he'd managed to save enough to purchase the year before.

Valentine cut his eyes toward his father without turning his head. If he looked at him full-on, he'd break and he knew it. He'd confess his sins in a blubber of tears like a boy and beg his daddy to give him some fatherly advice that would miraculously make everything right again. He half wondered if the man would take his belt off to him, hit him like Lilly Beth had. So he said nothing, shaking his head instead.

"You and Lilly Beth have a row?"

"No, sir."

"That's the only reason I can think of for a man to be a-eatin' at the breakfast table of his mama rather than his wife's."

Valentine hadn't thought of that. "Uh . . . Lilly Beth's just not feeling so good this morning."

They chugged through the center of town. It was cold outside, but Valentine cracked his window anyway. He felt as though he couldn't breathe.

From the corner of his eye he caught the movement of his father's hand swinging toward him, then felt the impact as it smacked between his shoulder blades. The slap was so hard and fast, Valentine bit his tongue. "What the—" He touched his fingers to the tender flesh, then drew them out, checking for blood. There was none, but he shot an angry glance toward his father anyway. His first one ever.

But the man was grinning, mouth half open and a gleam in his eye Valentine had never seen before. "What'd you do that for, Daddy?"

His father laughed then. "Mama and I were wondering how long it'd take you and Lilly to make us grandparents." His chin rose a fraction. "There's Nevan Nevilles standing on his side porch. Don't often see him there this time a-morning." His father raised his hand in a wave as Valentine flashed his eyes over to look out the dust-laden window. Stella's daddy's glare locked with the fear Valentine felt, and, unwittingly, he nodded his head in greeting.

Turning back to his own father, he said, "Lilly Beth's not expecting, Daddy. She's just not feeling well this morning."

Hope dissipated from his father's face; for a moment Valentine wished he could be honest. Hendrick Bach was, in fact, already a grandfather. The grandfather of what he knew for sure to be a beautiful baby girl. His child.

And, if his wife was willing, his and Lilly Beth's.

34

My appointment with Valentine Bach was to be shortly after lunchtime on the day following my visit with him and his family. I wasn't sure what that meant exactly. Lunchtime was relative.

I woke early, downed two Advil with a cup of coffee to push the mental cobwebs and physical pain from the night before out of the way of my work. I then rummaged through a few of the bags of merchandise I'd bought at Wal-Mart until I found a small digital camera. It was time, truly, to get to work.

Starting in the unheated living room and continuing throughout the house, I began shooting photographs of every nook and cranny within each room, envisioning each in its final form as I went along. The living room would require an extensive amount of detail in the decorating. "The proper parlor," the room was called in the days of my great-grandparents. This room demanded furnishings rich in patina and upholstery.

The sofa and other furnishings that had been in Aunt Stella's living room were not only outdated, they were—with the exception of the old table that held the box of photographs—useless for this project. I had begun to jot ideas in a notebook as to what I'd need to purchase to bring it to the vision I had for it. It included a note that the room was large enough for several groupings of furniture, but with the house to be used as a museum of sorts, I decided later it wasn't practical. The room should feel open enough for people to move around and through while at the same time reflecting the period.

Because the house lent itself completely to the Victorian era, I planned to—at some point—seek out antique dealers and fairs in the area. Mother would be a gem at helping with this, and blessedly it would keep her busy. Too busy to ask questions about or interfere in my relationship or lack thereof with Evan.

The next room was the bedroom Aunt Stella and Uncle Jim had shared. Unable to reconcile, even yet, that Uncle Jim was no longer alive and that he and Aunt Stella would never again spend a night there, I decided to convert it into a morning room. It was on the southeast corner of the house; the majority of its windows being on the east side. As I aimed the camera toward that wall, I imagined the morning's sunlight framed by floral chintz window treatments and sheers with a dotted Swiss design. My ideas included a sitting area made up of a chaise lounge and two chairs around the side table that had begun its days as a purchase by my great-grandmother for the living room but had, at some point, been moved into this room by Aunt Stella. I would set a gleaming silver tea set with two mismatched cups and saucers along with a short stack of books dated in the early 1900s I'd found amongst the treasures of the house. I'd also found a small, framed photo of Aunt Stella and Uncle Jim, taken at some point during their courtship, as well as various family portraits I intended to have reframed to suit the period. These would grace the mantel of the fireplace. Above them I intended to hang a portrait of my great-grandparents that, according to Mother, carried with it a most interesting story.

166

"Your Uncle Jim found it," she told me years ago after its discovery, "in of all places an antique shop." She'd called me that very afternoon.

"You're kidding me."

"No, I am not. I drove over to Cottonwood, begged those two couch potatoes to come with me as I did some shopping for Ginny Jones—you remember her, don't you?"

"Of course."

"Ginny is redoing her kitchen and insisted I help her find some items for it. She's wanting an old country kitchen feel . . . hand beaters, coffee grinders . . . you know what I mean."

I blinked. "But what about the picture of Grandmother and Grandfather Nevilles?"

"Oh, *that*!" Mother laughed. "I couldn't get Aunt Stella out of the house—she said she had some canning to do—but Uncle Jim was practically foaming at the mouth for an outing. It's been nearly six months, you know, since the doctor told him he could no longer drive. If it weren't for Uncle Bob's store being so close . . ." She trailed off. "Anyway, Uncle Jim went with me. I decided to head up to Augusta to the antique market there. We drove through Waynesboro. Have you ever been to the antique place there? It's on Main Street just before you get to the center of town."

"No, I don't think so."

"Chock full of stuff. You could spend days there and not see it all. At any rate, Uncle Jim took off in one direction and me in another and the next thing I knew he was standing behind me saying, 'Look-a here at what I found.' I turned around and was just amazed to see him holding a large portrait of my grandparents."

"Mother, you are kidding!"

"No, I am not. The dealer said he had no idea who the couple was; that he'd purchased the estate of a Mr. Henry Hawkins who was—and Uncle Jim remembered this—a photographer who lived in Cottonwood back when my grandparents were alive. Uncle Jim said he didn't remember Mr. Hawkins Sr. but he remembered Mr. Hawkins Jr., who had kept the photography studio going until he got a job working for some famous magazine, but he couldn't remember which one."

"*Land & Home?*"

"I have no idea."

"I love that magazine. It's been around forever."

"I know that, Jo-Lynn."

"I know you know that. I fell in love with the magazine because when I was a child I used to devour yours when it came in the mail. And I remember a photographer named Henry Hawkins. I love his work, mostly of the landscape portion of *Land & Home*. I wonder whatever happened to him."

"Goodness, who knows. Meanwhile, we found this portrait, and I said to the dealer . . ."

My memory trailed off with the sound of a car door slamming outside. I walked over to the window overlooking the driveway and split a couple of the blinds apart to see Karol walking toward the house. I met her on the front porch.

"What brings you out on this cold morning?"

"Good morning," she answered. "Got coffee in there?"

I shook my head. "Not fresh." I tipped my head toward the gas station. "But I know where we can get a cup and a warm room besides."

Karol followed my lead, and we headed down the steps and across the frosty lawn. The sun had yet to peek through the thick clouds. Though it was late morning, the lawn continued to sleep under a wintry sheet. "You and I should talk about the heating and cooling of the house. I don't know why Uncle Jim never added it. They were always content with what they had. Personally, if I weren't now over fifty and consumed by the ever-present hot flash you would have found me frozen in there."

When we got inside the store Aunt Mae-Jo offered us cups of coffee and ordered us over to "the fire to get warm."

"Jo-Lynn, are you working over there in that house without any heat, honey?"

I told her I was, but I was keeping busy enough. I turned to Karol. "By the way, Valentine Bach is an old builder around here. He's coming over after lunch so we can talk about the house."

Karol clutched her mug of coffee close to her face to warm it with the steam. "Speaking of the folks around here, do you know a man named Alfred Pitney?"

"Hold on there." Mae-Jo made herself a cup of coffee and joined us at the table. "Whatcha need to know about that no-good for?" she asked Karol.

"He's a holdout," Karol said. "The house he and his family live in is an exceptional beauty but in great need of repair. When we're finished with our work here it'll be an eyesore. I've tried to talk with him several times, but he won't even let me near the front porch much less inside so we can sit down like civilized human beings."

"That man's not human, that's why," Mae-Jo said with a shake of her head. She took a long sip of her coffee. "I don't know why Diana puts up with him 'cept she had those boys of hers to raise. I always told Bob if he ever got to acting as strange as Alfred Pitney, I'd leave him."

"What can you tell us about him, Aunt Mae-Jo?"

"That house belonged to his daddy and his daddy before him. Rumor has it that the family money—and believe you me, there is plenty of it—came in part from the Klan's financing. The old man—Alfred's granddaddy—was some muckety-muck in the organization. Not the Grand Wizard or even the Grand Dragon, mind you, but he was on up there." Mae-Jo paused for a moment. "The Grand Titan, he might have been."

I looked at Karol. "A part of our rich Southern heritage I'd just as soon forget."

"Well, honey, you can't sweep the nasty up under the rug and believe that it's not there. All that does is leave a lump under the carpet."

"How well I know." I said the words so softly I wasn't sure if they were heard by anyone.

"The Klan's influence may not be what it once was around here, but no one is foolish enough to think it's gone. Our colored population here, they lay pretty low. Not like it was years ago, them living in the old shanties along the outskirts of town—we called them the quarters—but nonetheless . . ."

I smiled again. "Aunt Mae-Jo, I don't think they like being called 'colored' anymore."

"Well, whatever. You aren't going to teach this old dog any new tricks."

Karol straightened. "Personally, I don't care where the money came from. We just want to see what we can do with the outside of the house and the lawns around it. It would be stunning with some cosmetic work. They could live like pigs on the inside—I don't care—but the outside . . . I've thrown the word *money* out to him, but he gives me a look that makes me think he's got a gun and he's not afraid to use it."

Mae-Jo laughed. "He does and he isn't. And money means nothing to him. He's got a farm back behind that house that does all right, I reckon. As good as anybody's these days. I understand he also owns some rental housing over in Raymore. For the college students."

"Then he is doing all right," I said.

We sat quiet for a minute before Karol said, "What about Mrs. Pitney? What's she like?"

"Like I said, she always depended on Alfred to raise the boys. She's not from here. I don't know where she's from, to be honest with you. Keeps to herself when it comes to her personal business. Bob said Alfred met her on one of his Klansman conventions or whatnot up in Atlanta somewhere." She looked at me. "This was years ago, mind you."

"So she's lived here for a while?"

"The boys—they were hers, not Alfred's—were about four and five when she moved here. Bob said she was married to some old man uppity-up in the Klan who was arrested, then released but killed before he could go to trial. 'Least that's the way I hear it. Someone told Bob that Alfred was told to marry her by the Klan, but I don't know how true that is. I'm not even sure the Klan has that kind of clout anymore."

"I don't know enough about the Klan to know," I said.

"That's just the gossip," Mae-Jo confirmed. "But you can bet some folk around here aren't willing to let *any* old habit die."

"Maybe the Klan hasn't died; it just changed its name," I said, thinking of the white supremacy groups I'd learned about in the news. "How old are the boys now?"

"Early twenties, I'd say. Twenty-one, twenty-two. You see one, you see the other. That Godwin boy's been hanging out with them of late, and I told Bob that's some good coming to no good."

Karol looked confused.

Aunt Mae-Jo continued, "Terry Godwin's mama is good people. She raises those children in the Lord. There's not a Sunday morning nor evening over at the church but what she doesn't have those children there. Wednesday night supper too. Those young'uns sing in the adult choir. Have since they

171

were no more than twelve each. Prettiest voices you've ever heard." She turned to me. "Speaking of which, when are you going to come to church, little missy?"

"Ahhh . . ." I had not attended church regularly since I'd married Evan, who preferred to make his appearance, as he once said, "Like all good sinners, Easter and Christmas." Evan had it all covered. Or so he thought.

"Tomorrow's Sunday. You can plan to go with me and Bob. Then Wednesday. You'll go with me to the supper." She looked at Karol. "You too. Good home-cooked Southern food and preaching besides. Our new pastor is a good one. He lives over there in Raymore. Course, why would he want to live here?"

Karol bristled kindly. "Give me one year and he'll want to live here. Mark my words. Everyone who is anyone will want to live here."

35

"So what are you going to do about Mr. Pitney?" I asked Karol as she climbed into her car.

She shook her head as she pushed the ignition button. "I don't know. I'm going to call Mark Michaels after I leave here. See what he wants me to do. Oh!" She turned her crystal eyes toward me. "Mark told me last night they think they've found a developer for this project."

At first I thought she meant the house. "What do you mean?" I looked at the house, then back to her. "I thought I was handling this alone."

Karol smiled. "Not the house . . . Cottonwood. Mark's been searching through the proposals of several development companies and said he thinks he's found one. Should have an answer on that pretty soon. At any rate, their representative and you and I should get together to talk."

"Me?"

"Sure. Why not? This place is going to be a focal point when it's finished, and whoever it is will want to know what you're doing inside and out. We want to make sure our plans . . . jive." She said the last word with a hint of jest.

"I haven't heard that word in a while."

"And I haven't been in church since I was confirmed, but

looks like I'll be seeing you there." She winked at me. "Do you think they'll have fried chicken?"

"That's like asking if the sun is going to rise in the East. No group of self-respecting Southern women would allow a church supper to happen without fried chicken . . . and potato salad and—in spite of this wicked cold—sweet iced tea."

Valentine Bach arrived just before one o'clock, driven by his great-granddaughters, who parked the family car in our driveway, waved a friendly hello to me, and then headed over to the store. Mr. Valentine—who insisted I call him just that—and I walked in and through each room of the house. Every so often the old carpenter would stomp on an area of flooring with his worn work boot or pull his hammer from the loop of his overalls and tap on a wall. He spoke in a contractor's language. "See this?" he said, having tapped his hammer on the wall of one of the first floor bedrooms. "These studs are twenty-four inch on center on top of one-inch-thick one-by-sixes. Right 'chere . . . tongue-and-groove boards. And the nails you'll find under here are the old cut nails. Don't see those anymore."

Inside the dining room he gave me a lesson I didn't need, but it seemed important for him to share, so I let him do all the talking. "All hand-cut lumber in those days. If a house caught fire they burned hot and long." He nodded as his eyes clouded, as though he were remembering a house or two that had lost its life in a blaze. Then suddenly he continued, "And what they did was—they didn't put up plaster walls, you know—they put up the lumber and then stretched canvas over it and then wallpaper on top of that." He placed his weathered hand flat against a wall and rubbed it as though it were a woman's back. "Wonder how many layers of wallpaper's under here."

"I don't think Aunt Stella ever replaced this wallpaper. Not that I can remember, anyway."

Valentine chuckled, shoved his hands in his pockets, and shook his head. "No, ma'am. Not Stella. But I've heard tell Miss Loretta liked to keep up with the times. So she may have added at least four or five layers here." He looked toward the wall again. "Feels like five."

Upstairs and in front of a bedroom fireplace he said, "Jim had the good sense back years ago to replace the fireplaces. But why he never added central heat and air is beyond me. But I 'spect Jim and Stella lived only in the rooms they needed and figured why go to the expense."

"I don't remember any rooms being opened except the living room and their bedroom," I said. "And one led to the other. The doors between the living room and the hallway were kept closed. The dining room was never used, so it was kept closed. All the bedrooms were closed off. The kitchen was heated in the winter by cooking at the stove and cooled in the summer by a small window unit. Same with their bedroom and the living room."

Valentine bent his neck backward and looked up. I didn't follow his gaze at first; I was momentarily mesmerized by the way his hair traveled down his back. When I did look up, I frowned. The ceilings in this house were going to be a challenge. "Heat rises," Valentine said, looking back at me.

I brought my eyes back to his.

"I understand you had some folks over here working for a few days."

I cocked my head. "How did you hear that?"

He smiled. "Word gets around." He shuffled out of the room, and I followed. "Think you can get them back? We could use a few hardworking men over the next few months."

"What about the women?"

He stopped then and smiled again. The crow's-feet around his eyes were deep and oddly appealing. "Whatever you think best, ma'am. It's your money."

"Sort of," I said and smiled back.

As we walked around the outside of the house he asked about termite inspection, and I told him that calling someone was on my list of things to do. "Best do that today," he said, to which I replied, "Yes, sir." It was then I realized that, in an odd sort of way, he was no longer working for me, but I for him.

He headed for the opposite side of Main Street, and as we crossed over he said, "Around here, termites'll bring your house down before the years even have time to blink."

"Hopefully Uncle Jim took care of that."

We reached the sidewalk across the street, and he turned back toward the house. I watched as he eyed it. "Only slight bowing in the walls. Jim always tried to stay on top of things where the house was concerned but not so much with the buildings out back once his farming days were over."

At the barn I told him of an idea I had. "I'd like to have a cottage where the overseer of the museum can live, if need be. This will have to be torn down, but maybe we can salvage some of the original lumber."

Valentine nodded. "Seen it done a-fore."

When he'd finished his tour of the property and Annaleise and Arizona had joined us back at the car, I asked, "So, do you think I've completely lost my mind? I know it's going to be a lot of work, but you do agree, don't you, that it can be restored?"

Valentine looked from me to the house and back to me again. And then he smiled a quiet smile and said, "Foundation's pretty stable, ma'am. If a foundation's good, anything can be restored."

In spite of the twinkle within, his blue eyes pierced my soul. For a moment I wondered what he knew about me . . . about my marriage . . . or better yet, about my life. As he'd said, "Word gets around." Difficult as it was, I managed to look away from him and to the girls, who stood lovely and patient in their waiting. So young . . . so full of an inner exuberance that shone from their faces. Obviously nothing had happened in their young lives to chisel away at the hope and future one could easily see awaiting them. I took a deep breath, in and out of my nose. I looked back to the old man then. "I'll take your word for it," I said.

36

After the sermon and a final song by the Godwin twins—who sang an unaccompanied version of "How Great Thou Art"—the man whom I now knew as Elder Timothy Lawrence approached me in the church's center aisle, obviously excited to see a new face among the few but faithful of his congregation. "You're Jim Edwards's niece," the young pastor said, pumping my hand after the Sunday morning service at Upper Creek Primitive Baptist Church. "I recognize you from the funeral. Again, so sorry about your uncle." The man's face went from grinning to solemn so quickly it seemed a rehearsed reflex.

"Thank you," I said. "He will be missed."

Shoulder to shoulder, with Karol, Mae-Jo, and Bob behind us, we stepped down the aisle toward the door of the chapel, where parishioners slipped out of the warmth of the room and into the cold outside air. "I understand you'll be staying for a while. To fix up the old house on Main Street."

"Is anything a secret in Cottonwood?" I answered with a smile.

He returned the smile. "My family and I don't live here, and still I manage to keep up with the gossip."

"You've not been here long, I understand?"

"No, ma'am. This is my first church as elder." From the aisle that ran along the front wall of the church and behind the rows of pews a young woman, pretty and modestly dressed, approached us. "There you are," he said to her. Then, back to me, "This is my wife, Cheryl." His arm went around her shoulder. His hand squeezed her in affection, and she smiled up at him, looking all of not yet twenty years old.

"Nice to meet you, Cheryl."

"Cheryl, honey, this is Jim Edwards's niece. Remember I told you I'd performed his funeral."

Performed his funeral. Performed . . . The choice of words struck me as odd. Elder Timothy Lawrence hadn't known Uncle Jim. Never really taken the time to get to know him, in spite of my uncle's refusal to step into the church building.

For the first time I wondered what had happened that had caused Uncle Jim to have such resistance to formal worship. By now we'd reached the door. I tightened the sash around my coat, said "nice to meet you" to the child bride of the young preacher, and turned to Mae-Jo and Bob. "Wrap your scarf around your head, Aunt Mae-Jo," I said. "Otherwise the cold might get in your ears." I sounded a great deal like Aunt Stella now.

Mae-Jo complied as Uncle Bob, handsome and strapping at seventy-four years of age, winked at me and said, "She has my love to keep her warm."

Aunt Mae-Jo bopped him on the chest with the back of her hand. "Oh, you," she said as though disgusted. But I could see she loved her husband very much, and for a moment, I thought of Evan.

Karol and I had Sunday dinner—lunch—with Aunt Mae-Jo and Uncle Bob, then returned to the big house around three in the afternoon. Mae-Jo had sent both of us out the door with plates heaped over with food and an admonishment not to do any work the rest of the day. "It's the Sabbath," she said. "Keep it holy."

I took her words to heart. I put the plate of food on the kitchen counter, the house so cold I need not open the refrigerator, then went upstairs, lit a fire, and curled up on the bed under a quilt for a nap.

I woke two hours later. I had dreamed of Evan, that he had been with me at the church, that he had placed a warm scarf over my shoulders and adjusted it around my head. "Here," he said. "I don't want your ears to get too cold."

Still lying on my side, I placed a hand over my exposed ear and pretended it had all been true. "Evan," I whispered. "Why don't we have what Mae-Jo and Bob have? Where did we go so wrong?"

I looked at my watch. It was shortly after five, and I thought to call Mother.

"Mae-Jo tells me you went to church with her and Bob this morning," she said after our hellos.

"I did. Karol went with us. Did she tell you that?"

"Why didn't you come to church with Daddy and me?" Mother expertly avoided my question. "You could have seen Stephen and had Sunday dinner with us."

"I hadn't really planned to go to church at all, Mother. Aunt Mae-Jo insisted and . . . I went."

"Did you have anything to eat?"

"Of course. Do you think I'm starving myself to death over here?"

"I still don't know *what* you're doing over there."

"Are we going to get into that again? Because if we are, I'll let you go."

Mother remained silent until she said, "Did you know Evan has been calling your father?"

"Still?"

"He misses you, Jo-Lynn. You two really should try to work this out."

"He called me."

"When?"

"Last night."

"And?"

"And we got into a fight. As usual."

"Oh, Jo-Lynn."

"Why are you blaming me?"

"I'm not blaming you, Jo-Lynn. I just . . . I don't know."

"Your tone says you think I'm in the wrong."

"Well, maybe I do. I believe marriage is for better, for worse. I believe that when you have problems, you stick with each other and work those problems out. Jesus gave a pretty short list of reasons for marriage to end, you know. 'We just don't see eye to eye anymore' wasn't on the list."

"I know . . ."

"And don't think for one minute that my marriage to your father has been all good. We've had our problems."

"I've never even heard a single cross word between the two of you."

"That doesn't mean we haven't had them. I never believed in arguing in front of children."

"Why not? If you argue and then make up, wouldn't that demonstrate that love covers a multitude of sins?"

"You sound like a preacher."

"Mmm."

"Why must you argue with me all the time, Jo-Lynn?"

"I don't argue with you all the time." The irony of my statement was not lost on me, and I smiled. "Just sometimes . . . like now."

"You shouldn't argue with your mother on a Sunday."

I felt my face break in a grin. "Oh, Mother. You're such a peach. Even when you frustrate me, you make me smile."

37

After my conversation with Mother, I called Doris. We spoke briefly—Aunt Stella was doing well, adjusting, ornery as ever—and then I asked to speak to our family matriarch.

"How ya doing, shug?" she asked when she came on the line.

"Good, Aunt Stella. You?" I sat in the rocker, feet planted on the floor, and swayed to and fro.

"I'm hanging in there. Missing Jim, no matter how busy Doris tries to keep me. Tell me what you've been up to. What's going on with fixin' up the house?"

I filled her in. When I mentioned Valentine Bach there was a pause. Then she said, "Valentine Bach will do a fine job."

"I met his family." I spoke with trepidation, remembering Aunt Stella's sentiments over the late Mr. Godwin. "Miss Bettina sends you her best."

Another pause. "Tell her I said hello," she said finally.

"I will. I also saw the family this morning at church. Miss Bettina's grandchildren sing so beautifully."

"You went to church? To my old church?"

Her *old* church. Another odd turn of phrase. "Yes. And I was thinking . . . Aunt Stella, can you tell me why Uncle Jim—or *you* for that matter—never went to church? I know you've had a strong relationship with God, but I don't ever recall, you know, seeing the two of you in a church building. Outside of a wedding or a funeral, I mean."

Aunt Stella didn't answer right away. "Things happen. Change how you feel about churchgoing. But you're right as rain when you say Jim and I have maintained a strong relationship with the Lord."

"What about when Doris was a child? Didn't you take her to church?"

"We did. Jim and I went to church until Doris was a teenager. She kept going and we stopped." Aunt Stella coughed a laugh. "Isn't that a hoot? Usually it's t'other way around."

I didn't answer.

"Listen, shug. Don't go worrying yourself about Jim and me. What's got you wondering this anyway? Did that young preacher say anything to make you think your uncle isn't in the hereafter with the Lord because he didn't attend a church service—"

"Oh no! Nothing like that."

"Well, that's good to hear. One thing I'm for certain on, your Jim Edwards is probably up in heaven planting vegetables for the Lord's table," she said. "And I won't be too long behind him, sugar foot. Not too long a'tall."

After I'd changed into my pajamas, I went downstairs and made a cup of hot white peach tea from the gift bag Mother had purchased for me at Trish's, then slipped back up the stairs to my bedroom. I turned the portable television on—the one I'd purchased at Wal-Mart and had hardly made use of—sat in one of the front porch rockers, and enjoyed an old

183

black-and-white movie, a tearjerker starring Cary Grant and Irene Dunne.

My cell phone rang around 10:00. It was Evan, and though my head told me not to answer, my heart was feeling sappy from the old reel-to-reel love story—so I did.

"I thought I'd try again," he said.

"Hi," I said.

"I've been a jerk, haven't I?"

I picked up the remote control and muted the television. "Is that a rhetorical question?"

He chuckled from the other end. "Yes," he said. "How's it going down there?"

"Do you really want to know? About me, I mean? How it's going for me?" I pulled my knees up to my chest and curled my toes—toasty in a pair of socks—around the edge of the seat.

"I do."

For the next half hour I told my husband about the house, about the emptying of it, about Valentine Bach and his family, about the crew of day laborers I'd hired and would be hiring again, this time under Valentine's leadership. I told him of the barn and everything I'd found there, of the downstairs bedroom and its treasures. I told him about the house being unbelievably cold and my bed colder still in spite of the electric blanket I now owned, to which I heard him give a deep sigh, causing me to wonder if he truly missed me or only missed me in a physical sense. Dismissing that thought, I told him I was thinking of using water source heat pumps for heating and cooling the house, and I asked his opinion about them.

"A surprisingly simple method for an old house," he said. "I can do some research for you if you'd like."

I initially thought to answer him no but, stunned by his offer, said, "If you have the time. I'm sure you and Everett are busy."

"I'll make the time."

I hugged my knees, drawing them tighter to my chest—my heart—and was about to tell him of the delightfully wacky Karol Paisley and M Michaels and the plans they had for Cottonwood when I heard a glass shatter from somewhere downstairs. Startled, I took in a deep breath and said, "What was that?"

"What?" Evan asked.

I uncurled myself and stood. "Something downstairs . . . it sounded like the breaking of glass."

"I thought the house was empty downstairs."

I walked over to one of the windows. "It is. Basically." I peered out into the dark of night. My eyes caught a fleeting movement, and I cocked my head, grateful there were no lights in the room but that from the television and the fire in the fireplace. Just as I'd seen weeks before, there were men running from near the barn toward the barren field, this time three rather than two.

"Jo-Lynn?" Evan asked. "You there?"

A light flickered from the right, and I craned my neck, pressing my face against the icy pane for a better view. At first I thought it a reflection from across the room, but then I realized . . .

"Evan!"

"Jo-Lynn, what is it? What's happening?"

"The house is on fire! Call 911! Call 911!"

38

I ran into the hallway and down the flight of stairs, grabbing the curvature of the wood at the base of the banister and swinging myself toward the kitchen, somehow intuitively aware that the fire was there. Rather than going from the hallway directly into the kitchen, I jerked the dining room door open, then pushed through the swinging door with such force, I slid on the old Formica floor and fell onto my backside. The heat of the flames, which by this time were engulfing the pantry—an L-shaped room that ran along the backside of the house off from the kitchen—caused me to forget the initial pain from the fall. Smoke billowed into the room from the open door between the two rooms, and I immediately began to cough. Covering my eyes with one arm, I crawled toward the stove, where the fire extinguisher I'd bought stood like a prepared soldier.

I'm not sure why I thought to do it; I pulled myself up at the counter, twisted the sink's cold-water knob, then pulled the coffee carafe from the cup holder of the Rubbermaid dish drainer. I filled it with water, poured the icy water over myself, soaking my pajamas—my hands shaking all the while, sloshing the water to a puddle at my feet—and grabbed the extinguisher. Having never used one before, I wasn't completely sure how, but I told myself I'd seen it done in enough movies and television shows. I pulled the pin, stumbled toward the pantry door, then aimed the nozzle toward the floor, to the base of the flames.

As they began to diminish, I moved in closer, conscious of the scorching heat before me and the cotton material plastered to my skin. At some point I was aware of sirens blaring in the distance and then of neighbors—those people who come in your hour of need—behind me, beside me, some with their extinguishers, a few with heavy blankets for beating out the last of the embers. I began coughing again, and then Aunt Mae-Jo's arms were around me, her hands gripping the tops of my arms, pulling me out the back of the house, pushing me down to the floor of the porch, and then drawing water from the well.

"Drink this, honey." She handed me the tin dipper. She was dressed in a blue flannel gown and an opened terry cloth robe.

I drank it like an old dog in from the hunt, then looked up at her. "Why? Why?"

She took the dipper from me, filled it again from the old bucket, and handed it back. "Drink some more. Why what, honey?"

"Why would someone do this?"

Aunt Mae-Jo squatted down beside me. "What are you talking about, Jo-Lynn?"

I finished off the water before I answered, "Aunt Mae-Jo. Someone did this. I saw them. Three men." I coughed again. I coughed so hard I lost my breath, then gained my composure. "My eyes feel like they're on fire."

Aunt Mae-Jo stood, pulled a handkerchief out of her robe pocket, dipped it into the bucket of water, and brought it to me. "Use this. I'll go inside right quick and get your Uncle Bob. You'll want to tell him what you just told me. Don't move, now."

187

Telling Uncle Bob was the easy part. I repeated it to the sheriff from Raymore—Larry Ganksy, tall and boyishly handsome in what I thought to be his early thirties—who took meticulous notes and said "Mmm-hmm, mmm-hmm" a lot. However, repeating it to Mother and Daddy, my brother Stephen, and everyone else that came by between the dark hours of Sunday night and the light of Monday was exhausting.

I asked Daddy to call Evan—who had repeatedly left messages to call him back—and give him the news. "I'm just too tired for any confrontations," I said.

Though Mother frowned at my request, Daddy agreed to make the call on my behalf.

I didn't think to wonder *how* my neighbors gained entry into the house to help put out the fire until much later in the night, after I'd crawled between the warm covers of a bed in Aunt Mae-Jo and Uncle Bob's house. By then I'd been seen by paramedics from Raymore, had my wounds bandaged, and was only partially lucid, what with having been given a mild sedative. But I knew enough to know I'd not given anyone entry.

Monday morning, over plates of fried eggs, grits, sausage, and toast I asked Uncle Bob, "How did everyone get into the house? One second I was fighting the fire alone and the next thing I knew, half the town was there."

Uncle Bob grinned at me. "You don't really think those old locks will hold in an emergency, do you?"

I frowned. "I'll get Mr. Valentine to put dead bolts on first thing."

Doris called my cell phone early the next morning, before I left for the big house. She was nearly hysterical. I told her if she breathed one word to Aunt Stella, I'd quit this job before it got started.

The sheriff pulled into the driveway at the big house just as I arrived. I'd made the walk easily from Bob and Mae-Jo's and had just cornered the large oak that shielded the big house from the highway when I saw the squad car bouncing over the ruts and then come to a stop. I waved to him as he stepped out of the car. He nodded, slipped an army green baseball cap with a gold sheriff's star logo in the center on to his head. "I see I timed my arrival perfectly," he said and smiled.

"Would you like some coffee? We can step over to the store. Uncle Bob left a half hour ago so I imagine there's hot coffee brewing there."

He shook his head. "I'll only be here a minute. Now that you've had some sleep, do you remember anything about the men you saw? Anything at all?"

"No. I'm sorry, but no. I couldn't see their faces."

"Build?"

"They were slender. Wore dark clothes." I paused. "I guess you can say they moved like young men . . . not older men."

"*I* can't say," he said. "*I* wasn't there."

"That's all I know." I shrugged. "Sorry."

Valentine Bach came by midmorning, surveyed the damage, and said, "Pretty damaged, but we can fix it."

"Mr. Valentine, first things first. I want dead bolts on every outside door before nightfall. Apparently, the locks on these doors are worth diddly-squat."

Valentine told me he'd get right on it. His great-grandson had been his chaperone this time. As always, the young man kept his eyes locked on me the entire time I spoke with Valentine, leaving me feeling as though I were still wearing the water-soaked pajamas now in the trash. Finally, when Valentine told him they'd need to go into Raymore to get the supplies, he looked from me to his great-grandfather and said, "Yes, sir, Pappy."

They drove off just as Karol drove up. "I came as soon as I heard," she said, slamming the car door shut. "It was all everyone was talking about in the hotel this morning."

189

"You're kidding me."

She grinned wide. "Nope. I have never seen small towns quite like these two. It's like they're sisters or something. Everyone knows everyone." She reached for my left hand then gently pulled back my oversized sweater sleeve. I wore a short-sleeved shirt because of the burns, because I had to apply ointment and change the bandages so often. Karol now looked at the patching of four-by-four gauze squares against the swollen and tender flesh. "Ouch."

"It's not as bad as it looks. Only hurts when I think about it."

"So try not to think about it."

I nodded. "Let's go inside."

After we'd taken tentative steps into the kitchen and peered around the damage, Karol looked at me. "You really think this was on purpose?"

I nodded. "I was talking to my husband on the phone, and I heard a glass break. When I looked out the window I saw three men running through the back and then saw the fire." I paused for a moment. "Two weeks ago, a few nights after Uncle Jim's funeral, I saw them then too. Only then there were two, not three."

"You told the sheriff?"

I nodded but said nothing.

Karol walked over to the sink and peered out the window, then turned back to me. "Mark Michaels is arriving here later today with someone from the company he's considering for the town's development. Oh, and get this: even Mark knew about it."

"About what?"

"The fire."

"Mark Michaels knew about the fire?"

"I don't know how . . . but he did."

190

39

I soon found out how Mark Michaels, a handsome guy who looked more like the Marlboro Man than a businessman, knew about the fire. Just after lunchtime, while Valentine and Terry drilled holes and added shiny brass dead bolts to one-hundred-year-old doors, I stood watching on the porch against the Main Street side of the house. Three cars pulled into the driveway. The lead car was Karol's. The second a red Chevy Trailblazer. The third was a familiar black Porsche 911 Carrera S, its driver a man I'd shared my life with for twenty-five years.

I leaned my shoulder against a nearby column and whispered, "Evan."

Valentine turned from the door and looked from the driveway to me and back to the driveway. "You know them folks?"

"The man in the black car is my husband. I suspect the other man is the one responsible for the changes Cottonwood is about to undergo. And you know Karol Paisley, I'm sure."

Valentine nodded. "Sure do." He crossed over to me then as though a protective grandfather, pulled a cigarette pack out of his pocket, and said, "You mind?"

I shifted to press my back against the column. "If I smoked,

I'd probably have one with you." I turned my head to look at the threesome approaching from the driveway side of the house. "I should have figured this would happen."

"What's that?"

"My husband's company . . ." I shook my head. "Never mind." I patted the old gentleman on his shoulder. "Excuse me," I said then ambled down the length of the porch.

When I got close enough to Karol, who led the pack, she mouthed, "I didn't know."

I smiled faintly toward her, then cast my gaze on Evan. "What are you doing here?"

But it was Mark Michaels who answered. "Mrs. Hunter?" He extended his hand. "I'm Mark Michaels."

Couples have a way of communicating by looking into the other's eyes. Nothing has to be said. Neither a word nor a syllable. Just a look. It lingers longer than a casual glance but not as long as if, say, the couple were carrying on a verbal conversation. Evan and I gave each other such a look.

His told me he was bent on being here.

Mine reflected my displeasure. I'd wanted to do this on my own. Without him or his input. "I should have known," my eyes flashed, "that your company would bid for this job and win."

I could barely contain my anger. "Anger," Evan had said to me during one of our frequent arguments of late, "is not a basic emotion. Anger comes from something else. A driving force. What I'm saying to you, Jo-Lynn, is that you have to know *why* you're angry and not simply react in anger as you tend to do."

As I led the threesome to the back of the house to view the fire damage, I tried to come up with an honest answer as to why it was, exactly, I was so angry.

"It's not as bad as it could have been," Valentine said from the door between the kitchen and the dining room.

The four of us, standing near the protective sheet-covered doorway between the kitchen and the pantry, turned to look at him.

"We can have that repaired in no time. Lucky thing here is"—he pulled his sweat-stained Jed Clampett hat from his head, readjusted it just so, then set it back in place—"Miss Jo-Lynn had the good sense to have doused herself with water before she tried to fight the flames."

"And the good sense to buy a fire extinguisher," I said, trying to lighten the moment. It didn't much work.

Evan slipped closer to me, picked up my left arm, and looked at the bandaging. "How bad are your burns?"

"I'll be fine, Evan. I have to put a cream on periodically. Change the bandaging. Take something for pain if needed."

He eased my arm down until my hand slipped into his. He squeezed lightly. "You could have been killed." His voice was just barely over a whisper. For a moment I was so keenly aware that—in spite of our current difficulties—my husband loved me. Loved me very much.

And I struggled with the emotions that revelation stirred in me.

40

Cottonwood, Georgia
January 1947

Stella came out of the movie theater in a daze. She'd just seen *The Best Years of Our Lives* for the third time. Each viewing was more moving than the last. She looked over at her date, a boy named Tom she'd gone out with for a few months, a young man just home from the war.

He gave her a slow grin. "Was it as wonderful for you this time as it was the last time?"

She nodded. "I love that movie."

"Whatever makes you happy."

Tom was a tall and lanky man and appeared even more so next to Stella's petite stature. He wasn't an overly handsome fellow; his jaw was too square, his nose too small, and he wore oval-shaped glasses. But he was always a gentleman with Stella, and for Stella that was just fine. She'd gone out with him at least two dozen times and he had yet to even give her a kiss.

Her mama was nearly planning the wedding, though Stella had told her more than once not to bother.

"He's not the one," she'd said.

But her mother would not be discouraged. She invited him to suppers and Sunday dinners, clucked like an old hen every time he came to the house to pick Stella up for an outing.

If Tom were aware of her mother's overzealousness, he never mentioned it.

In her mother's mind, Stella knew, Tom was from Raymore, and that made all the difference in the world. "So what?" Stella had asked her.

"Then he isn't from here."

"And so? What's so wonderful about not being from here? I happen to like it here."

Her mother was standing in Stella's bedroom. Together they were putting fresh linens from the line on the bed. One woman stood on one side, the other opposite her.

Mama blushed. "Stella. You know what I mean. I think it's best for you if you married some nice young man from somewhere besides Cottonwood. Settle down close by but far enough away. It'll be easier for you."

Stella cocked a brow. "You mean for you, Mama."

Since her "time away," as Mama and Papa preferred to call it, six years ago, she'd grown sassier. "Too sassy," Papa would say, but he never scolded her for it.

She'd also grown tough. She had to. After her return, she'd taken a job at Wright's, but when Mrs. Wright told her mama that she was flirting with too many of the male customers, her mother had forced her to resign.

It wasn't that she was flirting, so much, Stella had argued, though she knew she had been. But it was a safe flirtation. "If I never fall in love again," she'd declared as though she were Bette Davis on the silver screen, "it will be too soon." Love came at too high a price.

After Wright's, she'd gone to work for Dr. Terrance Bird, a physician fresh out of school with a world of new ideas for practicing medicine, a spark in his eye for Stella, and a very astute wife who kept her baby blues on them both. Most girls would have felt uncomfortable around Doc's missus, but Stella wasn't most girls. She squared her shoulders, kept the fair young doctor at bay and the wife appeased by concentrating on her work, which included general office duties and the occasional holding down of a small child for a shot when Nurse Alice was busy.

Stella had dated a handful of young men but never more than a few times each. The moment they appeared serious, she ended the relationship. None of them really did anything for her anyway. Dating was more for something to do and for keeping her mother's mournful glances from becoming too much to handle.

Tom was different. He hadn't tried to grope her the way most boys did; he enjoyed the movies and dancing. Taking long walks and talking, though they never really talked about anything important. He didn't talk about the war, but he often brought up places he'd visited in Europe. She didn't talk about herself from before her "time away," choosing to focus more on the here and now.

Sometimes they went to Poor Man's Pond to catch a mess of fish. These were the times Stella found herself casting more than her line. Every so often, she'd look over her shoulder, expecting to see a seventeen-year-old boy dressed in overalls ambling toward her, cane pole balancing on his shoulder. But he never came, nor did the man he'd grown up to be.

She caught a glimpse of him every so often, of course. More than a few times they'd run into each other at the feed and seed when Stella went in to pick up something for her papa. Some mornings she went out on the front porch to drink her coffee in solitude and she'd see him and his daddy heading toward their next job. He'd give a slight wave as though they were old classmates who just happened to be passing each other along the way.

She'd seen the little girl only once; Lilly Beth rarely came to town, preferring to keep their daughter—Lilly Beth and Valentine's—close to home. When Bettina was three years old, though, Lilly Beth and Valentine had been forced to bring the child in. She had a high fever and was vomiting and nearly convulsive.

Stella had managed to stay professional, though it nearly ripped her heart out. While Dr. Bird arranged admission at the hospital in Raymore and Mrs. Bird warmed up their 1941 Oldsmobile automatic sedan in the driveway, Stella helped Nurse Alice prepare cold compresses to bring down the fever.

"Place it right here." Nurse Alice sounded more like a drill sergeant than a loving health care provider. Stella didn't usually take bossy orders well, but this time she didn't argue. This time too much was at stake.

Bettina was lying—clothed only in her panties—on the table. Occasionally, impulsively she kicked her legs against the cold of the air and the icy compresses. Her mother stood at her head, holding it to keep her from thrashing about. Her father kept vigil over his wife's shoulder, made little shushing sounds, and cooed his daughter's name. "Bettina," he sang. "Papa's here. Papa's here, Bettina Rose." When he said her middle name his eyes shot to Stella and Stella's to him.

Just as quickly, she turned away and back to her role.

"Get the fan from Doc's desk," Nurse Alice said. "Hurry, Stella. We'll need to turn the fan on her." Stella ran into the doctor's office, removed the chrome-plated GE oscillating fan from his desk, and said, "Nurse Alice's orders" to the doctor who was standing with the phone still up to his ear.

She stopped at the door and looked back. "She's going to be okay, isn't she, Doc?"

He couldn't possibly understand the question. He thought she was concerned about a patient. "Take the fan on into the exam room, Stella," he barked. He was sweating, even in the chill of March, and the sight of him gave her no comfort.

Stella did as she was told. The breeze blew across the room, rustling the pages of a wall calendar, as Stella joined Nurse Alice at the table.

"What'd the doc say?" Valentine asked her. "Does he know anything yet?"

"He's still on the phone," she answered.

Her voice seemed to reverberate in the small room, became an electrical shock between them. It was their first real conversation since that evening so long ago when she'd told him he was going to be a father and he'd told her he was going to marry someone else. And that someone else was now standing between them.

Stella looked down at the child, their child—she'd allow herself to think it just this once—saw the silky curl of her brown hair and, for a fleeting moment, the dark brown of her eyes. They were her eyes. Stella's. And, in that moment, she remembered a childhood photo taken of her sisters and her at this same age. An almost identical image.

The doctor came in announcing that the car was ready. "Wrap the child," he said. The hospital was expecting them.

And then they were gone.

And Stella was left to worry and wonder, in spite of Dr. Bird's report that a doctor from Raymore had called later that day to say Bettina had stabilized. Then, at the end of her workday nearly a week later, she sat at her desk in the now-vacant front room, organizing files and folders. The front door opened, and Valentine shuffled in, looking decades older. He held his hat in his hands, crushed it as though it were paper. She wore a powder blue dress, scoop necked and tied together at the throat by a shoestring bow. It was an odd thing she would remember later. She pressed her hands against the files before her, leveled her shoulders, met his blue eyes with her dark ones. "Is she . . ." She couldn't say the word. Couldn't say "all right." Wouldn't say "dead."

His face was expressionless. Then he nodded. "She's going to be okay."

Stella nodded in return but otherwise didn't move. If she did, she knew a flood of tears would overtake her. Then Nurse Alice, who was in the next room counting vials of medicine, would know. Doc Bird, sitting at his desk in his office, would know too. Maybe even Mrs. Bird, who was across the lawn in the house, dressed up like Lana Turner, hot and restless.

"I thought you ought to know, is all."

Again, she nodded. "I appreciate it." She pushed the words past the lump in her throat.

"That's all, then." He turned to go then looked back over his shoulder. "Stella," he said. "Thank you."

"I was doing my job." It was a stupid thing to say.

"No," he said. "For Bettina."

"She's a good child, then?" She kept her voice nearly to a whisper.

"Couldn't be any sweeter." His body continued to face the door, but his eyes were fixed on her.

"Lilly Beth's a good mother."

"She is that."

"That's all that really matters."

He gave a quick nod. "I won't be telling Lilly Beth I came by," he said. Then he turned and was gone.

"So, what do you like so much about that movie anyhow?" Tom asked her as they ambled up Main Street toward the big house. It had been four years since she'd seen Bettina, now seven years old and, Stella figured, a second grader at Cottonwood Elementary. Lilly Beth rarely came to town, and the times she did she came alone. Stella figured it was on purpose, not wanting her to see the child. Not that she blamed Lilly Beth. She might have felt the same way had their roles been reversed.

"There's a line I connect with," she said. "Every movie should have a line you connect with."

"Oh yeah? I guess I never really thought about that. Typically I just like to connect with the dolls starring in them." He chuckled like a schoolboy then said, "So which one do you connect with in *The Best Years of Our Lives*?"

Stella thought for a minute, wondering if she really wanted to share the answer to that with Tom. Deciding it was okay, that he was safe, she said, "You know that part where Fred says, 'They're playing golf as if nothing ever happened'?"

"Yeah."

"That's it."

He gave her a questioning look. "What's so special about that line?"

She shrugged before answering, pretending it was really nothing at all. "Sometimes you just have to go on," she said. "You know . . . like nothing ever happened."

"Don't I know it. Boy-howdy, don't I know it." Tom gave a low whistle.

Stella clasped her hands, low and in front. "Me too," she said.

41

Early November 1947

"Stella," Papa said. "Come here, child."

Stella had her hand on the knob of the back door, ready to walk in after a long day at Dr. Bird's office. She started, unaware of her father's presence near the turn of the wraparound. He sat in one of the rockers facing the side of the house, bathed in the shadows of late afternoon. Only the side of him—his arm resting on the arm of the rocker, hand holding an unlit pipe—was visible to her, and his voice was nearly inaudible.

She closed the screen door, took deliberate steps to where he sat, the heels of her new shoes announcing her approach, then turned the corner. "Papa." She knelt beside him. "What is it? You look so pale."

Papa turned his head slowly—he'd been looking out across the farm, she figured—and peered down at his youngest child. "Ah, I'm just a little tired tonight," he said. "Got a lot on my mind." He looked up at her, pretending to smile.

"Is it—" She stopped herself before she said anything else, waiting, possibly for Papa to tell her what she'd always suspected, what she could never say, even after all the secrets they'd kept for each other.

"It's nothing. Nothing good Southern girls of your standing need to worry about. But I do need you to do something for me."

"Anything, Papa. You know that." She placed her hand on his arm, felt the cotton of his shirt. It was cold to the touch. "Papa, you're cold. You should go inside. It's nearly winter and you'll catch your death."

He smiled at her, this time for real. "I'll go in shortly. Run over to the feed and seed right quick, will you? They'll be closing soon and they're holding some supplies for me. I'll need 'em before morning."

Stella stood. "Sure, Papa. I'll go right now," she said. "If you'll promise to go inside and sit by a fire."

"I'm just a little tired this evening." He looked back across the land. "Just don't have it in me to go back and get what I need. Mr. Shelby will know what you're there for. I sent a list over earlier today."

Stella looked down at her watch. It was 5:45 and the store closed at six, an hour later than most of the stores and shops in Cottonwood. "I'll be right back," she said, then hurried across the path she'd just strolled up.

Five minutes later she entered the wide open doors in the center of the building's brick façade, her senses assaulted by the pungent aroma of feed and the sweetness of leather. Mr. Shelby and his assistant, Lin Walker, were behind the counter, doing what store owners and their workers do at the end of the business day. Stella saw a few lingering customers meandering in the back; one she recognized as Silas Pitney, who gave her the willies, and another—a tall, handsome-in-a-boyish-sort-of-way man—whom she did not recognize.

"Hey, Mr. Shelby. Mr. Walker," she said, approaching the counter.

The two men looked up at her, both smiling broadly. She smiled in return.

"I came to get something you're holding for Papa."

"Can I get some help back here?"

The three at the counter turned toward the back, and this time Stella saw the unknown man full on. It seemed he jutted his jaw at her noticing him, then he winked.

"What 'cha need, young man?" Mr. Shelby asked, taking a few steps toward him. He turned back to his assistant briefly, said "Take care of Stella, will you, Lin?" and then hurried toward the back.

"You're holding some things for Papa," Stella said.

"Yep," Lin Walker said. "Got it right back over here."

Stella studied Lin as he stepped to the far side of the back of the counter. He was only a year or so younger than she. Attractive in a Dana Andrews sort of way. He wore a light-weight flannel shirt tucked into pressed dungarees and tied off with a narrow leather belt. Fashionable, Stella thought, for a man who worked in a feed and seed. No doubt his pants had been starched and ironed by his wife, who Stella had heard was a most domesticated girl still in her teens. Late teens, but still . . .

"How's Mrs. Walker these days?" Stella asked, mainly for something to say.

Lin looked over his shoulder. "Betsy's fine." He gave her a half smile. "Busy with the house and the young'un. Another one on the way too."

"Oh? Congratulations. You have a little boy, isn't that right?"

"That's right."

"I've seen him over at Doc's office. He sure can scream when he sees a needle coming toward his rear end."

Lin was bent over, reaching for the box of goods her father

needed. In that position, with her talking about getting shots, she couldn't help but grin. She thought it looked innocent enough, but it was impossible for her to tell. Nonetheless, Lin Walker flushed, then hoisted the box up onto his shoulder, then to the countertop before her. "You'd scream too, no doubt," he said, eyeing her. He leaned over, resting his arm on the rough edge of the box's top. "Didja hear 'bout the lynchin'?"

Stella shook her head. "What lynching?"

"I overheard Silas Pitney and Mr. Shelby talking about it not ten minutes ago. Some darkie they said was making eyes at a white woman over in Raymore. The Klan took care of business, if you know what I mean."

Stella felt her knees go weak, but she managed to hold herself up. *Papa . . .* She took a deep breath, drawing her bearings in with the chilled night air thick with the smell of hay and feed. "Nobody's said anything about it over at Doc's, and that's where I spend most of my time. Helping him and Nurse Alice. We don't make time for such nonsense as that, and I'd suspect if"—she raised her voice for effect—"Silas Pitney"—then lowered it—"were to keep himself as busy as Dr. Bird, he'd have much less time for gossip about black men and white women."

Lin Walker kept his voice hushed. "You'd best be careful, Stella Nevilles. Talk like that could get you into a world of trouble."

"Trouble I can handle."

Lin gave her a sideward grin. "Speaking of the doctor, maybe you and I could play doctor someday."

Stella hadn't seen that one coming, but she was not rattled. These days it took a lot more than Lin Walker to unnerve her. She'd given birth to a married man's child, given the child away, returned home, and went back to as normal a life as she could. She'd dealt with the jealous wife of nearly every man in town, including her employer, and managed to keep her virtue. Neither trouble nor one more married man on the prowl was going to shake her. Not in the least.

She rested her forearms on the counter, leaned closer to the man opposite her. "Will your child bride be playing with us or is she too busy canning beans and ironing your dungarees?"

He straightened. "Don't talk about my wife like that."

"And don't you dare make another pass at me."

He snorted. "Everyone's talking, Stella."

She furrowed her brow, for a moment thinking he was talking about her and Valentine. "About what?"

"You and Doc Bird."

For a moment Stella felt relieved, then angry. "Don't listen to gossip, Lin Walker. It's not Christian."

"Gossip or not. People talk."

Stella stood back, now aware that the unknown customer was nearing the counter, Mr. Shelby close behind him. She kept her eyes on Lin, though. "Let 'em talk. They're just jealous I'm not home dusting furniture and shucking corn all day."

The man snorted again, shoved the box toward her, then smiled, phony but pleasant. "We'll put that on your father's bill," he said. "Tell Mr. Nevan I said hello, will you?"

Stella picked up the box. It was heavier than she anticipated. "What in the world has Papa ordered, Mr. Shelby?"

"Here, let me help you with that," the man behind her said.

The box in her way, she struggled to look at him. When she did she found his face, shadowed by a day's beard, handsome and his eyes soft brown and smiling. Though they warmed her from the inside out, she shook her head. "Thank you, sir. I've got it."

Determined to be a gentleman, she supposed, he took the box as though he were slipping a sleeping child from her, then balanced it with one arm, threw his one item into the box, and repositioned it again. "You lead the way," he said. "I'll follow."

Stella bristled then nodded. "Okay. Sure then." She took two steps toward the door. "This way." She sent a smile over her shoulder toward the two men behind the counter. "Good night, sirs," she sang.

"Night, Miss Nevilles," Mr. Shelby said. "My best to your mama."

Stella stepped out of the opening to the sidewalk, then allowed the man to pass by her as etiquette demanded. She took in a deep breath. He smelled of burnt leaves and cigarette tobacco. For Stella, the combination was intoxicating.

She began to walk, and he kept a quick pace with her, finally saying, "Are we racing for a reason, Miss Nevilles?"

She stopped and looked up at him. "How'd you know my name?"

He nodded his head back a notch. "The feed and seed. The store owner called you Miss Nevilles. I assume that's your name." He smiled.

Stella didn't answer at first. She just took him in. "You're not from around here."

"No, I'm not."

"Where are you from?" She turned, began to walk again, this time strolling, her hands clasped low and in front of her. She spied Charles Eskew coming out of the bakery across the street, pie box in one hand, the hand of his young daughter Mary Jo in the other. "Hello, Mr. Eskew," she called out, wanting her knight to know she was well-known in her own town. "Hello, little miss Mae-Jo," she called to the child, then smiled as they acknowledged her in return.

"Grew up in Red Bluff Landing," her escort said.

"Never heard of it. Where is it exactly?"

"Over in Screven County."

"That's not so far away. What are you doing here?" Stella looked up and past him; the street lamps flickered on.

"Came here to work for my mother's uncle. He owns a farm out a ways."

"Oh? And who would that be?"

"Gordon Carter. Know him?"

"Everyone knows everyone around here."

"'Cept you."

She stopped again. They were near the end of the business section, and she'd want to lead him across the street now anyway. "What do you mean by that?"

"You don't know me."

She started across the street. "Oh, I know you. You're Gordon Carter's nephew."

He threw back his head and laughed then. "I think, Miss Nevilles, you and I were cut from the same cloth."

They reached the other side of the street without a single automobile coming or going down Main Street. "What does that mean?"

"What that means is I heard the way you were talking to that clerk back there. I'd 'a climbed over that counter there and put my fist through his head if you hadn't 'a clobbered him with your tongue." He laughed again. "You're sharp. I like my women sharp."

"I'm sharp, all right. And I'm not your woman." She pointed toward her house. "My house is right there. We can cut across the yard and go in the back."

He stopped, leaving her to take several steps without him. She turned back. "What's wrong?"

"Can't go a step more."

207

"Why not? Is the box getting too heavy?"

"Box is fine."

She tilted her head. "Then what is it?"

"Don't know your name. If I don't know your name, I don't think it's proper for me to come up on your porch over there."

She cocked a brow. "You do too know it. I'm Miss Nevilles."

"That part I know. But when you go to introduce me to your father and mother, by what will you say is my name? Puddin' Tane?"

She pursed her lips. "Oh, I see." She pressed her hand against her chest. "I'm Stella Nevilles," she said. "And you are?"

He laughed heartily again, and when he sobered, said, "Jim. Jim Edwards. Pleased to meet you, Stella Nevilles."

She turned, hoping he hadn't caught her blush in the glow of the street lamp. "Likewise, I'm sure." She looked down, found the path in the lawn that connected the back of the house to the street. She asked, "How old are you, Jim Edwards? If you don't mind my asking."

"I don't mind. I'll be thirty-two Christmas Day."

"Thirty-two? Practically an old man. Are you married, Mr. Edwards?"

"No, ma'am, but I plan to be." He jostled the box in his arms, shifting it from both to one as they neared the back porch steps.

Stella looked up, saw her mother peering between the ruffled Priscilla curtains of the kitchen window, no doubt looking for her youngest child to come home so they could eat supper. The look on her face registered a question as to who the handsome man walking alongside Stella might be, and instantly Stella saw that flicker of hope that had dissipated in the spring with the announcement that she and Tom were no longer dating. Without missing a beat she asked, "Oh? Marrying a girl from around here?"

"I am." He sounded winded now.

"Anyone I know?"

"Everyone knows everyone, you said."

She stopped on the top step and looked back at him standing on the stoop. "I did say that, didn't I?"

"You did."

"So, who is she then?" She turned toward the door, not thinking to wait for the answer.

But his answer stopped her before she reached the screen. "You," he said.

42

Mark Michaels wanted to see Cottonwood before discussing the house project or, for that matter, the issue of the fire and the culprits who'd set it. Karol and I walked him and Evan up to the center of what had been the township. I pointed to various buildings, told him what I remembered about them. "That was the movie theater over there," I said, pointing to the end of the block. The marquee was empty of all but red lettering spelling "Closed," but the "s" had long been missing.

"The last movie that played there was called *Rachel, Rachel*." I looked at the threesome, who stared at the façade. "I remember because, for years afterward, the title of the film remained on the marquee."

Karol looked at me. "I remember that film. Joanne Woodward starred in it."

"I think so, yes."

"I saw it on TV a few months ago."

I jutted my chin. "Past that, to the left on Railroad, is the old train depot. It's been out of commission for some time, but the building is still there, an artesian well, and a leftover caboose sitting a ways off the tracks."

"An artesian well?" Mark asked. "Are you kidding me?"

I shook my head. "The best water in the world. It should be a drawing point for the town."

Karol spoke up. "I've seen it. My first day here. And the depot and caboose, which—by the way—is unlocked. There are seats inside, a couple of old travel trunks."

"Is it a cupola caboose?" Evan asked.

"A cupola caboose?" I asked. "What's that and how is it you know about it?"

Evan frowned at me. "All little boys know about trains. It may come as a surprise to you, Jo-Lynn, but I was a little boy once with all the little boy toys."

And now you have all the big boy toys.

"A cupola caboose had a projected roof with a window," Mark supplied, grinning at the two of us. "The crew could sit up in it and look over the rest of the train."

It was Karol who answered. "No. It was a bay window caboose."

I gave her a look, and she laughed. "What? I was a tomboy."

I shook my head as if to get the last few lines of conversation out. "Okay, then . . . if you keep going about another mile down Railroad, it curves and becomes Lake. That's where the old schoolhouse is."

"Isn't that a bit far out?" Mark asked.

I knew the answer to this. "A long—and I do mean *long*—time ago, my great-great-grandfather owned that land. It was part of his nonresidential farmland. When he began selling the land to retire, he decided to invest in America's future. So, he sold part of it and had a schoolhouse built on the other. Until then, the local school was a one-room type thing like what was on *Little House*. Great-great grandfather Nevilles believed most adamantly in education, so he built a large schoolhouse complete with a gymnasium. Mother

211

used to tell me that Friday and Saturday nights were nothing without being at the gym." I shrugged. "Cottonwood didn't have a hospital, but standing where we are right now, if you could look straight ahead and past two streets, Dr. Bird had a little office behind his house on Foster Road. My Aunt Stella worked for him before she married Uncle Jim—not that it's of any interest to you—but I do recall a penicillin shot I got once from Dr. Bird when I came down with the flu or some such illness while spending part of my Christmas break here." I smiled at the threesome. "From that moment on, I hated Dr. Bird," I said, and this time they laughed.

"I know the place you're talking about," Karol said, then looked at Mark. "The house is not being lived in, but it's a grand old thing. Would make a perfect B&B and the old office would be a perfect caretaker's cottage. I've done some research. It's owned by a Lance Bird." She turned to me. "Doctor Bird's son?"

I nodded. "I suppose so. I honestly don't remember. Mother would, though."

"Find out," Mark said to Karol.

His words gave me an opportunity I'd been hoping for. "Mark, can you tell me what are your plans here? To destroy or to restore?"

"Jo-Lynn . . . ," Evan said.

Mark raised his hand. "No, no. That's an honest question, and it deserves an honest answer." He pointed across the way, swinging his arm wide. "There's a lot here that can be salvaged. I saw that on my first trip through here. There's a lot that can't be. It wouldn't be safe." He leaned toward me while shoving his hands into the pockets of his jeans. "I'm not on a search and destroy mission, Mrs. Hunter. So if that's what's bothering you . . ."

That and so much more, not that Mark Michaels needed to hear about it. "Call me Jo-Lynn," I said in answer.

He gave a polite nod of his head.

"This was a mercantile here," I continued. I pointed behind me with my thumb, then took a few steps over to the dark and dirty windows of the double doors, painted green, and peered through as best I could. "A department store before its time." Inside were the scatterings of a few crate boxes, yellowed sheets of drop cloths, and crumbled newspaper pages. The counters—once filled with merchandise that gleamed in newness under the overhead lights—stood empty, barren like an old woman who'd outlived her time. "Dear me," I whispered. I glanced upward. Plaster fell in chunks from brick walls and single bulb lights hung forlorn from beadboard ceilings.

The others pressed their cupped hands to the glass and peered inside. "What a mess," Evan remarked.

I turned. "Over there." I pointed across the street. "Where you see what used to be a painted ice cream cone." The group turned. "That was called Scoops. Not original but a popular hangout for teens in Cottonwood back in the sixties." I looked at my soft leather ankle boots. "In its day," I added, as though speaking to the boots—worn, scuffed at the toe and heel—rather than the people behind me. "Quite the place to be. To the right of it was the drugstore and on the other side, the post office, then the bank. If you notice there's a door between the bank and the post office. That leads to the cellar. Uncle Jim used to say that was where the testosterone ran amuck."

"Meaning?" Mark asked.

"From what I gather, that's where the Masons met, and maybe even the Klan."

"The Ku Klux Klan?" Karol asked, then nodded. "Interesting bit of trivia."

"Welcome to the South," Evan mumbled.

"Where's the post office now?" Mark asked. "Surely with residents here there's a post office."

"There is. It's just down the road from the big house on the highway."

I took steps, paused to wait for the others to follow, then resumed. "The feed and seed store is at the end of this block, and it's still in operation. Clyde Walker owns it, but his daughter Donna runs it. Not that you won't see Clyde in there." I turned and looked at Karol. "Donna is married to Ty West. He owns the farm with the old windmill out on the highway heading toward Raymore."

Karol nodded then turned to Mark as I stopped and allowed the three of them to walk ahead of me. Evan gave me a fleeting glance. "The farm is outside the city limits so I've not really gotten to know the family. But the farmers depend on the feed and seed store. We'll have to move it before we can renovate what's already there."

Evan craned his neck to the left to obtain a better view of the store. "That's been here as long as I can remember." He straightened, shoved his hands into the pockets of his belted all-weather coat—the one I'd purchased for him at Nordstrom's, the one I knew cost more than most of the people in Cottonwood made in a two-week paycheck—and kept moving down the broken covered sidewalk. He made a face of disdain and said, "Smells like an old barn in there." It was at that moment his shoe caught on a raised piece of cement. He stumbled, righted himself, and swore softly as Mark questioned whether he was all right.

Evan crossed over to the ledge of a window. He propped his shoe upon it, leaned over, and brushed his hand across the toe. "These are Bruno Magli," he said, as though the sidewalk should have known better than to jut itself forward, or at the

214

very least Evan should have known better than to wear his expensive shoes in a place as simple as Cottonwood.

I smiled as I crossed my arms and leaned against a post. I thought of the care Evan gave to his shoes—lining them up according to name brand, color, and style; the way he fumed when our weekly housecleaning service managed to get them out of order while vacuuming. And then for some strange reason I remembered the day Percy and I had entered the nearly dilapidated barn, of how he'd shook his head and said, "Well, now, Miz Hunter, if you love the farm, you love the smell of it too. You can't have the glory of the crop without some sweat and stench along the way."

I looked at Evan fully then. I loved my husband and I didn't want to throw away a quarter of a century of life with him. But the sweat and stench along the way seemed to drown out any inkling of glory we might find with the harvest. The real question, I thought, was whether or not Evan's idea of glory and mine were the same thing. Perhaps Evan was planting cotton and I was planting chrysanthemums. In full bloom they were both pretty to look at, but with one decidedly less prickly to pick.

"I'd like to meet the residents who have decided to stay," Mark was saying to Karol as Evan righted himself and I straightened my thoughts to the here and now. "What can you do to arrange that?"

Karol looked at me then back at Mark. "Well, Mark, since you asked . . . on Wednesday Jo-Lynn and I are going to the church for the . . ." Karol faltered, searching for the right word.

"Church supper," I supplied. "It's a Wednesday night tradition here. In most Southern churches, as a matter of fact."

Evan cocked a brow as Mark asked, "And?"

"And," Karol said, "it might be the best way for you to meet a lot of the residents at one time." When Mark's stoic expression remained, she added, "Whilst dining on some fried chicken."

"And potato salad. And it *would* be the best way," I said. "Most of the folks who live here attend the church where most of my deceased relatives are buried." Then I smiled. "Not that we've buried any of them alive." I made a jab of my head toward my husband. "At least not yet." If there was any humor at all in my voice, Evan didn't hear it. He frowned at me in sincere disapproval; I turned and began walking back toward the big house. "I don't know what these other buildings were, but when we go to the church, we can find out then . . . or ask Mr. Valentine when we get back to the house."

43

Valentine and Terry were gone when we returned, the keys to the dead bolts left hanging in the keyhole of the one in the door to the living room. I couldn't help but smile at the irony, though Evan didn't think it funny. Karol and Mark left, promising to return the following day. "We'll talk details tomorrow," Mark said. "Meanwhile, I've got to get checked in to the inn." He looked at his watch. "It's after three now."

Evan slipped into the house as I stood on the front porch and waved good-bye to Karol and Mark. When they were out of sight, I jerked my head to look over my shoulder, then spun around and went into the house.

"What are you doing?" I asked Evan. "Why aren't you leaving too? Please tell me you have a room at the inn."

He stood in the center of the empty living room. He'd unbuckled the belt of his coat; it hung loose on either side of his small frame. His hands were splayed at his hips and his neck was bent to look at the twelve-foot ceiling. "This isn't the original ceiling," he said. He began pacing the room, peering up at the imperfections above our heads. "It looks like someone added this. Probably over the tongue and groove boards from the flooring upstairs." He stopped near the window that, now without curtains, exposed the barren, once prosperous farmland. The picture they made—the bleakness of the land behind the successful man dressed in a costly balmacaan—caused me to blink several times, speechless, though only for a moment. "Evan," I said. "Let me say this again: what are you *doing*?"

He looked at me then, studied me as he studied the framework of the house, then smiled. I pressed my lips together, my emotions lopsided. It was good to see my husband and yet it was not. There was no other developer I could imagine that would do a finer job on Cottonwood than Evan, yet I'd wanted so desperately to accomplish this project on my own. Though the town would be his and the house mine, still I knew he'd interfere in what I imagined would be my career's masterpiece.

And then there were the personal issues. Evan had promised a life of devotion to me. A life centered on me. How childish I'd been to think it would happen as he'd promised. How conceited of me now to be angry that it hadn't. I loved my husband, but I was tired of being his trophy wife.

Still . . . last night as we'd spoken on the phone, a familiar yearning had crept over me.

"I'm just checking things out, Jo-Lynn. What's your problem?"

I threw my hands up in the air like a teenager frustrated by curfew. "My problem is that you don't need to be here."

"There's a good possibility that Mark Michaels will hire me to do a job. I'm here to do whatever it takes to get the deal."

I had to think for a moment before answering. "Not *here* in Cottonwood, Evan. I know why you're here in Cottonwood. What I don't know is why you are *here* in the big house." I pointed to the door and beyond the door, the driveway. "Why aren't you following your possible new client to Raymore? There are no hotels here in Cottonwood. No inns, no quaint B&Bs." I took a breath. "Not yet, anyway."

Evan pinked briefly, then took steps toward the closed French doors. "I'm not staying in a hotel, Jo-Lynn. I'm staying here."

I watched, stunned, as he opened one of the doors and passed over the threshold.

"What are you doing?" I felt my chest tighten. My arm, under the bandages, began to throb. "Ow," I whispered.

His footsteps nearly drowned out his answer. "Coffee. I need coffee."

I followed behind him. "You cannot do this."

"You don't have coffee?" he asked without turning to look at me. By now he was at the dining room door, continuing down the hallway.

"Of course I have coffee. Evan!"

He rounded into the doorway of the kitchen. I walked faster, following until I, too, was in the kitchen, where the assaulting odor of the fire was strongest. Evan stood in its middle, again with hands on his hips, surveying it as he'd done the living room. This time, he was looking toward the undressed window.

"What are you looking at?"

He turned. "You know, I find it nearly impossible to comprehend that you're living like this." He pointed to the charred wall separating the kitchen from the pantry. "Look at this mess. Not a piece of furniture in the house, nothing but yellowed walls and creaking boards and a back pantry burned nearly to a crisp."

"There is too furniture in this house." It was an idiotic comeback.

"Where?" His face registered the challenge in the manner typical of the Evan I'd come to know of late.

"My bedroom is still furnished. I'm living here, after all. What did you think I was doing? Sleeping on the floor-boards?"

He took a few steps toward me, hands still splayed on hips. "I would think you'd be at the house on the hill. Your mother doesn't understand this either, Jo-Lynn."

My mother? *Traitor.* "This isn't about my mother, Evan. This is about me. How many times do I have to explain this to you? Or to her?" I felt tears then, hot burning tears, rushing to the surface of my eyes, spilling down my cheeks. My mother and now my emotions. Both of them traitors.

Evan's face softened, his shoulders sagged. He'd never liked to see me cry, but I wasn't crying to take advantage of that and I told him so. And then I completely collapsed in a river of tears, my face pressed into my hands. I sobbed, "Why would anyone want to do this?"

And then his arms were around me, protective and loving. "Do what, Jo-Lynn?" His voice, warm on my ear, was smooth as rich honey. I buried my face then between his shoulder and his neck. I took in a deep breath; he smelled of the luxury and heat of Bond No. 9 and the simplicity and cold of having taken a walk down Main Street in Cottonwood.

My arms conspired with my tears; they slipped around him, my hands crawled up his back. I felt the familiar leanness, the way the shoulder blades curved around when he held me, and I knew that in spite of our recent lack of communication, this man was more than all the arguments we'd had. This man was the husband of my youth. However we'd recently managed to grow apart, we had the foundation of the early years. A foundation built on love and admiration.

Valentine Bach had said it best: if a foundation's good, anything can be restored. But was it enough?

"Jo-Lynn? Do what? Why would anyone want to do what?"

I pulled back from him, wiping my face with my fingertips, then pointed toward what was left of the pantry. "This."

Evan stepped over to the sheet of plastic covering the pantry's doorway. "I've been thinking about that." His hands slipped into his pockets. He pulled out a pair of leather and cashmere gloves then wiggled his fingers into them. First his left hand, then his right. Finally he turned to me and said, "Is this the first incidence of something like this? Since you've been here?"

I shook my head. "No. There were a couple of other . . . incidents." I told him about seeing the two men in the early morning hours a few nights after Uncle Jim's funeral and about the evening I'd walked back from the store, feeling as though someone were watching me.

"So then the question is why would anyone not want you to restore this house?"

I looked at the old Formica below my feet, imprinted by soot and shoe soles, then back up to Evan. "That doesn't make sense. Why would anyone care if I restored this house?"

He shrugged and walked back to me. "Someone who doesn't want Cottonwood reestablished, maybe?"

I crossed my arms and burrowed my hands under the armpits of my coat. The chill of the room was getting to me, and I began to shiver. Or perhaps I imagined it was the chill of the room. "That could be any number of people. Aunt Stella told Karol that even the people whose homes should be demolished might not want the money they'd be given for their property simply because of family history to the land."

"That could be it."

"Could be?" My shivering turned more to quivers and, again, Evan wrapped me in his arms.

"You're freezing in here," he said. His eyes turned smoky, the lids heavy. "Hey. I've missed you."

"I've missed you too."

His eyes traveled upward. "Where'd you say the furniture in this house is?"

221

I stepped away from him. "No, Evan. You cannot stay here. You should not even be here. It won't solve anything."

"How about if I remind you that I'm your husband?" He gave me his little-boy-wants-a-cookie look.

I felt my knees go weak while my mind struggled to stay strong. "It won't solve anything," I repeated, this time in a whisper.

But he took me by the hand and drew me away from the iciness of the kitchen and through the hollowness of the hallway. "You should install curved casings in here," he said.

"I am," I answered, then mentally kicked myself for doing so. "Evan . . ." By now we were climbing the stairs. "Evan. Stop."

Not that he was listening.

Not that I meant it.

He opened the door to my room, a room he knew well with a bed he knew even better. Many were the times we'd snuck to it during family get-togethers, pretending to be sleepy after a Southern-cooked Sunday dinner. In need of a nap, we'd claim.

The room, without a fire, was just as cold as the rest of the house. Evan drew me to him by cupping my jaw with his gloved fingers, bringing me close for a kiss. When we parted he said, "I don't see any firewood."

"It's downstairs." Had he not been so close he would not have heard me.

He nodded a couple of times, said, "I'll go get it," then took a step from me.

I caught his arm with my hand. "Don't. There's an electric blanket on the bed." I arched a brow, giving him my most sensual look.

"Oh yeah?" His voice purred.

And then I smiled. "I bought it on sale at Wal-Mart."

44

We came downstairs a little after seven, slapped peanut butter and jelly on slices of Sunbeam, poured cold milk into coffee mugs, grabbed two apples from one of Aunt Stella's vegetable bowls I'd filled and placed on the countertop, then ran back upstairs to the warmth of our bedroom.

A little after eight, Evan went downstairs alone, this time for firewood. He came back, commented on the stillness of the house, and set about making a fire for us.

"Not like Atlanta." His eyes were intent on the logs that—with the help of pine cones—began to pop and blaze.

I was still in bed, sitting between the pillows, resting my back against the headboard, burrowed in a mound of linen, blankets, and quilts. My knees were at my chest with my arms locked around them, and my hair fell haphazardly over my shoulders as I placed one cheek on top. I knew I painted a picture of a woman who'd been loved and who had loved without reservation in return. "Mmm," was all I could say. Atlanta and Druid Hills within it were a million miles away and with them all the problems Evan and I were facing. Like Scarlett O'Hara, I chose to think about them tomorrow. To-morrow, after coffee and perhaps more time alone in this room, we'd address the issues. Tomorrow we'd begin to work on the foundation of our lives together.

Evan climbed back in bed with me, glanced over at the television, and said, "So how many channels do you get with that thing?"

I rolled my eyes, knowing as wives know where this was heading. "About three."

He gave me a look I knew well.

"Yes, you can turn it on," I said, then giggled. As he left the bed for the remote, I slipped down the mattress until my head came to rest on the downy fluff of the pillows. I yawned.

Evan fiddled with the remote, inching his way back to the bed, joining me again. "Sleepy?"

I nodded yes.

He kissed the top of my head and said, "Why don't you try to get some rest? It's been a long day, and I doubt you slept much last night. I'm going to watch a little television and I'll be right there with you."

I nodded again, closed my eyes, and within minutes, was lost in a dream.

I woke at six, startled first because of Evan's presence and secondly because the television—though its volume was turned down low—was still on. The fire was out and the room was cold. I pulled myself out of bed, scurried over to the chifforobe and into my robe and slippers. Evan stirred from the middle of the bed, opened one eye, and said, "Whereyagoin'?"

"Coffee," I said, smiling at him. "Remember? I think that's why you stayed yesterday . . . for a cup of coffee."

He grinned at me, devilish. "Oh yeah. That was it."

I opened the door, then went down the stairs, leaving the door ajar. As I came near the bottom steps I noticed two things. First, a putrid odor permeating the downstairs, no doubt a combination of the fire, its soot, and mud from the shoes of neighbors and firefighters. Second, the French doors were opened. Not wide open but open. No doubt Evan had left them thusly when he'd gotten the firewood.

I went into the kitchen, made our coffee, and then went back up the stairs, two mugs of steaming coffee in hand. Handing Evan his, I said, "You left the doors open last night."

Evan sat up, clasped the mug with both hands. "What doors?"

"The French doors." I came around to my side of the bed. "Not that it's any big deal; it's just that I always close them."

"I closed them."

I took a sip of coffee then got into the bed. "What do you mean?"

He looked at me. "I mean I closed them. I remember because, with the wood in my arms, I had to use my foot."

I pondered this a moment. "Maybe you didn't close them securely."

He shook his head. "I don't think so." He placed his mug on the bedside table and stepped out of the bed.

"Where are you going?"

"Downstairs."

I followed behind him. "Why?"

"I don't know, Jo-Lynn. It's just a feeling."

Together we went downstairs, my hand resting on my husband's shoulder. Evan commented on the smell about halfway down, and I gave him my theory. "Maybe," he said. "But I don't think so."

"No?"

"It's not like any soot and fire I've ever smelled." He opened the French doors and stepped into the living room, halting after two steps. "Good gosh."

"Oh, Evan!" I stepped around him, my hand covering my mouth, my fingers pinching my nose. The quivering I'd experienced in the kitchen the day before began again. "Who would do this?" I released the hold I had on my nostrils, then pinched them closed again.

Evan turned toward the doors as though leaving.

"Where are you going?"

"To call the police," he said.

Larry Gansky arrived forty-five minutes later and repeated Evan's sentiments verbatim. "Good gosh," he said, whipping his cap from his head as he stepped over the threshold of the front door.

Evan, by now dressed and presentable, pointed to the walls on either side of the fireplace, where words had been scrawled in animal excrement. *Go home!* they read. *Get out! You are not wanted here!* Swastikas were plastered above, beside, and below the words.

Larry pulled a handkerchief from his pocket and covered his nose.

"I opened all the windows," I commented. "It's helped some, but not much."

The front door opened. I turned to see Mae-Jo and Bob entering the room. "What in the world?" Aunt Mae-Jo said.

"Mercy," Uncle Bob said, simultaneously.

"Aunt Mae-Jo. Uncle Bob. What are you doing here?" I crossed the room to them.

Mae-Jo looked from Evan to me and then back to the graffiti. "We saw the sheriff's car. My goodness but doesn't this smell?"

The sheriff stuffed the handkerchief into his pocket and pulled a small writing tablet from the inside of his leather jacket. "Any idea on who did this?"

I shook my head.

"But obviously the fire and the vandalism are connected," Evan said.

"Obviously." The sheriff walked over to the door, to each window. "Any idea as to how the perp entered?"

Evan stepped closer to me. "Not a door or window was open," he said. "No screens cut. Nothing."

Larry gave Evan a hard look. "You were here all night?"

Evan nodded. I glanced toward Mae-Jo, who was looking at me, her eyes questioning.

"And you didn't hear anything?"

We both shook our heads. "Nothing," Evan answered.

"The TV was on." I swallowed hard. "Upstairs. And the bedroom door closed. To keep the heat in."

"I see." He glanced around. "You folks should think about central heat and air."

"I'll make a note of it," I said, my tone cynical.

The sheriff raised a brow, then asked a few more preliminary questions, took a couple of Polaroid photos of the "crime scene," and then said, "I suppose we'll need to have someone watching the house from now on." He replaced his cap and started to leave. "Do some drive-bys."

"That's it?" I asked. "Aren't you going to dust for finger-prints?"

The sheriff chuckled. "Let me guess. You watch *Law & Order*."

"No," I lied.

"Mmm-hmm. Well, tell me, Lenny Briscoe, just how many fingerprints do you think I'd find around here?"

My shoulders sagged. "I see your point." I looked around. "Who's going to clean this mess?" I asked as though I didn't know.

Mae-Jo joined me. "We are. Now let's find a bucket, some soap and rags, and see what we can do." She looked at Larry Gansky and said, "Do the best you can, young man. Two incidents in two nights. Surely it's not a coincidence."

"Yes, ma'am," the officer replied. "We'll be on it. Like I said, we'll have someone patrol the area." He looked at me. "Typically, we don't. Not out here. Nothing like this ever happens in Cottonwood. Not these days, anyway."

"My lands, no," Mae-Jo said. "Bob, how long has it been since we've seen a swastika on anything around here?"

"Long time," Bob said. "Mighty long time."

45

Mark and Karol arrived shortly after Mae-Jo and I finished the unenviable job of scrubbing down the walls, and she and Uncle Bob had left the big house, crossing the lawn and street for the store. Mark and Karol remained quiet while Evan explained what had happened, how we had been upstairs all night, how I had come downstairs and found the door open, how he'd suspected something was amiss. Mark turned to Karol. "Can you come up with any logical reason why this has happened?"

She shook her head. "What I don't understand," she said after giving Mark's question time to roll around in her head, "is why now?" We were standing out on the back porch near the well and where the trellises—once vibrant with color and bloom—stood bare and ashy. I'd made a fresh pot of coffee, and we drank steaming mugs of it in the cold. Karol and I sat on the steps as Uncle Jim and I had once done watching the rain advance toward us. Evan and Mark stood on the stoop, both with legs spread like coaches on a football field's sideline. Evan was dressed in casual dress pants, a long-sleeved shirt, and cashmere zip cardigan. Mark wore jeans that looked as though they'd been dragged through a field, and a collarless shirt under a denim jacket. They made quite the picture of opposites, in spite of the fact that Mark Michaels could, no doubt, buy Evan and Everett out five times over.

"What do you mean?" Mark asked.

Karol took a sip of her coffee. "Why not before? Why not when *I* first came to town? Or you, Jo-Lynn? You've been here two full weeks. If someone was trying to scare you away, why wait till now?"

"I guess so." A fleeting memory of being at the front door of the house after visiting with Mae-Jo in the store, of thinking I heard someone lurking nearby, of calling out and then . . . nothing. "There was one time . . . I thought . . . but . . ." I looked at the three listening to my ramblings. "I don't know if it was anything or not." I shrugged. "This is crazy. I'm just a designer trying to renovate my great-grandparents' house."

"Then maybe it's the house."

"The house?" Evan said.

Karol took another sip of coffee. "Well, if it were the town project itself, wouldn't one of the buildings downtown, so to speak, have been the target? I've walked that block or two down the street I don't know how many times, and believe me, there isn't anything there of any value or importance. The best thing that could ever happen to Cottonwood is renovation."

"So you think it's the house? Someone doesn't want the house renovated."

Karol shrugged and bobbed her head back and forth a few times, pursing her lips as though ready for a kiss. "Not necessarily. If they'd wanted to burn the house down, they could have, so the fire was obviously a scare tactic. That travesty back there was too. Think about it, you didn't hear anyone in the house, which means they—whoever they are—could have come upstairs and killed you in your love nest." She sent a warm smile my way.

230

I shivered. Someone had been in my family home. In the big house. Someone had desecrated it with animal excrement and symbols of horror, of power gone amuck. Someone had dared to try to burn it. Our heritage.

My legacy.

"What about something *in* the house?" Mark asked.

I shook my head. "There's nothing there. Other than what's in the bedroom where I sleep, and there's really nothing in there at all."

"Define 'nothing at all.'"

"Bedroom furniture. Two rockers, a television. A couple of boxes of memorabilia I've yet to go through. Not entirely anyway. One from the barn and one from a downstairs bed-room."

"Maybe you should do that, you two," Mark said, looking from me to Evan. "See if either of them holds any clues as to what's going on around here. Why someone wants you to stop renovating the house."

I stood. "Should we do that now or wait?" I turned to look be-hind me, then back. "Mr. Valentine will be here soon and—"

"And I need to get to work," Evan said. "See what's really what down there. So maybe later this afternoon. Or after dinner."

I looked at Karol, she at me. "That's right!" Karol said. "The blueprints."

"What blueprints?" Evan asked.

"Jo-Lynn's aunt gave her some blueprints that were drawn up in 1938, wasn't it?"

I nodded. "They're upstairs. In one of the boxes. I'd nearly forgotten."

Mark took a step forward. "Evan, take a look at them. Who knows? Maybe there's more than just white lines on blue paper."

Valentine Bach and his grandson, Buster, drove to Raymore early Tuesday morning, just after Buster returned from
his shift at the plant. They rehired the day laborers for an
extended period of time. "The first thing we need to do," I
said to Valentine, "is cut every last sprig and branch of this
foliage away from the house, the barn, and the stables. We
can't work on what we can't truly see."

"Call Melba and Irene," the old gentleman said. "Tell 'em
to start cooking."

After Karol and Mark had left, Evan—digital camera draped
around his neck and a notebook in his hand—had traipsed
down the sidewalk that had once shot straight toward town
but now appeared in a psychedelic state, waving like a wet
spaghetti noodle. Minutes later a truckload of men and women
drove up—Percy, wearing a huge grin as though he'd come
home, included—ready for a full day of work.

That evening, Evan and I went to the house on the hill for
dinner. As we neared my childhood home, he said, "I want
you to think about something."

I looked at him from the passenger's side of his car.
"What?"

"I want you to consider staying with your mother and father
for the next few months."

"What?" I shook my head and crossed my arms. "No."

"Jo-Lynn . . ."

"No, Evan. I can't believe you are even suggesting it."

"I'm not sure it's safe for us—and especially you when I go
back to Atlanta—to be at the house alone."

"What do you mean, when you go back? I thought you'd
be here for a while."

"Jo-Lynn, you know how my work goes. I'm only here long

enough to hire a surveyor, get some measurements and some photographs. I've got the photographs, I hired a surveyor this afternoon, I've got your great-grandfather's blueprints—thank you very much for saving me some time and expense—and I'll need to get back to Atlanta. If the firm gets the account from M Michaels, then most everything I need to do can be done from there."

Just when I was getting used to the idea of Evan being in Cottonwood, he was leaving. Maybe not tomorrow, but soon enough, anyway. "When?"

"When am I leaving?"

"Yes."

"I'll be here another two days. Tops. That's why I'm saying, Jo-Lynn. You need to be at your parents'. There's nothing in Cottonwood anyway; pretty soon you'll have to come out of that bedroom. You know that."

"It could be months."

"You're kidding yourself. What is it about that house that has such a hold on you?"

I looked out the windshield for a moment, thinking back to the lines in a book about renovating old houses. "What inexplicable magic do they cast over those who must bring life back to them?"

"Jo-Lynn . . ."

I jerked in my seat. "It's my family home, Evan. I thought we'd discussed all this. I thought we were on the same page. For once."

"Don't start, Jo-Lynn."

"Don't start?" My fingers splayed in front of my face. I stretched them as far as the skin and bones would extend as something animalistic came from my throat. Or, perhaps, it came from my belly. I could no longer be sure. I felt the car slowing in speed, and I looked over at Evan, who was looking at me as though I had two heads. Our eyes locked, then he looked forward and brought the car to the shoulder of the road.

"What is wrong with you, Jo-Lynn?"

I took several deep breaths, exhaling after each one, before I answered. "Look." I kept my voice calm and sure. "I don't know who it is that did this monstrous thing—these monstrous things—but I won't let them run me out of the big house. That place is my home just as much as the house on the hill and just as much as our place in Druid Hills." I shook my head again. "I won't do it. Go back to Atlanta. Go back to your office. I don't care. My office, if you will, is an upstairs bedroom in a one-hundred-and-fourteen-year-old house. Mark Michaels is a preservationist. He wants a museum that will draw people not only to my family's heritage but also to the heritage of an entire town, and he's going to get one. It will be a masterpiece and it will be mine."

I watched Evan's face change from hard and set to loving and tender. "Then as a possible associate on this project, I must insist."

I kept my voice steady. "Evan Hunter, you know good and well that if you were not my husband, you'd not bring up anything remotely close to this. If I were just another one of Mark Michaels's employees—"

"But you're not. You're my wife. I can't possibly look at you as just another employee." He reached across the seats, picked up a stray strand of my hair, and tucked it behind my ear. "So, as your husband—"

"Oh no you don't. No, Evan. I won't be bullied like this." I pulled the strand of hair from behind my ear. "Not even in your tender trap." I exhaled. "Besides, don't you understand? Whoever wants me out of the house will not be satisfied with my leaving it. Someone wants something. I can feel it. Something in the big house or near it, one. Aren't you curious?"

"Of course I am." He reached over, took my hand in his. "I'm just worried about you."

I pulled away. "Are you speaking to me as a husband or as a businessman?"

"Maybe a little of both."

I shook my head again. "I won't leave."

He didn't say anything at first. Then he asked, "Compromise?"

I couldn't imagine. "Define."

"You'll stay with Mae-Jo and Bob when I'm not here. It's not the house on the hill, but you'll at least not be alone in the big house."

I turned to look forward as a low growl escaped my throat. "Jo-Lynn."

"Deal." My shoulders fell forward. "Mae-Jo will be thrilled."

Evan pulled the car back onto the road. "Your mother will want you in Raymore. What are you going to say to her?"

He was right there. "I don't know." I looked over, pointed a horribly unmanicured fingernail at him. "But not a word tonight. Promise me."

He nodded. "Deal."

46

By Wednesday afternoon, Valentine Bach's crew of day laborers had cleared and hauled away all the overgrown shrubs from the house and from the buildings out back. Tomorrow, Valentine told me as we stood on the sidewalk near the front of the house, work would begin on the exterior of the house. "Replacing the foundation," he said. "That's first."

"Yes, sir."

"I've ordered the jacks for the job, and we'll start raising the house off the old foundation. You'll be a-wanting to stay out of the house for a few days."

"Will do," I said. Even speaking to me, his employer, he spoke as though giving orders to the laborers.

He looked at his watch and said, "It's about church time. I'd best be getting home, get washed up."

"You'll be attending Upper Creek?"

He nodded his head, pulled a cigarette out of the pack in his front pocket, and lit it. "It's the only church around here, you know. So when I go, that's where I go."

"I see," I said, for something to say. I crossed my arms and cocked my hip by placing my left foot at a forty-five-degree angle.

He squinted at me as he blew smoke away from us. "Do you?"

I was unsure what he meant or where he was going with his words. "Well, you're obviously going tonight, aren't you?"

"Wednesday night, every week."

I paused, then smiled wide. "Wednesday nights they have supper. That explains why I didn't see you on Sunday."

The old man chuckled. He took a slow drag from his cigarette, then exhaled the smoke as he spoke. "As a boy and a young man, I was German Lutheran. My family—my parents and I—went to a church over in Savannah. That's where I met my wife. Her father was the reverend there." He dropped the cigarette to the sidewalk beneath his feet, ground it out with a booted foot, and continued. "When my wife died and then my parents within a few years of her, I just quit going." He looked down, then back up, hardly moving his head. Just his eyes connecting with mine. "I've had my issues with God."

"Haven't we all." My words were not spoken in jest.

"That's a fact. You can't live this life and not have your issues with God."

"But you've lost a wife and both parents. That's a pain I've not experienced."

"Different. Different pains. Losing a wife—especially a wife in her prime—and losing your parents are two different things is what I'm saying to you. But pain is pain."

I felt myself growing colder by the moment. The late February weather was pleasant enough during the day, but once the sun tipped behind the trees, the temperature dropped fast. I rubbed my arms with my hands and said, "That it is."

He looked at me straight on. "What about you, missy? What have you lost along the way?"

I started to walk up the sidewalk, and he joined me. "I've never really lost a loved one other than Uncle Jim. I can't imagine losing my parents. My husband. I don't have any children so . . ."

"I've been left in this life with one great blessing, and that's my girl. She ain't hardly no girl no more," he added with a grin. "A grandmother herself. You get to be my age, you've watched 'em grow up, get married, have their own, then their own have their own. The circle of life." He drew an imaginary circle in the air with the tip of his finger.

I looked beyond the fading circle and up the road toward town; the now-familiar Geo was coming toward us from its outskirts.

"There's Arizona now," he said. "Coming to get this old man like the good child she is." He eyed me. "The young'uns's mother—Fiona—she's the faithful one. Bettina went to church with your mama when she was a teenager. They went to Upper Creek, so it just followed that Bettina took her boy there. When Buster Junior came home with Fiona as his bride, they started going there and they've raised the kids there." He smiled. "Finally talked me into going back with a fried chicken and some German potato salad."

"The best way to a man's heart, and all that?" I asked.

Valentine Bach chuckled as the car pulled up to the curb beside us. The passenger's window went down, and Arizona beamed at us from the driver's side. "Hey, cutie," she exclaimed, her dimples digging deep. "How about a date with a cute young thing?"

Her great-grandfather's laugh was hearty. "Who? You?"

"You know it, baby!"

"Be right there, sugar plum."

I placed my hand on Valentine's shoulder and said, "You're a blessed man, Valentine Bach. You've got great-grandchildren who adore you, a grandson who helps you with business when he can, and a daughter who lives close by."

"Bettina was my one reason for living when Lilly Beth, God love her heart, left this world. I don't know what I would-a done . . ."

"A child is a true blessing. I never had any, but I've always heard it said." I tilted my head. "What a pity you didn't have a house full of children, Mr. Valentine."

A pained look crossed his face. Then, as if to shake it off, he took a step toward the Geo and his waiting great-grandchild. Looking back at me he said, "You don't know, do you?"

"Know what?" I asked.

It seemed he looked through me then, past bone and tissue, past here and now. For a moment I saw something flicker in his eyes—brilliant blue as they already were—and a smile, tiny and cynical, came to his whiskered face. "Don't make no never mind," he said. "Didn't then. Doesn't now."

47

Elder Timothy's Wednesday night sermon was taken from Nehemiah 8.

Nehemiah, the story goes, came home to Jerusalem to rebuild a wall.

Opposition surrounded him, but the workers were plenty and ready to do what needed to be done to succeed.

The preacher said, "What Nehemiah is saying here is this: quit your crying about the past." I—in a new state of nervousness—flipped a few pages, back to front, of the opened Bible on my lap and began to read from the sixth chapter. I used my finger to run along a line that seemed to jump out at me. "But they were scheming to harm me; so I sent messengers to them with this reply: 'I am carrying on a great project and cannot go down. Why should the work stop while I leave it and go down to you?' Four times they sent me the same message, and each time I gave them the same answer."

I thought about the fire. The vandalism. Two times someone had tried to send a message to leave. Evan was keenly aware of it, but I refused to acknowledge it. "I will not go down," I whispered to the book spread before me, all the while wondering if, after two more such times, I'd feel the same. If there were, in fact, two more times. Maybe, because

I had apparently stood firm in resistance, those who wanted me gone had given up, realizing I was doing nothing more than renovating a house and helping to bring life and business back to Cottonwood. There wasn't a person in this tiny chapel that couldn't benefit from the work we—Karol, Evan, Mark, and I—were doing here.

I looked to the front of the church, where the preacher now stood on the right side of the podium, his elbow resting against it and his legs crossed at the ankle. He said, "We have an opportunity to rebuild this town," as if he'd heard my thoughts. I blushed, and he continued, "We are so happy to have Mark Michaels from M Michaels here with us this evening." The young pastor raised himself up on his toes with the word *thrilled* then came down to rest again on his heels as he continued. "His project manager, whom many of you know, Karol Paisley. And I'm sure everyone in this room knows Jo-Lynn Hunter—the niece of Mr. Jim and Miss Stella—and her husband Evan. Evan, as I understand it, is a contender to oversee the urban development itself."

The shifting of bodies and all eyes were on us. Evan looked at me and whispered "urban development" as though it were some great joke. I frowned in return.

"Mr. Michaels," the pastor continued, "would you like to come forward, sir, and say a few words to the congregation?"

Mark Michaels stood, walked to the front of the room, and turned to face what represented the majority of Cottonwood's population. For the next half hour, I watched as he worked the good Christians of the church like a politician in an election year. He began by telling a little about himself, his brother, their company, and what they had achieved in the past. He focused on one particular town in North Carolina that, like Cottonwood, had lost most of its business and, in time, its citizens.

"In the late twenties there was a run on the bank, forcing it to close its doors. Like Cottonwood, this town depended on farming. When mechanized farming came along, many of the farmers were put off the land."

Voices murmuring affirmation and understanding rippled through the room.

"My company—mine and my brother's—came in, got the people involved as we hope to involve you, and began to renovate, one step at a time. Some of your family or friends may own houses or buildings we've offered to purchase at fair prices. These are the places we see we cannot salvage." For effect, he rested his hands on his hips, looked down, then back up. "I know the land and this town mean something to you people. Most of you were born here, were reared here, have lived here nearly your whole lives. You have loved ones buried in the cemetery just outside these stained glass windows. I want you to know that I understand you have history here. And I want to help you make it a history to be proud of, not something that was and then was no more."

"Maybe we don't want your help," a deep voice called out from among the small crowd.

All eyes turned toward its direction.

"Maybe we want to be left alone just as we are," it continued.

"Oh, hush your mouth, Roy Morrison," Mae-Jo countered from nearby.

Elder Timothy took a step toward Mark. "Mr. Roy . . ."

"Ah, don't 'Mr. Roy' me." The older man stood and waved away any further comments. "I'm just saying maybe some of us like things the way they are."

Uncle Bob stood. "Look here now, Roy. I understand your feelings, but I also understand that my business is going under. I've watched this town—which was thriving back when we were young'uns—go down to near nothing. That may be fine for you. You've got one foot in the grave as it is . . ."

A ripple of laughter went through the room. I glanced from Uncle Bob to Mr. Morrison, who I only vaguely remembered, and then to Mark, whose face visibly relaxed. He had a friend in Uncle Bob, and he knew it. What he didn't know was that Uncle Bob carried a lot of weight in Cottonwood; Uncle Bob's approval was nearly all he needed.

"Ah, go on with yourself," Roy Morrison said.

"You go on, now."

Elder Timothy attempted to gain order. "Gentlemen."

Uncle Bob raised a hand. "Sorry about this, but it all needs to be said. We've got a chance here to put Cottonwood back on the map, and I, for one, intend to support what this young man and my niece over here are trying to do. Now, who's with me?"

Applause broke through the small attendance of parishioners, and Mark smiled. Thanks in part to Uncle Bob, he had them in his hand now; he was ready to take the next but all-important step. He asked each person to stand, tell their name, a little about themselves, and what they thought their role might be in this combined effort. When a man and woman sat together—sometimes with their children—the man stood and introduced his family, his family's history in Cottonwood, and what they did for a living. Most of the men were farmers but few were solely farmers. "Crops not been so good these past few years" was heard time and again. With each introduction—the unmarried and widowed women standing on their own accord—a firm sense of hope filled the room. And when we'd heard the last of the church's members—all but Roy Morrison, who'd left the church—and the final question had been asked of Mark and satisfactorily answered, Elder Timothy concluded the meeting by saying,

243

"I think God is doing a good thing here." He smiled broadly. "A God-thing, we like to call it."

Someone said "Amen."

I looked at Evan and him at me; again we read each other's thoughts. Mine said, "This is going to happen. I'm so happy."

I read his to say the same.

But as I later learned, I'd misread them entirely.

48

"You didn't have a chance to talk, really," I said to my husband as we drove from the church back to the big house. "I was hoping to hear what you had to say about the downtown area."

Evan laughed, turning for the moment to look at me. I saw his eyes glimmer in the winter moonlight, and in spite of the frigid cold outside, I felt toasty on the inside.

"I got a pretty good kick out of the term 'urban development' for that little strip of buildings in the center of town."

I feigned a pout and spoke in my best Oliver Twist voice. "'Ey, mister. It may not be much but it's 'ome."

Evan laughed lightly again. "Nice," he said. "You should join the local theater." His brow raised, and a finger went up in the air. "Oh, wait. That would require an actual theater."

I wiggled back in my seat and said, "There will be, you'll see. Oh, Evan." I turned to him again. "Can't you just see it?" Then I shook my head. "No, not yet you can't. But I can. I see Cottonwood as it will be . . ." I knew how to get my husband to join me in my excitement. "With a bakery that will feature Miss Melba and Miss Irene's goodies. Did you ever taste anything as heavenly tonight as their cakes? I made an absolute pig out of myself." I reached over and poked him in the side. "You didn't do so bad yourself."

"I admit it was delicious. And I admit you can't get food like that just anywhere."

I grinned. "Now that I have your attention . . . I can see antique shops and clothing stores. And, ha-ha, a local theater so the people here—who will be more than the sixty citizens Cottonwood now has—can go see a movie or perhaps have local plays. And if we can get the school up and running sooner rather than later, young families will move here with their children. Oh! What else can we have downtown? We'll need a realty office, of course. A bank. A café." As I said each new place, I held up a finger on my right hand, touching it with the index finger of my left. "A vintage hotel? Yes! Remember the hotel we stayed at . . . where were we? Florida?"

Evan nodded. He hadn't forgotten. "I remember. I also remember the train coming through every few hours and waking me up."

I reached over and wrapped my arms awkwardly around his shoulder. "I remember all those times you woke up too."

His eyes slanted toward me. "Vixen."

I slipped back to my seat, took in a deep breath, and sighed. "It's going to be incredible, Evan. How much of it can you save, do you think?"

He didn't answer right away, finally saying, "What do you mean?"

"Of the old? How much of the old can you save?"

I heard him inhale, then blow air through his nostrils. "Jo-Lynn, you have to understand something, sweetheart. It's cheaper and, to be honest with you, wiser to tear it all down and start over."

"What? Are you crazy? Do you know how old some of that brick is? The lights and shelving. The structure of everything is invaluable, Evan. Besides, Mark Michaels seems to agree with me on this issue, so there."

Up ahead, the big house came into view. Evan slowed the car and turned off the highway and onto the property. The car bounded along the ruts of the lawn until it came to a stop.

"For now," he said, then added, "Jo-Lynn, listen to yourself. You have a degree in interior design. You know what happens to walls and floors and ceilings over time when they are not properly cared for. I'm not so sure that we go into some of these buildings they won't fall in on top of us. Is that what you want? Some of these day laborers or local residents killed by a beam that lets loose while someone else two doors down is hammering? Not to mention the electrical disasters you'd be looking at. Plug one wrong thing in and the whole of your precious downtown could burn to the ground."

"Don't be so dramatic, Evan. Our theater isn't opened yet." I didn't speak in jest. I opened my car door and stomped toward the front porch. I'd left the old hanging lamp between the front door and the steps burning as bright as forty watts could shine, but it had apparently gone out while we were gone. "Great," I muttered.

Evan was not far behind me. "I thought you left the light on."

"I did. Like everything else around here, it's on its last leg."

Evan dipped into his pants pocket and brought out the key to the dead bolt. "That's what I'm trying to tell you, Jo-Lynn. Glad you see it my way."

I punched him in the shoulder. "We're not done with this discussion. I'm not going to let you flatten what's down there. It will lose its charm and appeal. Promise me you'll discuss this at length with Mark Michaels."

The front door swung open, and Evan stepped back to allow me entrance. "Of course, Jo-Lynn. I'm not the boss of this, but I'm an expert and I think Mark will at least listen to my opinion."

"He'll listen to mine too," I said, then pointed to the firewood in the copper pot. "Let's grab some of this and head upstairs. I'm freezing." I glanced over at the French doors.

As we trudged up the stairs, arms laden with wood, I spoke over my shoulder. "We're supposed to go through the boxes tonight, remember? See if we can find anything that might be of interest to anyone."

Evan sighed. "I'm tired. Let's do it in the morning."

I grew concerned that if we didn't do it tonight, the morning would come with all the work within it and we'd not get to it then either. But I no longer had the energy to argue with him. We reached the landing, and I stopped. The moonlight spilled into the unadorned windows at the ends of the hallway, granting enough light to the door of the bedroom, which was ajar. "Evan," I said.

"What's wrong?" He came up beside me.

"I know for a fact I closed this door on the way out. I remember because my coat belt got caught in it."

We stared at the door for several seconds, perhaps longer. Perhaps it was minutes or hours or days. It seemed forever until my husband finally whispered, "Come with me." He turned, barely making a sound, and we retraced our steps down the stairs and out the front door, the firewood growing cumbersome in our arms.

As soon as we hit the top of the porch steps Evan said, "Get in the car. Now."

It was not until we stepped off the porch that we dropped the wood, then ran for the car, slipping into its warm interior and locking the doors. Evan pulled his cell phone from his coat pocket and dialed 911 while I kept my eyes on our bedroom window.

"Nothing's moving around in there," I said, my voice barely audible.

Evan gave the information, then slapped the phone shut and turned to me. "Call your Uncle Bob. See if they've gotten home yet."

I didn't have Uncle Bob's cell phone number in my phone, but I did have Mae-Jo's. She answered on the fourth ring. When I asked where they were, she told me they were just pulling up in their driveway. "Can you come back here?" I said. "I'll explain when you get here."

Evan spoke from the driver's seat. "Tell Bob to bring one of his guns."

I turned my head to look at him, my mouth gaping open. "Evan," I said.

"Tell him."

I repeated my husband's order.

"Mercy sakes alive," Aunt Mae-Jo said. "What now?"

49

A county deputy arrived within ten minutes, followed by Larry Gansky, who got out of his car saying, "I should bring a sleeping bag and my toothbrush."

But he smiled at me, bringing my heart rate from racing to fluttering. Then he looked over at Uncle Bob. "Mr. Seymour, what 'cha got there?"

Uncle Bob glanced down at the hunting rifle hanging casually alongside his right leg. "Provisions," he answered.

"So I see. Tell you what; I'm here now, so why don't you put that thing back on the gun rack in your truck where it belongs."

Uncle Bob complied, though not happily.

The sheriff's deputy approached from the side of the house, an orb of light from his flashlight streaming on the ground before him. He walked as heedlessly as if he were strolling in a parade. "Find anything?" Larry Gansky called out.

"Nothing, Sheriff," the young deputy replied. Then he reached the five of us shivering in the cold and dark of the big house's front lawn and, looking at Evan and me, said, "But your room is a disaster."

I started for the house, but Evan caught my arm. "Wait, Jo-Lynn."

"What?" I looked from my husband to the sheriff and then to the deputy. "Are you telling me someone has ransacked our room?" I looked back at Evan. "The boxes."

"What boxes?" Larry asked.

Evan relaxed his grip on my arm and explained to the sheriff about the boxes in our room, about Mark Michaels's suggestion to go through them, and that we were going to do exactly that in the morning because we were tired, having had a full day and then church.

"Looks like somebody beat you to it," the deputy commented.

Larry Gansky sighed heavily. "Let's go see what we've got," he said. We followed him across the lawn, up the porch steps, along the porch, and into the front door like baby ducks behind their mama.

Once inside, he said, "Someone turn on some lights around here."

I reached for the switch and flicked it, but nothing happened.

Evan moved to another wall, another switch, but flipping it proved fruitless.

"Power's been cut," Uncle Bob said. "I'd bet my life on it."

"This is ridiculous," I said. "What in the world could possibly be in this house that would cause all of this?"

"Old houses keep dark secrets," Mae-Jo said.

"But this house is empty, Aunt Mae-Jo."

The sheriff and his deputy pulled standard-issue Maglites from their belts, and within a breath, the beams of light shot through the room, scanning it, coming to rest on the French doors. They were opened wide now.

I walked toward them and toward the staircase with my entourage behind me. I allowed the sheriff and his deputy to enter our room first. As their lights came to rest on the floor

251

where the boxes had been stashed, I gasped, Aunt Mae-Jo with me. "Oh my," she whispered.

I knelt beside the chaos. The light was veiled by the tears that refused to stay back as I picked up each piece of memorabilia, photographs ripped from their vintage frames, musty ledgers from my great-grandfather's farming days, each one shaken and tossed, and the old family Bible emptied of its treasures—curls of baby hair inside small onionskin envelopes, newspaper clippings of wedding announcements and family funerals, and recordings of births and baptisms—and pitched to the side like a bargain book at Barnes and Noble.

"Can you tell what's missing, Mrs. Hunter?" Larry Gansky asked. His voice was gentle, and I thought fleetingly that he understood innately what my heart was enduring.

I shook my head as my shoulders began to shake. "I hadn't really had time to go through it," I said between sobs and hiccups. Evan dropped beside me, cradling me in his arms as Aunt Mae-Jo said, "Bless your heart, Jo-Lynn." And then to her husband, "Bob, go call the power company. The least we can do is see about getting some power back to this house." But Uncle Bob didn't move; instead he said, "I'll take care of it in a minute, Mae-Jo."

"It just doesn't make sense," I said, pulling the Bible onto my lap. "Why would anyone want to do this?" I looked up at the sheriff. "I know I keep saying this, and obviously there is no answer to that question. I just don't understand it."

Sheriff Gansky squatted down beside me, handing me a handkerchief he'd pulled from his pocket. "My wife collects family heirlooms," he said. "I know how she'd feel if she came home and found some of her things strewed from one end to the other."

I nodded, wiped my eyes, and blew my nose as delicately as I could.

In the shroud of light that seemed to permeate the room I saw the skin around his eyes crinkle, forming deep crow's-feet. "You can keep that," he said, pointing to the handkerchief, and I laughed without meaning to. Then he patted my shoulder. "We may not have any answers right now, Mrs. Hunter. But we will." He stood, looked over his shoulder to his deputy. "Deputy Lee here will stay posted across the street until his shift ends. I doubt anything else will happen tonight, but it may make you feel better to know he's close by."

Evan had stood with him. "We'll stay with Jo-Lynn's aunt and uncle tonight." He looked from the sheriff to Bob and Mae-Jo. "If that's okay."

"Of course it is. You didn't even have to ask," Mae-Jo said, to which I began to weep again.

Evan and Bob walked the sheriff and his deputy out of the room. I remained on the floor, holding the family Bible, cradling it like a child, until Mae-Jo came beside me and said, "Come on, child. Let's get your things."

I placed the Bible on the floor, then stood. But instead of getting our pajamas and a change of clothes for the following day, I stepped over to the window to watch the men as they walked purposefully across the front lawn toward the parked cars. Deputy Lee, still holding his flashlight, flipped it off, then twirled it like a baton until he slipped it into its black ring on his belt. A pinpoint of moonlight reflected from its slick inky surface, seeming to wink back at me.

"Oh my gosh, that's it," I said as I brought my hand to my lips.

Aunt Mae-Jo came up behind me. "What's it, hon?"

"A flashlight." I turned to look at her. "The night I saw the two men walking toward the barn . . . one was carrying a flashlight. I didn't know what it was then, but now I do."

Mae-Jo placed a hand on my shoulder. "Well, darlin', no

one would dare walk without one in the middle of the thicket covering the yards the way they were then."

I raised my hand, index finger pointing upward as the others balled into a fist. "But it means more than that," I said. "It means they were looking for something. I can't pass off the fire or the . . . you know . . . the other. But a part of me wondered if seeing the two men was related. I think now all three—or four—are connected."

Mae-Jo went from the window overlooking the front lawn to the one peering over the back of the property. "You said they were going from the house to the barn?"

I joined her, careful of where I stepped. "Yes."

She turned to me. "Perhaps then whatever they were hoping to find in the barn they found that night."

I gasped again. "That's it! Aunt Mae-Jo, when Percy and I went into the barn, the contents of the desk were spilled on the floor. I thought it was negligence brought about by time or . . . something." I shook my head. "I don't know what I thought exactly. But I never connected the desk and the two men."

"Whose desk was it?"

"My great-grandfather's. Aunt Stella's father."

"And where's the desk now?"

"In storage."

She wrapped her arm around my shoulders. "Tomorrow, we'll go check it out. Can you get to the desk pretty easy?"

"Yes, ma'am."

"Tomorrow, then," she said. "Now, get your things together. You need a good night's sleep and so do I. Let's go home."

50

Sleep rarely comes easily on the wings of anguish and questions. While Evan's rhythmic breathing was a sure indication he had left his worries and concerns at the door of Bob and Mae-Jo's guest bedroom, I resorted to shallow breathing followed by the occasional sigh. My mind raced, bouncing between wonder at why anyone wanted to vandalize the big house and why anyone—particularly my own husband—wanted to tear down what remained of downtown Cottonwood. My thoughts spun out of control all night, first going room to room as I'd done with my camera, asking myself what in that particular room could be so important—both before vacancy and after.

Having eliminated any and all possibilities, my thoughts moved to the town and what I could do to salvage it. Electricians could be called in, drywallers, painters, carpenters, roofers.

Then I began to wonder who, already in town, might have the credentials or experience we'd need to renovate Cottonwood. This led to less immediate issues. A city government for one, with a mayor, city manager, and city clerk, perhaps its own police station or sheriff's office. If enough people moved here, we'd once again need city utilities rather than depending on service from the county.

We'd need to develop a mission statement.

City ordinances. No doubt Karol had this under control already and it surely wasn't my job or responsibility. Still, tonight it was on my mind, as real a challenge as the man lying in bed next to me.

I thought perhaps I could contact the National Register of Historic Places and see if the big house qualified for nomination. Mother, I decided, would be ideal for heading this. All I had to do was mention it ever so casually in conversation and she'd be all over it. I smiled at my ingenuity.

Then I frowned. I opened my eyes and stared at the ceiling for long moments, having the realization I was thinking in terms not of *being* here but of *living* here. Permanently. Somehow, inexplicably and without warning, the soul of me had left Atlanta and Druid Hills, the people who called me "friend" and those who pretended to be. My work, my career, my employers . . . I was separate from them all. The only glitch to this thought was my husband, who I knew would just as soon have a leg amputated as leave the opulence of Druid Hills, his standing at the country club, and his partnership with Everett. Unless, that is, I meant more to him than all those combined.

I shifted, and the box springs creaked. I touched Evan on his shoulder with my fingertips—ever so lightly—but he didn't move nor did his breathing change. I drew my hand to my lips, curling the fingers toward my palm, then squeezed my eyes shut against what I now knew to be true. I had, over the past few weeks, truly come home.

In my heart, lying there in the still and silence of the country bedroom in a rural home, I could hear an echo of my footsteps—clomp-clomp-clomp, thump-thump-thump—as I walked down the wide space of the hallway in the big house the day Uncle Jim died. I pictured myself walking the planks of wood along the wraparound porch as I'd done the day Aunt Stella left for Doris's home and the new life she would have there and the lights from Uncle Bob's store flickering as they'd done thousands of evenings before and would, no doubt, continue to do. I heard the squeak of hinges on the old glider at the end of the porch and the smell of burning leaves and the green and brown of foliage thick as the summer's air. The familiarity of it all resonated within me.

What do you have in mind? I lifted a silent prayer.

Like Uncle Jim, I wasn't what one might call a religious person, but I knew God personally. I'd gone to church my whole life. As a child, regularly. As an adult, semi-regularly. I knew all the Bible stories. I knew John 3:16 and the Twenty-third Psalm. And I knew the presence of God better than both of those.

Maybe it was the church service tonight and on Sunday. Maybe it was the love wrapped around Miss Melba's sweet potato soufflé and caramel cake. Or the easy way the preacher had of presenting a sermon, the way he leaned against the podium as casually as if he were waiting for a bus. Being in that sanctuary—twice now—felt like home. And the big house felt like home.

What do you have in mind? I asked again. Even as I prayed the words I felt my body grow heavy with exhaustion as though God answered, "For you to sleep now and leave the rest to me." My eyes fluttered open, then closed again, the lids heavy and determined. I was slipping, finally, to sleep.

And my last thought was that it was no wonder. I had, after all, finally come to understand—truly understand—why I was here. This time in Cottonwood was more than me renovating a house. God was renovating me.

Aunt Mae-Jo and I left the house before Evan and Uncle Bob had gotten out of bed. We met in the kitchen as the world changed from midnight blue to ashen gray, had a cup of coffee, jotted a note on a pad of paper so as not to alarm our husbands, then quietly walked out of the door and into Aunt Mae-Jo's Mercury Marquis. The engine hummed and heat met cold as a plume of smoke circled the car. Mae-Jo switched on the defrost, allowed it to do its job for an impatient half minute, then swiped the windshield with the wipers and we were on our way.

Twenty minutes later we were in Raymore and inside the storage unit.

"Good land of the living," my aunt said, looking up and around at the stacks of furniture and boxes of items I'd pulled from Aunt Stella's. "Who knew this much stuff was in one house?"

I pointed an index finger toward the metal ceiling as I turned sideways to shift between two rows of boxes. "And the barn. Don't forget the barn."

"Heavens, no."

I disappeared from her sight and neared the desk. "It's a big house, Aunt Mae-Jo. That's why they call it the 'big house.'"

"And too much house for Aunt Stella, I always said," she called over the top of the boxes. "I told Bob years ago they should knock that top floor off—goodness knows they never went up there—and just have the bottom half of the house. Doris always slept in the back bedroom, even when she was a teenager, and except for when the whole family came in, no one knew that second floor existed."

I found the desk and said so.

"Keep talking; I'll find you."

I heard her inching toward me, and I laughed as I began pulling the drawers from the desk. Other than old ledgers, a few fountain pens, some rubber bands that crumbled between my fingers, paper clips, and the like, there was nothing of any seeming importance.

"When I married Bob, back in '59," Aunt Mae-Jo said from

beside me, "Mr. Nevilles was dead already. Mrs. Nevilles too, though I remember them both, of course. Everyone knew everyone in Cottonwood, same as they do now." She reached down and touched one of the dusty leather-covered ledgers, tapping it with her pink-tinted nails. "Jim was running the farm—had been since he married Stella—and to my knowledge he never used the barn as an office. I would see him, sometimes, coming out of the dining room, and Bob would say, 'What are you up to, Uncle Jim?' and he'd say, 'Oh, just going over a few of the books.'" Mae-Jo paused. "Can't you just hear him saying that?"

I smiled and nodded.

"I never really thought about it, but now I wonder just where it was he was working at. There was never a desk in the dining room."

I looked at Mae-Jo, locking my eyes with hers. "The butler's pantry. There were always ledgers and almanacs and calendars and things like that in there."

"But the butler's pantry is no bigger than a minute."

I shrugged. "Maybe he brought the books to the dining room table. Then put them back." Something tugged at my memory. Uncle Jim, looking around the formal dining room, hands on hips, muttering, "Waste of space, this old room. If I'd built this house I'd-a left this room off the plans."

"Hmmm . . . ," I said.

"What?"

I shook my head. "Nothing. Just a memory knocking."

Aunt Mae-Jo began pulling the drawers out of the desk.

"What are you doing?"

She set the drawers—which smelled of dust and cedar—one at a time, on top of the desk, emptied the top one, and then flipped it over to reveal its bottom.

"What are you doing?" I asked again.

"Looking. If someone was trying to find something, it's because it was hidden. Bottoms of drawers are a good place for hiding things."

I frowned, but I joined her in her efforts. "I have a feeling our culprits thought of that already."

"Maybe. Maybe not."

When the third drawer had been emptied and flipped and nothing of any interest was discovered, we both silently began refilling them. Aunt Mae-Jo touched my hand. "Wait. This isn't a ledger," she said, picking up a small book. "This is a daily journal. Desk journals, we used to call them." She flipped the book open to expose the handwriting I had come to recognize as belonging to my great-grandfather. "Back then, businessmen and even housewives kept a daily diary of things they did, meals they cooked. They didn't try to express their feelings like people do today. It was all about what had to be done or what got done. Nobody cared how you felt about the fleetingness of life." She waved her hand in the air for effect, and I laughed lightly. "Farmers used them for recording plantings, harvestings, that kind of thing." She handed the book to me. "You can start reading on the way home in the car."

I looked down at the book. "I wonder why the men didn't want this, though. Maybe it wasn't what they were looking for. Obviously the financial ledgers weren't."

Mae-Jo gathered the ledgers. "Then we'll go over them with a fine-toothed comb. Who knows but what those men— whoever they are—didn't underestimate Mr. Nevilles?"

"You think this has to do with my great-grandfather?"

"What I think is this: one, they went first for Mr. Nevilles's desk. So it only makes sense that it has to do with him. And whatever it is or was, it wasn't buried with him. Two, I'm hungry, and you get to buy me breakfast. I'm not picky. McDonald's will do just fine."

260

51

Cottonwood, Georgia
February 1956

It rained the day they buried her papa. It began early that morning as a fine drizzle, but by midafternoon when the funeral was set to begin it had turned to bitter sleet. In spite of the thickness of her wool coat, it felt like razor-sharp knives pelting against Stella's body as she walked from the car to the canopied graveside.

She stood in the front row before the casket perched over the dug hole that waited to swallow it. Next to her was Mama, and together with the extended family and myriad friends huddled under large and dark umbrellas, they listened as the preacher—who knew and loved her father so well—spoke briefly, quickly, so as to get the good folks of Cottonwood out of the cold and back to the big house, where warm fires and hot food were being prepared. Stella strained to hear him; his words were barely audible over the flapping of the canopy's scalloped border and the *pfft-pfft-pfft* of the sleet against its canvassed top. But it was important that she do so; she'd want to remember these words until she, herself, drew a final breath.

She reached her right hand toward her mama—hunched over and paler than Stella ever remembered seeing her—and slipped her gloved hand into the crook of her arm. She squeezed, and Mama looked over at her, and then through her, as though having her youngest child so close was both consolatory and no consolation at all.

When the preacher had said his final amen and the attendees had spoken their hasty words of condolence, Stella looked across the sea of faces, searching for the most familiar to her now. When she spotted him—her husband Jim—he was holding their six-year-old daughter tightly in his arms, her bottom resting atop his forearm, her arms wrapped around his neck as though she were drowning in a sea of despair. Sometimes, Stella thought, no one loved "Pops," as the grandchildren called him, more than Doris. It was no wonder she was so distraught.

"You need to get that child out of the cold," her mother said next to her. Stella turned to tell her she would, but the older woman was moving toward the arms of her oldest living son, Conroy. Hersham, the eldest child born to Loretta and Nevan Nevilles, had died from a heart attack at fifty-two, and was lying in the ground already, soon to be joined by their father. Beside him was Galvin, their youngest son, one of the more than fifty thousand who had not returned alive from the Korean War.

It seemed to Stella life had too often been so unfair, so unkind. It had made her crusty around the edges, Mama said. But it had also given her Jim, the absolute love of her life, and after him, Doris. And, Papa always said, Jim had managed to penetrate the callused to bring out the sugary-sweet.

What Jim had failed to heal, Stella said, Doris had more than restored.

Stella muttered a quick "Yes, ma'am," then started for her husband. Seeing her approach, he did the same. "Let's go,"

Stella said to him. "We need to get to the house before the rest of the world does."

Jim took his free arm and wrapped it around her as she pulled the hook of her umbrella from over her forearm and opened it for the two of them. Jim awkwardly attempted to take it from her, to hold it over her, but she jerked it away and said, "I've got it."

Halfway to their car he asked, "You okay?"

"No," she said. "But I will be."

"Mommy?" Doris asked from the other side of her father's broad shoulders.

Stella cocked her head. Doris's cheeks, round and rosy, were streaked by her tears, and her curly white-blonde hair was wild about her face and held back by a black satin ribbon that threatened to slip off her head at any moment. "What, shug?"

"Did Pops go to live with Jesus?"

"Yes, my love."

"Is he with Jesus now?"

"Yes. I believe he is."

"Then who is that in the box-thing back there?"

Jim interjected, "Don't ask your mama so many questions, baby girl."

"It's okay," Stella said, resting her head against the top of Jim's arm. "She's just being a child."

They reached the car, and Jim opened the front passenger door for his wife, then placed their child on her lap. Stella watched through the rain-drenched windshield as he ran around the front of the car, opened the door of it, and slipped inside. "Let's go home," he said to his little family.

"Will Pops be there?" Doris asked.

Stella squeezed her daughter against her. "No, hon. Remember? Pops is with Jesus now." To which Doris, once again, began to cry.

The big house had settled down. Supper—including Irene Patterson's banana cream pie and her sister Melba Dawson's deviled eggs—had been eaten in spite of the family's mourning and the town's loss of Nevan Nevilles. Stella had shut the door behind the last of the guests, ignoring the brass key in the keyhole. She'd put the house back in order as the family prepared for bed, and when all had gone quiet, she'd stepped back into the living room to put the fireplace cover in front of embers that occasionally popped and sizzled as they lay dying. She turned off the table lamps, then slipped beyond the French doors leading to the back of the house.

Her mother slept in the middle room to the left of the hallway with her sister Lottie, who insisted their mother not sleep alone that night. Lottie's husband Charles and one of their sons bunked down in the back bedroom. Upstairs, other family members slept in three of the four bedrooms while a few of the cousins slept on beds and pallets in the rooms reserved as the nursery and playroom, first for the children of her parents and now for Doris. Stella had asked Jim to keep Doris with them in their room for this one night, and he'd agreed.

Stella looked up the stairs; Jim's form shadowed the landing. "Hey," he whispered down to her.

She placed her hand on the banister but made no move to climb the stairs. "Hey," she whispered back.

He came down the staircase slowly, then stopped on the bottom step and sat on the fourth. Stella joined him. "You're not quite ready to go to bed, are you?" He wore his pajamas and bathrobe and smelled of soap and toothpaste.

She shook her head no, then began to play with an imaginary

string between her fingertips. "I have a couple more things to do before I come up."

"Like what?"

She looked at him and smiled weakly. "Just a couple of things." She patted his knee.

"You're avoiding coming to bed."

"What do you mean?"

"If you don't go to sleep maybe you won't have to wake up in the morning and face the reality of your papa's dying."

She pondered that before answering. "No," she said at length. "I think I have come to grips with that."

He slipped his hand around hers and was quiet for several minutes before speaking again. "I saw Valentine Bach this morning when I went up to the store for your mama."

"Oh?" She didn't dare look at him now.

"He said to tell you he was real sorry about your daddy."

Stella nodded, keeping her gaze on her feet.

"He said your daddy was real nice to him over the years; a good man."

She nodded again. "Yes, he was."

"He said he'd never forget a long conversation he had with your daddy on the front porch steps. I asked him what it was about."

"And what'd he say?"

"He just said, 'Life and such.'"

Stella smiled in the semi-darkness.

"And he said to tell you he knows what it feels like to lose someone you love and that he and Bettina Rose would say a prayer for you and the family."

"Bettina Rose," Stella repeated the name.

"Sweet girl," Jim said. "She and Margaret have been such good friends over the years. They're like two peas in a pod. Hard to believe they're near-bout grown women."

265

"They are that. Margaret told me today she'll go to business school for sure in the fall."

Jim leaned over and kissed his wife's cheek. "I'm going to bed now. Don't be long."

"I won't," she answered. "I love you."

Her husband stood and looked down at her. "And I love you. More than you'll ever know."

When he'd closed the bedroom door, Stella stood then took deliberate steps to the back door. She plucked her coat from the coat tree, picked up the tin-plate lantern kept there, then opened the door and turned it on. It lit the path toward the barn, and Stella quickly made her way in the freezing cold. The air was crisp and veiled by chimney smoke. She opened the door wide enough for her thin frame, slipped inside and toward her father's desk. There she pulled open the bottom drawer and reached for a stack of papers in an envelope marked with the words *Thursday Nights*.

She didn't open it. She didn't need to. She'd known what was inside it from the time it was but a single page of paper. "Your secret is safe, Papa," she said to it, then placed it under the breast of her coat. "No one ever need know."

Stella hurried back to the house, back to the warmth inside it. She shut the door behind her, set the lantern down, then slipped into the stillness of the kitchen and from there into the dining room, where a feast of covered food was spread across the top of the dining table. She sidestepped it, making her way into the butler's pantry.

She closed the door firmly behind her then pulled the string overhead to light the miniature room. Only then did she allow the tears that had threatened to spill down her cheeks the whole day to fall. But she willed them to keep silent until she could do what she must do.

She raised herself up on her toes, pushed her hand between

two upright ledgers, then inched her fingers along, searching for a tiny lever. When she made contact, she pressed against it and heard the familiar click followed by the sliding of the wall. Then Stella waited for the panel to shift and allow her entrance to the place where only she and her father ever went.

And then she slipped inside.

52

Mae-Jo and I arrived back at the big house at about ten to find Valentine Bach and his band of merry men hard at work. "Aunt Mae-Jo," I said, pointing toward the laborers, "Evan and I will need to stay with you again tonight if it's okay. They're working on the foundation for the next few days."

Mae-Jo patted my knee and then opened her door. "You've always got a place to stay," she said.

I remained seated as I watched her walk across the street to the store. I then slipped out of the car and began walking the perimeter of the house until I found Valentine, hunched over, hands on his knees and peering into the crawl space under the house as he shouted orders to some invisible someone. "Mr. Valentine?"

The old gentleman jumped, then laughed. "You scared my mule," he said.

I pointed upward. "Is it too late to go inside?"

"'Fraid so. I would-a thought you'd had what you needed out by now."

I shook my head. "No, sir. We had another vandalism last night. My husband and I stayed with my aunt and uncle and . . ." I trailed off. The rest was understood. "Mr. Valentine, has the sheriff been by this morning?"

"No, ma'am. Ain't seen him. But I tell you what; I thought something must-a happened. I saw a deputy parked over on the other side of the store yonder. But once we came in, he left."

"I see." I looked toward the store, then back to the old contractor. "Is there anything I can do to help?" I smiled.

He returned the smile. "Stay out of the way."

I placed a hand on the droop of his shoulder and said, "Yes, sir."

I returned to the car, pulled the ledgers and journal from the backseat, then hauled them over to the store where coffee brewed and a warm fire invited me in. "Can I sit in here and look over all this?" I asked from the door.

Mae-Jo was sitting at one of the tables, already enjoying a cup of coffee. She raised the mug toward me. "You gotta love a coffeepot that will pause while you pour."

I laughed, dropped the ledgers on the table, and then poured a cup of coffee for myself. By the time I returned to the table, Mae-Jo was already flipping page by page through a ledger, leaving the journal for me.

We read for the next hour, one cup of coffee following the other until, sometime near noon, Miss Irene and Miss Melba came with lunch for the workers. Mae-Jo and I stopped what we were doing long enough to walk over and help set up a long table of food along with Chinet plates and Styrofoam cups for the piping hot coffee Mae-Jo supplied. Then, as though drawn by some primal force, Evan and Uncle Bob arrived "just in time." When the four of us had topped our plates with a variety of sandwiches and homemade potato salad, we walked back to the store, shoulder to shoulder.

"I've talked with Mark," Evan said to me after we'd gathered around a table apart from the ledgers, blessed the food, and began to eat. "And you're right. He's a preservationist. He

269

wants the numbers and drawings to reflect using the bricks and lumber that we are forced to tear down but saving as much as we can as is."

I beamed, licked my finger, and drew a "1" in the air. "That's one for Jo-Lynn."

Over lunch Evan discussed his thoughts and ideas and then Mae-Jo and I shared what we'd found at the storage unit.

"Anything of interest in the books?" Uncle Bob asked.

I shook my head as I bit into my ham and cheese sandwich. "Not yet. At least nothing on the surface."

Our husbands left shortly after lunch; Uncle Bob back to the house to "get some things done" and Evan to Raymore to find Mark and to discuss his findings from surveying the downtown property. "Want to come?" he asked me, but I declined. "I've got to go help break down the tables and throw away the trash," I said, jutting my thumb toward the big house. I also wanted to continue reading my great-grandfather's journal, which was—up till now—mostly what seeds were planted, what crops were harvested, what money came in, what money went out, and who was in his employ.

The weather outside had warmed up to a sizzling sixty-four degrees; I told Mae-Jo I was going to continue reading outside on one of the old benches. "Leave the door open, will you?" she asked. "I'll open the back door and get a nice breeze in here."

Before I sat down, I peered over at the big house for what felt like the twentieth time that day. Work was still in progress and I was still not needed. I was glad to have the journals and ledgers to keep me occupied.

At about three o'clock Arizona and Annaleise drove up in the Geo and pumped a few gallons of gas, and then Annaleise went inside to pay while Arizona joined me at the bench. "What 'cha got?" she asked, pointing to the book.

I closed it, placed it on my lap, rested one hand atop it, and then gave it a single pat. "My great-grandfather's journal." I leaned over and looked at the big house, then back to the teenage girl who was nothing short of beautiful. "I am not as fortunate as you. I never knew my great-grandfather. You have your great-grandfather living a yard away. You have his wisdom at your disposal any time, day or night."

She gave me an elf-like look, then asked, "What was his name? Your pappy?"

"Nevan Nevilles."

She wrinkled her nose. "They had such funny names back then, didn't they? I mean, look at Pappy. His name is Valentine. Like a card or, you know, the day. I mean, why didn't his parents just call him 'Love Child' or something?"

The screen door swung open; the quieter of the twins stepped down the time-carved cement steps. I slid over a notch or two and Arizona did the same. "What are you talking about?" Annaleise asked as she sat next to her sister.

"Weird names like they had a hundred years ago. Names like Nevan and Valentine."

"Pappy's name," Annaleise said, "is Valentine Pemrose, after his mother's last name. Pappy said he'd never tell anyone that when he was a boy 'cause the other boys would beat him up if they knew." She giggled, then added, "I guess he's too old to care now."

"Funny how what matters when we're young doesn't matter so much later on."

"And did you know Ga-Ga's middle name is Rose? I guess after Pappy's middle name."

"There was a Valentine *Penrose* who was a famous French writer," I informed them.

They looked at me and nodded as though I'd just explained quantum physics.

Arizona finally said, "So, the man who was with you last night is your husband?"

"Yes."

"How long have you been married?"

I looked past the old and modern gas pumps and the grease dotting the cement, over the top of the Geo and across the highway and into the thick foliage of untended land beyond. "A long time," I said. "Twenty-five years."

"Are you in love?"

"Arizona," Annaleise admonished with a roll of her eyes. She looked at me. "Excuse my nosy sister."

I shook my head. "That's okay. And, yes. I'm in love."

"How do you know?" Arizona asked.

I straightened. "Well, let me think . . . As aggravating as he can be at times, I can't imagine being with anyone else. His is the face I always seek in a crowd." With the fingertips of my right hand I touched the place where my heart beat a quick step. I wasn't accustomed to having such personal questions asked of me by such young women. "I guess love is a feeling that you just know when you feel it. When we're not getting along I'm engulfed by pain and when we are I'm engulfed by passion. It feels a bit overwhelming, actually."

"Like you're drowning in it?"

"Yes, Arizona. Like you're drowning in it." I crossed my eyes, teasingly. "But you don't want anyone to rescue you."

The girls laughed.

"How did you meet him? Your husband?" Annaleise asked.

I felt a half smile come to my lips. "After college, I moved to Atlanta and met him at a business function." I pointed to my eyes. "He had the most amazing sparkle to his eyes; that's what attracted me to begin with."

The twins looked at each other and giggled as young

women do. I laughed lightly with them. "He was quite the romantic in those days."

"Not anymore?" Arizona again posed the personal question.

"Well . . ." I shifted on the bench. "It's different after twenty-five years. I mean, you'd like to think it isn't, or at the very least that it shouldn't be, but it is."

"Not with our parents," Annaleise said. "They're disgusting they're so romantic with each other."

"It's mostly because of Mama," Arizona offered. "Daddy says he could eat her with a spoon."

"Yes, I saw your parents in action. I well remember."

We drew quiet again until Arizona said, "I think I might be in love."

"Here we go," Annaleise said, then frowned.

Arizona hit her playfully on the leg. "Stop it. You're just jealous."

"No. I'm not." She crossed one leg over the other and began to furiously pump her suspended foot up and down.

"Yes. You are."

"So," I interrupted, remembering all too well the ping-pong arguments my brother and I had when we were teens. "Who are you in love with, Miss Arizona?"

The perky blonde gave her attention back to me. "No, I *think* I'm in love."

"Okay. Who do you *think* you are in love with?"

"His name is Lance. He's in a youth group over in Raymore, and we met when our churches got together for a cookout about two months ago. He's been calling me ever since and he wants to take me out, but Mama says no way, that we're too young, blah, blah, blah . . ."

"We are too young," Annaleise, in all her sixteen years of wisdom, said.

"Hush your fuss." Arizona nearly jumped in place.

I raised my hand, a silent pleading that the girls come to a truce before an all-out war broke out. "Girls?"

"Sorry, Miss Jo-Lynn," Arizona said. "She really is just jealous."

"Well, let's not start that again. Why don't you just tell me about Lance and, Annaleise, see if you can be patient enough for her to do so."

Arizona wrapped her arms around herself as she talked, reminding me of myself at their age. As she spoke, my mind slipped back to the young man I'd dated exclusively in high school, the boy I thought I'd one day marry, have lots of children with, raising them in a big house with a picket fence and window boxes spilling over with flowers. Now, as Arizona spoke, I struggled to remember why we'd ended our relationship. We'd certainly dated long enough to commit. We'd been homecoming king and queen. We'd made all the "most likely to" lists. I was the "adorable Jo-Lynn Tatum-Teem" and he had been the "dashing Royce Coniff." Dashing, everyone said, because he wore English Leather, so much so that the scent of it often arrived in a room a full minute before he did and lingered long after he'd departed.

"Miss Jo-Lynn?" I heard Arizona say, pulling me from my memory.

"I'm sorry, what?"

"I asked why you decided not to have children."

I furrowed my brow. "How did we get from you and Lance to my not having children? Did I fall asleep?" I tried to smile.

"No," Annaleise said, leaning over. "My crazy lovesick sister here said that she and Lance have already decided to have three. They haven't had one single date and they don't have a clue as to when Mama and Daddy are going to allow them to go out, but they've decided they want three kids."

I pursed my lips and focused on Arizona. "I have to agree with your sister. Isn't this rushing things?"

She shrugged. "The heart wants what it wants."

"Well, that's true but—"

"And Pappy told me once that he and my great-grandmother fell in love when they were only, like, seventeen."

Annaleise shook her head. "They were eighteen when they married, Zona, and Mama told me it was an arranged marriage, that they hardly knew each other, so no way they fell in love before they married."

Arizona splayed her hands. "Papa told me he was seventeen when he fell in love the first time, Leesie. He said they met when they were seventeen. I remember Pappy telling me."

"That doesn't make sense," Annaleise said. "How could you be in love with someone you hardly know?"

Before the girls could continue their banter I reached over and placed a hand on Arizona's knee. "You know what is amazing to me, girls? You two, in the midst of sibling tension, just called each other by pet names."

In unison they said, "Oh, we always do that." Then Arizona added, "But only when we're stressed with each other. Daddy and Mama do it too. Daddy calls Mama—"

"Ona," Annaleise supplied.

"And Mama calls Daddy—"

"Gussie."

"Gussie?"

The girls laughed. "It's a combination of his names. The 'us' in Buster and the 'G' in Godwin."

I joined in their laughter, finally settling to say, "You young ladies are a stitch."

"Daddy says that when things get tense, if you call each other by funny pet names, then it's harder to keep stirring such a fuss."

275

"I'll have to remember that." I tried to think by what name I might call Evan. His middle name was Spencer, so—perhaps, I thought—Spence? I shook my head at the idea; there was nothing endearing, really, to call him. My name—Jo-Lynn—was already a nickname. My shoulders sank. We were a couple without "funny pet names." Oh well. I leaned over to get a better look at Annaleise. "Thank you for sharing your afternoon with me. This is the most I've ever heard you speak." Then to Arizona, "And you, my dear, keep the brakes firmly applied. Your great-grandparents lived in an era when it might have been okay for eighteen-year-old boys and girls to get married, but that's changed now. I was twenty-five, almost twenty-six, when I married."

"Do you have any regrets?" Arizona's bravado in question-asking again rose to the surface and spilled out her mouth. "'Cause Pappy said he didn't; only that she died so young."

I didn't answer right away. Then: "A few. I do wish I'd had children." I raised a finger in the air. "That is, if I could know for sure they'd be as wonderful as you."

The girls smiled at me just as a shuffling came from around the side of the building. Our gazes turned toward the sound, and within moments their great-grandfather stood before us. He placed his hands on his hips, gave the girls a brief nod, then looked at me. "Missy, I've got something I need to talk to you about."

"Okay."

He looked at the girls again. "Little ones," he said, his voice tender. "Go on home now. This is a private matter."

53

Mr. Valentine and I walked from the store to the house, taking short, slow strides toward it. The old gentleman shoved his hands in his pockets as we walked, kept his chin tucked toward his chest and his eyes on his work boots. He reminded me of a young boy returning home from school with a bad report card, hoping for one minute more before the ax fell. As though, if he waited long enough, the world would simply come to an end and the repercussion of the large red F would never have to be.

"Mr. Valentine?" I asked as we reached the sidewalk near the big house.

"Walk with me," he said, turning his head just enough to peer up at me from the brim of his hat.

"Okay."

We strolled the sidewalk along the front side of the house toward the town of Cottonwood. "We'll be done with this by tomorrow," he said. "Sorry about your things being inside."

"We'll be okay," I said.

"Just want you to be careful."

"I appreciate that."

We were then at the place where, now that the excess foliage had been cleared away, the relic of the old barn and stable and outhouse was visible. Mr. Valentine nodded toward it. "You still plan to use what the termites didn't get to?" he asked, stopping before it.

"I do. Hopefully there's enough there that's salvageable."

"Jim kept up with termite inspections on the house but never cared much for the houses out back. I would ask him from time to time why he didn't rent out the farmland rather than leaving it like that—a lot of people asked him—but he just wasn't interested. He'd made his money over the years, invested well, and he and Stella were not hurting for anything." He shrugged. "At least that's what he told me."

"You and Uncle Jim were good friends. I know you must miss him."

He didn't answer. He turned back toward town and ambled toward it. I joined, staying quiet until he was ready to speak. But he said nothing until we reached the center of town. He stopped and I stopped beside him. The temperature was beginning to dip again; I crossed my arms so that my sweater wrapped tight around me.

We were across the street from where the old mercantile had been.

"Were the girls bothering you much?" he asked.

"Uh . . . no. Not at all."

"That's good. Their mama and daddy has raised them to be respectful."

"They're good girls." I tilted my head and, looking fully at him, smiled. "They wanted to know about Evan and me. You know, about love and how you know you're in love and things like that." He raised a brow and gave me a half smile. "They said some nice things about you and your wife. That you fell in love early in life. I think Arizona is a bit of a romantic while Annaleise is more practical."

He nodded. "I met my wife, Lilly Beth, when we were sixteen. By the time we were seventeen our parents had arranged we'd get married."

"Really? That seems so . . . old country, for lack of a better word."

"Our folks were old country. Our parents were first generation born in this country so a lot of the old ways of doing things were . . ." He trailed off, then continued. "See that store over there? What used to be Wright's?"

"Yes, sir."

"The first year Lilly Beth and I were married, I had just enough money to buy her a little scarf—a pretty thing, just like her—for Christmas. We'd been married less than a year, had just enough money to cover the necessities and nothing for the extras, but I wanted her to have something nice." He eyed me again, this time keeping his focus on me. "See, missy, I didn't love my wife when I married her. Love wasn't the reason we got married. We got married because we were told to. Now, Arizona has told me she thinks she's in love." He chuckled. "That child would talk to a tree if she thought it would listen. And she tells me everything. Always has."

"She's much more open than her sister."

"Don't tell her any of your secrets," he said. "She'll blab."

I laughed; a winter's breeze picked it up and carried it toward the big house. I looked up. The sky was turning an ashen gray; dusk was hovering on the horizon. "Mr. Valentine, is there something you're trying to tell me?"

He nodded. "Yes, ma'am. Bear with me if you will."

"Okay."

"Now, Annaleise, you can tell her anything. She'll go to her grave with it."

"I can see that about her."

"She's like me in that."

"You've got secrets?"

He didn't answer. He turned, starting back for the house. I followed next to him, saying nothing. Finally he spoke. "I was

Jim's friend," he said. "But long before that, I was Stella's. We were friends before I married Lilly Beth, you see."

"But not after?"

"Married men didn't keep their single female friends back in those days."

"Oh." I thought about that for a moment before asking, "Lilly Beth and Aunt Stella weren't friends?"

"Lilly Beth didn't live here until I married her."

"I see."

We were now back at the house. Mr. Valentine pulled his right hand out of his pocket long enough to point toward it. "Missy, I'm not one to talk about things that have been placed in my confidence, but I'm worried about you. There are secrets in that house that I know about. Things your aunt told me."

"Like what, Mr. Valentine?" I felt my back grow straight.

He didn't answer right away. "I'm an old man, young lady. I don't have any energy left in me for the kind of battle I'd have to fight if anyone knew what I was about to tell you." Again, he eyed me from beneath the brim of his hat. "I need to know if you can be as trustworthy as Annaleise."

"Yes, of course. I mean, if you know something that . . . Mr. Valentine, there have been crimes committed here, and the lives of my husband and me have been in danger. If you know something, you have to tell me. You have to tell the sheriff."

He shook his head. "No, ma'am. If you bring the sheriff to talk to me, I will say I don't know anything."

My shoulders sank. "I don't understand, then."

"You're not in danger, missy. No one is going to hurt you. They're looking for something, and I know what it is. But they won't find it."

"What is it? What are they looking for?"

"Information. Information Stella would never want anyone to know." He turned fully toward me. "You love your aunt, don't you?"

"Of course, I do. What kind of question is that?"

"Then listen carefully to what I'm saying. Tonight, when things have settled down, get yourself a piece of paper and a pencil and draw the layout of this house. You know how to do that, don't you? They taught you that in school?"

"Yes."

"You do that and then tomorrow we'll talk more."

"I . . . Mr. Valentine . . . I . . . why can't we talk now?" I asked him. "Or why can't I just call Aunt Stella and ask her what kind of secrets this house holds?"

He raised his chin. "That would be a mistake. She'll deny knowing anything, and then you and I will have a mighty big problem between the two of us. I'd hate for that to happen."

"Then what are we doing now? Why are you telling me anything at all?"

"I've been thinking all day. If you can get the information and pull out the part Stella doesn't want anyone to know—if you've got the stomach for it—then you can give it to the sheriff, and these cowards around here will leave you alone."

"What do you mean 'the stomach for it'?"

I waited for an answer but got none; Valentine Bach stared at me a moment, then took five steps toward the back of the house. Then he stopped, looked over his shoulder, and smiled. "You look a lot like her, you know."

"I'm sorry?"

"Stella. Oh, what a beauty she was in her day." He turned again and said, "Still is." His words were barely audible, but I caught them.

And then he walked toward the barn and stable, leaving me to stand on the stoop near the steps leading to the front door. A door I could not safely enter, but a door, I now knew, that led to a secret so dark, my aunt would never wish it revealed.

54

Evan and I went to the house on the hill for dinner. Evan questioned my quietness along the way, but I chalked it up to having been immersed in Nevan Nevilles's diary for the better part of the day. I didn't tell him about my visit from the Godwin twins or about the walk I'd taken with Mr. Valentine.

When Mother and I were done with the dishes and Daddy and Evan were enjoying conversation in the living room, Mother turned to me and said, "Jo-Lynn, what's going on?"

I feigned surprise. "What do you mean?" I walked over to the coffeepot and began preparing coffee. My hands were shaking and I silently cursed them for it.

"I'll make the coffee," she said, taking the scoop and bag of coffee from me.

I pulled the coffeepot from the maker, walked over to the sink, and filled it with water. When we were done with our tasks and the coffeepot was beginning its final sighs, Mother walked over to the kitchen table, pulled out two chairs, sat in one, and then pointed toward the other. "Sit."

"Mother."

"Young lady . . ."

I knew that tone and without hesitation I became obedient.

She crossed her forearms and placed them on the table. "What is going on with you?"

"What do you mean?"

"Okay, if you want to play that game: with you and Evan specifically?"

I shook my head as I leaned back in the chair. "I honestly don't know. We've settled nothing between us. I could return to Druid Hills at the end of the renovation on the big house and find that absolutely nothing has changed. Or, I could find that everything has changed, though I doubt it."

"Has he given you any indication that the two of you are on the same page in your lives?"

"He's attentive as he used to be. He's listening to me when I talk about the renovation projects."

"Projects?"

"Yeah. The big house and Cottonwood."

"Well, darling, that's because *he* is involved. M Michaels will most likely give his company the job. He now has a vested interest."

I sighed. "I've already thought of that, to be honest with you."

"Did you actually discuss anything? About how you've been feeling over the past year? Your restlessness? Or his for that matter?"

"No."

"Why not?"

I had to think before I could answer. The coffeepot coughed and sputtered, and I took that as my cue to get up. Mother, who will never be accused of sitting idly by while someone else is moving about, joined me at the counter and prepared a cup for herself and one for Daddy. I stared at the two cups, then at the one before me. I'd not thought to prepare anything for Evan. Mother stopped what she was doing to stare at me for a moment, then reached in the cabinet for another mug. "Here," she said, followed by, "You're tired. Don't start kicking yourself over such a tiny thing. You've obviously got a lot on your mind. You hardly said three words at dinner."

I nodded, and in silence we took the mugs of coffee to our husbands, then returned to the kitchen. At the table, Mother said, "So. Talk to me. What exactly have you and Evan done toward working things out?"

I pouted. "We've made love."

"Jo-Lynn, don't be vulgar."

"Mother! That's not vulgar. We're married, after all. Didn't you always say that sex is God's gift to the bride and groom?"

She took a sip of coffee. "Yes, but I don't need to have it thrown in my face. I want to know what you've talked about, not what you've done between the sheets."

"Other than the projects and the vandalisms, nothing really."

"What vandalisms? Has something besides the fire happened?"

Mother's earlier reprimand to not kick myself leapt from its imaginary place on my shoulder, ran across the kitchen, jumped through the opened window over the sinks and into the dark of night. "Ugh," I said.

"Jo-Lynn."

"All right, but please don't go ballistic on me."

"I will make no such promises."

I told Mother about everything that had happened after the fire. She mulled my words over then said, "I will personally string my brother by his toes for not telling me this himself."

"Mother, no. I made Uncle Bob and Aunt Mae-Jo promise not to say anything. I didn't want you to worry and I know you well enough to—"

"Well, of course I worry. You are my child, are you not?"

I made a face at her. "That's what you keep telling me." I paused, allowed my finger to run a ring around the rim of my coffee mug. "Mother, do you know about any secrets inside the big house?"

"What do you mean?"

I relayed what Valentine Bach had said to me.

"He's an old man, Jo-Lynn. I have no idea what he's talking about, but I'd suggest that you leave it alone."

"He wants me to draw a diagram of the big house. Not a blueprint per se, but a layout of the rooms."

"Whatever for?"

"I don't know. That's all he told me. And he took me down to the center of town to tell me about buying his wife a pretty scarf for their first Christmas."

Mother said, "Lilly Beth Bach rarely, if ever, came to town. Bettina and I were twelve years old when she died; I didn't know Bettina well until afterward, really. I knew her; I even played with her and visited her in her home, but her mother kept such a tight rein on her. She kept her from all social functions that children typically take part in. But after her mother's death, Bettina became much more involved. Her father saw to that."

"Why do you think Lilly Beth kept Bettina so sheltered?"

Mother paused for a minute before answering. "I have no idea. Miss Lilly Beth always seemed like a sweet woman. And a good mother. Maybe she was just overprotective."

I sipped my coffee. "Could have been."

"She was always very tight-lipped around me."

"Bettina?"

"No, her mother. Bettina used to say that her mother was very fun-loving and talkative, but I never saw any signs of that. I remember feeling as though she were tolerating my being in their home but not really wanting it. Now, Mr. Valentine was another matter. He is now as he's always been, quite the character."

I smiled. "He is that." I paused. "Mother? Whatever happened to Royce Coniff?"

"Royce Coniff? Whatever made you think of him?"

I shook my head. "Oh, I don't know . . . you know how sometimes, you just think . . ."

Mother nodded. "I saw his mother not two weeks ago. She always asks about you, and I always tell her you are doing fine."

"And Royce?"

"He's married. Lives in Colorado, somewhere near Breckenridge. Miriam always brags about his children—to hear her tell it, they're perfect. And apparently, life is good in the Rockies."

"That's nice," I said. "When you see Mrs. Coniff, be sure to tell her I said hello. And say hello, for me, to Royce. And his wife." I pursed my lips. "And his children."

55

I sat propped against the headboard of the bed of Mae-Jo and Bob's guest room with a pad of paper on my lap and a pencil in my hand, the picture of concentration. Next to me, Evan looked the same. While his drawings were of the downtown area, mine were of the big house.

I'd not told him about the conversation I'd had with Valentine Bach nor of the details of the conversation I'd had with Mother. Only that she and I had talked and that she'd wondered where he and I stood.

We were on our way back to Cottonwood at the time. He took his right hand cupped around the gear shift between us, patted my knee, and then returned it to its resting place. "We'll be fine," he said. "I think you know that, right?"

I didn't answer him. The truth of the matter was that I was not completely sure we would. Mother was right in her concerns that we'd not actually talked about anything other than the immediate issues in our lives. I had no assurance whatsoever that life would be any different once I returned home to Druid Hills. And the unspoken issue of my heart remained, that Cottonwood was feeling—inexplicably—more and more like home. Druid Hills was nothing more than the place I lived.

So instead of answering him, I told him about my conversation with the Godwin twins earlier in the day. He listened but commented little.

Mae-Jo and Bob had already gone to bed when we arrived back at their house so we quietly made our way up the stairs and into the guest room, me toting a Wal-Mart bag of clothes from my childhood closet. As we disrobed I told Evan that unless we could get to our room in the big house by the next day, we'd have to get some shopping done for him. He rolled his eyes in response.

And then we sat up in bed like children with coloring books and crayons and drew our pictures. Only mine wasn't coming together. I wadded up page after page and tossed them next to the bed until what appeared to be a white rock pile was on the floor beside me.

"Problem?" Evan finally asked.

I shook my head. "Something isn't right." I had my next attempt of the first floor etched out on the page before me. I pointed to the wall between the dining room and the living room. "I've never noticed this before," I said. "But there's something not lining up here."

Evan leaned over. "I don't see a problem."

"Look." I pointed to the butler's pantry. "If the wall between the dining room and the living room meets in the center, then the butler's pantry would jut out like this." I retraced the lines of the tiny service room.

"Hmm," was my husband's response.

I shook my head, placed the paper and pencil on the bedside table, turned off the table lamp, and then scooted down the mattress with my hips. "I'm tired. This has been one very long day."

Evan leaned over and kissed my forehead. "It has. Sleep well. I'll turn off my light shortly."

288

I found both Valentine Bach and Larry Gansky in the front yard of the big house the following morning. It was early and Sheriff Gansky had come to report his findings over the past twenty-four or so hours, which were nil. "I've had a deputy here two nights in a row, and nothing else seems to have happened."

I looked at Valentine, who looked at his boots and kicked the dust on the ground. "Maybe whatever they were looking for, they found," I said.

"Well, whatever it is, we'll post someone here a few more nights. Hopefully the worst of it is over and the culprits—no doubt young men with too much time on their hands—will come to their senses and stop this nonsense."

"Hopefully."

Sheriff Gansky tipped his cap, then returned to his squad car. Valentine Bach and I watched in silence as he drove away. Only then did I pull the drawing pad of paper from under my arm and say, "I've got a problem with the drawing of this house."

Mr. Valentine pulled a cigarette from his front bib pocket, lit it, then exhaled across his shoulder. "I thought you might."

I had, by now, flipped the cover of the pad open to the rendering of my rough drawing. I pointed to the wall I'd shown to Evan the night before. "Here's the problem."

"Yes, ma'am."

I looked at him, studied his face carefully. "You knew this, didn't you? You knew I'd have a problem with this."

"You didn't hear it from me."

I looked down at the paper again, then to the big house, then back to the paper. I pointed to the wall with my fingernail, tapping the page a couple of times. "Is there . . . is there a room here?" My hand flew up to cup my mouth. "Oh my goodness," I said. I removed my hand. "That's it, isn't it? There's a room between the living room and dining room and behind the butler's pantry. Wait a minute. That's why the room is between the living room and dining room rather than the dining room and kitchen. It's not a butler's pantry at all. It's a gateway to a secret room."

"I can't say." He shuffled away from me, drawing on his cigarette as he went along. "Crew will be here shortly."

I followed quickly behind him. "Mr. Valentine, wait!" I caught up to him. "Tell me what this means."

He stopped. "I can't. I've probably said more than I should have said as it is. I promised your aunt . . . and I'm a man of my word. When I say I won't do something—or will do it—I keep my word. Always have." He shuffled away again, leaving me alone to think.

When I caught up with him once again, I found him behind the house, dipping his head to look under the house, surveying the work from the day before. "Mr. Valentine?"

He righted himself to gaze at me with his amazing blue eyes. "Missy?"

"Can you at least tell me this? You said you and Aunt Stella were friends, but I'm thinking you must have been pretty close to have been the keeper of whatever secret she has concerning this house. As close as she and I are, she's not said a word to me. Nor apparently to my mother, who couldn't imagine why you'd have me draw the house."

For the briefest of moments, Valentine Bach pinked. He looked away from me, turning his face toward town, toward Wright's Department Store, where he'd purchased a pretty scarf for his young bride their first Christmas together and perhaps, I thought, past town to the modest house they'd shared. The house he now shared with their great-grandson all these years after her death. He waited with his wrinkled face illuminated by the morning's sunrise as though expecting someone to say something to him, and then he turned back to me and said, "Stella and me were in love, missy."

I took a step back. "What?" My words were barely audible.

"I've taken quite a cotton to you. That's why I'm telling you all this. But I'm going to ask you not to say anything to anyone."

"Of course not . . ."

"Least of all Stella." He looked away again. "I would never want to hurt her. Not like I did . . . but that was a long time ago. Still. It haunts a man. Try hard as he may to make it all right. To make it all better. To pretend none of it ever happened." It seemed to me the man was having a conversation more with himself than with me.

"Mr. Valentine?"

He looked at me again, shook his head as though to clear it, and said, "Missy, that was near-bout seventy years ago." His voice was strong. "A lot can happen in seventy years."

"I—Mr. Valentine, what happened between you and my aunt?"

He looked to his feet, pulled another cigarette from the pack in his bib, and lit it. "I got married," he said.

I took a moment to digest his words. "Your parents' arrangement," I said in understanding.

"Life was differ'nt back then. Way differ'nt. But I loved Stella." He brought his blue eyes back to mine. They were suddenly vibrant, and in that instant I saw him as a young man, good-looking as he must have been. Handsome in his youth and the world at his fingertips. He'd been in love with one woman and forced to marry another.

I remembered my mother's recollection of how he'd loved his wife and I thought of his declarations concerning the pretty scarf. I said, "But you loved your wife too."

"Oh yes ma'am. In time I loved her very much." The sound of a truck pulling into the driveway shifted his attention. "Sounds like Buster is here with the crew. Good thing he works in Raymore and your laborers live there, I say." He took several steps toward the side of the house leading to the front then looked back at me. "Not a word, missy. Promise me that much."

I nodded. "I promise."

56

Sunday afternoon, after church in the morning and Sunday dinner, as it is called in the South, at noon with Mae-Jo and Bob, Evan returned to Atlanta and to our home in Druid Hills, to Everett and their company. Mark and Karol had joined us for church and the three of them had talked at length in the churchyard afterward while I'd been kept in a small huddle with Arizona and Annaleise, both who—I felt—now considered me to be somewhat of a new big sister, in spite of being old enough to be their mother.

When I'd asked Evan about the conversation between him, Karol, and Mark he replied, "Just business stuff," as though I were no part of it. To best circumvent the topic he then added, "What about the twins? What sage advice did they seek today?"

For reasons I cannot explain, I accepted the diversion.

Valentine Bach had given me the go-ahead to enter the house as of Sunday afternoon, a fact I'd told no one. Nor had I mentioned to anyone, including Evan, about Valentine's teenaged romance with my great-aunt. Additionally, I'd kept the secret room just that: a secret. Evan hadn't bothered to ask about it, and I'd not exerted the energy to tell him. But as soon as his car disappeared from sight, I told Mae-Jo I was going to the big house and I wasn't sure when I'd be back.

"Is it okay for you to walk around in there now?" she asked.

"Yes," I told her. "Mr. Valentine asked that I allow the work on the foundation bricks a few days to set and I've done so. Besides, I can't imagine what harm my one-hundred-and-twelve pounds could possibly render."

"You have a point," she said, then bid me farewell.

The cold inside the big house cut through my coat and the velour of the track pants and hoodie I'd changed into after lunch. I shivered as I stepped purposefully through the living room and toward the door leading to the butler's pantry. Being near the French doors—left opened—I glanced at the staircase and considered going up and into my room to right the wrong of the men who'd rummaged through the boxes. The desire lasted only momentarily. I had a more important mission today.

I opened the door to the pantry. "Good gosh," I muttered. The cold of the living room was like a sauna compared to the tiny space of parallel shelves and counters. I tucked my fisted hands under my crossed arms and looked around. Other than when we'd cleaned out the house, I'd never seen it devoid of items.

The room was dim, and I pushed both doors open to allow for more light, then reached over my head to pull the narrow cord connected to the overhead light. I studied the cracking of the shelves against the wall where I now suspected a secret room lay, swiped a layer of dust from one of the shelves, then tucked my hand back under an arm. I hunched and used my eyes to scan each and every inch of the counters. Finding nothing to indicate a way into the secret room, I squatted, resting my rear on my heels, and opened the cabinets beneath the counter. Though empty and the doors open, it was too dark to see well enough to determine if in fact there was a switch or lever. I frowned, thinking I should have brought a flashlight. I stood, closing the cabinet doors.

Under each countertop were two small drawers. I opened the two belonging to the secret room's wall, pulling them all the way out, peering under them and around them, but finding nothing. I slipped them back into the grooves and pushed them shut. I stretched to see if I could spy anything along the shelves just out of my natural eyesight, but at only five-foot-four and five-foot-five on my tiptoes, it wasn't much use.

I turned my back to the counter, pushed my rear up and on to it, then used the shelves as support to stand. I ducked my head to look under the middle shelf. It was then I found it, a small horizontal lever. I pushed it.

Instantly the counter and shelves shifted. I screamed as though I'd seen a mouse, and continued to hold on to one of the shelves. When the shifting came to a stop, it revealed an opening just large enough for a human body to inch through.

I gingerly sat on the counter then hopped to the floor on both feet. A blast of icy air pushed its way into the pantry, and again I shivered.

With a mixture of curiosity and anxiety, I pushed the door fully open. Then I slipped inside.

57

The room was not what I expected. I'd thought to find something akin to an attic filled with old relics and remembrances, items once found useful and then stored rather than thrown away. But what I found was something closer to a Victorian executive's office. The walls were papered and wainscoted; the floor was covered with a faded vinyl that was patterned with large pink roses with moss-green leaves on a background of colorful swirls. It appeared to have been tacked down along the edges with heavy-duty white flathead thumb tacks. A few had popped up, and the edges had begun to curl.

There was a narrow antique oak rolltop secretary/desk and a Georgian Queen Anne armchair against the left-hand wall, a small round double-tiered table devoid of any ornamentation other than dust in the left corner, and a four-drawer oak filing cabinet in the right. Next to it, a brass spittoon.

I stepped in slowly, looking overhead for a light, turning my body as I went along. I found a single bulb light alongside a framing of a hidden staircase, the cords to both hung parallel to each other. I pulled one, bringing light into the room, then the other and unfolded the ladder-type staircase that now hung suspended in the center of the room.

I took each rung carefully, unsure as to how stable they

might be after all these years. When my head had cleared the opening I peered around to find exactly what I'd expected to find on the floor below. Lopsided boxes were stacked upon lopsided boxes; there were discarded pieces of knickknack furniture covered in sheets or dust, lamps with and without shades, mirrors with and without cracks, framed works of art and photographs and the like.

I stepped back down the stairs, deciding to look for secrets in the newly discovered office before doing the same in the attic.

I pulled the chair away from the wall and over to the desk. I sat and then, avoiding the enclosed interior of the desk for the moment, opened the top drawer. It was empty of everything but a few rubber bands, paper clips, some type of putty, and an old No. 2 pencil. I picked it up and, coaxed by some unknown force, sniffed it. It smelled like the first day of elementary school.

I closed the top drawer and then opened the middle. It was filled with more of the farm's business ledgers. The third drawer revealed nothing but some old photographs of the house and farm during various seasons and crops. One, however, caught my attention. It was a somewhat bent eight-by-ten black and white of the big house taken from the opposite side of Main Street. In it, the barn and stables, storage buildings, and the old split-rail fences were visible as was the west side of the big house. Behind the buildings and fences was a line of massive oak and pecan trees, their naked limbs stretching toward the white of the sky. They appeared to be more spiderwebs than branches, and the entire landscape was covered by a thin blanket of snow. I flipped the photograph over and saw, in handwriting I didn't recognize: "To Nevan and Loretta. My friends always, HLH, II. 1941." I flipped the photo again to look at the glossy image, then nodded. This was the work of Henry Hawkins. I smiled broadly; it was as valuable as finding a random snapshot from the camera of Ansel Adams.

I set the photograph on top of the secretary and then closed the bottom drawer. I placed my fingers through the brass handles of the rolltop and attempted to push it open, but it wouldn't budge. I dipped my head to study it; it was locked. I stood, looked around the desk for a key, along the wainscoting, under the desk, but found nothing. Then I remembered how Aunt Mae-Jo had looked for a key under the desk drawers in the storage unit.

I pulled the top drawer from its place, flipped it, found nothing. Likewise with the middle and bottom drawers. I'd stacked them on the floor so that the first drawer was now at the bottom of the stack. I began pushing them back into place, starting with the bottom drawer, then heaving the middle drawer into place. I reached toward the floor for the top drawer, bringing my rear down into the chair and bending at the waist. As my hands touched the unfinished wood of the drawer's sides, I paused, then looked over my shoulder and up into the rectangular hole left by the drawer's absence. I sat straight then, leaving the drawer behind. I reached my hand into the opening, placing it palm up against the wood under the desk's interior. I patted around until I found what I was looking for, a small metal key held in place by a piece of putty.

The key fell into my hand with a light tug, and I opened the desk.

Inside were letter cubbies filled with stationery—yellowed paper and envelopes—a Bakelite rocker blotter, and an ink pad with a box-shaped stamp. Atop the green leather desk pad was a cast metal desk set comprised of an inkwell, a pen tray set on four cast feet, a letter rack, a stamp box, and a matching letter opener. I picked up the latter and held it toward the light. It had a slight nick on the tip of its blade.

I set it back in its place, then I pulled a piece of paper from one of the cubbies, took the ink pad and stamp, stamped the pad and then the paper.

Nevilles Farms
James Edwards
1 Main Street—Cottonwood, Georgia
Phone: 300

"Wow," I said aloud.

My voice echoed faintly in the narrow room.

I fingered each item of the desk set, thinking that a true gentleman had used this desk but knowing that the room and the items in it predated even him. Before Uncle Jim, Great-grandfather Nevan had used this room.

I found a key in the pen tray. I gathered it out of its longtime resting place and then walked over to the filing cabinet. As I suspected it would, the key fit the lock, and I turned it then pulled open the drawers, each filled, I discovered upon flipping through them, with folders of information only farmers would find of interest. Knowing they might add to the value of the museum, I pulled them from the drawers and walked them over to the desk, where I formed four short stacks.

By the time I'd gotten through the second file, I was sneezing, hopelessly near losing my breath.

And I was bored.

I stopped taking my time with each and every paper of each and every file, choosing instead to hold the other files on their ends and flipping as though thumbing through a book. When I'd placed the seventh or eighth file back in the cabinet I returned to the desk, picked up the next file, and stopped short. Sandwiched between was a large envelope with the words *Thursday Nights* penned in a handwriting I'd come to know well. My great-grandfather's. I picked it up, opened the flap, and slid a thick stack of papers from inside.

I furrowed my brow. "What in the world . . ."

Page after page, some filled with Nevan Nevilles's handwriting, others pasted with newspaper articles, all to do with the Ku Klux Klan. There were minutes to meetings—all held on Thursday evenings—details of activities, monies taken and monies spent, photographs of Klan atrocities, and addresses of "Folks KKK Will Deal With."

Two of the names caught my attention.

Henry Hawkins and Percy Robinson.

"Percy?" I said.

I pointed to the words under the names and read aloud. "Hawkins, Jew, real name: Hurwitz." Then, "Samuels, Negro, November 1947, Poor Man's Pond, S. Pitney (center)." Finally, "Robinson, Negro, December 1947, outside his home, S. Pitney (center)."

The next page showed two blurry photographs—no doubt taken in haste—of the man's body hung from a pine tree near a pond. His arms were haphazardly tied low and in front by a short cord of rope, his bare feet arched downward. His pants were soiled and his shirt—long sleeved and cotton—was torn. His face was swollen, his eyes bugged, his lips parted, and his tongue protruding.

Underneath this photo was another one more horrible than the first. Another black man, this one without a name under the picture, this one with his arms wrapped around a cross-beam and then secured by ropes, this one arched in agony— his naked chest bowed—this one burned to a crisp.

Two local men killed by the Klan. Two lives ended by two appalling deaths. And more inexcusable and unspeakable than the evidence of their murders and the agony etched across their faces were the stares and grins of the white ones—men, women, and even young children—who stood nearby, proud predators of their prey, as though they'd shot, killed, and dressed an eight-point buck on the first day of hunting season.

I gasped, bile rose to my throat, and on impulse, I swallowed. It burned as it returned to its source, and I flipped the page over so as not to see the photos anymore. If a single member of my family was among those in the audience, I didn't want to know. Not now, anyway.

Please, dear God, no!

I remembered, then, Percy recounting that his father had been forced to watch his own father being lynched. I released a breath I'd not realized I'd been holding. I sank back in the chair, feeling strangely exhausted, and with that exhaustion was the knowledge I'd just begged God not to reveal to me.

My great-grandfather was involved with the Klan. I shook my head no; muttered, "It can't be . . . it can't be . . ." over and over, waiting for the truth of those words to somehow plant themselves deep within my heart and then miraculously become truth. If Nevan Nevilles was a part of the Klan, that fact went against everything I'd ever heard about him from Aunt Stella and from Mother. Worse, it darkened my history—my family's history—in ways I couldn't begin to deal with. I began to cry, releasing great sobs that—as with my breath—I'd unknowingly held for far too long.

Renovating this house was supposed to be my legacy, not my shame. I slapped my hands down on the pages then quickly shuffled them together and thrust them back into the envelope. A cloud of dust flew up and I sneezed again. With that the bile returned, and this time with my lunch. My eyes blinded by a remnant of tears, I stumbled toward the spittoon near the oak cabinet and vomited until there was nothing left inside me.

Fifteen minutes later the secret room's door was standing guard once again and I was in my car, driving as fast as the speed limit would allow for the library in Raymore. Beside me was the envelope and information. On top of it, the black-and-white photograph by Henry Hawkins.

58

I could have gone to the house on the hill. I could have run into my father's home office, turned on his computer, and researched myself into oblivion, but I did not. Mother would become curious, and I wasn't sure I had it in me to answer any questions right now. But the public library—even on a Sunday in the South—would be open, and I could use one of the computers, search through decades of microfiche, piles of books and magazines, and without an inquisition.

I was dismayed, upon my arrival, to discover I had but a half hour to work. It was 5:30 and the library closed at 6:00. Having read the notice on a placard near the front door, I turned and went back to the car. There was no need in opening this can of worms now. Instead, I called Mother.

"Hi," I said, giving her my best "cheerful as always" voice.

"Hello, yourself. I just got off the phone with Mae-Jo. She says you've been at the big house all afternoon."

"Yeah, well . . . I'm not now. I'm at the library here in Raymore. Can I spend the night with you and Daddy? I'll want to come back in the morning."

"What are you doing at the library?"

"Mother, can I?" I leaned back against the headrest and

closed my eyes. A headache the size of Georgia was creeping up my spine, wrapping around my neck.

"You know you don't have to ask. But what are you doing at the library?"

"I'll explain when I see you. I need to call Mae-Jo now. I'll see you shortly." I disconnected, started my car, pulled out of the parking lot, and then—at the first red light I came to—dialed Mae-Jo's number. When she answered I told her I'd gotten some brilliant idea for the big house, had come to Raymore to do some research, and needed to come back in the morning so I'd spend the night with my parents. In her endearing way she told me to be careful, enjoy my evening, and she'd see me soon.

In spite of the cold, Mother was standing on the front porch in wait for me, reminding me of a cat preparing to pounce on a piece of string newly discovered in the carpet. She stood between the center columns, resting a shoulder against one, legs crossed at the ankles, dressed in charcoal gray wool slacks and a matching mock turtleneck top and quilted vest. Even from the driveway I could see the complementary sterling silver accessories she wore. Though petite against the massive framework of the Georgian colonial, she stood out like a model waiting for the shutter of a photographer to open and close.

I looked over at the black-and-white Henry Hawkins print in the seat beside me, pulled it onto my lap, then took the packet of Klan information and slid it under the front seat of my car.

"What's that?" Mother asked as I approached from the driveway.

"A photograph. I thought you'd be interested in seeing it." I extended it to her, and she took it. "What are you doing outside? It's getting so cold. Let's go in. Does Daddy have a fire built?"

Mother turned to go inside and spoke to me as she studied the photograph. "My, aren't you twenty questions this evening?"

I coughed out a laugh. "Aren't we the pot calling the kettle black?" I returned.

"Don't be sassy, Josephine Milynn. It isn't Christian on a Sunday, and it certainly is not becoming of a lady of your breeding."

I pretended to fold like a road map as we entered the foyer, where Daddy met us. "I don't know why she insisted on meeting you outside," he said with a chuckle and a hug.

"Hi, Daddy," I said, hugging him back.

"Come in, take a load off," he said, wrapping one arm around my shoulder and leading me into the warm glow of the living room, where a fire blazed, sending heat into the classic elegance brought by Mother's décor. "I just made hot cocoa, and there's a cup waiting for you on the sofa pouf."

I laughed lightly. Whenever my father said the word *pouf* he deliberately inserted a certain highbrow air. "How your mother got me to say the word *pouf*," he'd once said to me, "is anybody's guess."

Mother's pouf was hefty and skirted, large enough in circumference for an ornate silver tray topped with tall mugs of hot cocoa and marshmallows and a short stack of dessert plates and a serving dish of wedding cookies, my all-time favorite store-bought treat. While I helped myself, Mother handed Daddy the photograph.

"Well, how about that," he said. "Goodness, I don't know when I remember that number of buildings in the back."

I popped a cookie in my mouth, then moved to the central seating area and the camelback sofa with way too many pillows. I swallowed and then said, "I wanted to ask you about that."

"They tore several of those down when you were very young," Mother said. She sat then in her favorite chair while Daddy made himself comfortable in its twin a few feet away, cocoa mug cupped in his hands. "Uncle Jim said they weren't necessary anymore because even though he ran the farm successfully, mostly they were unused and becoming a danger to anyone who walked in them. Much like the one you're faced with now."

"I'm tearing it down," I said, taking a sip of my drink. "This is good. I was hungry and didn't know it."

Mother jumped up then and said, "Why didn't you say you hadn't eaten? I'll fix you a sandwich." She was out of the living room before I could blink.

I looked at Daddy. "Did I say I hadn't eaten?" I asked with a wink.

He winked back. "A mother's intuition." He flipped the photo over to read the back. "HLH?"

"I think that's Henry Hawkins. Well, I know it is. His father had a photography studio back when Mother's grandparents were young, and then his son took over. There's a photograph of Aunt Stella as a young woman I'd be willing to bet he took. It has his touch."

"What do you know about Henry Hawkins?" Daddy set the photograph on the table between the two chairs.

"He kept his father's studio going in Cottonwood for a while—I remember Mother telling me this—and then he left and . . . see, he became a famous photographer, Daddy. His photos used to appear in *Land & Home*. I was always taken by his work."

"Whatever happened to him?"

"I don't know. I—"

Mother entered the room then, carrying a plate with a sandwich and some coleslaw. "I don't usually allow eating in the living room, but I suppose you're grown enough not to drop your crumbs on the floor. You know how I hate to run the vacuum."

I made a playful face at her.

"Who were you two talking about?" she asked, never one to be left out of any conversation.

"Henry Hawkins. The second one."

Mother picked up the photo. "Why all this interest, Jo-Lynn? Henry Hawkins lived in Cottonwood, then he didn't."

I took a bite of my sandwich, making sure the plate stayed directly under it. I chewed carefully, then swallowed, following it with a sip of cocoa. "Mother," I said. I tried to keep my voice as nonchalant as possible. "What do you remember about Alfred Pitney?"

"Now why would you want to . . ." Mother gave me her best exasperated look.

"He's a holdout in the town project," I interjected, silently thankful for the information Karol had divulged about him.

"Oh. Well, let's see . . ." She crossed her legs then and leaned back in her chair. This was a good sign all the way around. "He's an old goat, if you'll pardon my expression."

I gave my father a quick look. He sighed as he rose and then walked over to the sofa pouf to replace his mug of now-finished cocoa.

"Okay. What else do you know?"

"He's married to a woman named Diana, who I remember well when she moved to town with her boys. I was grown by then, but Aunt Stella filled my ears with enough gossip to last a lifetime. Not that I partake in gossip. I abhor gossip."

Daddy returned to his chair, and I said, "Daddy, I think I feel a Shirley Jackson short story coming on."

"Whatever are you talking about, Jo-Lynn?" Mother asked.

306

"Shirley Jackson. We had to read her in a high school lit class. She was a somewhat modern gothic writer . . . she wrote . . . oh! She wrote *The Haunting of Hill House.* Maybe she had this house in mind when she wrote it." I raised my brow.

"Don't try to be cute, Jo-Lynn."

I laughed heartily then and felt an afternoon's worth of tension slip from my shoulders, down my spine, and into the soft cushions of the sofa. "I needed this," I said. "Anyway, she wrote a short story called 'Strangers in Town' in which the lead character states that she abhors gossip and then does nothing but gossip the rest of the story."

"Well, I really do abhor gossip. Now, do you want to know about the Pitneys or not?"

"Sorry. Pray continue."

59

According to Mother, Diana Pitney moved to Cottonwood in 1982 when her sons were young—she estimated about five and seven years of age. Perhaps older, she said, or perhaps younger, but not by much. Alfred Pitney, whose family had ties to the Klan, had gone to Atlanta and had returned married and the new father of two very rambunctious sons. Alfred adopted the boys, who Mother estimated to now be in their thirties. Neither son, to her knowledge, was married and—as far as she knew—they both continued to live with Alfred and Diana. "Mae-Jo would know," she said. "Ask her."

I told her I would.

Diana, Mother said, was at least twenty years Alfred's junior. It was rumored, she continued—not that she repeated rumors—that Diana and Alfred had separate bedrooms, which was why they'd never had biological children between the two of them. "Uncle Jim used to say that wasn't true," she said. "He told me once that when a man is as mean as Alfred Pitney, he doesn't have sons, he has demons, and the good Lord knew Cottonwood didn't need any more demons."

"Meaning?"

"Meaning, I suppose, that . . . well, I don't know Jo-Lynn! Why don't you go ask your aunt Stella?"

I didn't respond except to say, "Go on."

"What else do you want to know?"

"Who was Alfred's father?"

"Earl Pitney. Now, him I remember. Not that I don't remember Alfred. Alfred was a year younger than me and used to brag all the time about how bad his father was and how he was going to do thus and such. A real menace in the school. He was expelled so many times I'm not even sure he graduated, though I guess he must have. Today they would say he had ADD or some such, but in those days we just said he did bad things."

"Like what?"

Mother waved her hand in the air. "Oh, I don't know. That was so long ago, Jo-Lynn. Why do you want to know all this?"

I walked over to the table where the Henry Hawkins photo still lay and, walking back to the sofa, said, "Mother, what do you know about the Jewish population in Cottonwood? Back when you were growing up there?"

"The Jewish population? There wasn't a Jewish population, Jo-Lynn. This was Cottonwood."

I turned the photo side of the picture toward her and my father and said, "I have reason to believe that Henry Hawkins was Jewish."

"Jewish?" my father asked, suddenly a part of the conversation.

"Whatever gave you a notion as crazy as that? Not that there's anything wrong with being Jewish, mind you. Jesus himself was Jewish."

"Yes, Mother, I know. But as to Henry Hawkins . . . all I can say right now is that I've got a hunch. A pretty solid hunch, but just a hunch nonetheless."

"And this hunch is based on?" Daddy asked.

I pressed my lips together. "I'd rather not say at this time. But, Daddy, I wouldn't even say it here in the privacy of this room if I didn't suspect it were so." Just as I said the words, my cell phone—buried in the crevices of my purse and my purse still in the foyer—rang.

I stood. "Probably Evan." I glanced at my watch. "He's due home about now."

I walked into the hall, retrieved my phone—which by now had stopped ringing—saw that the call was from Evan, and then said, "I'm going to call him back upstairs in my room."

They both nodded as I turned and bounded up the stairs.

I elected not to say anything to Evan about my day other than, "Oh, nothing much. I'm at Mother and Daddy's now. Thought I'd stop by and visit. I'll probably spend the night here and go back tomorrow. Gas prices and all that."

He seemed unfazed, instead telling me that he and Everett had talked during half of his trip back to Druid Hills and that Everett, like Evan, was excited about the prospects of getting the M Michaels account. "Who knows where this could lead," he added, then—for good measure—threw in, "Everett says to tell you to hurry home."

The words stopped my breathing until I managed to say, "And why is that?"

"Oh . . . well . . . I stopped by their place on the way home and he says I'm looking much better since my time with you." He chuckled. "I have to agree with him. Hurry home."

"Or maybe you can hurry back to Cottonwood," I said, my voice timid and unsure.

"What does that mean?"

I felt funny somehow, then. My ears clogged, my head

spun, and I could hear my heart beating from deep inside me. Finally I said, "I mean, wouldn't you be coming back here before I'll get back there?" Now, I decided, was not the time to tell him how much at home I'd come to feel and that I wanted desperately to stay in Cottonwood when it was finished.

"Oh, sure," he answered. "Of course I'll be coming back there. *If* we get the nod from Mark."

"You know you will. He seems quite taken with you, and if you give him the right specs, well then there's no doubt you'll get the job."

"Yeah, I feel that way too," my husband said.

When I went back downstairs my father was standing in front of the fireplace and my mother was nowhere to be found. "Where's Mother?" I asked.

"She's cleaning away the dishes in the kitchen."

He pointed to the sofa where I'd been sitting earlier. Next to the faint indentation of where I'd sat was a book. "What's this?" I asked, picking it up.

"I remembered that when you went upstairs. It has a lot of information I think you're fishing for but not quite using the right bait."

I looked from my father to the cover of the book. Its title, *Knights of Terror*, was written in red. The background was the commonly used white hood of a Klansman. I looked back at my father. "Why do you think I want to know about this?" I asked.

"Alfred Pitney? Hawkins being Jewish? Even I know about Alfred Pitney's reputation, and I'm not from around here." He took a step toward me. "What are you looking for, Jo-Jo?"

I smiled at him. "Jo-Jo" was an endearment he'd used for me when I was a child. I hadn't heard it in years and it made me feel warm and safe. "Daddy," I answered, shaking my head, "I really can't say right now."

311

From the kitchen the faint sounds of Mother "closing up shop" could be heard.

"Best hide that," Daddy said, "before your mother sees it. If she thinks for one second you're wanting to know about the Klan, there's not a torture technique she won't try to drive it out of you."

I nodded, dashed out of the room, and managed to drop the book into my hobo purse before the tap-tap-tap of Mother's shoe heels hit the marble floor of the entryway.

Before we went to bed we watched a little television, made small talk, and then said good night. I prepared for bed quickly, then propped up in bed with the book Daddy had given me. I opened the book to the middle, where the story of Viola Liuzzo, a thirty-nine-year-old white civil rights activist from Michigan who, horrified by the news reports of the attacks against marchers at the Edmund Pettus Bridge and against the concerns and wishes of her husband, drove to Alabama to volunteer as marchers—along with Dr. Martin Luther King—came to protest. She went alone and in her own car, the story said, leaving at home a husband and five children.

I inhaled deeply. Mrs. Liuzzo and I had something in common, I thought. Though I had not come to Cottonwood because of my convictions about civil rights, I'd come against my husband's protests. "Sometimes," I said aloud and to no one, "a woman has to do what's in her heart, no matter what."

I returned to the story. It was March 25, 1965, and Mrs. Liuzzo—along with a nineteen-year-old African American named Leroy Moton—had just heard Dr. King deliver a speech. "How long will it take?" he asked the enraptured crowd. "Not long," he answered. "Because mine eyes have seen the glory of the coming of the Lord." Together—and with others—Viola and Leroy ferried marchers from Montgomery to Selma. With a load of passengers dropped off, she and

Leroy headed back to Montgomery for another load. When they stopped at a traffic light, another car—a blue Ford—pulled alongside.

Ford, I thought, closing my burning eyes. Henry Ford was well known for his anti-Semitism. I breathed out heavily. "How is it," I spoke aloud, praying in nothing above a whisper, "that so much ignorance can survive in a land where men came to worship you freely?"

I continued reading. For twenty miles the blue Ford, filled with four Klansmen, chased Liuzzo's car, at times up to one hundred miles per hour. I felt my heart race, wondered at what might have gone through the mind of this young wife and mother, what words screamed between her and Leroy or the two of them toward the maniacs giving chase might have occurred. I shuddered but kept reading.

After twenty miles the Ford overtook Liuzzo's Oldsmobile. As they sped along the highway, Viola Liuzzo turned her head to look at the Ford, staring in the face the coldhearted man who would then murder her by sending two bullets into her head. Liuzzo fell against the wheel, and Moton—splattered with blood—grabbed the wheel, turned the car to the right, and applied the brakes. They soared down and up a ditch then came to rest against a roadside fence. Leroy Moton faked death until it was safe for him to leave the car. He ran until he was picked up by a fellow marcher.

Inside the blue Ford was Gary Thomas Rowe, an FBI informant who later aided in the arrest of the three others.

I sat a little straighter and kept reading. A trial began May 3, 1965, and an all-white jury was selected. It ended in a mistrial. Days later the three men took part in a parade that ended with a standing ovation for them.

I sighed in disgust.

It wasn't until October of that year that another trial was

set, another all-white jury selected, and—two days later—an acquittal was handed down.

Eventually justice prevailed. In a federal trial the men were charged with conspiracy under the 1871 Ku Klux Klan Act. By the year's end, the three men were found guilty and each sentenced to ten years in prison.

Viola Liuzzo had not died in vain. In addition to her murderers being convicted, her death helped aid in the resulting Voting Rights Act being passed by Congress.

After finishing the story, I flipped to the index and looked for information concerning the Klan and Jews. I read for another hour, then fell asleep with the book spread wide over my heart.

60

I left my parents' home early the next day and went to Trish's for a cup of tea and a cranberry scone. The morning was absolutely glorious, a hint that the winter cold was nearly at an end and the spring was upon us. I sat by a plate glass window overlooking the district's center and looked out as storefronts opened to welcome patrons to their businesses. A couple of young men stood near a street lamp, one leaning his shoulder against it, the other standing no more than a yard from him, both sipping on cups of steaming coffee served in to-go cups with "Trish's Tea Room" scripted around them. The two men were deep in conversation, as though time held no boundaries or schedules for them. As one spoke, the other smiled, and then, a moment or so later, the roles reversed. Every so often they bellowed together in laughter. They were, without a doubt, friends.

Several shoppers passed between the two men and the window behind which I sat. None appeared to be in any particular hurry. Intermittently, a few dog owners and their pets strolled by, leashes pulled taut by animals more ready to get where they were going than the humans who held them.

For at least a half hour I watched and observed life in Raymore as it rose to a new day in the upscale, newly refurbished business district. I sat alone and quiet, thinking thoughts that had not occurred to me in so long I couldn't remember when they'd last crossed my mind.

Two men talking . . . one black, one white. Dog walkers . . . some black, some white. Shoppers . . . many races, many backgrounds.

I turned my attention to the inside. *Trish's patrons . . . mostly white, some black. White servers waiting on black patrons . . .* I thought about the days of my great-grandfather and even of myself when I was younger. Could they or we have ever guessed it would be this way? Could they have guessed, even, that not only would our country see a rise in biracial births but that we would have elected a biracial president?

I thought about the "colored" signs. Signs such as "Coloreds Enter in Back" and "No Coloreds Served." I remembered the two water fountains in the center of town, long ago ripped from their stations. I thought about the day the two black kids—no longer willing to be relegated to the tiny pool on Anderson Street—showed up at the "white" recreation department's Olympic-size pool and how most of the white swimmers had glided to the sides of the pool, watching intently to see what they would do.

Thinking on it now, I knew those two young people were as nervous and unsure about being there as we'd been. They entered the pool area from the shower rooms, shoulders back, eyes scanning the lay of the land. Having their bearings, they walked all the way to the deep end of the pool, climbed down the ladder, slipped into the cool refreshment of the chlorine water, swam a couple of laps side to side, then pulled themselves from the water and walked back toward the shower rooms, which served as both entrance and exit.

They'd made their stand and it was time to go home. Or perhaps back to Anderson Street, where they'd tell their peers about what they'd done and what we'd done. Or hadn't done.

I happened to be in the shallow end at the time, near the wide steps leading from the cement perimeter and into the water. It was from there I'd watched the whole thing, not moving, not saying anything, only listening to the hush of wild children and the occasional whispers that said, "Just don't look at them. If we don't make a big deal out of it, they'll leave."

But when they'd passed by me—me, all of eleven or twelve at the time—I'd looked up at them. Their dark skin was so foreign. Other than our maid, I'd never been close enough to study a person called "colored."

Sitting in Trish's I recalled how the water still clung to their lean bodies, giving them the appearance of sleek eels, and beaded on the tight curls of their hair. As they passed by me, one caught my eyes with his own, and unexpectedly I said, "Bye now."

He smiled at me—straight white teeth prominent against black skin—and I smiled back. And then he winked and shook his head.

I wondered now what had ever happened to the two young men. They never returned. In fact, not a single black person the rest of my growing-up years in Raymore visited the pool. But the two had set a precedent, and a curtain had been lifted. Two months later a handful of black students were bussed to our school. The year after that we were bussed to theirs. By the time we'd graduated high school we—both black and white—knew at least one universal truth: all men might be *created* equal but not all men *live* the same.

I supposed, sitting in the upscale tea room called Trish's, that the blight and horrors of the Civil War were to America what the Holocaust was to Europe.

I glanced out the window again and noticed a glint of sunlight against metal near the doorway of a business across the way. I leaned over the table and squinted, turning my head in

317

an attempt to make it out. It wasn't the address numbers and it wasn't a part of the security system. I tilted my head a bit more, felt the bones in my neck pop, said "Ow," then nearly jumped out of my seat as a voice behind me said, "What are you looking at?"

I turned to see Karol standing behind me. I pointed across the street and she leaned over the table, pointing her nose toward the glass pane of the window. "That," I said. "That piece of metal near the door of the jewelry store."

"Moskovitz's?"

"Yes."

She pressed closer to the window then stood back and said, "Oh! That's a mezuzah."

"I'm sorry?"

"A mezuzah." She sat at the table across from me and continued. "It's a parchment inscribed by hand and then put in a protective, usually ornamental, case and hung on doorposts of Jewish homes and businesses."

I furrowed my brow at her. "A parchment?"

"Yeah. It has Scripture from the Torah on it. From Deuteronomy, to be specific."

I was about to ask how she knew this when one of Trish's servers approached with a teacup and saucer and a small teapot steeping an aromatic brew. Karol asked if she could join me, I said of course, and the server placed the items on the table. I was asked if I'd like anything more; I said no, and when the young woman had stepped away I said, "And you know this because . . ."

Karol sat, began to prepare her tea—seemingly nonplussed—and said, "Remember stepdaddy dearest?"

"The game show producer?"

She placed the teapot on the table and took a sip of tea. "One in the same."

318

"Yes."

"He's Jewish. Not a practicing Jew, if you know what I mean, but his mother—*Bubbee* Taubie—now, she was in every way Jewish! Ask me anything about the high holy days, Hanukkah and Purim, bar mitzvahs, matzo balls . . ."

I laughed as Karol's accent changed while speaking the last few words, and she laughed with me. When our voices had died out, I again looked out the window. We remained silent until I said, "Isn't it funny."

"Isn't what funny?"

I shook my head, unsure whether or not to tell Karol what I'd learned in the last twenty-four hours. Although we certainly were more acquaintances than actual friends, I'd come to trust Karol. She never tried to be anything different than what she was: direct, outspoken, funny, open to try things, ready to listen, intuitive, and—for lack of a better word—basic. The old saying "what you see is what you get" fit her, and yet I knew there was so much more to her than one could learn in a lifetime. I also knew that even though I'd known Karol in *days* and I'd known Everett's wife Kit in *years*, I would trust Karol over Kit with what I now knew about my family's sordid history.

I finally settled on, "I hadn't really thought so much about Jewish families being in this area until yesterday and now—twice in two days—it's right here in front of me."

"Well of course there are Jewish people in this area. Savannah boasts the oldest Jewish congregation in the South; didn't you know that?"

"No. And, pray tell, how did you know that? Surely Bubbee Taubie didn't tell you that."

She grinned at me. "No. But, like I've told you before, it's my job to know everything."

"Mmm-hmm."

Karol took another sip of her tea and then added more

from the teapot to the cup. "Did Evan make it back to Atlanta okay?"

I nodded then took the last bite of scone. "You aren't hungry?"

"No," she said. "I had dinner last night with Elder Timothy and Sister Cheryl." Another Cheshire cat grin was sent from across the table.

"No way."

She nodded proudly. "Yes way. They called me at the inn yesterday afternoon and asked if I'd like to join them." Karol patted her stomach. "I may not eat again for a week. Cheryl had a spread—that's what she called it, a spread—like nothing I've ever seen—which is what *he* called it. 'Isn't this like nothing you've ever seen?'" She sipped at her tea again, then added, "I don't care how young you Southern women are, you certainly know how to cook and you cook a lot for one meal. It must be inbred."

"May be," I said.

Karol studied me then. "What's on your mind, kiddo?"

I shrugged. "Nothing really." I focused then on the rim of my teacup.

"Are you missing Evan?"

I looked up at her, felt my face grow warm. Truth be told, I hadn't had time to miss him. But instead of being honest about it, I said, "Sure. Of course I do."

She narrowed her eyes. "But that's not it. That's not what's bothering you."

I leaned over the table, placing my forearms against the edge of it, one folded over the other, and said, "Can you keep a secret?"

She mimicked my position and asked, "What kind of secret?"

"Does it matter?"

"No, but . . . okay. Shoot."

I took a deep breath and blew it out my nose. "I've found a secret room in the big house."

"A secret room? Define please."

"Do you remember the butler's pantry oddly situated between the living room and the dining room?"

"Rather than the dining room and the kitchen? Yeah."

"It's not a butler's pantry. It's an entryway to a hidden room. There's an office behind the shelves. That and a flight of stairs leading to an attic of sorts. Not the attic of the house, mind you, but sort of a hidden junk room."

She paused; to think, I suppose. "Is there something more to this?" She shook her head. "A skeleton chained to the leg of a desk or something?"

I frowned. She might be amused, but I wasn't. My family was linked to things I could barely think of, much less talk about. "Sort of. I found files that show my great-grandfather was a member of the Ku Klux Klan."

Karol leaned back in her seat and crossed her legs and arms. "Jo-Lynn, I thought you were born and reared here."

"I was."

"Then surely you know—you, a smart and educated woman of the South—that most people who have ancestry here would be able to make the same statements."

I shook my head. "No, you don't understand. It's worse than that. I found proof that my great-grandfather was involved in the murders of several black men." I waved my hand. "Not that their being black has anything to do with—I mean, it has something to do with it but . . . what I'm trying to say is *men* were murdered. Black or white, makes no difference to me. Karol, I was a part of the desegregation of the South. I remember it well; every positive and negative thing about it."

"Like?"

"Like . . ." I felt the cheeks of my face grow hot. "Like I remember my mother not thinking twice about the fact that a black woman came to our home twice a week to clean and help with laundry, but when I wanted to bring a black girl home from school with me because we were supposed to work on a science project together, my mother had a fit. It was one thing if they came into the house to work but quite another if they came into the house to study with her daughter."

Karol raised her chin. "Go on."

"Shari Franklin. I still remember her name. The smartest girl in our class. By virtue of the fact she was my partner, I was guaranteed an A on the project. I was so excited."

"Because of the A?"

"Certainly. I struggled to make Bs, Karol. This was a guaranteed A. I remember telling my friends—my white friends—how excited I was. Shari Franklin was coming to my house—the house on the hill—and we were going to study together. I remember my friend Jennifer saying her mother would have one natural born hissy fit if she brought a black girl home. To which I replied, 'Oh, I'm quite sure my mother will open wide the doors.'"

"Only she didn't."

"No. And I had to go to school the next day and lie to Shari that Mother was having the house repainted and the house reeked of Dutch Boy and could we meet at the library instead." I felt my eyes sting with tears.

"You've never really gotten over that."

"No. Shari Franklin didn't buy it, either. She didn't hold it against me, but she didn't buy it. And she didn't bother to ask if I'd like to come to her house instead."

"What did she do?"

"She pressed her lips together and nodded and said, 'Oh, I understand. That's fine. We'll just meet at the library. No problem.' But it was a problem. It was a huge problem. I promised myself that when I grew up and could have people in my home I'd not be bigoted like Margaret Tatem-Teem."

"And have you?"

I opened my mouth to answer, then closed it, then opened it again. "Have I what?"

"Opened your home to anyone, no matter their race?"

"Of course."

Karol gave me a sideward grin.

"I do."

"How often?"

I crossed my legs. "I don't know. I don't think about it, really. I don't have—" I stopped short.

"You don't have what?"

"I don't really have a lot of friends. Of any race."

Karol sat stunned. "Are you serious? You? You're so . . . so . . ."

"So what?"

Karol straightened. "So friendly. You have impressed me as being one of *those* girls—you know, like from back in our school days? The cheerleader, the homecoming queen, the class princess . . . whatever."

"Oh well. *Here* I had a lot of friends because I grew up here. I lived in the house on the hill, for heaven's sake. My mother was Margaret Tatem-Teem."

"And in Atlanta you live in Druid Hills and your husband is Evan Hunter. That's equally as impressive."

"But it's just not home." I felt my eyes widen. "Oh my goodness, I've never said that out loud before." I giggled without control as I watched Karol fight to compose her expression.

"So then where is home?" she asked me when I'd sobered.

I closed my eyes slowly and then, just as slowly, reopened them. "Cottonwood." I nodded twice. "Home is Cottonwood."

61

Karol tagged along with me to the library—an average-size building stocked with shelved books that smelled like elementary school sans the old librarian's pungent perfumes—where we spent nearly an hour looking up any and all information on Henry Hawkins. Henry Lewis Hawkins Jr.—famed landscape photographer—was born in 1898 in Cottonwood, Georgia. In 1918 he'd married Ellen Gibbons. Their daughter—an only child—was born in 1920.

"Jane Hawkins," I said to Karol, who stood behind the bar stool I sat upon as we perused the Internet via one of the library's four computers. I turned my head slightly and spoke over my shoulder. "I remember that name. She and my great-aunt were best friends when they were children."

"Keep reading," Karol said. From the tone of her voice, I could tell she loved a good mystery.

We continued in our search.

Jane Hawkins had married famed photojournalist Lyn Blackstone in 1942 and lived with him in Chicago, where they raised four children.

Henry Hawkins Jr. died in 1995 at the age of ninety-seven, in the home of his only child. Jane Hawkins Blackstone returned to her Southern roots, one article said, in 2004 at the age of eighty-four and resides with her daughter, novelist Kirstin Blackstone Stein.

"Wow," I said. "That's the woman who writes all the mystery novels."

"I've never heard of her," Karol said.

I glanced over my shoulder and snickered. "What? You've never heard of Kirstin Blackstone Stein? And here I thought you knew everything."

"Nearly. I'm just not a big novel reader."

"I only know of her—to be honest—because Mother insists on sending me her books every time they release. Autographed personally to me, by the way."

"Do tell."

I swung around on the bar stool. "Kirstin Blackstone Stein lives in Savannah. I'm not sure how well she knows Mother, but Mother makes out like she's practically on her Christmas card list."

Karol stepped around me and tapped on the monitor's face with her fingernail. "Only I don't think Mrs. Stein sends out Christmas cards."

I shook my head. "No, probably not. Then again . . . I was reading a book last night about the Klan. According to it, a lot of Jewish people changed their names, especially in the 1940s when the Klan joined the German-American Bund."

"Which was financed by the Nazi party."

I sighed. "Back to your being smarter than me."

She patted my shoulder. "Bubbee Taubie, remember? I'll tell you something else I know; Bubbee's maiden name was Schwartzstein. A lot of Schwartzsteins changed their name to Blackstone."

"Are you serious?"

"As a heart attack. So you think the Hawkins family was originally Jewish?" Karol asked.

"I know they were. The paperwork I found yesterday stated that before they were called Hawkins, their last name was Hurwitz."

"Where is the paperwork?"

I leaned down and pulled my hobo purse from the floor. I opened it and pulled the large envelope of information from its insides. "It's musty and dusty, but it's all in here."

Karol took the envelope as she nodded. "So what do you want to do now? Now that you know a brief history of the Hurwitz/Hawkins family."

I swung around on the bar stool to look at the monitor again. "Jane Hawkins Blackstone lives in Savannah. If we can find her daughter, we can find Jane. Maybe we can find out more about what happened in 1947. Namely why her father's name was on the list of people the Klan was to deal with and yet he wasn't . . . dealt with."

"At least not that you know of."

"Yeah." I faced Karol again.

Karol balanced the envelope against her middle and flipped through a few pages before she looked up at me. "Why is this—all of this—so important to you? Because your great-grandfather was involved and now you think we'll have to place this little revelation in the museum?"

"Not entirely, but yes."

"Look, Jo-Lynn," she began as she pushed the papers back inside the envelope. "All praise and honor to the Daughters of the Confederacy and all that, but we *can* keep this on the DL if you'd like. Mark Michaels would kill me if he knew I'd said that, but believe me when I tell you I know what it's like to have some family skeletons in the closet."

I looked down at the envelope she was extending toward me. Taking it I said, "It's not just that."

"What then?"

I slid the envelope back into my purse then hopped down from the stool. "I think I now know what those men were after. And I think it's right here inside my purse," I said, then walked away, leaving Karol to stare after me.

I called Mother from the car with Karol sitting beside me. "Mother," I said, sounding as upbeat as possible, "you'll never believe what I found out."

"What's that?"

"Do you remember the photograph I showed you last night?"

"Of Aunt Stella's house?"

"That's the one." I looked over at Karol and winked. I was using my car's Bluetooth system, allowing her to eavesdrop on the conversation. "Remember I told you it was taken by Henry Hawkins?"

"Yes, I remember."

"Well, turns out—are you ready for this?—Henry Hawkins is the grandfather of your favorite author, Kirstin Blackstone Stein."

"Are you serious? Oh, how absolutely fascinating, Jo-Lynn. You know, I bumped into her recently—well, this past Christmas—at a charity event over in Savannah. A lovely luncheon at Savannah Station—"

Karol cupped her hand over her mouth to keep from laughing out loud while I said, "Well, Mother, here's the deal. I'm on my way now to Savannah and I'd like to talk with Mrs. Stein about her grandfather."

"Oh, Jo-Lynn. Really, now . . . this has gone far enough, don't you think?"

"No, Mother, I don't. You can help me find this woman or you can hold me up, but I will find her. If I have to hit every bookstore in Savannah, I'll find someone who knows her and where she lives."

Mother gave me her trademark sigh. "Oh, all right. Hold on. I have her address here somewhere."

I heard the plunk-thunk of the phone as Mother set it down against a hard surface, I imagined the kitchen countertop. I glanced over at Karol, who was looking at me. "That was easy enough," she said, to which I replied, "It's not over yet. I'll probably have to have dinner at her house for a month."

The rustling of the phone being retrieved cut our conversation short. Mother spoke, saying, "Do you have something to write with? No, you're in your car."

"It's okay, Mother. I have a memory like an elephant's."

"Mmm," Mother said, then gave me the address.

I hung up the phone after thanking Mother profusely and then said, "I hope she doesn't live in a gated community."

"I hadn't thought of that," Karol said. "Oh well. Time will tell."

62

Kirstin Blackstone Stein did not live in a gated community. In fact, the subdivision she lived in was anything but ostentatious, giving me quite a chuckle. I was certain that the great dame of the house on the hill expected nothing less than a modern akin to the type of homes that stretch broadly along the azalea-blossomed and palm-tree-lined Victory Drive.

Karol and I approached the front door. I said, "Do you think this is really it?"

"I expected something more," she said. "After all, she's a bestselling author."

I shrugged. "Well, who knows?"

I rang the doorbell and we waited. A moment later footsteps came from within and then the front door opened wide. Before us stood a woman no more than five feet tall, with long black hair that curled wildly to her shoulders and had a shock of gray near the temple. Her jaw was square and her eyes bright as she peered at us and blinked. "Oh," she finally said with a laugh. "I thought you were my son. He's always forgetting his key."

I looked at Karol, who looked at me, and then together we turned back to the woman framed by the door. "No," I said. "Are you Kirstin Blackstone Stein?"

She breathed out heavily. "Oh, please don't tell me you're a fan. Not that I wouldn't love to see you—if you are a fan—but I'm afraid my house is not 'adoring fan' ready."

"No," I said again. "Actually, my name is Jo-Lynn Hunter." I glanced at Karol. "This is my friend Karol Paisley."

"Karol with a K," Karol said, extending her hand for a handshake.

Kirstin rested her hand against the edge of the door, no doubt ready to close it in our faces. "Look," she said. "I'm not sure who you are, but if you are with a church . . . I'm Jewish and I'm not interested in converting. If you're selling magazines, I have more than I can read now. In fact, if I start reading the stacks in my living room and don't quit till I die, there will still be a mountain of them to bequeath to my children. And if you are taking a survey, I have no opinions today. Maybe tomorrow, but don't count on it."

I couldn't stifle my laughter. "Mrs. Stein, my mother is Margaret Tatem-Teem—"

Eyes widened as she said, "Margaret Tatem-Teem? Good land of the living, what brings Margaret's daughter here?" She took a step back. "Come on in. My goodness, why didn't you say so?"

Karol and I stepped into the foyer as I reached into my purse and pulled out the photo of the big house. Kirstin took note of my movement and stopped to stare at the photograph. Reaching for it she said, "My grandfather took this?"

"I think so," I said. "How did you know?"

She laughed. "The light. He always said, 'Follow the light and you'll get the best shot.'" She pointed to the light behind the house. "And there's just something about his touch. I can spot it anywhere."

I looked around us then. The foyer—short and wide—was heavily decorated in framed photography that could belong to no one but Henry Hawkins. "Yes," I said. "Me too. His work was phenomenal."

330

"Are you here to talk about my grandfather?" She crossed her arms, my photograph dangled beside her waist from between her fingers. "Are you reporters from Raymore or something?"

I shook my head, but before I could answer, she added, "Would you like a cup of tea? Mother and I were just about to sit out in the garden and have a cup. What a lovely afternoon after this recent cold snap." She turned and made her way into the house; Karol and I followed. Shortly afterward, we—Kirstin, Karol, and I—were seated in thickly cushioned teakwood chairs around a matching low table while Jane Hawkins Blackstone lounged in a chaise with a thick plaid throw covering her legs. Her arms were kept warm by a bulky red sweater that pulled out the pink in her cheeks and made her white hair look all the more cottony. Though she was the same age as Aunt Stella, I could not help but see the differences in them. Aunt Stella was still—at over ninety years of age—full of spitfire. Jane Blackstone seemed more like a fragile china doll than a human being and, like a collector's doll, far too delicate to touch. In the first moments of our teatime, she looked at me with watery brown eyes and said, "So, you are Stella's great-niece. My, my . . ."

When we'd each had about a half a cup of tea and all the comments that could be made about the beauty of the garden had been made, I turned to Kirstin and said, "I'd like to come right to the point, if I may."

She smiled at me; tiny crow's-feet formed at the corners of her eyes. "I was hoping you would."

I reached for my purse, which I'd dropped at my feet when we'd sat, and pulled the large envelope from its satiny insides. Handing it across the table I said, "I live in Atlanta, Georgia, but I'm currently staying in Cottonwood to renovate the house my great-aunt grew up in."

"Such a lovely house," Jane Blackstone said in her fairy-like voice. "I played many a day in that house."

We all looked at her, and I smiled. "Miss Jane," I began. "I found some papers in the house." I glanced over at the envelope Kirstin had yet to open. "Papers indicating that Henry Hawkins—your grandfather—was of Jewish descent."

"Yes?" The word was more a question than an affirmation, but the question was left open-ended and I read it to say, "And your point?"

"You know this."

"Of course I know this."

Kirstin opened the envelope then, slid the paperwork from inside, and began to leaf through it.

"Miss Jane," I said, then took a deep breath and exhaled. "What can you tell me about the Klan in Cottonwood?"

"The Klan?" Kirstin asked, stopping in her personal investigation with the paperwork. Then looking down again she said, "Oh, this is horrible."

"You want to know about the Klan?" Miss Jane asked.

"Specifically in Cottonwood," I said.

"Why do you want to know about something like that?"

I took another deep breath and fought back the tears I feared would surface. "Miss Jane, I have reason to believe my great-grandfather was a member."

She chuckled then. "I would find that hard to believe . . . but in those days it was difficult to know."

"Can you tell me more about your family?" I asked. "And about how your grandfather went from Hurwitz to Hawkins?"

"In those days it was often necessary—or it felt necessary— to change your name and to attempt to fit in with Christian society. It was not an altogether uncommon practice. Then, of course, there was the Holocaust. World War II. It was not safe to be Jew or Japanese, though the threat came not from the same source."

"You left your name as Hawkins, but I assume you've returned to your Jewish faith?"

"Yes. What we practiced in secret we eventually could practice in public. This was one reason why I wanted to live in Chicago."

Just then Kirstin pulled a legal-sized yellowed envelope from the back pages of the envelope, those I'd yet to read through. I watched as she flipped the back flap and then pulled several sheets of tri-folded pages. She read the first page, then pulled it away from the rest and read the next and the next until she'd reached the end. Her face seemed intent, her lips moving ever so slightly as she read. A true writer, I thought, is first a researcher.

"Anything of interest?" I asked.

"I really wouldn't know." She looked at her mother. "Mom," she said. "You and Stella Nevilles were good friends when you were girls?"

"Oh my, yes."

"Did you know a . . ." She paused as she glanced down at one of the pages. "Valentine Bach?"

"Mr. Valentine?" I asked, reaching for the papers. "What does he have to do with this?"

Kirstin extended the papers over the table toward me. As I began to read—first the birth certificate of a baby girl born to Stella Nevilles in December 1939 in Rome, Georgia, and the next several pages the legal adoption of the child by Valentine and Lilly Beth Bach—my hand flew to my mouth. "Oh my . . . oh my . . ." Tears once again rushed to the corners of my eyes, but this time I willingly allowed them to spill down my cheeks.

"What is it?" Karol asked, reaching for the papers.

Blindly I handed them to her. "It's too much," I said. "That's what it is; it's too much."

63

I sat in the passenger's seat of the car while Karol drove my Lexus on the darkening road to Cottonwood. She said little while I read and reread every word, every line, and examined every jot and tittle. Every so often I exclaimed my frustration at this new revelation in what seemed to be an overwhelming list of revelations, usually in loud sighs.

"What is it," Karol finally asked, "that is really bothering you? That your aunt had a child you didn't know about or that Valentine and Lilly Beth Bach adopted her?"

It was then that the impact of who this child was and is fully hit me. I sat straight and grabbed Karol's shoulder. "Bettina Bach Godwin."

"What?"

"Miss Bettina. Bettina Bach Godwin is Aunt Stella's daughter."

"Well, of course. I know the birth certificate just says 'baby girl Nevilles,' but are you just now getting that?"

I pushed myself back in the seat and stared straight ahead. It seemed to me the dividing line in the center of the highway was coming at us too quickly and the place where the road disappeared was much too far away. It was as if we'd travel on for days or weeks or perhaps even years, and though we'd stay on course, we'd never reach our destination. The foliage on either side of the road sped by in deep shades of green and brown and gray. Trying to keep my eyes on it—trying to focus on just one tree or just one branch or one cluster of leaves—made me dizzy and nauseous.

At least I told myself that was what it was. I closed my eyes against the scene and tried to wrap my mind around what my heart was trying to come to grips with, the knowledge I'd gained in the hours of one day. My great-grandfather, a man I'd never known but had grown to respect by virtue of legend and story, was a murderer. My whole life I'd heard the singing of his praises. Even in the meager population of Cottonwood, he was a man still today revered and respected. How could I possibly expose him for what he really was? Perhaps in the 1930s and 1940s it didn't matter but . . .

"But even then they wore sheets."

I wasn't aware I'd spoken out loud until Karol cut her eyes toward me briefly then looked back at the road. "What?"

I blinked a few times, then said, "I was just thinking that if I expose my great-grandfather for being a murderer rather than this icon I've always been told about, I will hurt my family. After all, they wore sheets, didn't they? Why? So people wouldn't know who they were."

"But don't you think, Jo-Lynn, that most people from around here know that their grandparents or great-grandparents—if they were of a certain skin color—held the same beliefs your great-grandfather did? The photos you have—even those very few—show exposed faces of men, women, and children near the bodies of those murdered. They're standing there looking like they've come to see the opening of Barnum and Bailey, for crying out loud." She took a much-needed breath. "Look, I've been here for a couple of months, and I can tell you the prejudices around here—and they go both ways—are thicker than blood with some of these people."

"I know, I know."

"So do you really think you're going to shock anyone? Sheets or not?"

"I don't know. I only know that my family has been held in the highest regard in both Cottonwood and Raymore as long as I can remember. I don't want people to miss the good they've done because of the evil they've done."

"Not *they*, Jo-Lynn. *He*."

I shook my head. "Not just him. My aunt had a child, Karol, out of wedlock, in a place and period when girls of her . . . breeding didn't do things like . . . *that*. And more than that, my aunt has lied to me. She's lied to everyone. She has a child, a daughter, living not five miles from her the child's whole life and she treats her like any one of Doris's school chums. Bettina is her daughter, Karol. Her child." I began to sob, crying so hard I bent over and wrapped my arms around my knees in some awkward form of comforting myself. This was not, I decided, simply a moment of disappointment in the character of my family members; this was lamentation at no longer knowing who I really was.

I sat up and looked at Karol. Brushing the tears from my cheeks and jaw line, I said, "Do you know how long I've wanted a child?"

"No."

"Since the day I married. No, since before that. Since I was a child."

"So why didn't you have one?"

"Evan didn't want children. I would have given anything if I could have convinced him otherwise, but he was set in his ways. Every so often I'd get down about it and I would think

336

surely he would love me enough to relent. To see my pain and think maybe we should . . ."

"But he didn't."

"No." The car began to rock lightly over the broken asphalt in the road, an indication we were nearing Cottonwood.

"And so you made your career your child?"

"I worked mad hours, for sure, but I did love what I did. And I loved—love—Evan. I enjoyed our life together, and other than the childlessness, I had no complaints."

"And then?"

"And then Evan began to change. He became absorbed by who we were in the community and at the club and—"

"A lot like you."

"What? What do you mean, 'like me'?"

"You've been absorbed by who you are in the community of Cottonwood and in Raymore. That's why being here is so important to you. You lost your job in Atlanta—"

"I didn't *lose* it."

"Jo-Lynn, let's not split hairs here. You know chances are you never had any intention of going back."

I swallowed hard. She was right. How was it, I wondered, that someone who had only known me a short period of time could read me so well?

"It's my job," she said from the other side of the car.

"What?"

"You're wondering how it is that I know you so well, right?"

I felt my eyes widen. "My gosh! How do you do that?"

She laughed, the tiniest bell of a giggle, and then said, "I keep telling you my job is to know everything."

"Maybe that's why I was so quick to forgive Evan and allow him back . . ."

"Into your bed?"

I didn't answer. My gosh, but she was good. Finally, in an effort to get the subject away from me, I said, "I just don't see how Aunt Stella could have possibly given away her child and then stood by and watched another woman raise her."

Karol was silent. I felt the car slowing and instinctively looked to my right. We were approaching the big house, now no more than 150 yards away. Dusk's shadows had settled around it, and I could see that Valentine's crew was gone. Sitting in front of Mae-Jo and Bob's store was a county squad car, empty of its driver. No doubt he was inside getting a cup of coffee to keep him warm.

Karol pulled into the driveway, turned the car off, and then turned to me. "Isn't it funny? You've been agonizing about the fact that your aunt had a child she didn't keep while I have completely different questions."

I turned to her. "You do?"

"Jo-Lynn, are you so wrapped up in this that it hasn't dawned on you that I am only—what?—five years younger than you and that I've neither been married nor do I have any children?"

I opened my mouth to comment, then closed it. I rubbed my fingertips hard against the pounding flesh of my forehead then looked at her. "No, I guess I thought . . . well, I don't know what I thought."

She laid her head back against the headrest as she barked, "Ha!" Cutting her eyes at me she said, "Listen, my new fledgling friend . . ."

Her choice of words brought an unexpected giggle to my throat.

"Listen. I work in what is predominantly a man's world. I travel all over the globe—mostly in the U.S., but I travel constantly and meet people of all ethnic, religious, and financial backgrounds—and I've never once met a man who so knocked me off my feet I'd be willing to give up anything, much less my job, for him. I can sit here and tell you I've honestly never been in love, Jo-Lynn, though God knows I've wanted to be."

"Never?"

"No."

"Not even in high school?" I thought of Royce Coniff and the "love" we'd once had.

"Well . . . who can count that? I mean, what do we really know about love at sixteen and seventeen?"

I picked up the bent papers—the telltale birth certificate and adoption records of Baby Girl Nevilles—and said, "Or eighteen?"

"I think life was different then. A girl of seventeen or eighteen in the 1930s was far and away from girls of the same age in our day or today."

I thought of the photo of Aunt Stella, the one I supposed taken by Henry Hawkins Jr. I thought of the maturity in her eyes and yet the hope in the unexpected joys of what tomorrow might bring. Then I thought of myself in high school and—once again—of Royce Coniff and of those fleeting emotions we'd called "love." I thought of Arizona and Annaleise. Arizona fancied herself to be in love with a boy she hardly knew. Annaleise seemed put off by the prospect of love for her sister.

Karol was right. There was a vast difference in then and now.

"So," Karol said, breaking my reverie. "You're wondering how she could give up a child, and I'm wondering who she'd had a child with. Where is *that* love story? Because surely there is one."

I thought on this for a moment. "Oh my gosh."

"What?"

"Valentine Bach told me he and my aunt were in love seventy years ago."

Karol shifted in her seat. "So you think . . ."

I shook my head. "No, I . . . no. He said they broke up because he got married." I waved a hand in the air. "I'll explain that later."

"I'll wait."

"So then . . ." I took my time, trying to imagine the scenario. "Maybe because she'd loved him at one time and she knew he loved Lilly Beth enough to break off their relationship . . . maybe Aunt Stella thought then they'd be likely candidates. Lilly Beth never gave birth, I don't think, so . . . maybe . . . maybe because she didn't, she couldn't and . . ." I sighed. "I need Sherlock Holmes for this one."

"But you don't think your aunt gave birth to Valentine's child?"

I remained quiet for a moment, then said, "What kind of woman would raise the child of her husband and his old girlfriend?"

Karol laughed. "A pretty good one."

I rubbed my hands together in the cold of the car. "If I'm going to find out who Bettina's father is I'm going to have to take drastic measures."

"Go right to the source."

I looked at her then and nodded as I gave a wistful smile. "I'm sorry you've never been in love."

She reached across the seat and took my hand in hers. "And I'm sorry you never had a child."

I breathed in deep through my nose and sighed it out. I squeezed her hand and she squeezed back. My new best friend, I thought, and I smiled.

But Karol didn't return the smile. Instead she said, "Just see to it you don't throw your love away. My gut tells me Evan and you haven't begun to work through anything really. Allow me to stick my nose in where it doesn't belong and say, 'Work it out, Jo-Lynn.' Whatever you need to do, do it. Talk it out, scream it out, hug it out. Whatever it takes. Just don't throw anything of value away."

"I won't," I said, a mere whisper in the night.

Then she smiled. "Now, let's walk over to see Mae-Jo and tell her I'm spending the night tonight."

I blinked. "What?"

She spread her arms, bent at the elbows, and waved her hands around the driver's side of the seat. "In case you haven't noticed, sister, I'm without a car."

64

I woke to bright sunlight blasting its way around the blinds and draperies of Aunt Mae-Jo's guest bedroom. I squinted against the shock of it then blinked several times in an effort to try to figure out where I was and why. Like a memory best left asleep but shaken nonetheless, the previous days' events came back to me. Finding the secret room at the big house, the horrors of the photographs and the notes and records my great-grandfather had made and kept. Learning about Bettina Godwin . . . about Aunt Stella . . . wondering who she'd loved enough to become pregnant by and who'd not loved her enough to marry her when she'd become with child.

I rolled over onto my back, pushed wisps of hair from my face, raking it with my fingers, then rested the palm of my hand against my forehead, applying pressure as though to force some sort of understanding into my overburdened brain. For several minutes, in the dissipating chill of the room, I struggled to remember everything she'd ever told me about Valentine Bach. Nothing, I decided after several minutes, was indicative in any form that she'd had a relationship with him, much less that she'd trusted him enough to give him her child to raise.

The now familiar and warming smells of coffee and fried bacon stirred me from my thoughts. I breathed in deeply and stretched, then tossed the covers off my body, swung my legs over the side of the bed, and reached for my robe at the end of the bed and my slippers nearby on the floor. I descended the stairs, once again warmed by the pleasant familiarity of being here—not just at Mae-Jo and Bob's but in the countryside township known as Cottonwood. With a smile I made my way to the kitchen, where Karol sat at the table, munching on scrambled eggs. "Well, good morning, Mary Sunshine," she said. "Mae-Jo here was just saying if you didn't wake in a minute or two we'd call the coroner."

I smiled as I shuffled over to the counter and picked up a plate and coffee mug, threw a kiss at Aunt Mae-Jo, and then waited dutifully for my plate to be topped with grits, bacon, eggs, and toast and my mug filled with coffee. "I'm going to gain a hundred pounds if this keeps up."

Mae-Jo beamed in pleasure; no greater compliment could be paid a true Southern woman. "You could use some weight on those bones."

"Look who's talking," I said as I made my way to the table and sat with a plop. I looked at Karol and mouthed, "Have you said anything?"

She shook her head no. "Did Evan call last night?" she asked.

"He did."

Karol raised her brow, and I shook my head. No, I hadn't said anything to him about what I'd learned. Mostly he'd rattled on and on about life in Druid Hills and at work. The more he talked, the more I realized how little I connected Druid Hills to home.

Mae-Jo joined us at the table and asked, "So, what's on the agenda for you two businesswomen today?"

I looked at Karol. "I need to get you back to Raymore," I said.

"That you do," she said as she crumpled her napkin and placed it on her foodless plate. "Mark Michaels will have my hide if I don't send him some positive reports by this evening. I still have a few folks who are holding out for more money or just not wanting to see any changes come to Cottonwood, but part of my job is to shower charm on folks." She grinned at us and we laughed.

I took a sip of coffee. "I'll take you to Raymore, then head back to the big house. I've got to check on progress there and then I'm going to Luverne to see Aunt Stella."

"Whatever for?" Mae-Jo asked. "It's not the weekend."

Again I looked at Karol, she at me, and then back to Mae-Jo. "I've got some questions, Aunt Mae-Jo," I said. "And she's got answers."

Hours later I pulled into the driveway of the big house where Valentine Bach stood on one side of the wraparound porch, pointing toward the threshold of the door and speaking words I could not hear to one of the workers. I sat and stared for a moment. This man, this aging man with wild hair and stooped shoulders, was somehow familiar enough to Aunt Stella to take her child. Her infant daughter. I pondered a moment a conversation I'd had with the old builder; the first I'd had with him after moving to Cottonwood. He'd stood not ten feet from where he was standing now and he'd spoken of my great-grandmother. He'd commented on Stella's lack of housekeeping . . . of my great-grandmother's ability to keep a nice home. But, he'd said, he'd only heard this. He'd never come inside until after they'd died.

Remembering this made what I now knew all the more odd.

I got out of the car and walked toward the house. Seeing me, Mr. Valentine nodded, spoke a final word or two to his worker, and then joined me. Reaching me, he tipped his hat from his head then returned it to its place. "Didn't see you yesterday," he said.

"I was in Raymore and Savannah," I answered. "Mr. Valentine, I need to ask you a couple of questions." From the corner of my eye I saw Arizona pull the Geo up to the curb.

I glanced over as Mr. Valentine said, "She's bringing me my pills I forgot to take this morning." He took a step toward the car.

"Oh," I said. "Mr. Valentine, I really need to talk to you."

He turned back to me. "No, ma'am. You're going to ask me about whatever you found in that room, and I can't answer you. I promised Stella a long time ago."

"That's just it, Mr. Valentine. *Why* did you promise her? What kind of relationship—other than dating—did you two have?"

He turned fully to look at me as the car door opened and Arizona stepped out. He placed his hands on his hips and said, "We didn't date, missy. We were in love."

I opened my mouth to reply but then shut it. There was something about his voice, something strong and commanding. Something haunted by a memory I had no business trying to bring to mind.

Arizona reached us then, and Valentine turned toward her. She extended a small bag to her great-grandfather along with a plastic bottle of water. "Here ya go, Pappy. Ga-Ga said to tell you that you can run but you can't hide and that I'm to stand here until I see you take the pills."

She grinned at him, blue eyes sparkling in the late-morning sunlight, as he opened the bag and muttered, "That daughter of mine can sure be a nuisance."

I was struck then with the sense of falling and spinning, all at the same time. I looked from the old man—Bettina's father—to his great-granddaughter. *She has his eyes*, I thought. *She has his eyes!*

I took a step back.

"Miss Jo-Lynn?" Arizona peered at me with her head cocked. "You okay?"

I nodded, taking another step and then another. Valentine Bach turned his head from staring at the contents of the bag to peering over at me. Santa Claus looking from his bag of goodies to the longing, hopeful child. Taking in my expression, he straightened.

"She has your eyes," I said.

Arizona shoved her hands into the pockets of her jeans. "Of course I do," she said. "I'm his great-granddaughter, after all."

"That's right, missy," he said to me, understanding flooding his face and softening his weathered features. "That's right."

65

I arrived in Luverne and the home of Doris and her family within an hour. Several times during my trip I realized I was speeding. Other times I had those out-of-body experiences people have when they are so deep in thought they blink and realize the last five minutes are a blank to them. Evan called—just checking on me, he said—and I told him I was on my way to see Aunt Stella.

"Any particular reason?" he asked.

"No," I said, my voice a little too high in pitch. "Just wanting to see her."

When I got close to Doris's house, I called to let her know I was in town and wanted to drop by to see Aunt Stella. "I hope this isn't an inconvenience," I said.

"Honey, this is the South. Since when does anyone call to ask before dropping in on friends and relatives?"

I knew that already, but in all fairness I wanted to give her a chance to straighten her typically immaculate home. No matter what we say, Southern women do not like to be caught unaware.

Doris bustled about when I entered, asking me to "excuse the mess" and offering a cup of coffee, which I accepted, then buzzed into the kitchen like the proverbial bee to prepare it. She called back to where I stood in the living room and said, "Mama'll be out of her room in a minute. She's getting properly dressed."

"Where are the kids?" I asked.

"School," she called back, as though anyone should know this.

Aunt Stella was surprised and pleased to see me; her face broke in a wide grin and her eyes danced behind her glasses. I asked her if we could go somewhere to talk privately, to which she replied, "Of course, shug. Where do you want to go?" I looked out the arched doorway leading from the dining room to the sunroom and beyond to the massive backyard. Spotting a cozy settle of two Adirondack chairs and a small table, I suggested we take advantage of the warming weather and go out back.

I took two mugs of coffee from Doris, who said she had plenty to do inside while we chatted. When I'd settled Aunt Stella and all niceties had been executed, I got to the point.

"Aunt Stella," I said, pulling the yellowed legal-sized envelope from my purse. "I found this the other day." I passed the envelope toward her.

She set her cup of coffee next to a collie dog ashtray on the table between us, then took the envelope. Slipping its contents from inside, she unfolded the papers. I watched as her eyes became hooded and she shook her cottony head from side to side. "My, my . . ."

"Aunt Stella, it's none of my business, of course, but . . ." It dawned on me then that I'd not thought through what I was going to say to this loving matriarch.

"But you're wondering who this child is? Did I really have a child out of wedlock—shock, shock?"

I laughed lightly, more out of nerves than anything else. "Aunt Stella, I know people have been having sex outside of marriage since the beginning of forever but . . . I . . . you . . . I just never imagined." I swallowed. "Aunt Stella, was your child the child of Valentine Bach?"

She took her eyes away from the papers and gave me a hard look. "What brought his name to mind? What's he told you?"

"That he loved you . . . a long, long time ago."

"A very long time ago. I'm surprised he admitted it. We never spoke of it after he married Lilly Beth."

"Aunt Stella . . . why? What happened?"

Aunt Stella looked from me back to the papers. A tiny smile broke across her lips, so faint I almost missed it. A memory, a sweet and blessed memory had floated across her mind, I thought, and left a small treasure.

Finally she spoke. "People change history, baby doll, but time will change people and how they react to things like this." She lightly waved the papers.

"Meaning?"

"There's a girl living next door—Linda Settle's daughter—seventeen, I think Doris said she was. Anyway, she just gave birth to a baby boy."

"And?"

"And there's not a wedding ring to be found on a single one of her fingers. I asked her the other day when we went over to take a little gift why she wasn't married and she told me she wasn't ready for marriage. Now, if that's not something."

"Ready for motherhood but not marriage."

"That's right. Now me. I was a little older than her when I found out I was pregnant with Bettina. I was ready to marry Valentine. I was ready to settle down and be a good wife and a good mother. But things were different back then, and he had obligations I'd not known about before we got pregnant."

"To marry Lilly Beth?"

She nodded in reply. "In those days girls didn't have babies and raise them on their own. They might have said the daddy was in the war and died, but few people bought that."

"And Cottonwood was a small town."

"Very small. Papa and Mama would have been humiliated. I loved them too much for that. Especially Papa."

"But, Aunt Stella . . . Bettina was your *child*. And you just gave her away . . . how could you have done that?" I checked my voice, careful not to spill any accusations but rather only raise a question.

"You think I gave her away? I didn't give her away. I gave her to her father and to a woman I knew would bring her up in love. I didn't know Lilly Beth personally, but I figured she must be special enough. Valentine had chosen what his parents wanted—Lilly Beth—over his feelings about me. He wouldn't have done that if she'd been a bad person, I figured." She coughed a sad chuckle. "As difficult a decision as it was, I managed to rationalize it as best I could at such a young age." She looked at the papers again. "Don't think for a minute I didn't love my baby. I did. That's why I could do what I did. I loved her. Still do. That never goes away."

I thought for a moment before asking another question. "Did Uncle Jim know?"

"No ma'am, he did not."

"You never told him."

"Nor Doris. No one knew but Valentine, Lilly Beth, Papa, Mama, and me. And some attorney over in Savannah who is long dead and buried. Now you. But that's enough. No one ever needs to know about this. Some secrets are best kept just that way." She looked away then took a drag on her cigarette and exhaled into the cool springtime air. "Believe me on that one."

I sat back in the Adirondack chair and crossed my legs.

For several minutes we sat in silence—or maybe it was only a moment—me watching her, her looking out into the thicket beyond the yards. Sometimes we took sips of coffee, but mostly we just held onto our mugs. After she'd finished hers, she lit another cigarette, an action I'd seen so many times I'd preserved it in my memories.

I thought about the packet of information concerning the Klan and how her father—her beloved Papa—had been such a part of it. A man she loved so dearly, a murderer. She was right in saying that some things were best left unspoken, but I felt I had to know.

"Aunt Stella, what do you know about the Klan in Cottonwood?"

Aunt Stella took another long drag from her cigarette, fixed her eyes straight ahead, and locked her jaw. I sat still, waiting. Waiting for an answer I knew may or may not come, according to her mood. Finally she said, "Nothing. The Klan wasn't something we talked about then, and I'm not going to talk about it now."

I nodded in acquiescence. "Yes, ma'am."

I heard the back screen door open then, and I turned to see Doris, who called out to us, "Y'all okay out there?"

"We're fine," I called back.

"Mama, do you need a lap throw?"

Aunt Stella muttered, "It's killing her to know what we're talking about. Tell her if I'm cold I'm old enough to let her know."

I smiled. "She says she's fine."

"Mama, you sure?"

"Have mercy," Aunt Stella said, then ground her cigarette out in the collie dog ashtray.

"She's fine, Doris," I said.

Doris turned and went back inside.

"She means well," I said.

"So does a shot of penicillin, but you don't see anybody lined up to get one for the fun of it."

I laughed lightly then said, "I suppose having Doris helped make up for Bettina."

Aunt Stella whipped her head around to face me. Her expression was fixed, almost angry. "Don't think for one minute one child can take the place of another, Jo-Lynn."

"No, I . . . I mean . . . of course not."

"Listen here, shug. One child can't replace another. And a husband can't replace a child." She smiled at me then, letting me know everything was all right between the two of us. "And a job can't replace a husband."

I raised a brow. "But a great-aunt can sure dish out a lesson."

She looked ahead. "That's my job, shug." Then she smiled broadly at me. "You're a good kid. Always were. Margaret didn't know how blessed she was to have you, I always said."

I placed my hand on hers and nodded toward the house. "And maybe you don't know how blessed you are to have Doris."

"Oh, I know. Don't think for a minute I don't. At the end of my life—and this is the end of my life, the good Lord willing—I can't complain. It wasn't always easy, but it was always about the choices I made."

"Hmmm," I answered back.

"See, shug . . . you want to blame Evan for the fact you had no children. But he made his choice not to have children, and you made your choice to marry him knowing he didn't want to have them."

I nodded. "I think I've made another choice too, Aunt Stella. Only I don't know how he's going to react to it. I guess it will depend on his choice concerning my choice."

"And what choice have you made?"

"I've fallen in love with Cottonwood. Even with all its secrets, it's full of promise. I see the way it can become. Charming. Exciting. A respite in a storm. And I want to live there.
I want to live in the cottage I'm going to have built behind
the big house."

"Say that again?"

I nodded. "I wake up morning after morning knowing it. I
never really felt at home in Raymore, and I've never lived in
Cottonwood until now and . . . if just feels like home."

"Evan will never go for it."

"Maybe he won't. Maybe he will. I guess I'll just have to
ask."

"The answer is always no until you ask." She patted my
hand. "Take me inside, shug. I'm getting cold."

"Aha."

Together we stood, and she took my arm. "Just don't tell
Doris I said so. It'll make her smug. Last thing I need at this
old age is a smug child."

66

It was nearing five o'clock in the afternoon when I pulled my car into the driveway at Mae-Jo and Bob's. One look at the house—opened blinds into darkened rooms—and I knew the two of them were not home. I started to put my car in reverse, to drive the few yards from their house to the store, then decided my legs could use a stretch. I was exhausted from the events of the last three days, and the air was turning chilly; a walk, I decided, was the pick-me-up I needed.

I locked the car and walked down the highway, passing the big house and arriving at the store minutes later. My face felt wind-burned, but my mind and spirit were clearer than they'd been in days. When I pushed open the heavy door and stepped in, I was greeted by a blast of warm air and the mingled scents of coffee and burning wood. It was altogether pleasant.

Mae-Jo was standing behind the counter near the cash register. Uncle Bob, also behind the counter, was near the back helping a customer, a woman I didn't recognize.

"Hey, Aunt Mae-Jo," I sang as I shut the door. It rattled back in place. I stepped over to the coffeepot and prepared a cup of coffee as I spoke.

"The wayward child returns," she teased. "I don't know

what is going on with you, but something is cooking, make no mistake about it."

"You're right there, but I'll never tell." I hoped the lilt in my voice would hide the angst my heart was feeling.

"How was Aunt Stella?" Mae-Jo asked me. She had the store's ledger spread wide before her, a calculator next to it. She returned her attention to her task, staring intently from the pages to the machine, and she used the eraser of the pencil for pressing the numbers and the lead of the pencil for jotting down sum totals.

"She was good. Doris is good. The whole family is good." I reminded myself of the day Aunt Stella had asked me about Evan and I'd answered, "He's good. And fine. He's good and fine." Aunt Stella hadn't been fooled by my answer then; I wondered if Mae-Jo would be now. To keep suspicions at bay, I placed my purse on the counter then propped my elbows next to it and leaned over. "Aunt Mae-Jo?"

"Hmmm?"

"What would you do if you found out something about someone . . . *dead* . . . and if you revealed it you would hurt the surviving family members, but if you didn't you'd be keeping a secret that doesn't deserve to be kept?"

Mae-Jo stopped in her tasks and gave me a puzzled look. "Say what?"

I shook my head. "I know it makes no sense—this question—and I can't really go into any real details. I'm sorry. What if you found out about—"

Mae-Jo glanced toward the back, and I allowed my eyes to follow. Uncle Bob and the lady customer had turned to make their way toward the front of the store, and I heard Uncle Bob say, "If you look on the second aisle there, you should find it."

"Thank you, Mr. Seymour," she said.

I watched until all but the top of her head disappeared down the second aisle of food items. Turning back to Mae-Jo and Uncle Bob, who'd now joined us, I continued, "Aunt Mae-Jo, what if what you knew concerned a murder?"

"A murder?" Uncle Bob nearly barked.

I glanced behind me to see if his customer had been alarmed by what she'd heard. The top of her head was not moving and facing the nearest shelf. I imagined she was busily trying to decide between the cream of tomato and chicken noodle soups. I looked back at my aunt and uncle and said, "Shhh . . ."

"Who's been murdered?" Uncle Bob lowered his voice, but it was loud enough just the same.

"Nobody has been murdered." Nervous, I laughed lightly. "I'm just posing a hypothetical question."

"Right specific for a hypothetical question," he said.

"She wants to know what we'd do if we found out that someone who is already dead killed somebody before he died." Mae-Jo had dropped her pencil onto the counter by this point.

"Well of course it would have been before he died," Uncle Bob shot back.

I straightened. "Okay, you two." I took a long sip of coffee, which allowed me to take time to think through what I should and shouldn't say from here. When I'd lowered the mug from my lips I said, "Let me ask this a bit differently. What if you found out that someone in your family murdered someone—and that family member has been dead for a long time, a long, long time—would you tell or would you let sleeping dogs lie?"

Mae-Jo nodded. "It's a sense of justice you're looking for?"

"I suppose. The murders were senseless and—"

"Murders?" Uncle Bob interrupted. "There's more than one?"

I rubbed my forehead with my fingertips. "Uh . . ."

"That makes your hypothetical question more ominous. And I don't think it's so hypothetical. What's going on, sugar-foot?"

Shuffling behind me told me the customer was ready to check out, so I moved to one side, smiling at her and her at me as I did so. "I'm sorry," I said. "I'm in the way here."

"Not a problem." She spoke kindly.

Mae-Jo began the process of registering her items in the ledger as Uncle Bob slipped the few purchases into brown paper bags. I remained silent, watching the flow of the movement between the store owners and their customer until the woman, her crooked arms filled with packages, walked toward the door. I jumped to position then, dashing over to open the door for her, feeling more at home than ever.

"Thank you," the woman said.

"Not a problem," I said, repeating her words to me just minutes ago.

She smiled and I smiled back. She called over her shoulder, "Bye, now" to which Aunt Mae-Jo said, "Anytime, Diana. Come again."

67

Some things are best left unspoken; I decided after Mae-Jo and Bob's customer left that I'd leave questions concerning ancestral murders like sleeping dogs. I'd let them lie. Mae-Jo tried to press the issue, but I waved her away and told her I was going to go to the big house for a while, then I'd walk back to their house. "If you don't mind another night of company," I said. "Evan doesn't want me in the big house alone."

"When do you expect him back?" Uncle Bob asked as I slid my purse onto my shoulder.

"I'm not sure. I was hoping he'd love it here as much as I do, but when we talked earlier today . . . he's fitting right back in at home."

Uncle Bob smirked playfully. "That boy has never belonged anywhere close to here, I can tell you that much."

I frowned as I stepped out of the store and into the encroaching darkness that had enveloped the world outside. I hurried across the street and, as I crossed the lawn, dipped my hand into my purse to retrieve my keys. Unable to locate them by the seek and find method, I stopped in the middle of the porch and opened the purse wide, then pulled the envelope and its contents—those awful papers and forms and photos that had haunted me now for days—out to allow more light to filter in. I held the purse toward the streetlight a few yards away and, spying my keys, retrieved them and then quickly moved into the house.

There was enough light from nature and the street lamp shafting into the room to get me to the passageway between the living room and dining room. Inside the narrow secret room I pulled the light cord, lowered the attic stairway, then climbed the ladder-like stairs, leaving the desk and filing cabinet behind. Tonight I wanted nothing more to do with the Klan or the farm's activities, its failures and successes. I didn't want to know anything more about my great-grandfather and his vicious crimes. I only wanted to know more about my great-aunt and the elements of her life that I'd never before considered. I suspected I'd find this treasure of information in the attic I'd never known existed until a few days before.

When I'd switched on the light, I placed my purse in the corner of a room on the floor next to an old end table and beside a box I intended to go through first. Down on my knees I pulled the box top's four sides—carefully folded together—apart and peered inside. I smiled. At only the first box, I'd already hit pay dirt.

I pulled stacks of scrapbooks from inside, shifted to my backside, and began to flip through a history I'd grown to both love and despise. Birth certificates, locks of hair in brittle and yellowed envelopes—each scrawled with the name of the child the hair had belonged to—were displayed between theater tickets, church programs, newspaper articles, and photographs. I lingered over each item, periodically standing to stretch my back and legs, until I could no longer sit on the floor. I located an old cane bottom chair, dragged the box over to it, and continued with my research.

My phone rang from within the depths of my purse across the room and I jumped, then hurried over to answer it. Aunt

Mae-Jo was on the other end of the line, clearly concerned as to my whereabouts.

"What time is it?" Even as I asked, I glanced at my watch. "Oh, 9:30."

"Now you know why I was getting worried."

"I'm sorry, Aunt Mae-Jo. I'm in the big house still. I found some interesting scrapbooks dating all the way back to my great-great-grandparents. Karol will be thrilled at what this will bring to the museum." And I, I thought, was even more thrilled. The more good I had to offer to the way of life 150 years ago, the less we had to think about the bad.

"Do you need Bob to come get you?" she asked. "I don't like the idea of you walking back by yourself."

"Oh . . . I hadn't thought about that." I thought for a moment. "I'll probably just stay here tonight. I don't want Uncle Bob to have to wait up, and I'd really like to spend some more time here."

"It'll still be there tomorrow," she said.

"Yes, along with a dozen or more workers. No, I'm sure I'll be fine. Just don't tell Evan."

Aunt Mae-Jo was quiet, then said, "You know the deputy isn't out there anymore. I don't like the idea of you there by yourself."

I hadn't known that, but I wasn't surprised. Whatever the three men were after, they probably had given up. "Seriously, Aunt Mae-Jo. I'll be fine."

I hung up and called Evan, but he didn't answer—neither the house phone nor his cell. I dropped the phone back into my purse then shuffled back to the chair and my find.

At some point I must have fallen asleep, even in the uncomfortable upright position in the chair. I suppose I heard the voices below and was startled by them. I don't know. I'll probably never know for sure.

I do have a final moment of remembrance. A voice, clear and masculine, mocking and taunting, saying, "Well, what do we have here?" And I remember seeing their faces; two I did not recognize and one I did. Terry Godwin, looking wild-eyed and tough in a make-believe sort of way, the way Stephen used to look when he played "army" with his buddies.

I remember pandemonium. I remember throwing the scrapbook at them in some mockery of defense. But I don't remember anything after. I have no recollection of being hit— beaten—until I lost consciousness. I have now—for the hours between waking in the attic and waking in the hospital—only the story as Larry Gansky told it.

And for me, it is enough.

68

More than a week passed before I was able to talk to anyone or have what anyone said to me make sense. I have vague memories of waking in a hospital room, of seeing tubes and IV bags, of hearing the beeps and sighs of machines monitoring my heart, my breathing, my intake and my output. I have mental snapshots of the faces of my parents, my brother, my husband, and even Karol standing over me, telling me I was going to be all right and not to worry. These faces—like photographs scattered on the black pages of an old photo album—mingled with those of doctors and nurses and other medical personnel.

I wasn't worried. I didn't have the energy or the awareness to worry. I only knew an excruciating level of pain I'd never before imagined possible. It wasn't until much later that I knew—or cared to know—the details of my injuries. I had a broken leg, two broken ribs, and a head injury.

When the doctors allowed, Larry Gansky—along with Evan, who sat next to the bed gently caressing my hand with his thumb—asked what I might be able to add to what they already knew. He stood opposite of Evan and held his cap in his hands.

I told him what I could remember, which wasn't much. I

faltered over whether or not to reveal the name of the one man I could identify. I had grown to love Valentine Bach and his family and I didn't want to see any hurt come to them. They were, after all, *my* family.

My concerns were for naught. "We've arrested the three men who were in the attic," Larry said. "We also arrested Alfred Pitney and Roy Morrison for their role in it."

Roy Morrison. The man at the church. The man who'd not wanted change to come to Cottonwood. "Oh."

"You seem disappointed."

I ran my tongue over my lower lip, still swollen and cracked. Evan reached for a piece of ice from the bedside table's plastic pitcher and ran it over my lips. I smiled at him in gratitude. "I'm not disappointed," I said then. "I just didn't know, and I . . ." I closed my eyes. "I'm just sorry Terry Godwin was involved. He's like family."

"You mean he *is* family."

My eyes opened, but I remained quiet.

Larry looked at Evan. "She doesn't know?"

"We haven't told her anything yet," he said, speaking to Larry but looking at me.

I looked from the man standing to the one sitting and asked, "What's going on?"

Evan leaned in as he spoke. "Valentine Bach told his daughter everything . . . that afternoon."

"She knows? About Aunt Stella?" I felt a wave of disappointment and shame wash over me. All these years of keeping secrets, and with my interference it had all come spilling out.

"Pretty much everyone knows now. And it's okay. But what we've gathered from Terry is that after Valentine told Bettina, he brought the whole family in and told them. Terry then got a call from the Pitney boys—they're the men you saw that night, the ones who've been trying to get into the

363

house or get you to leave it all along—who knew you'd found something in the house."

"How'd they know?"

"Their mother," Larry interjected. "She was in the store and overheard you talking about murders and ancestors. She went home, told her husband, and he rallied up his boys, who called Terry."

"Only Terry now knew you were his relative and—in spite of his ties to the faltering white supremacy group around here—he loves his great-grandfather and his grandmother. He went along to the house, he says, because he didn't know what else to do."

"How did they know I was there?" I asked, remembering my car was at Mae-Jo and Bob's.

"They didn't," Larry answered. "At least according to Terry. They just came up on you. Their intent was to make one more mad search for the records that would implicate their families to the Klan and to the murders of probably a half-dozen men around here."

I nodded. "Instead they came up on me."

Evan drew closer. "When the confrontation with you got out of hand, Terry ran out of the house and into Bob, who Mae-Jo had ordered to go get you. If it hadn't been for that, you might not be with us now." I watched his Adam's apple bob up and down as he fought for composure then gave way and allowed himself to cry.

I cried with him, and when we were done we apologized to the sheriff for our emotions.

"Think nothing of it," he said with a smile. "And I want you to know that Terry is turning evidence on a lot that's been going on around here. It won't keep him out of prison, but it will cut his time and hopefully make him rethink his position of hatred of those different than him."

"What I don't understand," I said after several moments of mulling it over, "is what difference it made to these men. These murders took place so long ago; no one there is alive now. Or if they are, they're so old I can't imagine them being convicted and serving time."

Larry breathed in and out before answering. "We won't know for sure until we're through all the papers. What you had in your purse—and by the way, we have your purse—was just the tip of the iceberg, as they say."

I closed my eyes. "But why did they wait so long? Didn't they have ample opportunity over the years to come into the house and search?"

"No, ma'am. According to one of the Pitney boys, your Uncle Jim had a way of keeping people out of the house. They were more afraid of Jim, I think, than having the murders exposed."

"Uncle Jim? He was involved too?" I felt my heart breaking into a million pieces. It was one thing that a great-grandfather I'd never met was with the Klan. But not Uncle Jim.

"Yes, ma'am." He seemed almost pleased.

I frowned at him. "Well, I don't happen to think it's such a great thing that my great-grandfather and my great-uncle were at the center of Klan activity." I heard the beeps of the heart monitor increase.

Evan squeezed my hand again. "Honey . . . ," he said.

Larry furrowed his brow at me. "Uh . . . no, ma'am."

I ignored my husband's silent plea that I remain calm. "I saw the proof. I saw the papers."

He chuckled lightly and nodded. Raising a hand he said, "Promise me you'll calm down so the nurses don't kick us out, and I'll tell you a story."

I took a deep breath and exhaled, heard the beeping return to a natural rhythm. "When I was a kid—when I was in high school—I took part in the Explorer's program. It's designed for young people interested in law enforcement.

"I worked down at the sheriff's office doing anything and everything the old sheriff could find for me to do. When I was in my senior year of high school the new courthouse was built. That meant the sheriff's office had to be moved. Part of my job was to help pack up boxes of old information, files, that kind of thing."

"I see."

"No, I don't think you do. Sheriff Regan hounded me like crazy because I was taking so long. That's because every time I came across a file that I thought might be full of interesting nuggets—which was most of them—I'd sit down and start reading."

I gave him a weak smile. "I can understand that."

"So, anyway . . . I came across a file from back in the forties, chock full of information about the Klan."

I closed my eyes then reopened them.

"Mrs. Hunter, have you ever heard of a man named Gary Thomas Rowe?"

"I read about him in a book my father gave me. He was an FBI informant who was involved in the Viola Liuzzo murder."

"Viola Liuzzo was the only white woman killed during the civil rights movement; did you know that?"

"Yes."

"Well, ma'am, what I'm trying to tell you is that before there was a Gary Thomas Rowe—long before—there was a Nevan Collins Nevilles."

"He was an informant for the FBI?"

"Not for the FBI, but for the local sheriff's office, yes. His testimony went straight to the FBI, have no doubt about it." He winked. "There were a few decent sheriffs in the South, even back in those days."

"Are you sure? I mean, about my great-grandfather?"

"Yes, ma'am." He ran the palm of his right hand along the brim of his cap, now clutched in his left hand. "I think what you found in the house over there in Cottonwood were copies of Nevan's records."

"But what about Uncle Jim?"

"Jim had the good sense to keep secret what needed to be; to walk quiet and carry a big stick, as they say."

"Did Aunt Stella know? About her father and her husband?"

"I have no idea."

I had to think about that for a moment. Somehow, I doubted it. Somehow I believed she believed her husband and father were involved in lawlessness. "There's something else I don't understand. With the evidence gathered, why wasn't anyone ever convicted for the murders of Percy Robinson and the others?"

"Silas Pitney was arrested, but they couldn't pin anything on him, even with the mountain of evidence your great-grandfather had."

"But they were able to convict the three men who murdered Liuzzo."

"The Liuzzo case is complicated at best. The three men were convicted, yes, but of violating her civil rights, not of her murder. I could take you to the library today and we could pull a good dozen or so books off the shelf, each one telling a slightly different version of the murder, the trials, and the fate of the four men who were in the car that fired at her and Moton. Everybody pointing fingers at everybody else. Even the Liuzzo children bringing charges against the FBI in the 1980s concerning her death and Rowe's involvement." He paused. "Like I said, complicated at best."

I blew air out of my mouth. "I don't get it. I don't understand how there could have been so much legal confusion." I shook my head. "We always talk about the good old days. Maybe they weren't so good after all."

"Well, Mrs. Hunter, if it's any consolation to you today, at least Pitney got his. The ATF got involved, and eventually he was arrested for running moonshine. He went to jail and was killed in a—and I quote—'inside job.'"

I raised my hand. "I'm not sure I want to know anything else right now." I closed my eyes for a moment, then said, "My head is beginning to throb."

I opened my eyes to see him nodding then placing the cap back on his head. "I understand." He looked at Evan. "I'll leave her to get some rest now."

"Rest, yes," I said. "I just need to rest."

69

Raymore, Georgia
Present day

Stella talked Doris into driving her to Raymore to see Jo-Lynn on Monday. "It was time," she'd said on Saturday. "Phone calls are fine, but they aren't the same as being there."

"I know, Mama. Let me get the kids off to school and then you and I will go on over."

It was a long drive. Not so much in distance as in time. And not so much in time as in memory. Knowing what Margaret had driven all the way to Luverne to tell her, knowing that her family and Valentine's family all knew the truth, made it a little uneasy for her.

A lot uneasy.

"Makes me wonder why I bothered at all," she muttered, then drew on her cigarette and blew the smoke out the opened window of the passenger's side of Doris's car.

"Bothered with what, Mama?" her daughter asked.

But Stella only shook her head. What was the point, really, in talking about it? Since learning the truth about Bettina Bach Godwin, Doris had done little else but ask questions. Sometimes with her voice; sometimes with her eyes. Too many questions. Questions with not enough answers.

"It must be quite a shock," Stella had said to her daughter, "to find out your mama had a history before you came into being."

"Everybody's got a history, Mama," Doris had said. "I'm just trying to take all this in."

They arrived in Raymore a little after 10:30 that morning. Doris came around to Stella's side of the car and opened the door for her, took her hand and wrapped it around her arm. "Hold tight, Mama," she said. "I'm sure we have a ways to walk, even with parking in the handicapped spot."

Soon enough they were in Jo-Lynn's room, looking at her bruised figure, tinier than it ought to be. "You need to eat," Stella said.

"I'm doing all right," Jo-Lynn argued. "My appetite just hasn't caught up yet."

Stella kissed her niece, first on the forehead, then on each cheek. Something she hadn't done for years. She wasn't one for such demonstrations of affection, but she wanted Jo-Lynn to know how she felt. "I love you, little girl," she said. "If I'd 'a known what you woulda faced just to redo that old house . . ." Her voice quivered, then faded.

"Stop that now," Jo-Lynn said to her. "You didn't know."

"I didn't expect those papers were known by anyone but Jim and me. And he was gone."

Jo-Lynn closed her eyes then reopened them. "When we have time, I want to talk to you about that. I want to tell you some things I think you ought to know." She swallowed. "When we have time. Not today."

"Whatever you've got to say, say it now. I may not be around when you get ready to talk."

"Mama," Doris said. "Don't say that."

"Well, it's the truth."

Jo-Lynn looked at Stella as if to say she knew her aunt was right. "Aunt Stella," she began. "The truth is . . . the real truth is . . . your father wasn't involved with the Klan as I believe you've suspected all this time."

Stella felt her face grow red, then drain itself of any and all blood that might be left there. "Suspicion has nothing to do with what I know."

Jo-Lynn swallowed hard. Stella knew it was difficult, in more ways than one, for her great-niece to say what she had to say. Sensed it as well as saw it. "You don't know everything." Her niece struggled with her words now. "He was an informant, Aunt Stella. For the law. And it's his work that links itself to the hate that still exists here."

"Mercy," Doris whispered. "It's like Pops has come back from the grave and declared judgment and righteousness."

Jo-Lynn grimaced then.

"You in a lot of pain, shug?"

Her niece nodded, almost imperceptibly, then added, "You?"

"Not as much as five minutes ago, though I can't help but think if I'd turned over what I hid years ago a lot more justice would have been served."

"Maybe. Maybe not. It is what it is."

"God is in control, I reckon."

"He is that." Jo-Lynn smiled a half smile as though one part of her were capable and the other not.

"We'd best be going," Stella said, then looped her arm with Doris's. "Take me home now."

Doris looked at Jo-Lynn. "I'll send a nurse in to make sure you're okay."

Jo-Lynn nodded, then closed her eyes to rest.

They were near the first floor lobby, nearing the wide glass sensory doors that slid to either side and opened the whole wide world up to those who would enter or exit. They were exiting—Stella and Doris—just as Valentine and Annaleise were entering.

Doris stopped, halting Stella too. "Mama?" she said. "You all right?"

Stella looked from her old friend to her daughter and said, "Why wouldn't I be?"

And then they stood face-to-face for the first time since their secret had been exposed. She looked into his eyes—truly looked into them—for the first time since the day he'd come to Dr. Bird's office to thank her for her part in Bettina's medical care. "Valentine," she said. He was uncharacteristically dressed in casual pants and a long-sleeved cotton shirt.

"Stella."

There was a pause. An awkward moment where no one said a word or moved or even breathed. Finally Valentine pointed toward a grouping of retro chairs and said, "I suppose there was a part of me thought you might be here today. Mind if we have a word? Just you and me?"

Stella patted Doris's hand and said, "I don't see why not." Then looking at Doris she added, "Why don't you take this young lady to the cafeteria and get you both something to drink?"

When they were gone Valentine walked Stella over to the seats, helped her into hers, then sat in the chair next to it. He sat near the edge, one elbow resting on one knee, chuckled lightly, and waited.

"Well, you wanted to say something?" Stella asked him.

Valentine cleared his throat. "Shoot, I don't even know where to start." He took a deep breath, exhaled. "How about this: did I ever tell you about the day your daddy told me I was a father?"

"No, I don't believe so."

"I don't know if I was more scared then or the day I told you about me and Lilly Beth."

Stella decided to say nothing.

"Funny, isn't it?"

"What's that?"

"There was a time when you and I were as close as a man and woman can get, and right now I'm trying hard to say something to you and can't seem to get the words to form."

"Just say what's on your mind, Valentine."

He nodded, swallowed a few times, then began. "Stella, I want you to know something. If I'd been the man then that I am today—sure of myself, knowing who I am exactly—I would have fought against . . . I would have fought for . . . for us. For you and me."

Stella looked away. "You really want to go there now?"

"I do. I want to tell you how sorry I am. Sorry I didn't do right by you . . ."

"You did do right by me."

Valentine shifted. "I don't understand."

"You never did. That was your biggest problem too. You never understood. Let me make it simple enough. I loved you. I let you go. I could have stopped that wedding, and don't think for a minute I didn't lay in my bed that night and think about doing it. 'Cause I did. But sometimes loving someone means letting them go. So I did. I let you go." Stella glanced around the lobby. "I sure wish I knew why folks can't smoke in public places like they used to."

Valentine chuckled, then extended a hand. "What's say we go outside in the sunshine for a few?"

Minutes later, leaning against the statue of some famous somebody and smoking their cigarettes, Valentine said, "Remember how I used to go down to Conroy's store and buy us smokes?"

"I remember."

For a moment, it was all that was said. Then, "Valentine, listen to what I'm going to say to you because I'm only going to say it once. You took Bettina like I asked. You told Lilly Beth the truth about you and me, and for me that was something. If you could do that, I reckoned, you could love our daughter enough to give her a good life."

"I do love her, Stella. More than I ever thought I could love another human being."

"And you loved Lilly Beth."

He didn't answer right away. "Not at first. Not like I loved you, exactly. There's only one first love. But in time I loved her very much."

Stella took a long draw on her cigarette, then dropped it to her feet and crushed it with the toe of her shoe. She blew the smoke from her lungs, pushed it out with a strength she didn't know she had, then said, "Look here. Let me finish what *I* need to say. I don't regret any of it. Maybe I had my fair share to go to God with, to ask forgiveness for, but I don't regret it. God takes the messes we make in our lives and turns them into something good if we let him. I loved you. I lost you. I gave birth to Bettina, and some would say I lost her. But I never did. Not deep down where it counts. And then I met Jim Edwards, and God smiled on me one more time with Doris. So I want you to know what I never said to you before now. I don't regret loving you and having your child. I don't."

"That's good to know," he said, then paused. Finally, "She's taking it all pretty hard, you know." The March wind blew through the limbs of nearby dogwoods, finding its way through his mane of white hair.

Stella watched it shift over his shoulder before she spoke. "Is she?"

"She'll be all right. Just needs time."

"Time." Stella chuckled. "That's all any of us needs." Then she winked at the man she'd loved so many years before and said, "I reckon that's one thing you and me are about to run out of."

Valentine cast his eyes far off. "I can practically make out the pearls on the gates now."

Stella laughed again. "You always could make me laugh, back then."

Valentine returned his eyes to hers. "I think I can say what I wanted to say now. There were times, after Lilly Beth died, that I would ask God why. Why did I lose you? Why did I lose her? Why couldn't I have her back? Why couldn't I have *you* back? But you had Jim by then and you was happy. That much was for sure."

Stella closed her eyes.

"But I'm a man. A human being. And it didn't stop me from asking. From wondering why two people who loved each other as much as us couldn't just find our way back together."

Stella opened her eyes again. "It wasn't meant to be."

"No, I reckon it wasn't."

"I had Jim and I loved him."

"Sometimes I felt like I'd gambled and lost. Then I'd look at Bettina and think maybe I'd gambled and won. It sure was a confusing time back then."

"So what kept you from marrying one of those women that practically threw themselves at you after Lilly Beth died?"

This time it was Valentine who laughed. "Ah, Stella. I just figured what were the chances of any one of them turning out right. I'd had silver and gold in you and Lilly Beth. Loving two women in a lifetime ought to be enough for one man. It was surely enough for this one."

Stella was quiet for a moment. "I guess we'd best get back inside before they get back and wonder where in the world we went."

Valentine extended his arm. "Shall we?"

Stella's smile came slow, but it came. She slipped her arm into his and allowed him to guide her toward the hospital's entrance. Halfway there, she dipped her head and watched as he slipped his free hand into his pants pocket then drew it out again.

"I've been carrying this around since Jim died," he said. "Thinking I might run into you. Thinking maybe it was time to return it."

"What's that?" she asked. And then she recognized it.

A thinning and yellowed linen handkerchief, embroidered with faded flowers and a fine letter *S* in their center. After all these years, she thought, he was letting her go.

70

I think stories like this one—stories like mine—should end in some sort of climactic moment. Other than, that is, being beaten nearly to death by three men and living to not remember it. But this one doesn't. Not really, anyway.

I entered a rehab facility a few weeks after the attack and, in time, was able to move from the center to the house on the hill, where Mother waited on me and Daddy encouraged me with each baby step of progress.

Evan drove to Raymore every weekend. When M Michaels gave his firm the job, he moved there to finish his work in Cottonwood. Six months later we stood before the nearly completed big house and a quarter mile from what was becoming everything I'd dreamed Cottonwood would be right down to an upcoming county fair. I told him then I wanted to relocate, that I wanted to oversee the museum and live in the barn-like cottage behind the big house. "I've grown to love the people here. Arizona and Annaleise treat me like a second mother, and that, Evan, has filled an emptiness I've always known I had but dared not mention." When Evan said nothing, I continued. "I've become family to a family that was mine all along, but I'd—we'd—never known. Even visiting Terry once a month has become important to me. And there's work here to be done. A good work. There's still so much of the dream yet to realize and . . . Evan, say something."

He looked down at his Bruno Maglis and nodded a few times. I wrapped my arm through the crook of his and leaned my head against his shoulder then stood back to watch his down-turned face. Finally, after a moment or two of lip biting, he said, "I knew this was coming."

"And? I want to know what you think."

He looked up at me then. "What do you want me to say, Jo-Lynn? You want me to leave behind my work? My career? My life?"

I kept my face as expressionless as I knew how, then said, "I want to be enough for you."

"What does that mean?"

I pulled my arm from his and pushed my hands into the pockets of my capris. "Do you remember when we went to Ireland . . . when you proposed?"

"Of course."

"You said you wanted me to give up the idea of children and that you wanted to be enough for me."

His face registered remembrance. "I said that, yes. And until a year ago, I thought I was enough for you."

"Until a year ago you were. But one person cannot replace another and a child born cannot replace a child lost and a career cannot replace love. That's what I've learned—what I learned—before that night . . ." I looked toward the second floor of the house. "And sometimes God brings you back home and allows you to start over. Evan, I want to start over."

"And where does that leave me?"

The sun hiding behind the thick foliage of oaks and pecans and pines peeked through their branches. I squinted at my husband and said, "I've found something here . . . something I want to share with you. Something I hope you'll share with me. It's . . . it's a sense of belonging. A sense of peace. Every week we go to church now, and I find myself talking to God more and leaning more on his understanding than my own, and I think that—in spite of not going to church—this is the way Uncle Jim lived his whole life." I took a breath. "It's like my life began the day his ended. Or, at the very least, the day we lowered him into the ground." I paused. "The day the angels danced on air."

"Okay, now you've completely lost me."

I extended my hand and he took it. Pulling him toward the front porch of the house I said, "This house is nearly ready for Mother and me to do what we do best . . . to get all those fabulous things we've found or purchased or refinished and place them back inside. And I keep asking myself, *And then what?* What happens to me when I have to go back to Druid Hills?" I stopped before the freshly painted front door and faced my husband, drawing both his hands into mine. "Do you know I've not missed it up there? Not once in all this time?"

"I know."

I remained silent.

"So now you want me to give up everything I've worked for and move down here. What will I do, Jo-Lynn? Become the mayor of Cottonwood?" He smirked at his own humor, and I giggled. "Seriously," he said. "What? Go to work for your brother?"

"Of course not. You're on the road so much anyway, Evan, you could drive up a couple days a week and do the rest of your work from here. What difference does it make where your house is? Isn't it more important where you call home?"

He pursed his lips and chewed on the inside of his mouth for a moment, then tugged at my hands. "Come here," he said. He wrapped me in his arms, and I sighed. "You've got a point. And I'm willing to think about it."

I tilted my head to look at him. When I smiled, he smiled back. "Won't that be something?" I asked.

He kissed the tip of my nose and said, "Just don't let it get out."

I hugged him close. "It'll be our secret."

Two years to the day after we'd buried Uncle Jim and as the sun shone in magnificence, we laid his sweet wife next to him. There were no angels dancing on air, but as I sat between my husband and my mother at the graveside I imagined they sang a hallelujah chorus when she entered heaven's gates.

Bettina Godwin sat between Mother and Doris, and as family often does, they held hands while Elder Timothy spoke about a woman he didn't know but had drawn enough information from those of us who did. And when the final prayer had been prayed and the family had been acknowledged by those in attendance, I whispered a prayer of thanks to God that before this beloved woman had left this life, she'd learned the truth about her father and her husband; that their lives had been lived out in good, not evil. I thanked God that she'd had the opportunity to hold her oldest child in her frail arms and express all the love she'd had in her heart for her and what joy she'd been given in seeing her grow up, whether she was known as her mother or not. And I thanked him for the lessons she'd taught me at the end; that life is about sacrifice and in that sacrifice we are more oft to receive than to give.

A week later we were in the cemetery once again, this time to bury Mr. Valentine. As Timothy spoke to the living about the dead, I pondered the things the old contractor had said to me the first day he'd come to the house asking for work.

We'd been speaking of my great-grandparents, and he'd

said, "Died one week of each other . . . I suppose that's the sign of true love right there. Maybe the purest kind, I reckon."

"Maybe," I said now in a whisper. Mother looked at me and raised her brow, and I shook my head. There was nothing to share. She would only argue with me that Mr. Valentine and Aunt Stella had grown apart and had found another love—the deepest kind. And I would argue back that theirs was not the deepest kind. Theirs was the rarest kind.

The next day Evan and I took part in the Southern tradition of visiting the freshly turned grave of the deceased. We stood there, just the two of us, me in front of him, his hands on my shoulders and my head resting against his chest. His heartbeat kept rhythm with my own, and I spoke into the cool spring air. "If a foundation is good, anything can be restored."

I felt Evan squeeze my shoulders. "What's that?"

I nodded. "I'm just remembering something Mr. Valentine said."

Evan chuckled. "I'm sure it was full of great wisdom."

"Oh yes."

A breeze blew then, blew from across the farmland beyond the cemetery and toward us. I closed my eyes, felt the chill of it across my face, and breathed in deeply, reminded of the day we buried Uncle Jim and the moment the wind had skipped upon my shoulder, whispering, "I'm not there."

I blinked open my eyes and scanned the rows of granite marking the births and deaths of those who had come and gone before us. Realizing there was nothing of those I'd loved in this place, I turned my head and glanced over my shoulder.

"Well, Mr. Mayor," I said with a wink, "let's go home."

And then we did.

Acknowledgments

This is not a true story. It is based, however, on a place very near and dear to my heart. At least twice a month my family—my mother, father, brother, and I—would go there, a half hour's drive from home. This was the home of my great-grandparents, the childhood home of my grandmother for whom I was named, and the present home of her sister, my great-aunt Della, and her husband Jimmy. This house, this wonderfully fabulous house with rambling rooms filled with treasures and secrets, has a large wraparound porch with nearly a dozen old porch swings and a drawing well at the back door. My brother and I spent hours exploring both it and the land around it. (Oh, how I'll never forget the day we discovered the old outhouse. To this day my mother laughs about our expressions when we came running back inside to tell of our find.) The house lies broken and nearly barren now, but always and forever in my heart it will be one of my childhood homes.

In spite of this story being fabricated, it required a lot of research, and for those who aided me, I am forever grateful. Thank you to Dori Grantz, who explained the difference between an interior designer and an interior decorator and who spent valuable time answering my questions about both; to my mother, Betty Purvis, who met me in the declining town where our ancestrial home lies in near-ruins and who walked the broken sidewalks, explaining the way life used to be when it was vibrant and hopeful; to Charlie Seitz who—after renovating an old farmhouse—shared some of the problems and pleasures therein; to Nancy Kruk, who helped me understand some of the finer details involved in renovating an old house; to Rhonda DeLoach from Register, Georgia, who sent old newspaper articles to further my research; to Miriam Feinberg Vamosh, my dear friend, who shared with me some of the issues concerning Jews in America during the 1940s (may we never see those days again); and to Gayle Scheff, my Southern-girl reading buddy, who read every line as I wrote it, rewrote it, and then rewrote it again. Thank you for helping me catch those "vacant" spots.

And, of course, to my editors: Vicki Crumpton, who said, "I really like this!" and Kristin Kornoelje, who took what Vicki sent and made it sing an even prettier song. Thank you, everyone at Baker Publishing Group for everything you have done and continue to do for me as a fiction writer.

Thank you to my agent, Deidre Knight. You are a TRUE GRITS: Girl Raised in the South! Thank you, thank you, thank you, sweet lady!

Finally, a huge thank-you to my family: husband Dennis and daughter-still-at-home, Jo-Jo. Thank you for giving up your time with me and my precious time with you (all the more important) so I could write this novel. It had stirred for so many years, and we, together, can now hold it in our hands. I love you for that.

Eva Marie Everson